Titles by Katherine Sutcliffe

MY ONLY LOVE
ONCE A HERO
MIRACLE

DEVOTION

KATHERINE SUTCLIFFE

JOVE BOOKS, NEW YORK

DEVOTION

A Jove Book / published by arrangement with
the author

The Putnam Berkley World Wide Web site address is
http://www.berkley.com

ISBN: 0-515-11801-X

A JOVE BOOK®
Jove Books are published by The Berkley Publishing Group,
200 Madison Avenue, New York, New York 10016.
JOVE and the "J" design are trademarks
belonging to Jove Publications, Inc.

PRINTED IN THE UNITED STATES OF AMERICA

My thanks to the best literary agent in the business,
Evan Fogelman.
My friend.
What would I have done this last year without you?

And, as always,
To my family.

I love you all.

FATHER OF LIGHT

Father of light, to thee I call;
My soul is dark within.
Thou who canst mark the sparrow's fall,
Avert the death of sin.
Thou who canst guide the wandering star,
Who calm'st the elemental war,
Whose mantle is yon boundless sky;
My thoughts, my words, my crimes forgive,
And since I soon must cease to live,
Instruct me how to die.

—George Gordon, Lord Byron

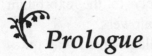# Prologue

Maria Ashton stood near the rectory door, waiting for it to be opened. The sooner the better—best to get the ugly affair over with as soon as possible. What could she have been thinking, to answer the advertisement like she had? Desperation could make fools of the hardiest souls, as could deception. Oh, but she would pay *dearly* for *this* deception! The hair shirt stinging her flesh would seem mild punishment compared to what would certainly follow this "breach of decency and trust," as her father, the Vicar Ashton, would term it.

Reaching into her skirt pocket, she withdrew the wrinkled and smudged article she had torn from the *London Times* a full six weeks earlier.

> Position offered. Desire live-in companion. Tutor. Nursemaid. Yorkshire district. Wage compensatory with experience. Prefer healthy, strong male. Reply to . . .

Her fingers closing around the paper, Maria moved to the window and noted the miserable weather without. From here she could see the steep roof of her home rising through the mist at the far end of the village, its slate roof a shocking opulence compared to the humble thatched cottages surrounding the Vicar Ashton's well-appointed house—due completely to the exorbitant tithes demanded of the church followers.

Unlike her own home, the village green was unremarkable. Grass grew among the pavement stones and the very rooks on the leafless trees seemed half asleep. All appeared as still and quiet as the local cemetery, which was not surprising, considering the vicar expounded at every opportunity on the sins of frivolity and cheerfulness. As if to add to the dismal mood, the entire village was filled with a dense white mist, rare indeed to the mostly clear atmosphere of the village set high on a hill. When the mist set in, it did so with an intense cold that pierced to one's very soul.

Odd, however, that she did not feel it. In truth, she felt little of anything but numbness.

"I forbid it!" cracked the vicar's voice suddenly, causing Maria to cringe, to glance toward the door, her mind on escape. But where would she go? Inevitably she would be forced to face the vicar's wrath. Best to steel herself and get the confrontation over with . . . as she always had. She had learned young in life that it was better to bear, for a short time, the wicked bite of her father's punishment than to live under the lingering cold fear of eventual discovery.

There came from the adjoining room a rumble of

angry voices—her father's, another man's . . . a woman's—not her mother's, certainly. Her mother would be cowering in the corner, her white, emaciated, unhappy face turned in dread and shame toward the wall. That, more than any fear of facing her father, gave Maria pause, made her shudder with self-recrimination. While she gave not a double damn about the distress, or fury, this caused her father, her mother was a different matter.

Because of Maria's recalcitrance, Mary Ashton would be cannonaded by blame. Her mother would be reminded that it was because of her own beauty that Maria had been born an object of the devil, too beautiful by far. Had Mary's own sensuality and comeliness not caused the young vicar's temporary dalliance with the demon lust—which resulted in his marrying the girl, not out of love by any stretch of the imagination (God was his only love; God and the godly position He would grant Vicar Ashton upon his demise), but out of repentance.

And obviously, Maria had inherited her mother's penchant for factiousness. Did her tongue not continually challenge her father's authority? (Which was tantamount to challenging God himself.) Was the vicar not repeatedly forced to punish her, as he had Mary in those early years, before he broke her spirit completely, when she valiantly refused to bow to his twisted sense of authority?

Maria closed her eyes. What could she have been thinking to have responded to that advertisement? Dear Lord, who could have imagined that *royalty* would appear on her father's doorstep to interview her for a position she had applied for on a whim—because she had listened too closely to newly married Sarah McCann's discourses on the amazing delights of the world outside this village (not to mention the marriage bed), and she had watched a little too long, and longingly, at the fine coaches and their ultra-fine passengers who passed through on their way to the city.

But mostly, because she had wanted desperately to save a certain young man—a very special young man—from making the grave mistake of falling in love with Vicar Ashton's *offspring of the demon lust*. But most of all, she had wanted, selfishly, to save herself from marrying into the same sort of life, and fate, as her mother. And she wanted to save her mother.

Maria smoothed her hands down over her skirt, and for a brief moment, before reminding herself of the sins of vanity, wished for something nicer to wear—something brighter than the grave simplicity of the black she was normally forced to don. Her brother, Paul, had often vowed to someday purchase her a blue dress (he would order it from one of those posh books he had once seen some fancy lady perusing in her fancy coach) the same blue as her eyes—"blue as spring skies"—that would accentuate her "breathtaking beauty."

Maria did not consider herself pretty at all, but very . . . plain. She had fair skin and flaxen hair that would always remain flaxen—never gray. She generally wore a sort of half-cap of black lace, which she considered the most becoming head attire for a young lady of her age and complexion. As far as intelligence was concerned, she had never been thought of as clever.

She could read, and write, mostly thanks to Paul, whose grandest dream had been to teach—not as their father taught the lads of the village—no hail of fire and brimstone—no espousing of Scriptures to punctuate the evils of modern literature or the ideas and ideals of philosophers—but to enrich the mind, heart, and soul with an appreciation of true, uncensored knowledge.

The door opened behind her.

Maria turned, her heart skipping and her breath catching. Her father filled up the doorway, eyes ablaze, his wide, wrinkled face aflame with anger, fists like ham hocks clenched at his sides. The air suddenly became unbreathable.

"Witch." His voice rattled deep and low in his chest. She knew that voice, reserved for those wretchedly sinful individuals whose souls he would, without compunction, damn to eternal hell.

He closed the door gently—too gently to be menacing, and she backed away, coming up against the wall, pressing into it as if she could become one with the rectory's rich mahogany panels.

"You won't touch me again," she stated with a conviction she didn't feel in the pit of her stomach. He was her father, after all. He could treat her in any manner he so desired—or so he had always convinced her. "I'm not a child any longer. I'm a grown woman and if I desire to leave this place—"

"Wicked girl. Rancorous and spiteful sinner that you would humiliate me in this manner."

Backing into a corner, she glanced toward the door, the window—no escape—to flee now would only infuriate him further, and there was her mother to think about . . .

Raising her chin and planting her small feet apart, she met the vicar's eyes, her look one of challenge and defiance that made his face turn a slow, burning red.

"I won't allow you to hurt me any longer, Father. I'm leaving this place and when I'm capable I'm returning for Mother—"

"Insolent fiend! Satan's daughter! Just like her—Eve of temptation, despoiler of righteousness. Destroyer of man's discipline and judgment." His eyes raked her. Towering above her, his surplice shifting over his massive frame like a shroud of power and doom, he hissed through his teeth, "Succubus. Worming your way into a man's dreams, despoiling his virtue, filling his mind with lustful appetites so he deviates from the dictates of moral and divine law."

She turned her face away. "I won't allow you to break me like you have Mama."

"Whore—"

"You won't rob me of my youth and spirit—"

"Wanton—"

"Of my dignity! You're a wicked man masquerading as God's disciple and were it in my power I would see you defrocked and cast from the church. I would tell the people of this village who so fear and revere you just exactly what sort of man you are!"

"Silence!"

"I would tell them that the tithes you demand of them are exorbitant. That the miracles their precious monies buy are nothing more than false promises from a man whose own wealth is growing by extremes, who someday hopes to see himself bishop—"

"Blasphemer!"

"I fully intend to return here and take Mama away from your cruel and insensitive abuse before she ends up like Paul."

"How dare you mention that heathen's foul name to me!"

"Because of you he's dead—my only brother is dead—"

"Falsifying slut."

"You stood aside and allowed that evil man to raise his fists against your own son. Because of you my brother spent the last two years of his life in unbearable pain—"

"Vengeance is mine, sayeth the Lord!"

"Yet he continued to love you the entire time he lay there dying little by little. With his last breath he begged you for forgiveness—"

"'Tis God's judgment not mine."

"*He was your son!* Your own flesh and blood and you refused to speak to him for two years because he fell in love with a woman—"

"A harlot! An adulteress. Branding her and casting her from my village was mild punishment. I should have burned her at the stake."

"Cruel, vindictive man. I'll save myself and my mother from you if it's the last thing I do."

He raised his hand to hit her. In that moment the door opened.

James Thackley, the duchess's assistant, a tall, gray-

haired man wearing wire-rimmed spectacles and a
somber but smartly (and expensive) tailored suit, entered the room and paused, his expression one of
surprise at the vision of the vicar with his fist raised and
shaking, his brow beaded with sweat, and Maria backed
into a corner, chin thrust outward, feet planted, and tears
streaming down her cheeks. At last, he smiled—not
smiled, exactly; the occasion did not lend itself to such
lightness. His expression was one of pleasantness,
which was obviously meant to assure Maria that all
would be fine.

With a last speaking glance at her trembling parent,
she dashed for the room where the Duchess of Salterdon was waiting, a hovering portly and balding physician named Ethan Edgcumbe at her side.

The steely, all-condemning gaze of Vicar Ashton fixed
on Maria as she somewhat clumsily curtsied to the frail
Duchess of Salterdon, a matriarch in her eighties with
jeweled fingers and silver hair and a countenance severe
enough to stop a clock. Such a look would have made
most young women of Maria's age, having just turned
nineteen, tremble in trepidation (certainly respect)—and
obviously the duchess knew it—practiced it—prided herself in it—which was no doubt why the old woman's
silver brows drew together when Maria responded, not
with the anticipated cowering of the typical timid ninny,
but with a lift of her chin and a narrowing of her
eyes—the same obstinacy which her father termed
"nerve of Satan" and which would invite a thorough
lashing with a thin leather strap.

"So, we finally meet," the duchess said in a surprisingly strong voice, considering her age and obvious illness. Her unsteady hand lifted Maria's letter from her lap and she appeared to peruse it before looking up at Maria again. "Tell me, Miss Ashton, why you applied for this position when I clearly stated I wished to fill the position with a male."

Maria swallowed, cleared her throat, and did her best not to look at her mother, who sat on a milk stool near the wall, shrunken inside her clothes and her eyes, like dark, lifeless hollows, staring into space. Once— according to whispered gossip—Mary Swift had been beautiful, full of fire and energy, not unlike Maria, and desired by every unmarried man in the village. But that was before the Vicar Ashton arrived to win her over with promises of a heavenly paradise that awaited any woman who companioned him on his trek to save every damned-to-hell soul in England. Poor Mary. Poor Mother. Her beauty, her youth, her dreams, all wasted; now she had passed the age where she cared. Oh, yes, it was not age alone that had produced the dull severity of expression that Mary wore, the eradication of all of youth's restless emotions, but disappointment, disillusionment, and the loss of hope. Her eyes were constantly dull, her face blank and immovable, like a landscape from which the sun had faded away, leaving it all gray and dark.

"Miss Ashton," the duchess prodded.

Drawing back her shoulders, Maria met the dowager's sharp gray eyes. "I fail to see what difference gender makes; if a female is equally as qualified for the position—"

"Are you qualified for the position, Miss Ashton? I need someone physically strong, mentally capable, emotionally rigid. Your charge, should I decide to employ you, can be occasionally difficult."

The statement appeared to cause the duchess a certain outward pang; her close-set lips quivered once or twice then she resumed her bearing, which seemed habitual to her. She looked Maria up and down and with a dismissive flip of her thin hand, added, "You're little more than a whiff of a child. An infant! I find it impossible to believe you could adequately handle the . . . situation. What makes you think you are physically and emotionally mature enough to work with the . . . infirm?"

"My brother was an invalid," she blurted, cursing the desperation she heard in her own voice. "He was beaten unmercifully by a man who was thrice his size, and who had no regard whatsoever for human compassion. My brother's back was broken in three places. For two years I was at his side, day and night. I fed him. Clothed him. Bathed him. For hours I read to him, encouraged him, pleaded with him not to die. I watched him rally at times, and then sink. I exercised his legs and arms because he couldn't. He could do nothing, Your Grace, but lie there with his ever-sharp and clear mind and watch his body deteriorate. 'Twasn't his injuries that ultimately killed him, Your Grace, but his broken heart."

Silence filled the room, interrupted only by the brief, pitiful sob of Maria's mother. Still, Maria refused to lower her eyes. "I read, Your Grace, thanks to my brother." She smiled. "When we were much younger we would hide away in the forest and he would teach me all that our father had taught him throughout the day. He taught me to write as well. And cipher. Your Grace, I do very well with children."

"I'm less concerned with that than I am with the caretaking of one's heart and soul, Miss Ashton."

"I won't allow it," railed the vicar again, his big hands fisted in his parish cloak and his wide face going purple. " 'Tis a world of sin and corruption, Your Grace. Look at her. An object of temptation, she is, with as willful and decadent a soul as you'll find. 'Twould do no good to unleash her sort of wickedness on the world."

"I was speaking to the girl," interrupted the duchess, her gaze still locked on Maria. "You're very young and beautiful. Obviously, you have little experience outside the boundaries of this village. I fear you would use this position as a means of escaping your obvious . . . predicament."

She had nothing to say to that because, in a manner, it was true. When applying for the position she had had no thought of philanthropy in her mind.

Almost wearily, the duchess discarded Maria's letter into her assistant's hand, then she unsteadily left the chair. The physician hurried to her side, wrapped one arm gently around her thin shoulders, offering support. The duchess stood motionless for a moment, as if uncertain of her strength, her jeweled fingers working nervously in the folds of her velvet skirts. When her eyes returned to Maria, however, they were gray as flint and just as sharp.

"I'll expect you at Thorn Rose at the end of the week. Mr. Thackley will see to the arrangements."

"I beg your pardon," Maria cried softly, her surprise evident. "Do I understand correctly, Your Grace? Have you offered me the position?"

"Obviously." Anticipating the vicar's outburst, the duchess turned to face Maria's father. "As for you. We'll speak privately before I leave."

As if in a trance, ignoring the heated exchanges between her father and the duchess, Maria moved toward the door, gasping slightly as her mother's hand came up suddenly to fiercely snatch her arm and stop her. Those normally dull, dead eyes now glittered; that usually blank face reflected desperation and fear.

"Would you desert me?" Mary cried in her hoarse, desperately unhappy voice. "Would you abandon me here *alone* to live with him? Oh, God, first Paul and now you. What shall I do? *What shall I do?*"

Maria peeled her mother's fingers from her arm then fled the rectory, refusing to look back as she ran, with the bitter wind stinging her face and fingers, down the winding, cobblestone pathway through the cemetery to her brother's grave. She dropped onto it, leaned back against the cold, hard headstone, drew her knees up to her chest, and buried her face into them. Again and again her mother's anguished face rose up before her—the pleas, the tears—always when Maria showed any signs of escaping.

"Maria," came the soft voice from the fog. As Maria looked up, the figure she had dreaded most to see came toward her, scattering mist, his clergy's collar shimmering white in the dull day.

"Go away," she called. "My father may well come looking for me. He won't look kindly on his prized curate associating with such a fallen soul as me."

"Maria," John Rees said, and dropped to one knee beside her. His slender hands caught her face. His kind, searching brown eyes regarded her intensely. "Tell me what I've just heard is untrue—that you plan to leave us. Tell me that you intend to turn down Her Grace's offer—"

"Nay, I shall not, John Rees! Not for my mother's sake. Not for you. I'm leaving here, John, and I shan't return until I'm capable of providing my mother a refuge from my father."

"Then marry me, Maria. I beg you! I've commissioned the archbishop for my own rectory. We'll take your mother with us—"

"Nay, I won't allow you to suffer by his hand as I and my family have. I care for you too much."

He grabbed her in his arms, pressed his lips to her forehead, and lingered there, stroking her fallen hair with one hand. "I'll speak to your father about us."

"No!"

"He would bless our marriage, I'm certain of it."

"He would pray for your soul, John, and see you cast from the church." She pulled away suddenly, causing her hair to cascade over her shoulders, to form a waving, curling triangle around her face. Her skirt brushing the flowers from her brother's grave, she sat back on her heels and stared at her father's young assistant, who regarded her with something just short of worship.

"Do you truly love me, John Rees?" she asked.

"Aye. I've loved you since the night I moved into your father's house. You were no more than a child and I . . . suddenly found my passion for God battling with my passion for you. I've seen how he treats you and your mother. I saw him turn his back on his only son—"

"Yet you did nothing to stop him because you fear him as much as the rest of us. You would do nothing to jeopardize your position with the church, because if he truly is appointed bishop then you yourself will rise to his place as parish vicar. 'Tis that part of you that frightens me, John Rees. I fear you are too much like my father."

"What do I have to do to convince you that I love you more than anyone—"

"Nay, not more than God! More than the almighty God, sir? Need my father remind you that *he who loveth father or mother, or wife, or sister, or brethren more than God is not worthy of heaven?*"

For an instant, John looked thunderstruck. His hands fisted and buried in his flowing surplice and cassock. Confusion furrowed his brow.

Narrowing her eyes, Maria leaned toward him. "Kiss me," she whispered. "Nay, not on my brow, I'm not a child any longer, John. My lips, John. Kiss my lips. I'm nineteen and have never been kissed. Not by you. Not by anyone. And do you know why? Because there isn't a solitary man in this village who would risk my father's wrath. Not you because, despite what your body feels, your heart belongs to God."

He turned his face away, and his eyes downcast.

"Would you turn away from me on our wedding night?" she demanded. She grabbed his hand and pressed it to her breast.

John gasped and tensed. His gaze flew back to her face, then to his hand which she held fiercely upon the fullest part of her bosom.

Her lids growing drowsy, her breath quickening, Maria smiled. "Is this not a part of love, John? The giving of one's body, as well as their soul?"

He made a choked sound in his throat, and his eyes brightened with a sort of light that made his expression one of fiery pain. Then he pulled his hand away.

"God have mercy," he said shakily, and pressed his fingers to his eyes, as if to block out the image of her, her riotous hair tumbling and drifting in the rising breeze, brushing lightly over her breasts that pressed almost brazenly against the too-tight bodice of her child's dress, despite the fact that she was forced, by her father, to bind her chest to alleviate her "appearance of flagrant wantonness."

Sinking back on Paul's grave, Maria turned away, the heat of his hand still burning her breast while the cold air and desolation sent shivers down her spine.

"Nay, I could never marry you," she declared wearily, her eyes filling with tears that spilled down her cheeks. "Mayhap my father is right. I was spawned of lust and am therefore doomed to a life of licentiousness. Nay, I could never make you a goodly wife, John Rees . . . any more than you could make me a proper husband."

Chapter One

Thorn Rose Manor
Haworth, Yorkshire, England
1805

Maria tried not to think about the odd looks she had received from the folk in Haworth the moment she announced that she would be employed at Thorn Rose Manor—companioning the Duchess of Salterdon's young grandson. Surely, the expressions of consternation (and sympathy?) were nothing more than her own imagination, which, on occasion throughout her life, had proven to be the stem of a great deal of trouble. Had her father not vowed that such "dream worlds" that she concocted were machinations of Satan? And that inevitably she would find herself sucked into the demon pits of unreality to languish forever?

Balderdash! The only *demon pit of unreality* she had ever been sucked into was her own father's house and his fist-flailing Sunday sermons.

The road from Haworth entered a valley, at the bottom of which sprawled a striking, awe-inspiring building, entrancingly luminous under winter's clear dusk sky. The structure was a hodgepodge of architecture, with deliriously sloping roofs and many-sided towers, whose sharp and steeple-like pinnacles speared the horizon dramatically. Her head and shoulders thrust through the window of the coach, Maria blinked away the icy sting of cold and stared in disbelief at the imposing manor she would, very soon now, call home.

What had she expected? Mayhap some grim, ancient rock of a country home with bleak, lifeless windows! Not this . . . magnificence—this . . . palace, set amid stark gray hills that heaved up round the horizon. She could well understand now why the duchess's eyes had shone so when she spoke of Thorn Rose Manor. As far as her eye could see stretched artificial lakes, bridges, and formal Renaissance gardens. There were towering filigreed spires and massive walls of stained glass that reflected the failing sunlight in streaks of blues, greens, and golds. Her father would decry it, of course. Pronounce its ostentatiousness fit only for the gluttonous appetite of the affluent—who were undoubtedly doomed to eternal hell for reveling in their wanton opulence.

Oh, yes, Maria could appreciate the fondness she had witnessed in the duchess's eyes. What she had not understood, however, was why those steely eyes had grown so dark and distressed when discussing her family—the lad—the obvious chink in the grande dame's aristocratic armor—the boy who resided here, alone but for the scattering of servants who occupied the domicile. The lad who, the duchess proclaimed, could prove to be difficult, at times stubborn, angry, belligerent—obviously in need of patience, tenderness, and understanding. Was Maria up to it?

Of course I am, she told herself with a lingering shudder of doubt. She would dance with the devil himself before returning to her father's house! She would *bed* the devil himself if it meant acquiring the finances somehow to get her mother away from the vicar's unseemly influence—before it was too late.

The coachman deposited Maria and her single valise on the manor steps, tapped his hat brim with one finger, and murmured something about "the lunatic" and "how many of ye comin' and goin's it gonna tek afore they finerlly put it away."

"I beg your pardon?" she cried as he cracked a whip over the pair's massive croups, then watched as the conveyance lumbered down the potted drive. For an instant she considered running after it; then, drawing back her shoulders, said aloud, "You've come this far, lass; there's no turning back now."

Still . . .

She looked up, up the formidable ancient walls that were littered with brown ivy. The windows were dark, and growing darker as the sun slid beyond the purple horizon.

Taking a breath, she mounted the steps that were made of rough stone, so pitted that beaded spiders' webs glistened in the fissures. For a long moment she stared at the pair of matching lion's head knockers that had grown green with age, then she rapped hard on the door with her fist.

Nothing.

Again, harder, then glanced toward the dark mullioned windows, her mind racing through memories of stories Paul had once embellished upon her while she sat trembling in bed, the pillow pulled over her head in an attempt to muffle tales of banshees and headless knights who wandered castle galleries in search of "pretty lasses" to eat. Nothing about the windows or house felt remotely reassuring, and frowning, she turned and stared after the coach as it disappeared through the tunnel of denuded trees in the distance.

" 'Oo's there?" came an intolerant voice from behind the door.

Flooded by relief, Maria laughed at her own nervousness and cried back, " 'Tis I, here at last—"

" 'Oo the blazes is I? I 'oo? I ain't openin' this bloody door for nobody name I."

"Maria Ashton!"

"Don't know no Maria Ashton, ain't expectin' no Maria Ashton—"

"I was sent by Her Grace, the duchess—"

"I know 'oo the blazes 'Er Grace is—lud, do I look daft or wot?"

"I wouldn't know," she replied as patiently as she could manage, considering her toes and fingers were fast becoming numb. "If you will only open the door—"

"I ain't openin' no door for nobody unless I've explicit instructions from the housekeeper—"

"Then let me speak to her—"

"She ain't here!"

Dropping her valise to the step, Maria focused on the tarnished knocker and did her best to bite back her frustration and growing agitation. Then she remembered. "The letter!" Snatching up her reticule, she dug into it and produced a paper. "Will an order written by the duchess herself benefit?" she called, smugly smiling at the knocker and waving the notice beneath the lion's green snout.

Silence, then . . . the door cracked, just barely, enough to allow a thin nose to protrude through the opening. A pair of close-set eyes peered out at her, growing round, then narrowing conspicuously as they acknowledged Maria.

Her smile widening, Maria flipped open the paper and held it up for the sentinel to see. "Mayhap this will change your mind."

"Wot the blazes do I look like? A bloomin' magistrate? That damn piecea litter could say aught as far as I know."

For an instant, as she was struck with the realization that the servant could not read, her bravado failed, then rallying, she thrust her nose to that of the door guardian and added, "Aye, you're right, but will you risk the chance that I'm telling you the truth? What do you think Her Grace's reaction will be should she learn her written directives were ignored?"

"Bloody 'ell," the voice muttered, just before the door slammed closed, rocking Maria back on her heels. No more than a second passed before the door was flung open, revealing the scrawny form of a housemaid, her apron twisted lopsidedly around her waist, her scraggly blond hair spilling from beneath her crushed cap. "Well?" she barked. "Wot the blazes are ya waitin' for, a bleedin' engraved invitation? Hurry the hell up, for the love of a drunken Pete, afore I bloody freeze, not to mention allowin' ever' connivin' highwayman in the county access to the manor's silver chests."

"Highwaymen?" Hefting up her valise, Maria hurried into the foyer, her mouth dropping open as she scanned the dim interior of the house.

"Aye, highwaymen. Folks ain't safe in their own homes these days." The servant kicked shut the door, the slam reverberating down the half dozen corridors leading off the entry. Hands on her hips, giving Maria a thorough going over with her eyes, the girl added, "No more'n a fortnight ago Lord Middleton's majordomo answered the door to some gel who said she was there by invitation of Lady Middleton 'erself. No sooner did she step into the 'ouse than a dozen 'ooded bastards come bustin' in behind 'er. The next hour they, includin' the silly bitch who weren't no friend of Lady Middleton's at all, tied the whole damn family up with drape cords and robbed 'em blind." She sniffed. "Lady Middleton still 'as fits of vapor ever'time she thinks 'bout it."

"That's dreadful," Maria replied absently as she ran her fingers lightly over the ornately scrolled wainscotted walls and the carved mahogany cherubs peering out at her from deep alcoves.

"Dreadful's puttin' it mildly, I'd say. And by the way,

from now on 'ousekeepers come and go by the back entry—"

"Oh, I'm not a housekeeper." She picked up a china vase and held it up to the flickering oil sconce on the wall. "I'm here to companion young Salterdon."

"*Young* Salterdon?" The girl snatched the vase from Maria's hands and plunked it back on the table.

"The duchess's grandson. He's ill, of course. An invalid?" Tiptoeing to the foot of a staircase, lightly placing her fingertips on the shining balustrade, she peered up through the dark at the landing above. "I should like to meet him immediately, of course."

"Right." The voice sounded curiously tight with humor. Then the servant stepped around her and, none-too-gently brushing Maria's shoulder with her own, started up the stairs, her slender hips swaying from side to side in an exaggerated manner. "She'd like to meet 'im immediately, she says, as if she were the bloody duchess 'erself. Next thing ya know she'll be tellin' me to unpack 'er damn bag and press 'er frilly knickers . . . as if I ain't got nothin' better to do with me time off . . . not as if I get a whole lot of bleedin' time off."

Obviously her fantasies of being greeted by cheerful servants in starched uniforms and frilly white mobcaps had been just that—fantasies, as were the images of her being met by some kindly majordomo who would, of course, be stiffly proper and look down his slightly bent nose as he announced her arrival to the staff. The housekeeper would sweep her away to some tidy warm space near the kitchen fire and reward her with hot tea and warm crumpets swimming in fresh butter and cream.

Instead Maria was led through one rambling passageway to the next, given little time to inspect her vast surroundings, which, she surmised, would look immensely more warm and welcoming, if not spellbinding, during the daylight.

Virtually running to keep up with the recalcitrant servant's long stride, her sight grabbing the occasional glimpse of galleries stretching north and south, oaken staircases curving up into the dark where paneled walls formed rich wooden horizons far above her head, Maria dragged her carpetbag behind her and attempted conversation.

"I didn't realize the journey from Huddersfield would take two days. We hardly stopped to eat, just briefly this morning, a tavern just out of Lancashire . . . I suppose I've arrived too late for tea?"

No response.

"I hate to admit it, but this is my first venture away from my home and family. Have you worked at Thorn Rose long?"

Nothing.

Maria frowned.

The air felt chill and vault-like; windows and passageways rose from the floors forming soaring arches with flying buttresses. It all seemed so cheerless and vacuous, despite the lavish accruements, hardly the sort of environment for a sickly child. No wonder the lad whom she had been employed to companion could prove to be difficult. "Without light, there could be no joy.

Without joy, there could be no life!" Paul had often-
times declared with his brilliant smile.

Shadows had set into the tiny room where Maria was
led, up four flights of stairs to the locus of tiny servants'
cubicles, neatly lined up like pins, all the same size and
with just enough space to get in and out of bed. Only a
sliver of failing sunlight spilled through the drawn
curtain of the single window, forming a pale streak on
the floor near her bed. The servant, having entered
before her, fumbled with a lantern, and once lighting it
turned to stare at Maria with suspicious, disapproving
eyes.

"I can't reckon why the duchess would send the likes
of *you* to take care o' *'im*. She's slippin', I vow. Up 'ere,
I mean." She tapped her head with one finger and
looked Maria over again, shaking her head. "She's
paraded men thrice yer size through this house, thinkin'
they would accomplish miracles—and all of 'em 'ave
packed it in within a fortnight, vowin' it would be a cold
day in 'ell afore they spent one more day with . . .
'the monster.' "

"What a very cruel thing to say! There's not a solitary
human heart and soul that cannot be saved with
patience and kindness."

Her eyebrows going up, the servant huffed. "You
ain't met *'im* yet, I vow. Well, never mind. You'll see
for yerself soon enough, I 'spose." Moving toward the
door, she added, "I'd lock this if I's you. Never know
who ya might wake up to find standin' over ya in the
dark. Just last month the Viscountess Crenshaw woke
up to find the man fondlin' 'er under 'er nightgown

weren't her 'usband at all, but some masked man, 'oo spent the next two hours ravagin' er right there afore 'er own 'usband. If there weren't bad enough, they went and stole 'er entire wardrobe of underclothes. Two days later 'er most revealin' chemise was discovered flyin' from the old gibbet down at Nigel's Hollow.

"And by the way," she added with a pause for effect. "This side of the row is the *women's* rooms, the other belongs to the men servants. Any nighttime escapades is cause for immediate dismissal, if ya know wot I mean, and by the looks of ya, I 'spect ya do."

She sniffed and regarded Maria with a disapproving glint in her brown eyes. "There's a washroom at the end of the 'all. It suffices for us all. Gertrude, she's 'ead 'ousekeeper, is promisin' to get us our own washbasin in each cell—that is if she can convince the local shopkeeper to advance us any more credit—a bloody cold day in 'ell that'll be, I tol' 'er, not the way *'e's* mucked up 'is credit. We do well to eat 'round 'ere. 'Til then, ya bathe there and be quick about it."

"When shall I meet Master Salterdon?" Maria called after the servant, then hurried to the door when getting no reply. As the faint shape of the housemaid disappeared into the shadows, silence swelled up in waves to surround her. She glanced first one way, then another, visions of highwaymen and headless knights parading across her mind's eye. With a lift of her chin, she reentered her room and shut the door. She fell against it with a sigh.

Dare she admit, even to herself, that she felt overwhelmed by these last days' events? In the past four days she had found herself employed by the Duchess of Salterdon, removed from the only house and village she had ever known, and thrust into as foreign a world as she had ever imagined. For the first time in her life she was alone—truly alone. The routine, mostly harsh life in which she had existed the last nineteen years had vanished like smoke with one flourish of the duchess's pen.

She was free . . . free of her father's sobriety, of his cruelties administered in the name of God. Free not to wither emotionally and die like her mother. So where was the elation?

The small window overlooked a barren patch of dirt and a dying, leafless rowan tree, its skeletal limbs lined with roosting rooks. Finding no solace in the bleak panorama, Maria sat on the edge of the bed, hands clasped in her lap, and stared at the wall, too weary and hungry to even visualize the tiny room decorated with a picture or two, or the floor made warmer by a colorful rag rug.

If she were home, she would be preparing her father's supper: perhaps a leg of mutton donated by a member of his parish. Bread would be crisping in the oven. Soon the kitchen would grow overly warm. She would shove open the Dutch door and allow the cool evening breeze to kiss the sweat from her brow. If her mother could manage to rouse herself from her ennui, she might chat softly of her life as a young girl in the village . . . when the lads would parade by her house in hopes of catching a glimpse of her. Mother and daughter might share a laugh . . . before the vicar came home. They might even grow brave enough to talk of Paul.

Dear Lord, she was tired. The last days of tolerating her father's threats and recriminations and her mother's weeping had made for sleepless nights and an endless barrage of second-guessing her decision to leave home, and the only man who dared to love her despite, or because of, who her father happened to be.

Dear John . . . would this separation force her to realize her true feelings for him?

Minutes ticked by.

With a sigh, she at last left the bed, moved to the door and eased it open.

Where was 'the monster' now? Poor, misunderstood, misbegotten lad: What could have happened in his young life to form such a notorious character? She knew only that his parents were dead. That a little over a year ago there had been an accident which had left the young man . . . impaired, though to what degree the duchess had refused to elaborate.

Maria moved quietly down the corridor, retracing her way down staircase after staircase, her curiosity compelling her to search beyond the occasional open door, each time feeling stunned by the overwhelming riches that greeted her in the form of mirrored or marbled walls, crystal chandeliers, marquetrie floors, and gilded columns.

By the time she at last found her way to the lower floor, several servants were busily lighting lamps and the immense chandelier that they had lowered by way of a cable and winch. The hundred or more candles cast brilliant light over the grand staircases, sculpted reliefs, tapestries and marble walls as well as floors that were set off by large ferns and palms potted in great Chinese vases.

Still, she continued to wander, deeper into the heart of the grand house, back into the shadows until the hallways became narrow and the marble and paneled walls became brick and stone and the sconces on the walls cast vague light and shadows. From some source, there came warmth, and the smell of food. It lured her, thawed the growing chill from her face and fingers, causing her stomach to growl in hunger.

Coming to the top of a narrow flight of winding stairs, Maria paused. She peered down the crude staircase, toward the dashes of flickering red and yellow light reflecting off the stone wall and listened to the oddly disturbing sounds from below—voices muffled by distance.

The kitchen. Of course. Mayhap once she explained that she had had little more than porridge early that morning for breakfast, the cook would supply her with a bit of bread and butter, perhaps a cup of warm tea. Anything to quiet this jittery sense of nervousness settling in the pit of her stomach. Perhaps she might even coerce a moment's conversation from him—anything to quiet her mounting discomposure.

She moved lightly, silently, down the spiraling steps . . . and froze at the entry.

The bodies lay entwined upon the trestle table before the fiery hearth—both naked, their flesh glistening with sweat, arms and legs thrashing as if for dominance, hands twisting into hair, faces contorted in a manner of both pain and pleasure.

"Give it t' me, Thaddeus. Quick! Afore someone finds us," the servant Maria had met earlier cried in a hoarse voice, and clawed at the young man's bare, flexing shoulders that reflected the firelight like smooth marble.

"Ain't no one gonna find us, Molly," he reported, and pumped his hips up and down between the girl's thighs. "I've seen to it. God, lass, but yer lovely. Such lovely tits," he cried, and buried his face between them, kissing them and fondling them with his tongue and lips.

Maria swallowed, but could not move.

Molly locked her ankles around the young man's waist and ground her loins against his, thrashed her head from side to side, her white breasts swinging like heavy pendulums with his every thrust, with each contraction of his muscled buttocks, each flex of his straining arms. Sweat poured from beneath his unruly crop of reddish-brown hair and rained down his brow, his temples.

"Oh God. Oh God," Molly whimpered, as he pumped harder and faster. "I'm dyin'. I'm dyin'."

"Dear God," Maria heard herself whisper, and when the man threw back his head, his dark eyes locking with hers, she could do nothing but open her mouth in silent surprise.

His eyes widened, briefly, then narrowed. They captured her, froze her, as did his grin, for though he was driving his hard, lean body into Molly's, it was

Maria to whom he was making love—right up to the moment he threw back his head and cried aloud.

Maria gasped and backed away, turned on her heel and ran on her tiptoes back to the foyer where her kid-soled slippers slid on the polished marble, causing her to dance in place before grabbing a table for support. Face burning, heart racing, she froze there, suspended above the floor, balanced on one leg, a hundred of her father's sermons on "sins of the flesh bringing untold damnation to the soul" flashing one after another through her memory. No doubt he would have a few choice phrases for this "den of inequity" in which she now resided—and the fact that she had just watched the entire sordid act with a shocking sense of fascination.

She fled up the stairs, taking little notice where she was going, ran down one long passageway after another, until, winded and realizing she had become disoriented, she fell against a wall and closed her eyes, only to have the indecent scene displayed in all its glory upon her mind's eye—every last detail emblazoned and wringing a heat from her that she had only vaguely experienced before—a few times in John's company (though it obviously had not been mutual)—other times when Paul had whispered secrets of his times spent with the village blacksmith's strikingly beautiful, and amorous, young wife. Now, however, unlike then, her body shook. Her mouth felt dry as chalk.

It seemed she stood there an hour, hugging herself. Until the heat of her body became chilled by the surrounding cold and the disturbing physical feelings she had experienced those eternal minutes she had spied on the lovers became one of bemused chagrin.

Collecting herself, realizing at last that she had become hopelessly lost in the labyrinth of Thorn Rose's corridors, Maria wandered from gallery to gallery, too numb to notice her grandiose surroundings, growing more intensely frustrated and angry over the quandary in which her body seemed to be captured. She wanted only to return to her room, to hide there forever, if necessary. To forget the last moments had ever happened. Still, she would find no respite there from her growing anxiousness. Silence would hardly stem the sense of disquietude that had begun to set in the moment she first saw Thorn Rose—when the realization finally set in that there was no home and hearth to rely on now. She was a solitary soul adrift in a universe of strangers.

Nay, she must not dwell on it. "Plan for the future and dwell less on today, for today is already history and cannot be changed," as Paul had often said . . . even as he lay wasting away in his deathbed. Oh, to be as cheerful and resolute when faced with such an unsurmountable adversity as impending death. If she were only that strong and brave . . .

Maria nudged open doors, peered into rooms with furnishings covered in dusty sheets. What odd and unhappy circumstances for a child. There was little here denoting cheerfulness, lightness; where was there a solitary toy, any evidence at all that a living human being, aside from servants, occupied the stately manor?

What could the duchess have been thinking to imprison a lad here in such secrecy?

She grew more determined by the moment to find her charge and introduce herself—they would pass the evening hours in becoming acquainted—perhaps she would teach him a song or two—together they would conquer this abysmal solitude and, eventually, become fast friends and companions and confidantes; these bleak hallways would ring with the child's laughter— she would see to it!—and when the duchess arrived on the morrow any doubt she might have had that Maria could successfully cope with the lad and his problems would be vanquished.

Upon coming to a well-lit corridor, Maria paused. The furnishings appeared well dusted—no ghostly sheets tossed over settees and chairs. The ornamental brass sconces on the walls were highly polished and reflected candlelight brightly.

Ah, this was more like it! The walls exuded grandeur and elegance. The air smelled of the many bouquets of fresh flowers in crystal vases that glittered from the dozen or so tables placed along the long gallery.

Most doors lining the sprawling corridors were open. Each drawing room, dressing room, and bedroom was a masterpiece of exquisite museum-worthy furnishings. Never, even in her own wildest imaginings, did she ever visualize anything so masterful and awe-inspiring. Her heart lifted. At last she managed to put the last days and hours from her mind long enough to grasp the thread of hope, which had compelled her to come to Thorn Rose in the first place.

She spun on her tiptoes, arms thrown wide. Biting her lip, covering her mouth with her fingertips, she cast a startled look around, half anticipating her father to come roaring at her from the shadows, fists raised as he expelled biblical recriminations regarding such frivolous, outrageous behavior.

Sweet relief when only silence greeted her! She almost hugged herself in happiness.

Hope and promise having replaced her former doubt, she moved down the carpeted hall, humming cheerfully to herself, intent now upon locating her young, *difficult* charge.

At last, she happened upon a closed door, and stopped. Cautiously, she knocked. No reply. Easing open the door, she peered inside at the vast, dim room whose windows were hidden behind heavy velvet casings. The air felt as still and cold as that in a mausoleum, and the smell—

Maria covered her nose, those last months of her brother's dwindling life rising from the vault of her buried memories. How well she recalled the scent of impending death and decay. It hovered in the impenetrable air like the grim reaper himself.

Easing the door open further, her senses focusing, Maria moved into the terrible chamber.

Broken china lay cast across the floor: delicate shattered tea cups, splintered dinner plates. A wheelchair sat, disposed, in the furthest corner of the cold room. No minute coal glittered amid the dank ash in the hearth. Only a solitary candle guttered in its own melting wax near the head of the bed, its flame, having grown much too long on its unsnipped wick, dancing dangerously close to the sheer curtains draped from the bed's overhead tester.

"H-hello," she called softly with a dry and trembling voice. "Is anyone there?"

No response.

"Master Salterdon?"

Silence.

Swallowing, covering her nose and mouth with the back of one hand, Maria cautiously stepped over the shattered china and moved toward the massive bed, her heart thudding, her knees growing weak.

"Master Salterdon?" she said again in a dry as dust voice.

She caught the curtain with her unsteady fingertips and nudged it aside.

There was a form there, hidden within the shadows. She narrowed her eyes, focused harder. No child's form, certainly, for it was big and broad and—

"Oh. Oh, God!" she gasped aloud and stumbled back, vaguely hearing the splinter of china beneath her feet. "Oh, God," she repeated more loudly, then blindly spun and ran for the door, flinging it open wide, stumbled over a fold in the carpet and ran down the long corridor until coming to the top of the staircase; grabbing the balustrade with all her strength, she called, "Help! Someone! Anyone! Oh, God," she wept to the figure that materialized through the shadows below. "Come quickly," she cried. "There is a *dead* man in yonder room!"

Chapter Two

Certainly, she was dead. How could she doubt it? Above her, St. Peter, dressed in his flowing, celestial gown, his long white hair flying out behind him as he gripped the book of judgment in his arms, glared upon her with eyes full of fiery condemnation. Obviously, her father had been right. Her wanton soul (certainly it was wanton or she might never have watched the earlier spectacle of two people thrashing together on a kitchen table!) had no right in heaven and St. Peter, with his choir of angels behind him, was on the verge of casting her soul, in the name of God and all that was divine, to the pit of eternal hell.

"She's awake," came a whisper near her ear.

Suddenly, St. Peter's fire and brimstone face became blurred by the ruddy-cheek image of a black-capped housemaid with eyes round and shiny as new copper farthings.

"Here now." The servant showed her small white

35

teeth in a smile. "Are ya awright, lass? Gor, but ya give us a fright, faintin' dead away like ya done."

"Wh-what happened?" Maria closed her eyes and wondered at the cyst of pain throbbing on her forehead. Obviously this was not hell unless hell was a palatial existence of crystal chandeliers, Italian marble mantels, and delicate lace sheers flowing over the bed . . . and Lucifer had a visage and tone as kindly as an angel's. "Where am I?"

"Lud," the servant clucked her tongue. "Ya must've hit yer pretty head harder than we thought last evenin'. I'll have Molly—she were the gel who greeted ya upon yer arrival—I'm sure she weren't at all cordial; she wouldn't be toward a lass as comely as you; she's accustomed to demandin' the lads' attention 'round here; greedy lass, I wouldn't trust her as far as I could pitch her 'round me own husband, if I had one. I'll have her fetch a poultice, aye. Ye'll be right as rain in no time."

"Molly!" she barked, causing Maria to wince—to recall in a flash the torrid image of Molly spread out on the trestle table, naked as the day she was born, her legs wrapped around some man's pumping hips. "Fetch me bag of herbs, ya know the one, and heat the kettle to boilin'. While yer at it see that the duchess gets her chocolate. Ya know what she's like after her trip from London." She winked at Maria, her brown eyes twinkling. "The old dear has a weak spot for chocolate, ya know. Says it's wot's kept her alive this long . . . that and bein' cantankerous," she added under her breath, then chuckled. With a wider smile, the servant added,

"Me name is Gertrude, luv. I'm head housekeeper." She jangled her immense ring of keys hanging from a chain around her waist. "I only arrived home this mornin'— family sickness in Devonshire, ya see. I would've been here to greet ya, had I known, but I wasn't aware that Her Grace had employed *him* a new companion."

Drawing in a deep breath, clearing the cobwebs from her confused mind, Maria sat up straight and grabbed the startled servant's arms so fiercely the woman squeaked. "The body!" Maria rasped. "The body in the bedroom—the dead man—oh, merciful Lord, I recall now, the terrible stench, that dreadful personage—like some horrible beast, covered in foul clothes and hair and—"

"Hush!" The servant patted Maria's cheeks as if to instill some sense in her babblings. "Don't be lettin' Her Grace hear ya speakin' of him like that—she gets upset enough—"

"He's dead!" Maria wailed.

"Nay—"

"I saw him—lying there, his dull, lifeless eyes staring up at nothing—"

"Aw heck, lass, he *always* looks like that."

"But he *must* be dead," she reasoned frantically. "No living being could look so or . . ." She shuddered. "Who, pray tell, is he?"

Righting herself, both chubby fists propped on her equally chubby hips, the servant frowned and worried her lower lip between her teeth. "It's him, o'course," she finally replied.

"Him?"

"Aye. *Him.*"

Little by little the servant's meaning sunk in. Sliding her feet from the bed, momentarily closing her eyes as the throbbing on her forehead sluiced through her temples, Maria shook her head. "But that's not possible. I was employed to companion a child, not some—"

"Lud, the old dear must be gettin' desperate—or daft. She *tol'* ya he was a child?"

Raising her eyes to the servant's, Maria opened and closed her mouth. "Not in so many words, but . . . I assumed . . ."

"I reckon he were like a child," said the maid, her expression becoming sad, her eyes distant. "Aye, it breaks me heart to see him now, so helpless and mindless, wastin' away."

Pulling a linen from her apron pocket, Gertrude dabbed at her eye and sniffed. "I've worked for His Grace goin' on eight year, seven of 'em a pleasure, I vow. He were always a decent master, if not a bit tempestuous. He were that way, once, ya know. Tempestuous. Full of the devil, he were, in and out of mischief's way, causin' his family a lot of bother—"

"His Grace?" Disbelief settled around Maria in a red haze. "That . . . *being* . . . in yonder room is—"

"My grandson," came the firm voice from the doorway. Gertrude jumped aside, revealing the dowager duchess's frail form on the threshold. Weight resting on the crook of her cane, her sharp gray eyes scanned the opulent bed chamber before settling again on Maria. "That *being* is my grandson, Miss Ashton: the Duke of

Salterdon. Heir to my dear, departed husband's title. Heir to my fortune when I, myself, am gone."

"How dare you?" Maria cried, causing Gertrude to squeak in dismay and dash from the room, muttering under her breath. Maria slid from the bed, swayed with dizziness before drawing back her shoulders with an effort that sent a sharp pain down her back. "With respect, Your Grace, you lied—"

"At no time did I insinuate that your charge was a child, Miss Ashton."

"But anyone would assume—"

"I fail to see what difference it makes. Had I thought you incapable of adequately filling the position I wouldn't have employed you."

"But he isn't human! He's . . . he's . . ."

"A monster?"

A servant bustled in with a silver chocolate service, which she placed on a table near the distant, cheerfully crackling fire. Only when the housemaid had departed did the duchess make her way to the cluster of winged-back chairs grouped around the hearth. She eased down into a tapestry seat before saying, "I will ask you to hear me out before making any snap decisions concerning your continued employment at Thorn Rose."

"I cannot imagine *what* you could convey that would alter my opinion, Your Grace."

The duchess poured chocolate into a pair of china cups. "Do you like this room?" she asked, reaching for an ornate silver spoon. "It's yours, if you wish. I hadn't intended for you to be put in with the other servants."

"I don't want the room," Maria declared. "I won't be bought—"

"It was my husband's favorite. The mural of St. Peter depicted on the ceiling was taken from a painting he once saw hanging in the Louvre in Paris. My husband was a very religious man. He felt that any hurdle we confront during the course of our existence on earth is nothing more than His way of teaching us how to be worthier of heaven."

With the gold rim of the cup poised at her lips, the duchess gazed off into space and, with a crease in her brow, said thoughtfully, "Although I cannot imagine what lesson could come of this . . . problem. My grandson, though occasionally reckless and willful, and more often than not lacking in moral fiber, was not evil, nor wicked. I fail to see, Miss Ashton, why he should be made to suffer so." Turning her glassy eyes back to Maria, she pleaded in a more feeble voice, "Please, young lady, sit and hear me out."

Maria sat, but when the duchess attempted to hand her the cup of steaming chocolate, she shook her head and said, "You cannot convince me, Your Grace. I won't remain here."

"Then what will you do? Return to your father's home? Is that sort of hell more to your liking?"

"You *are* cruel," Maria declared with a lift of her chin. "And devious. I'm sorry I ever thought to reply to that dreadful ad."

"But you did and here you are. You don't strike me as the type of young woman who would flee from adversity. If that were so you would have escaped your father's house long ago."

"I'll go to London," she said with conviction.

"And do what? You have no formal education, other than that which, according to your mother, was taught to you by your brother, unbeknownst to your father, who, once learning of your's and Paul's scandalous behavior, stropped you both and refused you food and water for three days—hoping such deprivation would cleanse the sin of deception from your minds and hearts."

"He meant well," Maria said, disbelieving her own words as the memory triggered hot color into her face.

"Did he?"

Maria jumped to her feet. "I shan't be bullied. Nor will I be manipulated. Had you prospected into my past as thoroughly as you say you'd realize that I am not easily intimidated. In truth, Your Grace, I'm well-known for my penchant for being unreasonably determined not to yield under pressure. My remaining here, companioning that . . . *man* is immoral and impossible and . . . I demand that you return me to Huddersfield immediately."

"And then where will your dreams be, Miss Ashton? How will you manage to save enough money to provide your mother with a way out of her predicament? How do you intend to provide her a home, should you convince her to leave your father? Oh yes, my dear, I'm well aware of those aspirations as well."

Maria fled the room, took the stairs two at a time, losing her way along several passageways before locating the tiny chamber that had been her quarters upon arriving at Thorn Rose the evening before.

Flinging herself onto the bed, she buried her face into the musty pillow. The knot on her forehead throbbed pitiably, but it was the sense of disappointment that troubled her most; disappointment, not, surprisingly, at her circumstances or even the cold thread of shock that shivered like an icicle through her entire being, but at her behavior. Anger was not admirable, and such temper tantrums were unforgivable. Dignity came with equanimity. God frowned on such ill and grievous outbursts. Her father would have locked her in a box for such behavior.

She would face the duchess again, of course, and more calmly explain her reasons for wishing to leave Thorn Rose. Certainly, the duchess would find someone else—preferably a man—to tend her grandson, the Duke of Salterdon, or what still existed of him.

What *did* exist of him—that terrible corpse of a man, the beast, the monster lying so lifelessly in a bed fit for royalty, surrounded by more wealth than a thousand men would know in their entire lifetimes?

Gertrude entered the room, bestowing Maria a concerned, understanding smile. "I'll see to that bump on yer head now. Oo, that's a good one that. It'll be right blue for a while—"

"I don't want the poultice," Maria announced, and rolled toward the wall. "I should suffer dreadfully for my selfishness. 'Twould serve me right."

"'Tis everyone's reaction when they first see him, 'specially those who've known him before . . . family and friends, I mean. 'Cept there ain't much family and friends who come round anymore. Just his brother and the duchess . . . and them leeches Thackley and Edgcumbe," she added under her breath, and frowned. Shuffling round the bed and plopping herself onto the sagging mattress, the cherub-faced Gertrude tenderly placed the pungent bag of hot herbs on the swelling. Maria winced but offered no further resistance.

"I reckon it's just too painful to see him that way, knowin' how he was before and all. I often thought it a mistake to hide him away out here, but the duchess's advisors felt it would be less humiliatin' for her and him. Knowin' His Grace, I imagine he wouldn't care to have society paradin' through his home, starin' at him like he was some curiosity."

"Is he dying?"

Gertrude pursed her lips. "I don't rightly know. Edgcumbe"—her voice became tight—"says he's dead in here." She tapped her temple. " 'Tis only a matter of time before the body dies as well. Course, if it were left up to Edgcumbe, His Grace would've long since been buried at Menston."

"Menston?"

"Royal Oaks Hospital for the Mentally Infirm at Menston. Oo, lass, it were a dreadful place. Full of lunatics and folk possessed by awful wickedness. The poor souls are chained and beaten like animals."

Maria swallowed.

Gertrude wrung her hands. "The idea of His Grace bein' interned there . . . it makes me furious when I see how Edgcumbe and Thackley are wearin' down Her

Grace's resistance, constantly tellin' her that he would be better off there . . . and so would she. She ain't been the same since all this happened. It seems all the life has gone out of her."

"How was he injured?"

"Thieves wot jumped him as he left Epson Races. Aye, he were a rogue then, a real rakehell. He and his brother, Lord Basingstoke, were once the most eligible bach'lors in all England. Prime, they was, and handsome—twins, ya know. *Identical.* Then Lord Basingstoke up and married a lass from Wight and His Grace was left to fight off *the marriage noose*, as he always called it. He just lies there now, makin' his life and ever'one else's hell, rousin' only when he's a mind to, which ain't often. Only then it's to roar like a dragon or fling china at our heads."

"Can he neither speak nor walk?"

Gertrude's expression became odd, her hands nervous. Finally, she sighed heavily and tucked her wrinkled linen back into her pocket and started for the door.

"Gertrude?" Maria called, causing the servant to pause at the door and reluctantly look back. "Is he insane?"

"That ain't for me to say, lass."

Maria barely noticed the servant's exit, but lay with her head nestled into the pillow and stared at the ceiling. What next? Last evening's escapade was enough to put her in shock . . . now this.

She shivered, buried her face in the pillow again and tried to put the "beast's" image from her mind. Impossible! Unlike her brother, this man's personage was terrifying, his physique massive, and *he was quite possibly demented.*

Oh, merciful Lord in heaven, was this to be her punishment for turning her back on her family and goodly John Rees, who personified virtue and uprightness? Was she simply to walk into this unseemly and questionable situation like Daniel into the lion's den? A lion would certainly seem less threatening!

She would not do it! She *could not!* Headstrong and determinedly willful she might be, but she was not irrationally stupid. She would request a day or two to consider her circumstances then ask—nay—demand that she be transported to some safer and more acceptable domicile. Until that time she would be in no way responsible for the duchess's ugly and grievous grandson.

At last, much to her consternation, she found her way back to that terrible place of illness and impending death, where she discovered the duchess, flanked by Thackley and Edgcumbe, standing at her grandson's bedside, weeping softly. Despite her earlier anger, Maria's first instinct was to run to the frail duchess and comfort her, but then she sensed that few people had ever witnessed this particular woman in a weak moment. Still, the need to console her was strong. Despite her revulsion of the appalling premises and its inhuman inhabitant, she understood the feeling of helplessness and despair. As the duchess felt for her grandson, so had Maria felt for her brother. Her Grace felt that his life was as her life, and that his death, or the very contemplation of such horror, would make the world so black that to look upon it drove the pain of loss to the very core of her soul.

"Trey, Trey, my darling boy," the duchess wept, her voice quivering in grief and anger. "What shall we do now? How could they have allowed you to become this . . . monster? How could they have treated you so despicably? You are my grandson! The Duke of Salterdon . . ."

"There, there, Isabella," comforted Edgcumbe. "You shouldn't be here. You shouldn't see this. My own heart is broken that Trey has come to this. You know I have loved him like my own son over the years—"

"As have I," Thackley said.

Having joined Maria, Gertrude gasped, her round face becoming flushed as she discovered the terrible condition of the room. "Lud," she groaned, then hurried to the duchess, offered an abrupt curtsy, then proceeded to wring her hands.

"Beggin' yer forgiveness, Your Grace. I ain't been on staff in a fortnight—only arrived back just a few short minutes before you come. Rest assured, Your Grace, that this terrible situation won't happen again."

The duchess said nothing, just stared down at the still as death form in the bed.

Gertrude gave Thackley and Edgcumbe an impertinent sniff then turned on her heels and exited the room, not so much as glancing toward Maria. There came heated voices from the hallway: Gertrude's and Molly's.

"Daft girl, wot the bloody hell were ya thinkin' to allow His Grace to get in that condition?"

"I'd like t' see you risk a conk on the noggin—'e's dangerous, I vow, 'urlin' china at our 'eads—"

"More likely you were occupyin' that blazin' stable boy Thaddeus. I wouldn't blame Her Grace if she dismissed you. I'd see to it meself if—"

"Ya won't be seein' to aught, ya silly ol' bugger, cause ya know ya won't be findin' anyone else willin' to put up with his stuff. And we both know the duchess don't want the rest of England to know what a bloody idiot he's become."

Maria closed her eyes and sank against the wall. "Blazes," she whispered. "Blazes."

"You'll write me the moment there's been any change," said the duchess as she boarded her coach, along with Thackley and Edgcumbe.

"Of course." Maria stood aside as the coachman closed the door and latched it.

Peering down at her through the window, her face slightly ashen and her eyes a trifle red, the duchess managed a smile. "Are you certain you like the room? You may change at any time, if you so desire. I felt your being near him would help—"

"The chamber is lovely," she assured her.

The duchess gazed up the facade of the immense house. "I've informed the staff that you have total control over this house and my grandson's welfare."

"'Tis a tremendous responsibility, Your Grace."

"Of which you are perfectly capable," she replied

with a touch of her old authority, then added with a dignified lift of one thin eyebrow, "I sensed it the moment I saw you—your strength and moral fiber. You shall do him good, I think."

" 'Twould do him better to be with his family and friends, I think," Maria stated boldly, causing a twinge of despair to cross the duchess's brow. "Would you depart so soon, Your Grace? Would you not remain a day or two, to assure yourself that I'm competent for the task, if nothing else?"

"Were I yet young at soul as well as heart . . . but my soul is weary and my heart is broken, my dear. I cannot stand to see him that way for very long. I was never strong where my children's welfare was concerned. Please understand . . ."

With a lift of her hand, and a last faint smile, the duchess bid Maria goodbye and the coach rolled under way.

Maria gazed after her, long after the stately conveyance had disappeared over the horizon and silence and winter's emptiness had filled the world again. She thought about calling after the duchess, of explaining one last time that the thought of spending one moment in her grandson's presence filled her with a fear she had not known even with her father.

A thin snow had begun to fall. It covered the countryside with sheer white, allowing patches of dark earth to show through. All seemed peaceful and she could not help but turn her face up and allow the cold sprinkles to dust her closed lids and nose and lips.

Ah, but she and Paul had loved the snow—had loved

to sneak away from their father's stern eye to frolic like puppies, to build snow castles, to slide daringly across the perilously thin pond ice. Many a time, in those last months of his life, they had gazed out his window and watched the snow fall and shared their most intimate secrets: secrets about would-be lovers strolling through snow-dusted wheat fields together . . . of kissing until their noses turned red from cold and their mingled breaths formed sparkling icicles on their mouths.

Alas, 'twould be her first winter without Paul.

Wearily, she reentered the manse and, shutting the door behind her, leaned back against it and closed her eyes. When she opened them again, she looked into the wide-eyed watchful eyes of the curious staff.

Gertrude beamed her a reassuring smile. "I'm glad ya stayed, lass. I sense y'll bring some life to the old place. Ya might even do His Grace a bit of good."

"I hope so," she replied simply, though she was not at all certain of it herself. She felt a bit light-headed with nervousness; her stomach ached and she wondered if it were from trepidation or because she had not eaten since yesterday morning.

"If ya ask me"—Molly's voice came from a nearby doorway—"she won't be lastin' out the week. 'E'll be eatin' the likes of 'er for his bloody tea by the end of the day . . ."

"Hush!" Gertrude threw the servant a withering look. "There'll be no more o' that talk in my company. If the duchess feels the lass is capable of handlin' the . . . His Grace, then that's that. In truth, it might do His Grace a bit o' good to have such an angel watchin' over him. We all thrive with a bit of kindness and compassion now and again."

" 'E'll break 'er in two joost like that," Molly sneered then snapped her fingers for emphasis.

Maria gasped.

Molly sauntered toward the group, her hands on her hips. "Maybe we should tell 'er joost wot he done t' the others, eh?"

Gertrude made a sound and the others muttered to themselves.

"Conked 'em, 'e did, right on the ol' noggin' with this or that dish. If he could get 'is 'ands on 'em 'e flung 'em like they was puppets across the room—'cept Mr. Doherty who he pitched out the window, headfirst. It were an ugly mess, I vow." She shuddered. " 'Is arms is strong as ten men's, I wager, and when 'e snarls—"

"Enough!" Gertrude cried. "He weren't that bad, love," she said to Maria, who felt herself go cold inside at the image of the "the beast" snarling and mauling any hapless ninny who thought to help him. "Granted, he has his moments, but who wouldn't, considerin'. He were once an energetic and virile man, not to mention handsome—"

"Handsome," Maria said in a tone of disbelief.

"Aye," another young maid declared with an air of dreaminess. "A real rogue, he were. Weren't a mamma in England wouldn't have given her right tit to get her daughter matched up with him . . . if she couldn't have him herself."

The group snickered, and Molly added, "Most of 'em did. 'E made a cuckold of 'alf the husbands in England,

I wager. By the time 'e used up one there were another
waitin' in the background. Course, them days are gone
now. The silly bitches wot used to come sniffin' at 'is
'eels wouldn't come within a mile of 'im now. Not even
that fancy-knickered Lady Laura—"

"Ye'll not be spoutin' on about his personal affairs,"
Gertrude declared in a tone that set half the servants
back on their heels. "Yer just jealous that he wouldn't
have aught to do with you. And speakin' of jealous,
you'd best keep yer talons out of Miss Ashton or ye'll
have me to answer to. The lass has got better judgment
than to be sniffin' after the lot of ne'er-do-wells you
invite under yer skirts."

With a squeal of indignation, Molly marched from
the foyer, slamming a door in her wake.

The image of a naked Molly and companion writhing
over the kitchen table brought a discomfiting flush to
Maria's cheeks—even more so than the thought of
venturing up the stairs to confront the devil himself. So
collecting herself up, filled with a purpose she had not
experienced since the passing away of her brother, she
moved toward the staircase. " 'Tis no better time than
this to get to know him, I suppose," she said more to
herself than to her companions.

The line of servants trailed up the staircase behind
her, their footsteps reverberating like marching soldiers
on the carpeted floor.

The corridors to His Grace's room were lined with
gold-gilded friezes and busts of kings and queens (no
doubt the Salterdon ancestors), and life-sized portraits
of wide-eyed, pale-faced young boys (identical in every

manner) lounging with dogs or sitting rigidly on the backs of saddled horses. Only as Maria paused outside the duke's door did the idea occur to her that one of those cherubic visages belonged to the Duke of Salterdon. So much for innocence . . .

Allowing herself a glance back at Gertrude, who encouraged her with a weak smile, Maria nudged open the chamber door, bracing herself for the rush of cold, fetid air and gloom. Regarding the littered floor, the dim light, the bed blanketed by shadows and testers, and the vague form silhouetted within, Maria cleared her throat and stepped over the threshold, feeling not unlike Beowulf entering Grendel's lair.

She made her way through the broken china, past tumbled furnishings and discarded clothes (long forgotten) tossed over chair backs. Arriving at the window, she took a fortifying breath and flung open the drapes, scattering dust that danced in the dull winter's light spilling through sooty windows.

"Gertrude," she called.

"Aye, Miss Ashton?"

"From now on these casings will be left open during the day."

"Aye, Miss Ashton."

"We'll begin by cleaning this room. Bring hot water and soap and brushes. Remove the carpets and beat them. I noticed fresh flowers—"

"They come from the conservatory, miss."

"I want every table, every nook and cranny filled with flowers. Yonder chandelier is to be polished, and light it."

"Immediately, miss."

Turning to her underlings, Gertrude barked out orders and clapped her hands, causing her subordinates to scatter. Turning back to Maria, Gertrude looked from her to the bed then back again, her expression now one of concern and wariness.

Maria gave her a reassuring smile and approached the bed, hesitated as she reached for the curtain, then taking another deep breath, drew it aside.

His Grace, the Duke of Salterdon, or what she could see of him beneath his tangle of dark, slightly curly hair and bearded features, lay just as he had lain the previous evening, twisted in his bedclothes, his dull eyes open, staring at the roof of his bed. Cautiously bending nearer, pressing the back of one hand against her nose and mouth, she studied hard to see that his chest was slightly moving.

Closer, holding her breath, she tried her best to study his unkempt features, which were even more frightening than she had first thought. Surely, this personage could not belong to anything human—certainly no one sane! Those sunken features—or what she could see of them behind the wild growth of facial hair, heavy brows, and tangled mop of hair spread out over the entire soiled pillowcase—were corpse-like. Trembling, she passed her hand over his face and eyes, prepared to snatch it back at the least hint that he might rouse from his trance-like state to attack her. Yet he did not so much as blink.

Turning again to Gertrude, she asked, "How long has he lain here like this?"

"I can't rightly say, miss. Like I told ya, I've been away for a fortnight. But even afore I left he'd decided to hole himself up in here like some dragon in a cave. He wouldn't have aught to do with anyone tryin' to rouse him. We was forced to leave his meals on a tray by his bed. Sometimes he managed to feed himself— other times . . ." A sadness passing over her features, Gertrude wrung her hands. "Other times he'd go for days, as if he were willin' himself to starve, until the hunger became so bad he'd break down and . . ."

Gertrude turned away. Maria hurried to her, wrapped one arm comfortingly around the housekeeper's shoulders, and regarded her pained profile. "And what, dear Gertrude? Tell me. I must know everything if I'm to help him."

Gertrude shook her head, as if the memory were too much to bear. "I'd find him attemptin' to feed himself, food crushed in his hands 'cause he ain't got the coordination no more to find his mouth. It broke me heart, it did, to see him that way, knowin' how he use to be and all—so dignified and handsome—aye, he was the epitome of aristocracy. We was all right proud to work for him."

Her own throat tight with emotion, recalling how her own brother had become a mere shadow of himself, Maria gave the grieving servant a reassuring hug. "Then that shall be our first endeavor, dear Gertrude: to do our best to restore our master to his former distinguished self. Will you help me?"

"Aye, lass."

"Our first objective will be to clean this room from top to bottom, then focus our energies on His Grace. I'll need your help to assure the staff that no harm will come to them."

"It won't be easy, miss. Betty, she's the uncomely wee one with the crossed eyes and the underbite—her job is to empty the grates and clean and polish 'em with black lead—the last time she come in here he flung a china vase at her—smacked her upside the head, it did, right here." She pointed to her right ear. "She's been hearin' bells ring ever since. Says it'll be a cold day in perdition before she sticks a big toe over that threshold. And who could blame 'er."

"But he seems docile enough now." Maria cast another precautionary look toward the bed.

Gertrude lowered her voice to a whisper, and her face became a mask of fear. "That's the devil of it, ya see. Ya just never know when he's gonna rouse. One minute he's lyin' there starin' off into space, the next he's grabbin' ya 'round the neck and wringin' the very life from ya. Ooo, I shudder to think about it!" With a gasp, Gertrude covered her mouth with her hands and squeezed her eyes closed. Her entire body took on a trembling that made Maria's chest restrict. "Promise me ye'll be cautious at all times," the housekeeper pleaded.

Her mouth dry, Maria nodded.

"Then I'll see to the others." Gertrude moved toward the door, where the others continued to crowd, brows knit in consternation and anticipation. Stopping, she looked around, chin quivering, her face twisted in a sort of despair, which made Maria feel as if she were about to be hanged and slung from the gibbet.

"Good luck to ye," said the maid, then she scurried from the chamber.

Chapter Three

From her bedroom threshold, which adjoined Salter-don's immense chamber, Maria watched as a small army of servants paraded into his room, arms loaded with dustbins, wash pails, brushes and flakes of lye soap. They set about their grueling task with fierce purpose, occasionally glancing warily toward their master as if anticipating his rousing any moment to devour them.

Soon the displeasing stench of sickness gave way to the pungent smells of soap and fragrant beeswax, and with each improvement Maria's spirit lifted, despite the extreme fatigue she felt over her lack of food and sleep. Twice she attempted to lend her energies, little as they were, to the task of cleaning, but Gertrude would not have it.

"The duchess has left explicit directives that yer one and only concern is to be His Grace. And that we're to treat ya as if you were a member of Her Grace's family."

"But I'm unaccustomed to such idleness," she explained.

"Ye'll not be idle for long," Gertrude declared with a lingering look at the apparently unconscious man in the bed. "He'll come 'round eventually, and then . . . well, miss, ye'll see for yerself soon enough."

Little by little, the cleaning crew dwindled, until only Betty remained, frantically polishing the fire grate and casting terrified glances toward the shadowed bed. Any attempt on Maria's behalf to console her only managed to agitate the skittish servant more. At last, with a groan of relief, the mousy little maid tossed kindling onto the coal, lit the beeswax candles in the girandoles scattered over the walls, and made a hasty retreat from the room, slamming the door behind her with a finality that shook the windowpanes.

Alone at last, her hands clasped together at her bosom, her toes slightly turned in and peeking from beneath the hem of her black skirt, Maria glanced about the sprawling masculine-appointed apartment and listened to the murmur of a tall case clock on the adjacent wall.

" 'Tis silly to feel so frightened," she said aloud. "He couldn't possibly be any more menacing than Father. Or more cruel. Could he?"

Forcing her feet to move, she crossed through the gloaming shadows to stand at the foot of Salterdon's bed. Through the pale sheers she could barely make out his form. The servants had done a respectable job of tidying his bedclothes, which lay neatly molded to his body. They had even managed to contain his wild mane of hair so it no longer spread out over his pillow. Still, there was little they could do to soften his feral mien. He looked as terrifying as before, and she shuddered all the way to her shoes.

From the tall case clock came a click and groan. The felt-covered hammer struck a muted seven times. With each strike Maria attempted to force herself nearer the bed; her duty, after all, was to see to her master's comfort as well as his welfare. She could hardly accomplish that while standing here, at the foot of his bed, her only thoughts on the awful stories about Salterdon the servants had divulged during the long, exhaustive afternoon.

Cautiously, she eased to the side of the bed, nudging open the sheer with one slightly shaking fingertip. If he made a grab for her she would scream; Gertrude assured her that all she need do, if the circumstances arose, was to cry loudly or give a good yank on the bell-pull. Someone would *eventually* hear her.

Unable to see him clearly, she reached for the lit candle on the nightstand and concentrated on keeping it steady as she lowered it near his face. As always, his dark, vacant eyes were open and staring. The reflection of the flickering candle flame gave the only life to those maniacal orbs; she suspected that when they were aware, they would be full of fire and condemnation . . . like her father's—no, not like her father's. There would be no threat of hellfire in these eyes . . . but something far different . . . but just as frightening—mayhap more dangerous. When, she wondered, would the dragon rouse?

"Your Grace," she called softly, tentatively. "Can you hear me? My name is Maria Ashton, Your Grace. I've come here to help you. Blink if you comprehend me."

Nothing.

Lowering the candle near his face, she leaned more closely over him, noting the strong bridge of his nose and how deeply set were his eyes. He had a fine brow, she realized, now that the servants had brushed the hair back from his temples, and his mouth, though mostly hidden behind the untended facial hair, looked not unbecoming. His lips, she thought, looked as if they would be quick to smile, to quip, to slash to the heart with one murmured indignity.

Frowning, she drew away, put aside the candle, and retreated to her room.

She wrote a letter to John Rees, and another to her mother detailing every minute of her time since arriving at Thorn Rose. Terms like Goliath, fierce, and horrifying continued to pepper her dialogue, along with palatial, sumptuous, and opulently awe-inspiring until, frustrated, she crushed the stationery and tossed it to the floor.

How did she convey to the two people she loved most in the world that her very welfare might well be in question? And would it not seem inelegant to wax on about her pampered and sumptuous manner of living? John Rees would fear for her decadent soul. Her mother . . . if her mother would only realize that

Maria was doing this for her with hopes of someday providing her with a haven safe from the Vicar Ashton's influence and not because her childhood fantasies had, at last, corrupted her priorities as her father had always vowed they would.

She was not Satan's Angel using her body to manipulate men's souls to sin. How could she, bound up like some medieval maiden so that her woman's frame was as flat and shapeless as a boy's?

" 'Tis no wonder that John Rees showed so little in the way of manly appetites," she mused aloud, her wide blue eyes looking on her image in an oval looking glass. The prim collar of her dress fit snugly around her throat. Her lips forming a slight pout, she flipped open the trail of tiny buttons until her throat was exposed to her collarbone. Another two, then another, until she could just discern the shadowy line of the cotton bindings beneath her simple, coarsely spun linen shift.

There came a sudden rap on the door. Grabbing closed her collar, jumping from the chair, she spun toward the entry as Gertrude poked her head in and smiled.

"Yer up yet. Good. I thought y'd be likin' a bath. The lads have brought yer water."

Her face flushed, her fingers clumsily stumbling with her blouse buttons, Maria mutely nodded, her jaw dropping as Gertrude flung back the door, allowing the entrance of several strapping lads hefting steaming water in great buckets hanging from yokes over their shoulders.

Gertrude hurried to the sprawling Japanese-lacquered

room divider taking up one corner of the chamber, and with a grunt and groan, wheeled out an immense ornate object whose curving sides reached as high as Maria's waist. A highly detailed lid fit snugly over the top. Gertrude placed it before the fire.

"What is it?" Maria eyed it suspiciously.

"A bathin' tub, o' course." Gertrude flipped back a notched section of the cover and nodded at the waterboys. They filed by one by one, depositing water into the tub, enough to make the nearby windowpanes turn blurry with condensation.

"Gracious," Maria declared. " 'Tis deep enough to drown in."

"Aye. Ya wouldn't know it now, but His Grace believed in cleanliness if nothin' else. He designed these tubs himself, even this contraption." She pointed to the cover. "It keeps the heat and steam in longer. If ya ask me I'd feel like a bleedin' lobster in a pot, but then, who can figure the aristocracy, eh? Me dear ol' mum used to say that more'n one bath a month was sorely puttin' yer health in jeopardy." Lowering her voice, she added, "His Grace won't bath in aught but rain caught in the water butts. Says its purities cleanse the pores and softens the skin better than water fetched from wells or becks. Has his horses bathed in rainwater as well."

"Horses?"

As the last of the waterboys left the room, Gertrude closed the door and hurried back to Maria. She began fussing with the remaining closed buttons on Maria's dress. "Horses," Gertrude stated. "Dozens of 'em. Arabians."

"Arabians?"

"Incredible, they are. Elegant as any graceful woman, and beautiful to boot. They became a passion of His Grace's the last few years—ever since his brother married a lass who had a devotion to 'em. Always had an eye for horseflesh, did Salterdon."

"Horses," Maria mused a bit dreamily. "I've always dreamt of owning my own."

"He were unlucky at the gamblin' table, but never failed to leave the track with a purse full of winnin's." She clucked her tongue. "It were Epson Races that were his undoin'. Gorm thieves wot jumped him and his friends as they left Epson that night."

If Gertrude found Maria's bindings uniquely strange, she didn't show it. Instead, the portly maid walked to a chiffonier and pulled open a drawer. "Feel free to use any of these salts, love. A dash or two of these and ye'll be smellin' sweet as a flower. I'll be givin' ya yer privacy now. One of the gels will see to yer dinner."

Without another word, Gertrude quit the chamber.

After a moment's hesitation, Maria allowed the shift to slide from her shoulders, then the bindings, which pooled around her ankles and feet.

Ah, sweet freedom! Cupping her breasts in her hands, she rubbed away their numbness, enjoyed their feeling of heaviness, the idea occurring to her that this could well be the first night in years that she would sleep without the confinement of bindings. At last there would be nothing to fear. Her father was far away—no more terrifying nights of waking, startled, to discover him standing over her, his hands on her bound breasts . . . making certain, he'd said, that her licentious femininity was sufficiently suppressed.

After dumping the entirety of a bottle of violet-scented salts into the steaming water, Maria carefully climbed in, holding her breath and sinking slowly into the hot water; her flesh tingled with heat, and the scents rising with the steam cocooned her in wild fragrance so she began to feel heady.

Oh, but this was decadence! She really shouldn't indulge herself so; she might become accustomed to such superfluity, and then what? She would become exactly what her father had predicted, and besides, who could say whether she would remain at Thorn Rose for long? Should *the beast*—His Grace—prove to be as difficult to handle as the servants vowed, she might do well to survive their eventual meeting!

Still, what harm could come from enjoying such a bath this once?

The door opened behind her, then gently closed.

"You may put my dinner tray there, next to the bed," she called, her eyes drifting closed as she slid a lathered soap ball over her shoulders and smiled. "I feel dreadfully sinful. Silly, isn't it? Do you know I've never bathed in anything other than a foot tub? The only time I've managed to submerge this much was when my dear brother and I sneaked down to Jones's beck to swim. It, of course, wasn't warm nor did it smell of violets. In truth, it was frequented by Jones's pigs—a dreadful lot of boars who made haste to chase us away with immeasurable grunts and shrieks." Laughing lightly, she cupped the scented water in her palms and allowed it to trickle over her face. "One bit my brother on his naked behind. He howled all the way home, then told my father that he'd been butted by a goat. I told him he'd been *butted* all right . . ."

Laughing again, she stood, allowing the water to slide like fluid silk down her body as she added, "Father never found out Paul was lying. I, however, had my mouth washed out with soap for speaking so fresh. Will you hand me that toweling, please?" She pointed to the linen Gertrude had provided for drying.

"I'd be more than happy to," came the male voice, "just as soon as I deposit this coal near the fire."

Without thinking, she spun around, her eyes flying wide, her jaw dropping open as Thaddeus, Molly's kitchen lover, bestowed her a toothy smile.

Thaddeus Hartley Edwards looked quite different with his clothes on. Maria failed to recognize him at first, dressed as he was, in loose cotton breeches and a checked flannel shirt that was dusted with hayseed. His hair was neatly brushed back, and his jaw appeared freshly shaven. As he directed those dark laughing eyes to hers, and his mouth curved in a grin that was reminiscent of the one he had bestowed on her the evening before, the realization that she stood before him unabashedly naked struck her.

"Oh!" she cried. "Oh my. Oh . . ." She dropped back into the tub, sending water spraying over the sides.

"Gorm." He shook his head. "Yer even comelier than I thought—"

"Get out!"

"No wonder Molly's got her knickers in a twist. And

to think I tol' 'er ya wasn't nothin' more than some flat-chested chit I wouldn't spend a ha'penny t' poke."

"I beg your pardon!"

He sauntered across the room, a hob of coal cradled in his arms. "I reckon this makes us even, don't it? We've both seen each other naked as the day we was born. Now that we've got the 'I'll show ya mine if ye'll show me yers' over with we can get down to more serious business."

"The only business we shall 'get down to' is your leaving my room without hesitation!"

"*Yer* room, is it? Ain't we got cozy all of a sudden." Dropping the hob to the hearth, then propping his hands on his hips, he added with a lift of his eyebrows, "Looks t' me like you ain't got much room t' barter, Miss Maria Ashton of Huddersfield, unless ya want t' come out of that barrel and make me."

"Perverted fiend. Gertrude was right about you."

"Gertrude is a meddlin' ol' bat who's jealous 'cause there ain't an eligible bastard in the entire county who'd have her."

With a furious huff of exasperation, Maria grabbed for the tub cover and folded it down around her. Only her head protruded through the opening as she continued glaring at her intruder. "If you don't leave here immediately, I shall inform Gertrude, and the duchess as well, that you and Molly have been . . . fornicating on the kitchen table."

"Ouch!"

"I mean it!"

"Fornicatin' is an awful sinful word for the vicar's

daughter to be spittin'. Then again, I ain't ever seen no reverend's daughter wot looked like you. You can take that as a compliment, by the way."

"I take your entire existence at this moment as the worst grievous insult. Now, for the last time—"

"Right. I'll get out. Just wanted to drop by and welcome ya to Thorn Rose, and t' let ya know that I've got a broad shoulder t' lean on when ya need it. And ya *will* need it soon as 'e rouses. It'll be right curious to see wot 'e'll do about you. 'E's just liable to eat you alive, lass. Aye, y'll be lucky t' come out of this with that lovely little backside intact. 'Ave a real good evenin', Miss Ashton. Enjoy it while ya can."

From the void there came voices, muted as always, at least while he dwelt here, in the foggy recesses of unconsciousness, floating lightly as if on air, sunlight and shadow shifting in and out of his obscured vision— eternal days of lying in this crypt-bed—his entire world now a distant cacophony of sounds—birdsong, the infrequent comings and goings of servants who stopped talking or humming whenever they entered his "lair"— unending nights of waiting for daylight to return so he could, at least, look forward to the idiots' company— brief as it was. Oh, yes, a man of any intellect could go insane removed from an intelligent society. His own thoughts could drive him insane. The monotony of breathing could drive him insane. The monotony of routine, or the lack thereof, could drive him insane— had driven him insane.

Ah, yes, he must surely be crazed—out of his

mind—else the visions of blue-eyed angels with porcelain skin and hair as soft and silvery as spun clouds would not have stirred him from his bleary senseless sleep. Certainly, he was losing his final, tenuous grip on reality to imagine that he could smell violets, that the lyrical tune of a woman humming, and the alluring tinkle of splashing water were anything but conjurings of a frighteningly disturbed mind—a mind which, too often, grappled with the memories of beautiful women: long-limbed, sweet-smelling women who would have sold their souls to perdition to sleep with him— once . . . no longer.

He was a beast. A monster. A lunatic, after all. A woman would have to be desperate to spend time in his company.

Chapter Four

He was a monster. A beast. *A lunatic!*

Maria dreamt of awakening to discover the Duke of Salterdon standing over her, features barely discernible behind his lion-like mane of hair and wild beard, his staring eyes lit by fire, his hands on her breasts. Only it was her father's voice growling from his throat, proclaiming her to be possessed of witchery, an instrument of lust. What *God-fearing* man would care to associate with such a slattern?

At just after three in the morning she sat up in bed, her swollen eyes fixed on the deep shadows near the door to his room. Was it open? She was certain she'd closed it!

Scrambling from the bed, she ran to the door and flung herself against it, heart racing, hands fumbling with the knob only to discover that the door was closed solid and locked. She tried to breathe evenly; attempted to slow down her frantically racing heart and to rationalize. There was nothing to be frightened of. Her

69

monsters of the dark were behind her . . . at least those with the Vicar Ashton's face.

Yet, now there was this other—a man who terrified and abused his staff; a beast-man with the temperament of a dragon; a man so large and fearsome that to come within a room's length of him, even as he lay there as if dead, made her tremble with fear.

Dear God, which abomination frightened her more?

Gertrude clucked her tongue and, taking Maria's face in her hands, shook her head. "Ye've not slept a wink, I vow. Yer lovely blue eyes are sunken and shadowed. Tell Gerti the truth; are ya homesick, lass?"

Offering her friend a weak smile, Maria pulled away and swept up a paper. "I've spent the last few hours contriving a plan with which to deal with His Grace's circumstances. What is most important is to coerce him out of his ennui."

"We've attempted that for the last year, to no luck. I reckon when a soul decides to give up there's naught you can do about it . . . and ya didn't answer me question. Yer family, lass: are ya missin' 'em?"

"There comes a time in a woman's life when she'll do better for herself on her own, Gerti."

"That's a lot of muddlycock. A lass like you ought to be married by now and bouncin' a pair of bairns on her knees." Glancing about the chamber, noting that Maria had already made her bed—not to mention seeing that the tub had been emptied the night before and her ewers filled with fresh water this morning, Gertrude sighed. "By the looks of this place ye'd make an adequate wife.

Not many gels I know could tuck corners as neatly as them." She pointed to the well-made bed.

"My father was a perfectionist. Only those individuals who are entirely without flaw and who meet supreme standards of excellence in all that they do will reach heaven."

Her merry eyes narrowing as she regarded Maria, Gertrude shook her head. "I reckon that don't leave much hope for the majority of us, does it?"

Maria said nothing, just slid on her kid slippers and adjusted her skirt over them, doing her best to hide the fact that the shoes were worn thin.

"Does yer father's idea of perfection have aught to do with the bindin's ya wear?"

Maria turned away.

"Ye've got no reason to wear them here," Gertrude pointed out.

"I simply feel more comfortable with them."

"Comfortable or secure?" Again, Maria didn't respond, just made busy with collecting the notes she had jotted through the sleepless predawn hours.

"From wot I can see," Gertrude said, "ye've got a right nice figure beneath all them wraps. It's a real shame to waste it 'cause of a lot of archaic ideas. Well, never mind. I reckon there'll come a time when ye'll be feelin' the need to shuck 'em . . . like when ya meet that special lad ye'll be wantin' to impress . . . or maybe ye've already met him . . . ?"

"What makes you think so?" Maria cast her curious friend a sideways glance.

Gertrude pointed to the scattering of wadded papers

littering the top of the writing desk. "Looks like ya were havin' a bit of trouble puttin' yer feelin's into words."

"Perhaps," she replied, thinking of John Rees with a touch of melancholy. Did he miss her? Was the emptiness and loneliness she felt due to this separation from someone who had been the only close friend she'd had, aside from Paul?

"Never mind, luv. It'll all work out. Wot's meant to be is meant to be. As me dear ol' mum use to say, 'The goodly hand of fate don't do aught for nothin'. If we listen to that little voice wot whispers loudest into our ear tellin' us wot choices to make, we'll always tread the proper path to our destiny.'"

Maria pondered the idea. "You're saying our lives have already been laid out for us? And only if we follow the true path that fate has dealt us will we discover absolute peace and happiness?"

"Aye, lass. When it seems that life is at its bleakest, rest assure that yer not experiencin' the difficulty for naught. There's a lesson to be learned; a strength to be won by meetin' the challenge and risin' above it. If ya believe that, the dark times won't seem so insurmountable. The trick is not to dwell on the hopelessness of the situation, but on the hope."

Taking a deep breath, Maria laughed. "Well, my dear Gertrude, I fear if we don't dwell on our chore at hand we might find our own situation insurmountable . . . meaning His Grace, of course. Our path at the present is to find a manner in which to rouse him."

"Ye'll soon learn that His Grace don't do aught that

he don't want to do, when and how he wants to do it. It's the way of the aristocracy, love."

"Occasionally we're all forced to do things we wouldn't necessarily want to do. Our purpose is to give His Grace the desire to continue living, my dear Gerti."

"Long as we don't lose our own ability along the way," Gertrude muttered, and followed Maria through Salterdon's bedroom door.

A pair of stocky boyservants looped the duke's long arms around their shoulders, and with much effort, raised him to a sitting position, his weight like that of a dead man's. Once they caught their breaths, they then heaved him into the wheeled bathchair, where Gertrude propped him up with her hands on his shoulders.

"Fetch me a rope!" she cried to Maria, who scrambled around the room until spying a drapery cord which she yanked from its harbor. Gertrude then anchored the duke to the back of the chair and stepped away, breathing hard, perspiration beading her brow and upper lip. "I wouldn't want to be in this room if he was to come to right now. I ain't so certain he'd appreciate bein' trussed up like some Boxin' Day game fowl. It ain't exactly ennoblin', is it?"

"There is little about His Grace that remotely resembles the ennobled," Maria replied, keeping a safe distance from the duke, her kerchief pressed to her nose. "'Tis hard to believe this is the same man who bathes, or bathed, in such sweetly scented water as I washed in last evening."

"Oh, he didn't bath in that." Gertrude mopped her

face. "That was for the ladies he invited to stay over—his mistresses and such. No doubt about it, he made certain his paramours wanted for nothin', includin' Parisian toilet waters." She chuckled. "When ye've settled in a mite I'll treat ya to a peek at their wardrobes. They'll make ya turn ten shades of pink, I vow. Scanty dainties such as them would make yer judgmental father drop dead of shock," she whispered behind her hand, and giggled again.

"Hard to imagine," Maria said softly, unable to stem the shiver of aversion she experienced each time she was forced to share space with the offending duke. Still, for some odd reason she could not help staring, her gaze locked on his profile.

His head fallen forward, hair a tangled web spilling over his shoulders, he looked like some Huddersfield bone grubber—hardly the sort who could tempt beautiful women down the path of damnation. Then again, if she were to believe her father, the sort of woman who could be tempted down *that* path deserved nothing better than Satan's damnation.

"Push him to the window," Maria directed.

With a grunt, Gertrude rolled the cumbersome chair to the window, placed it in a shaft of pure, pale light flooding the floor, then moved away.

"Bring food," said Maria. "Then a bath. Make the water steaming. And bring pails of the coldest water you can find. A plunge into a hot bath followed by a plunge into cold does much to purge the poisons from one's flesh and rouse one's spirit."

"Does much to rouse the temper as well, I imagine.

Are ye certain ya want to undertake such a scheme—I mean until yer fully aware of wot yer up against?"

Peering at Gertrude over her hanky, she declared, "I would rather cope with his sore disposition than his smell. And while you're at fetching water, bring me a few bottles of those bath salts. The violet was very nice."

"Aye, lass." Gertrude scurried from the room, and, with some caution, Maria settled into a nearby chair, hands clasped in her lap, her gaze locked on the Duke of Salterdon, slumped in the invalid's chair, chin resting on his chest, his dark brown mane lying limply over his concave shoulders that seemed very wide but very thin inside the dingy nightshirt.

She thought aloud, "You look so like Paul did in those last horrid days, when his soul hovered on that fine line between life and death. The Vicar Ashton believes such disasters are God's way of punishing His lambs who go astray. Paul's punishment was loving a woman forbidden to him, yet in his own heart and mind he did nothing wrong, Your Grace. Her husband abused her unmercifully in every unimaginable way. He flaunted the fact that he carried on . . . illicit acts with every tavern slattern in two counties. He treated her like chattel, Your Grace, whipping her publicly if she so much as questioned his authority."

Spreading her hands before her as if pleading her point, she said in a choke-filled voice, "When my brother happened upon the brute beating her, his only sin was attempting to stop him. Was not the crime, sir, in this man's breaking my brother's back? Of causing

his eventual death? Yet . . . the Vicar Ashton proclaimed it the *bastard's* right to do such!"

She hesitated, her entire body turning warm with
anger, and the fact that she had spoken such profanity so
openly and easily. More angrily she added, "The Vicar
Ashton, Your Grace, turned his back on his own son
and, even until Paul's dying day, would not set eyes on
him again. If a man as good and charitable as my
brother deserved such a cruel and destructive rod, then
what, Your Grace, do you deserve?"

Dust motes hovered in the sun-drenched air around
his head. The light reflected from his hair in little
auburn rainbows. Leaving the chair, she moved cautiously around her charge, never taking her gaze from
him. The sleeves of his nightshirt having been rolled
back, exposed his forearms; they were strong, she
noted, and had once been darkened by sun (had he
ridden shirtless on his much prized Arabian horses?)—
their once tanned color having grown jaundiced-looking
over the last many months of hiding away in this dark
and grim cavernous chamber. And his hands: Their
frame was there, as well as the muscles, standing forth
like the guttering of a candle; there were broad blue
veins going up the back and crossing every finger, but
the color—there was no color save the yellowishness of
his flesh—no flame of life, nor spark of evidence of
what he once had been.

"Is he decently situated?" Maria asked, her back
toward the tub.

"Aye," Thaddeus replied. "I reckon this ought to do him."

Taking a fortifying breath, Maria turned, hesitated at the sight of her patient's naked torso, his head back and resting against the ornamental tub, a deep black enamel fixture painted with golden dragons. The tub, however, was even grander than the one in which she had bathed the previous night . . . large enough for two, she thought with a wicked lift of one eyebrow, then felt her cheeks warm with dismay as she looked up to discover Thaddeus watching her, mouth drawn into a sarcastic tilt, eyes glowing with something other than humor.

She cleared her throat and grabbed a fire poker from the hearth, used it to lift the duke's nightshirt from the floor, and thrust it toward her smirking companion. "I suspect Gertrude will be waiting for these."

Thaddeus and his companion stepped back, their shirtfronts spotted with dampness, their faces flushed by rising steam. Maria rewarded them with a nod of dismissal. The young man, whose name she had not caught, shuffled from the room, while Thaddeus continued to stand his ground, ignoring the proffered clothing.

"Have you something to say?" she asked, avoiding his eyes, feeling her cheeks become as flushed as they had been the previous evening when she stood before him wearing nothing more than violet-scented bathwater.

"Aye," he replied, and shifted his weight to one hip. His stance looked cocky if not outright arrogant. His countenance was smug. "I'm wonderin' why you ain't tol' Gertrude yet about me and Molly."

" 'Tis none of my business," she replied shortly, casting him a glance from beneath her lashes.

He grinned again but made no show of leaving or taking the shirt.

"Is there anything else?" she asked.

He shrugged. "I was just thinkin' that I ain't ever seen hair the color of yers. It's a little like moonlight, ain't it?"

"Moonlight?"

"All silvery white and shiny soft."

Maria smoothed back the loose tendrils at her temples and lowered her eyes briefly, the nagging image of him and Molly making her frown.

"I wager it's beauteous when it's loose," said Thaddeus more roughly.

She said nothing more, and finally he grabbed the nightshirt and quit the room, pausing only long enough to glance back at her, then to His Grace, at which time his face became stony with an odd emotion.

Maria continued to stand very still after Thaddeus departed, long enough to contemplate the last moments, acknowledging that the young man had flirted with her, recognizing too that his sober reflections on her hair had caused a ripple of thrill in her breast. To encourage such compliments (especially in light of what she had witnessed between him and Molly—and especially what had taken place between Thaddeus and herself the previous night) wouldn't be right. Even to acknowledge them to herself would plant the dreadful seed of vanity in her mind.

She forced her gaze back to the duke, finding the

diversion did nothing to help her rattled senses. Steam rose in a cloud around the dragon tub. The duke's flesh had turned rosy, his hair and beard beaded with moisture.

How natural he looked, as if he were finding a delightful respite in the deep tub of hot water. Had it not been for his eyes staring off into space . . .

She wrung her hands, paced partially around the tub, trying to focus on anything other than that there was a naked man in a tub large enough for two whom it was her responsibility to bathe. A naked stranger—no innocent, kindhearted God-fearing young man like her brother . . . but a man with *body* hair . . . not only on his face but on his chest and arms, both of which were growing glossy with steam and sweat . . . a man who was nearly old enough to be her father . . . a man who had hurled one of his companions out a window.

"Dear Lord in heaven . . . if You will only see me through this I promise to . . . never entertain an uncharitable thought about my father again. I realize I've vowed as much before, but I mean it this time. After all, I'm only doing this in order to help my mother escape the bast—" She bit her lip and muttered, "Blazes. Surely You wouldn't challenge one with so charitable a motive in mind . . . ?"

She swept up two ornate crystal bottles of salts from a sterling silver tray, ran her thumb nervously over the swirling *S*, and approached the tub. Refusing to allow her gaze to drift toward the water, she flipped open the hinged lids and dumped the entirety of the two containers into the bath.

A waft of violet-scented steam mushroomed over the tub.

She took a deep breath.

Her fingers deftly rolled up her blouse sleeves, just to her forearms—further would verge on impropriety—it was enough that she was plunging her hands into water wherein lay a naked stranger! Slowly going to her knees beside the tub, gaze fixed on her charge's immobile features, she eased a cloth into the water then wrung it out.

Yet, she did nothing but stare at his face that seemed more bestial than human, lost as it was within that dark mane of hair that curled and waved from the bite of humidity coiling around him. She felt involuntarily captured by curiosity, as drawn to his inhumanness as she was repelled.

Salterdon's brow was broad, his eyebrows jetty and heavy, framing deep-set eyes the color of cold ash. His nose, high cheekbones, and mouth were all firm and strong, the latter being grim, having long since lost the ability or desire to smile.

"Hello," she said softly, watching those eyes that registered nothing. "Are you there, Your Grace? Can you hear me?" Guardedly, she swept the wet cloth over his brow—swiftly, then jerked back her hand—then again, more slowly across his cheeks, touched it lightly to his cracked gray lips.

"I'm called Maria, Your Grace. I've come here to help you. Can you hear me?" she asked softly and urgently. "Are you alive yet? Would you give me some sign? Some hint that you're here? A blink of an eye, a twitch of your lips?"

Nothing.

Sinking back on her heels, her arms hooked over the tub ledge, she regarded his still features, until the water grew tepid and the flush of heat drained from her master's flesh and he became marble-like again—less human and more frightening.

"Daft girl, what's come over me?" she said aloud as she set about scrubbing his arms that were long and heavy. "I've never been one to jump at her own shadow, yet, here I am on my knees mentally praying and outwardly shaking, and for what? Treat even a wild animal humanely and it will eventually comply. 'Tis no animal here; only a man."

Water ran from the cloth, down over his broad chest. Her hand looked like a child's against it, she mused, and the realization occurred to her that he had once been a powerful man, and, according to Gertrude, appealing to the ladies.

Laughing to herself, she glanced away, then back. Appealing to the ladies? Why, she couldn't guess. Reflected in that personage was no hint of grandeur or manner. She suspected the ladies of his class appreciated an aristocratic mien: debonair, handsome enough to make even the most fickle maiden swoon in appreciation—like her brother Paul, who had captured the fancy of every eligible young woman in the village.

His Grace, the Duke of Salterdon's bearing was frightfully imposing, unlike Paul's. But then, Paul had been no stranger. She had watched him grow to manhood. Had caught glimpses of his male body throughout her lifetime, therefore nothing about him had seemed foreign or frightening . . . unlike John Rees, the only man she had ever truly felt a certain affection that could, remotely, be deemed as love. Good, kind, constant John . . . had she agreed to marry him she would not be in this predicament now, both mesmerized and repelled by this man who was the very antithesis of what she had always deemed acceptable in a human being, much less a man.

Water dripping from her hands, she moved away from the tub and perched on the edge of a chair near the hearth, finding the heat did little to warm the chill from the room. Her body shivered.

Why could she not take her eyes from him?

Little of His Grace was revealed to her now but his profile, still in repose as he stared off into his private universe. A wave of long damp hair trailed over the back of the tub and lay limply in the still air.

Gertrude bustled into the room. "Have ya done, miss? Shall I have the lads come fetch him from the tub now?"

Her gaze captured by the singular curl spilling over the tub ledge, Maria nodded. "Yes. Or rather . . . no. His hair . . . we should wash it?"

"Would ya like me to see to it, love? Yer lookin' a wee bit pale yerself." Gertrude rolled up her sleeves, and with arms as stout as a milkmaid's, she proceeded to grab a pail of water, a handful of soap flakes, and made busy with scrubbing her master's head, while

Maria remained on the lip of the chair, her fingers twisted into the damp washcloth that had, by now, painted a great wet splotch on the front of her skirt.

"It ain't as if the help wanted to ignore him," Gertrude explained as foam worked up between her fingers. "He just ain't always obligin' to our administerin's."

"His Grace has a right to be angry." Maria watched a thread of white bubbles spill onto the duke's bare shoulder. She looked away, toward the window, noting the sun had disappeared again behind gray clouds. Snow was imminent.

"Aye, but he don't have to take it out on the rest of us. Anyhow . . ." Gertrude heaved up a pail of cold water and poured it over his head. "I don't reckon it matters now, poor sod. It's obvious that he's left us in spirit if not in body."

Their meal was delivered in that moment. For His Grace, there was a bowl of cold porridge, for Maria a plate of buttered scones and honey as well as porridge.

Frowning at the sleepy-eyed boy servant, a lad no older than herself, Maria declared, "But this won't do. Cold porridge for His Grace? I think not, sir. Take it back—"

"He won't eat it anyway," Gertrude declared as she attempted to wrap a fleecy towel around the duke's head.

"Nor would I," Maria retorted with a pique of anger. "Bring him poached eggs and ham. And a bowl of hot porridge, if you please. Heap it with almonds, if you have them, and brown sugar to fortify his strength.

Mayhap you all forget that he is *still* your master, and thereore deserving of your respect and loyalty. Mayhap you forget that he was once a man—nay, is *still* a man, not an animal, no matter how fierce he looks or behaves."

"Aye, miss," the boy said, his countenance full of discomfiture. Only when he had hustled out of the chamber, the tray of unsatisfactory food clattering in his hands, did she turn to discover Gertrude staring at her, the servant's eyes swimming behind tears. She nestled her master's head against her ample breast and stroked his wet hair. Her chin trembled.

"Ashamed I am," Gertrude announced with a catch in her voice. "We've buried him already and him still breathin'."

"And we'll have no more of *that* sort of talk either," Maria told her sternly, and shook one finger at her. "How would you feel, trapped in a body and unable to speak, but hearing all that is said about you, and all that is spoken is of impending death?"

Gertrude gasped. "Lud, do ya think he can hear us, lass?"

"Because the will or energy to speak has left him doesn't necessarily mean his ability to hear has fled him as well. Nay, Gertrude, man must endure everything that God sends. Perhaps he will stagger under God's burdens awhile, but he who believes in His causes will not be crushed. No burden ever crushes the human soul but the weight of sin and corruption itself. I . . . don't know the sort of man His Grace was, and is. Only he can know the sort of good or evil that wages war in his heart, dear Gertrude. The battle waged there is between him and the angels. Can he hear us? How can any of us know? Know only that the blessed things are the small charities of life, which throw us out of ourselves, our cares, and struggles, and draw us tenderly back within the circle of human interest. In short, dear Gertrude, do unto others, I always say, and regret will remain a stranger."

His Grace was sat in the wheeled chair before the window. With the help of the servants, and in compliance with Maria's directives, he had been dressed in some of his finest clothes: a soft white linen shirt and a white silk stock, splendid nankeen breeches and black boots. The clothes, however, hung on his frame, driving home the realization to Maria that, most assuredly, the duke had once been a most magnificent specimen.

Still, this most dapper wardrobe was a stark contrast to the savage-like personage. Clean and dry, his dark hair was a riot of cascading waves and curls that framed his face in a rich halo and spilled several inches beyond his shoulders. The untrimmed beard hid all aspects of his lower face.

Having drawn a chair up beside him, and placing herself comfortably into it, Maria attempted to entice his consciousness with the poached eggs and fried ham.

"A small bite, sir," she coaxed him softly. Egg and fork poised at his closed lips, Maria gazed anxiously into his vacant eyes, seeing only the reflection of the windowpanes in their gray irises. "Then mayhap you prefer the porridge, sir. 'Tis rich in cream and butter and brown sugar. 'Tis certain to warm you. Your hands are very cold, you see." Tentatively wrapping her own hand over the back of his, she held it until the chill of his flesh became as warm as her own, and then a while longer . . . because it felt so large against her own, much like Paul's had been—an anchor on which to hold when the waves of despondency would rise up to swallow her. Only Paul's hand had opened to accept hers, to grip hers, to offer strength and encouragement even as he lay dying.

"Even now I'm ashamed that it was he who comforted me," she thought aloud, and squeezed the duke's hand more fiercely. "I shall endeavor to remain strong this time, to offer you the consolation and strength I was too weak and frightened to give Paul."

With that, she once again attempted to feed him. His Grace only stared out the window, while the day grew dull enough to lay dark gray shadows on the hills that stood grand and cold around the fell.

The food having long since grown cold, the room having been scrubbed spotless, each table covered in cheery flowers whose aromas swirled in a perfumed cloud around her, Maria sat at her charge's side, silent, her blue eyes regarding him now and again while her mind wandered and a weariness crept over her, causing her lids to grow heavy, her mind dull as the distant hills.

She dozed and dreamt of Paul lying in his bed, a smile on his face even as his body wasted away. She dreamt that he left his bed and informed her that he was cured, and to prove it he danced across the floor on legs that were as sound and strong as tree trunks. Suddenly, they were children again, flying across the downs as fast as their legs would carry them, chasing butterflies and newborn lambs—oh! How the innocent children and animals had loved him, so pure of mind and spirit was Paul, collecting wayward and wounded souls with a smile and a laying on of his hand that seemed to Maria to burn with a divine, healing light.

"Have faith and look to me for hope and courage. I'll never leave you, sweet sister," he had promised as a child. And so too he had promised as, with his final breath, he'd slipped gently over the threshold of eternal life, and into God's welcoming arms.

A noise awoke her. Her heart racing, Maria opened her eyes, only to discover that the sound had been nothing more than her own sobbing. Leaving her chair, she moved to the window, pressed her feverish brow upon the frosting pane, watched as her breaths fogged the glass, her own image becoming blurred by the condensation.

Righting her shoulders and raising her chin, she turned back to her charge, hurriedly brushed the tears from her cheeks as she regarded His Grace, who continued to sit so still and stare . . . at her.

Not, not at her, certainly. Those glassy orbs reflected a bemusingly sad and thoughtful look. Perhaps he gazed at yon hills that had fast become dim with swirling snow. Mayhap his mind was lost in the memories of his riding swift as the moor wind on his horses . . . or perhaps he dreamt of some beautiful lady whom he had once seduced there.

But he was *not* staring at her.

Were she to believe that, she would be forced to acknowledge that the . . . beast was rousing; that her well-being, and even her employment at Thorn Rose might surely be in jeopardy very soon.

Maria backed away, then scolded herself for allowing herself to become so selfishly mired in her own problems. "Ashamed I am," she declared aloud, and forced herself to adjust the woolen throw over Salterdon's lap, tucking it under his knees as swiftly as possible before moving away.

"Paul would kindly remind me that no matter how burdensome our own lives occasionally become, there are those who are far worse off. That we should continually count our blessings and thank God if we have a roof over our heads, plenty to eat, good, or at least passably good health, and friends. My father, on the other hand, would lift the strop of God's vengeance and . . ."

She shuddered.

"No," she said thoughtfully. "We shan't go into that, Your Grace. Suffice it to say that the good vicar believes that God's way of dealing with the corrupted soul is to hail upon the sinner a goodly amount of painful retribution—fierce as firebrands. I, on the other hand, believe Him to be patient and kind and all forgiving—no matter what the sin, or sins. His hand is always outstretched. All one needs, Your Grace, is faith and courage, and a repentant heart."

She sat in a chair before him, elbows rested on her knees.

His hands lay on his lap and the temptation was

strong to touch them. *"Do* you hear me?" she asked softly, studying his bearded features, the realization occurring to her that she had never ventured so gravely close to this man. Her breathing quickened at the thought; her heart raced. As her nervousness and fear threatened to overwhelm her, she briefly closed her eyes and swallowed it back. "There are some faces to whom hard lines come naturally," she stated with forced lightness. "Faces born to grow sharp and dark; how unnatural it seems on you, whose eyes look as if they once flashed with wit and mischievousness. Whose lips look as if they were once quick to smile, to impart a playful barb to a close friend, an outrageous flirtation to a pretty young lady. 'Tis a pitiful thing to see these features plowed into unnatural harshness. If you *are* there, sir, rise up and allow me to help you. Take courage in the knowledge that I shall be here to assist you and encourage you, not only for your grandmother's sake, whose existence is dependent upon her seeing you well once again, but for your own sake as well."

A movement at the door; Maria looked up. Gertrude walked on tiptoes to the tray of forgotten food placed beside His Grace's chair. "No progress?" the servant asked in her sympathetic tone.

"None," Maria replied, and sat back.

Clucking her tongue and shaking her head, Gertrude regarded the plate of uneaten eggs and ham. "I'll be havin' the cook prepare somethin' special for ya tonight. A wisp of a girl like you shouldn't miss too many meals."

"Point taken, dear Gertrude. I'll try to eat more tonight, I promise."

"Ye'll rest better this evenin', lass. I'll have the cook brew up some of his special rum tea. Ye'll sleep as sound as a bairn, I'll guarantee."

Maria followed Gertrude to the door, watched the pleasant servant hurry down the corridor, open a panel in the wall, and disappear into it, her footsteps descending the servants' hidden staircase swiftly muted as the door closed behind her.

True to Gertrude's word, dinner was a veritable feast of watercress soup, roasted fowl with a cream sauce, rosemary potatoes, and, finally, syllabub to finish her off. She ate only after attempting to serve His Grace, who now, having been repositioned into a chair near the fire, stared into the flames, his features illuminated by red and gold firelight.

Nestled deeply into her soft chair, grown drowsy with repletion, Maria regarded her charge's strong profile. "Had I a book," she mused softly, "I would read to you. Paul always enjoyed that. He said, 'Words drawn with such beauty of tongue will paint vivid rainbows upon the imagination.' You look like a man who would enjoy books. Your brow is broad and noble, a certain sign of intelligence. No doubt you're a man of great passions, who exalts in extremes, who challenges mediocrity, and embraces diversity. Yet, you continue to hide there, somewhere deep within yourself. Why, I wonder? What, sir, are you frightened of? Because you fear the world may not respect the man you are now? A man is what he makes of himself, I think."

Leaving the chair, she strode around him, her fingers trailing along but not quite touching his shoulder (how bold she was becoming!), skimming over his disheveled hair, lightly, teasingly brushing his beard. Was it not a part of her responsibilities to treat him kindly and respectfully, to encourage his dignity and well-being?

"Only a fool would imagine that you're less of a man because of this." She paused with her back to the fire, her gaze falling to his long legs, and the black leather boots hugging them to the knees. Gertrude had spent a quarter hour polishing the expensive Hessians until they shone.

"They're very nice boots," she mused aloud, her gaze following the well-cut and fitted leather up the curve of his calf, to his knee. "They suit you," she added, slowly lifting her gaze back to his eyes that seemed to be looking directly into her own.

Maria eased to the floor, took hold of one heavy leg, and with a little effort, slid the boot off his foot, then the other, placed the pair to one side of the fire before taking his stocking foot into her lap and rubbing it, her fingers making their way in a constant, circular fashion up calves that felt cold and hard, up to his knee, then back down again, as she had done Paul's those many months he had lain on his back, unable to move. Paul had made a performance of enjoyment, sighing in contentment, though Maria had known that her brother had really felt nothing. The pleasure had only been in his mind.

"I'm told this helps the circulation," she explained, and massaged a bit harder, hands molding to the shape of Salterdon's muscles, to the curve of his ankle, squeezing and releasing, until it seemed as if the flesh warmed in her fingers. Occasionally, she looked up, to his face.

"The firelight reflects kindly from you," she told him. "It flushes your skin and ignites your eyes." Gently, she slid her hands over his knee, gripped his thigh firmly, noted the hard length of muscle even there, and how his breeches clung to the leg like a velvety skin. The firelight reflected from the nankeen in prisms of color.

Like a thin stream of pale light, the memory of Thaddeus and Molly took shape in her memory, rousing like two ghosts, stirring not fright, but that barely recognizable restlessness and discomfort she had experienced only briefly in John's company—when she'd allowed her curiosity and imagination to take hold—an ache that was as deep and low and disturbingly bestial as the man sitting before her now. Her eyelids growing drowsy, her gaze softly dropping to Salterdon's lips, then to her hand resting lightly on his hard thigh, her mind teased with the image of her standing in that kitchen door, watching two people writhe and twist on the table, sweating flesh glistening with firelight . . . only it was the duke's eyes that flashed up at her . . . and the woman beneath him groaning and gasping with such delicious fervor was—

"Miss Ashton?"

She jumped, gasping softly.

Thaddeus emerged from the shadows near the door.

Her heart racing, Maria pressed one hand to her bosom and averted her eyes. "You frightened me— coming out of the dark and silence like that. For an instant I thought . . ."

"That it was him speakin'?" Thaddeus barely glanced at His Grace. He grinned and hooked his thumbs over his waistband. "I reckon that ain't too likely."

"Have faith, Thaddeus. Miracles do happen." Collecting herself, struggling to put the shockingly outrageous image from her mind, as well as the lingering flutterings of disturbance still swirling around inside her, Maria struggled to her feet, only to discover her knees shook like aspic.

"I've come for yer dinner tray," Thaddeus declared.

"Please pass on my appreciation to the cook. The food was splendid." She moved around the duke's chair, placing it between her and her watchful companion, her discomfiture growing as he continued to stare, obviously enjoying her mounting sense of unease—as he had last evening. "I would prefer that you leave Salterdon's food. I may try one last time before bed to get him to eat."

"Yer just like all the rest," he said.

"The rest?"

"All them others wot come here to companion him, thinkin' they could do wot the one before him couldn't. 'Course, he was different then. Least he had some fight left in him, for whatever good it did him. He were little more than an idiot—"

"Thaddeus!" she cried. "Take care how you speak—"

"It don't matter. Even if he were still alive inside his head he ain't got the good sense God gave to a bleedin' goose. All he once were was wiped out with that damned blow to his head." A look of intense anger coming across his gaunt features, Thaddeus glared at his employer. "He didn't have no memory—didn't even know his own grandmother or brother. He couldn't talk, or walk. For six months he didn't do aught but choke in his own drool and roar like some—"

"I beseech you," Maria implored, "stop this horrible account!"

"It's the truth. Best to let 'im die. Put him out of his misery, and us too."

"I intend to speak to the duchess about this contemptible—"

"She won't do aught, and do ya know why?" He reached for her tray of food, leaving Salterdon's on the table. " 'Cause she won't have me loose out there, informin' the entirety of England just wot an imbecile the duke has become."

He started for the door, then stopped at the edge of the firelight, his gaze going once again to the duke. His eyes becoming distant, his voice softer, wearier, and oddly forlorn, he added, "He ought not to have fought them bloody highwaymen. He shoulda just given 'em over the money. He'd be alive and well now if he had. Damned fool. Bleedin' hero."

As Thaddeus exited the room, Maria stared after him, her eyes burning, not with the anger that had, at first, assailed her, but with a sudden wave of sorrow, not only for Salterdon, but for his friends and family as well. She empathized with their pain, facing his slow disintegration day after day, becoming a shadow of himself. The grim reaper hovered over their lives like a plague. They waited for the inevitable fall of its sword, but when would it come? Aye, impending death was a foul prison to the living as well as the dying.

Upon completing her toilette, dressed in her white nightgown, Maria reposed before the fire in her bedchamber, allowing the comforting heat to dry her hair that curled softly around her face and over her shoulders. Absently, she ran her brush through the pale strands, her mind running its course, from Paul, to John (she would write him again tonight—mayhap she would find the right words with which to convey her confusing emotions), to her father, to her mother who, as she did this time every evening, went to her knees with her husband and prayed to be forgiven for any unworthy thought or action she had committed during the day.

Since they were old enough to understand the difference between right and wrong, Maria and Paul had been there as well, praying until their knees had become sore and their necks weary and the candles had burned low enough to douse themselves in their own gutter. Paul had prayed feverishly, believing in his prayers, believing they would make a difference, while she had watched him from the corner of her eye and prayed that this torture in the name of God would hurry and end. She had not gone to her knees and prayed since leaving her father's house, and would not, despite the pang of guilt gnawing at her now.

Maria sighed and finished her tea, grown bitter with cold. True to Gertrude's word, the drink had relaxed her, made her drowsy. With an effort, she gathered up a candle and made her way to Salterdon's room, stood for a moment on the threshold, flickering light raised before her as her eyes adjusted to the dark.

She tiptoed to the bed, the hem of her gown sliding against her ankles.

Salterdon, having been dressed in fresh nightclothes, lay on his back in the clean linens, his dark hair spread over the pillow. As always, his eyes were open. His hands lay peacefully upon his chest atop the folded back sheet and counterpane.

She bent over him, regarded his face in the flickering candlelight, lightly brushed a heavy curl from his brow, and adjusted the down blanket more snugly over his shoulders, allowing her hand to linger along his jaw— so, his beard was not nearly so coarse as she had imagined, but soft and thick, gleaming like bronze in the faint light.

Timidly, she drew her fingers down over his lids, closing them, holding them closed while her small hand grew warm on his flesh and the candle dripped hot wax on the fingers of the other.

"Sleep well, Your Grace," she bid him softly, and removing her hand, stared fixedly at his eyes that remained closed.

Mayhap it was the trick of flickering light that made the harsh lines around his eyes appear to ease, the deep grooves between his heavy brows to lessen, and even to brush faint spots of color over the rise of his cheekbones.

Surely, 'twas only her imagination.

The night grew deep.

He lay in his massive tester bed and stared at the ceiling. Occasionally, his gaze drifted toward the distant door, which was opened only enough to allow dim candlelight to intrude into his dark chamber. Now and then there came a subtle noise, a tinkle of glass, a splash of water. A shadow moved over the threshold then disappeared.

He swallowed and forced his eyes to wander the room that was so different now, since her arrival. It seemed grand again, and livable. A few hyacinths in glasses created an abiding perfume, faint but delicious. Other scents came to him as well, wafted in at times through the half-opened door of her bedroom: feminine scents: rose water, scented soap.

He turned his head, focused his thoughts on the dying fire whose embers sparkled out from a hearth made picturesque by painted China tiles, and glimmered with a softened light on two exquisite heads, Night *and* Morning, *which formed the supporters of the white marble chimneypiece. But the sounds and scents emanating from the adjoining room nagged him, dragged his gaze back to the door while the memories of other women who had occupied that room, some whose names he could not even remember, tapped at his subconscious.*

The door creaked open, just barely, and a form

appeared, draped in soft, flowing white cotton, a guttering candle dripping wax held aloft in one pale hand. She floated toward him like a vision, moonlight hair shimmering in the candlelight. Up until now he had thought he had dreamt her.

"Do you sleep, Your Grace?" came her whispered words, and she bent over him, regarded his face, his eyes, her own reflecting the bright flame in her hand. Her smell washed over him, sweet and clean and feminine. He felt dizzy, and desperate, but when the familiar anger roused inside him, something about her child-like look captured him; he lay still, barely breathing, like one in the company of a fawn. If he so much as blinked she might flee . . .

She looked so frightened. So tentative. Of what?

Him of course. He was the monster.

The angel smoothed the counterpane over his chest, lightly touched her fingers to the spray of hair on his pillow. "I'm certain you don't mean to be cruel, Your Grace. 'Tis the anger and the belief that God and mankind have deserted you. Trust, sir, that they have not . . . Until tomorrow, good night, Your Grace," she bid him softly, and drew her hand down over his lids, closing them. He did not open them again until she had quit the room, taking the light with her.

Lying in the dark, he thought:

Don't go. *Please* . . . don't go.

Chapter Five

She awoke with a start, stared blindly through the blackness of her room, her mind registering that her candles had burned out, as had the fire in the hearth.

There were sounds—women's high-pitched voices. Weeping? Men shouting.

Flinging back the counterpane, she dropped to the floor, feet flinching from the cold, shaking fingers gripping her nightdress at the collar as she hurried to Salterdon's room, and to his bed. All was dark and quiet, but for the sound of his light breathing and the case clock ticking.

Again the shrill voices.

Hurrying from the room, she ran down the corridor until reaching the top of the stairs. There were lights below, and yes! a woman was weeping.

"Look wot we've got here," Molly said so suddenly Maria jumped. The servant shook her head as Maria leaned back against the balustrade and briefly closed her eyes, willing her heart to stop racing. "I'd ask wot the blazes yer doin' dashin' 'ere and there about the place dressed only in yer dainties but I already got a goodly idea of wot that is."

"I beg your pardon? I only—"

"I beg yer pardon?" Molly mocked. "Got airs ain't ya, Miss Ashton? Talk as if ya was blue as the duchess 'erself."

"There's no decree of which I'm aware stating that one must be royal to acquire an acceptable vernacular."

Molly huffed. Hands plunked on her hips, she narrowed her eyes. "Where is he?"

"He?"

"Don't be daft. Ya think I ain't seen the way ya eyeball 'im? Think I ain't heard the way he talks about ya? Always Miss Ashton this and Maria that—"

A woman wailed somewhere below.

Frowning, Maria tiptoed down several steps, leaned over the stair rail to better determine the commotion.

Molly pressed up against her, causing Maria to grab the rail for support. The girl's breath was rich with bad gin.

Lips thinned, Molly said, "I seen 'im comin' from yer room three night ago—all flushed and bothered. 'Is piece was hard enough for me to see at the opposite end of the bloody hall."

"Don't be daft!"

"Will ya deny ya give 'im a peek at yer bottom while ya was bathin'?"

Her face coloring, Maria backed down the stairs.

"Well, Miss Goody-Goody Reverend's Daughter? I reckon I've got ya backed into a pig's pit, ain't I? Deny it and ya lie; admit it and show yerself for wot ya really are—which is wot I've tol' ever'one all along—yer naught but a—"

"Molly!" screeched Gertrude from below, and Maria let loose a sigh of relief as the inebriated servant made a clumsy grab at her lopsided cap and staggered down the winding staircase, the heels of her too-large shoes clomping against each step. "Silly bugger," Gertrude exclaimed. "Ye've been pintin' it down at the Hound and Stag, ain't ya? No wonder ya didn't come when I called." Looking up the staircase at Maria, Gertrude shook her head. "We'll be beggin' yer pardon, love. We've got ourselves a bituva tiddlydoo—"

"What's happened?" Maria lightly, swiftly, descended the stairs after Molly, who grumbled and sneered before stumbling over Gertrude's toes. "I'm certain I heard a woman crying."

"It were travelers wot got laid low by them damn thieves—"

"Thieves!" shrieked Molly and clutched her flat bosom.

"Ye've got naught there the lot of cutthroats would have," Gertrude exclaimed, and shoved the girl away.

"The travelers, are they all right?" Maria asked.

"There were a woman and her two daughters, miss—"

"Were they injured?"

"Purses filched and a bauble or two. Seems they conked the driver on the head, though. He ain't come to yet. But that ain't the worst of it, I fear. All this took place just down the bend—"

Molly let go a shriek that made Maria and Gertrude grab their ears. "They'll be comin' 'ere next! Stormin' through them doors and takin' us hostage. They'll be usin' me body for their pleasures—"

"More likely you'll be usin' theirs," countered Gertrude angrily. "God help 'em . . ."

More softly Maria said, "Is there danger?"

Gertrude nodded somberly. " 'Tis well-known that 'Is Grace is in residence and . . . poorly. Take a good look 'round ya, love. There's a king's ransom in silver alone tucked away in chests. We'd be wise to unlock the arms room, I think. Maybe pass out a few weapons to the lads. Thaddeus is down at the stables," she said more loudly for Molly's benefit. "Seeing over the foalin' of His Grace's favorite mare. I'll make certain he shutters the lower windows and barricades all the doors."

Maria nodded. "I'll dress and see to our guests."

Lady Draymond wept into her hankie. "It was horrible. Horrible, I tell you. The fiends came at us from the dark—at least a dozen of them, their heads covered in black masks, their eyes leering at us through those terrible slits. I feared for my precious daughters' lives . . ."

Maria glanced toward the pair of rotund young women dressed in velvet and ruching who appeared to be around the same age as herself. Unlike their distraught mother, their attentions were on the plate of confections Gertrude had coerced from the cook's store of sweetmeats, as well as on their surroundings. "There,

there," she comforted the Viscount Draymond's wife. "Tomorrow this will all seem like a bad dream."

"If we all live to see tomorrow," Molly interjected as she plunked a tray of teapots and cups on a table. "If ya asked me, they was all lucky to get away with their lives."

The viscountess let out a shrill rail again, and with an exaggerated gasp for effect, collapsed back in her chair in a swoon.

"Gorm," muttered Gertrude as she shot the now hungover Molly a scathing look. "Fetch me a vinaigrette and be quick about it." To Maria, she added softly, "I might do well by leavin' her out. I ain't so sure I can put up with much more of this caterwaulin'. I ain't so certain Cook is goin' to be pleased 'cause his stores have been depleted; by the looks of them two there won't be a crumb left in this house by the time they finish."

" 'Twould be cruel and unchristian to turn them out," Maria said.

"I didn't say aught 'bout turnin' them out, love. I had more in mind of gaggin' 'em."

Molly returned with the smelling tin. "This could all be a trick as far as we know," she pointed out. "Could be naught more than a ploy to get inside—"

"Aye, and I'm really King George in masquerade," Gertrude declared with a roll of her eyes, then to Maria said, "I'll see the lady to a room, luv, then I'll make certain their driver is comfortable. Will ye see to her daughters?"

With Maria's nod, the Viscountess Draymond was hefted from the settee and ushered from the room. A scattering of sleepy-eyed servants stood around, staring first at Maria, then at the Ladies Charlotte and Florence, who continued to mutter to one another between mouths full of sweetmeats and cast disdainful glances at Maria.

"Mayhap the ladies would care to adjourn to a bed-chamber," Maria said. "Considering the misfortune which has occurred tonight, I'm certain your ladyships are much wearied and eager for a respite."

Florence, her cheek bulging with a sugar-coated almond, made a moue with her full lips that were dusty with sugar sprinkles. She appeared to consider the offer before turning to Charlotte. "Who is she, do you think?"

"No one of import I should think, not dressed in that manner," replied Florence who was a thinner version of her sister, but no less pompous. "A scullery maid perhaps."

They giggled and brushed crumbs from their velvet-skirted laps onto the floor, then Florence glanced at her empty tea cup, which sat directly beside the sweating pot. "I should like another spot, and this time I'd like more sugar."

A moment's hesitation, then Maria moved to the tray.

Charlotte reached for another almond. "Imagine our finding our way to Thorn Rose. A few months ago I might have been terrified, considering what became of His Grace."

Maria heaped two spoonsful of sugar in the bottom of Florence's cup, willing her hand to cease trembling.

"Shocking!" exclaimed Florence and swept up a petit four. "Lady Penelope Farnsworth-Shriverston mentioned the last time she called on His Grace after the accident he was a total loon—that he attempted to choke her and railed unintelligibly at her in so raised a voice she burst into tears. If that weren't enough he looked like some disgustingly filthy mongrel one would leave starving on the side of the road."

"Often," Maria said softly as she poured milk from a tiny pitcher into the cup, " 'tis the good-hearted soul who offers kindness to the stray who finds themselves the beneficiary of the animal's lifelong devotion. I cannot imagine anyone with . . . conscience leaving even an animal to starve beside a road."

"Regardless," Charlotte said with a toss of her brown curls, "the duchess did right by confining him in that dreadful sanitarium. Not a fortnight ago I spoke with Lady Rothblatt and she said she heard from Lady Adeline Gloag who heard from Lady Lily Hartcup that Lord Drabble had reason to visit an acquaintance at St. Luke's and while there actually happened on His Grace. They came face to face, Drabble declared. Salterdon was bound in leathers and howling like a cur. I shan't go into more detail, but I assure you the very recounting of the sordid moment engraved upon my memory a most horrifying image that I shan't forget soon. And to think Mama once entertained the idea of my marrying him. I shiver to imagine. Why, I would rather have been ravished by those dreadful thieves than to be forced to spend one night with such a monster as Salterdon."

"There, there, sweet sister." Florence patted Charlotte's chubby hand reassuringly. "There's nothing to worry over now. He's far, far away from here—"

"Actually," Maria interrupted, her lips forming a flat

smile as she offered over the cup of steaming oolong. "His Grace is not so far away at all."

The sisters blinked. "No?" they said in unison.

"Just up the stairs, m'ladies."

"Here?" Charlotte's mouth dropped open.

"At Thorn Rose?" A nut slipped from Florence's fingers and bounced off the china saucer in her lap.

"Locked away in his dark chamber . . . I'm certain you'll hear him once the house has grown quiet again. If I were you . . ." She lowered her voice and frowned. "I would hurry to your own rooms before . . ."

The women leaned forward, eyes wide, jaws dropped.

"As for myself," Maria turned toward the door. "I will leave you in Gertrude's capable hands and return to my own chambers—"

"Wait!" The Ladies Draymond leapt from their chairs, scattering cake pieces and almonds, and clattering china. Skirts and curls bouncing they hurried after Maria, gripping one another's hands and muttering between themselves.

He awakened from a fog.

Light came to him in a pinpoint at first, then grew, little by little, forming shadowy shapes that, like a twisted kaleidoscope, swirled with confusing colors and sounds.

No. No, not again! It was better there, in the dark and silence. Sleep was the elixir. No pain. No shame. No uncontrollable anger. Buried in his catacomb of unconsciousness there were no pitying faces weeping for what he once had been . . . would never again be, accord-

ing to the string of physicians who had paraded through his life the last year.

Why couldn't they understand? He simply wanted to be left alone with the thoughts in his head. There, at least, he could hear his own voice, not that belonging to an idiot who could not seem to make his mouth move correctly, who could not hold on to a thought long enough to communicate it.

Oh, yes, it was safer here, in the gray recesses, but something had disturbed him, had roused the sleeping tiger of frustration and dragged him back, struggling, into the blinding light.

A voice . . . soothing amid the savage cacophony of thoughts in his head. Music amid the melee. Often during the last endless days and nights it had disturbed him, conjured images of angels, and he had wondered if he had, at last, died and gone . . . no, not to heaven. There was no room in heaven for the morally corrupt Duke of Salterdon.

Concentrate, idiot. Focus, if you can. There! Somewhere amid the sun that was shining on his face, and the brisk breeze kissing his cheeks—the angel's song, lyrical, rising and falling. God, the light hurt his eyes.

A movement there. Focus. Ah! At last, the form takes shape. Concentrate.

She moved to a bench beside a tree and closed the book from which she had been reading aloud. Good God, who was she? The shape of her head was magnificent. Her hair—what a rare and beautiful shade it was, silken in texture that rolled in waves over her brow and framed her eyes, which were startlingly blue and clear and warm as they looked up from her readings to regard him with a sort of wonder-look, as if they saw what no other eyes could see. They were calm eyes and resolute, but with such a depth of passion in them that he felt instinctively the soul that they reflected.

Her nose was perfect, the mouth utterly temptable and smiling sadly. All were spiritualized by her clear, perfectly colorless complexion. Yet . . . she was little more then a child, with a child's guilessness and innocence.

Damn those eyes for their fear and pity. Damn them.

"What a wondrous day, Your Grace! Mayhap spring is near. The sun is at last warm, the sky perfectly clear. Were I able, I would carry you myself to yonder lake. Look there, someone is boating—a tenant, perhaps? Fishing for his supper, no doubt." Maria left the bench and swept gracefully around the massive elm trunk by which she had been lounging and reading to her master from a book. Sighing, enjoying the warming breeze in her face, she watched the fishermen with dreamy eyes.

"Oh, sir, if you could only see the water. It laps at the keel of the little boat and glitters like ripples of crystal around it. 'Tis almost as if the boat floats in the sunshine instead of the water. And see the sky, so bright even the hills seem asleep."

Leaning back against the elm, Maria listened to the breeze shift through the empty branches. It toyed with her hair, which she had allowed to fall loose that morning, and blew several long strands across her face.

A squirrel darted down a branch and leapt to the ground, mere feet from Maria; she gasped in delight, and easing to the duke, where he sat in his wheeled chair, eyes fixed on the distant countryside, she put her hands on his broad shoulders and leaned toward his ear.

"We have a visitor," she whispered. "Isn't he grand, sir? Such a pompous little scamp—nearly as pompous as those dreadful Draymond sisters who continue gnawing their way through your larders. I think we shall never be rid of them, Your Grace. Not until the driver sees fit to rally and tear himself away from Gertrude. 'Twas love at first sight, I think." She smiled. "Our dear Gerti is singing from morn till night these last days. Ah, love. 'Tis amazing what the emotion can do to one's logic."

She pointed to the squirrel. "See how he stares at us, as if we were the intruders. Shall we see just how brave he is?"

Laughing, Maria took a tentative step toward the furry creature, who regarded her with an unblinking perusal and a twitch of its ginger-colored tail. "How do you do?" Maria said, slightly bending at the waist.

The squirrel stood straighter, and cocked its head.

Maria smiled, and eased to her hands and knees, her pale hair spilling over her shoulders and trailing over the snow-covered dirt beneath her. "My dear mister squirrel, you look as if you wish to dance. I'm willing, of course, but you'll have to teach me."

With a bob of its head, the squirrel leapt onto the tree trunk and scurried to the lowest limb, where it commenced its loud chattering and stared down at Maria.

"Kindly mister squirrel, I fear I should fail miserably if this particular dance entails my dashing up a tree!"

Laughing, sitting back on her heels and dusting leaves and grass from her hands, Maria watched the squirrel make a startled leap to a higher limb. Only then did she sense a movement behind her, and slowly, she looked around, first spying a pair of highly polished knee boots, her gaze then traveling up, up a man's tall frame clothed in immaculate, splendidly tailored clothes, to a pair of most startling gray eyes, which regarded her with perplexity, if not outright amusement.

She gasped; the eyes she recognized—that noble brow, that lush mane of hair—though shorter, perhaps; even those lips were slightly familiar. Yet, *these* lips were not so grim, but curled in such a droll manner hot color rushed to her cheeks.

"Miss . . . Ashton?" the man said in so refined and mellow a voice Maria was left momentarily speechless.

The stranger offered his hand. "Shall I help you up, or shall I come down there?"

"Oh." Meekly, she accepted his hand and struggled to her feet, stepping on her skirts, which were littered with bits of leaves and grass and dirt. She made a grand show of cleaning herself before stepping away and rewarding the man with an apologetic smile and as dignified a lift of her chin as she could manage, considering the circumstances. "I *am* Miss Ashton," she declared.

"I was afraid of that," he muttered in reply, regarding her person in a most bemused, if not exasperated manner. "You're a child, for Godsake. What could she have been thinking?"

"She?"

"The duchess, of course."

"I hardly think it matters," Maria replied matter of factly. "*She* is the duchess, after all. I imagine *she* can and will do just as she pleases . . . and it pleased her, I suppose, to employ me . . . child or not."

The man raised one eyebrow. "Touché, Miss Ashton. So tell me, how is my brother?"

Her eyes widened. She swiftly looked beyond the intruder, to the duke, who continued to stare off into space. "Lord Basingstoke," she said more quietly, forcing her gaze back to the duke's twin brother. "I should have known immediately, my lord. My apologies." She hastened a quick curtsy.

"Nonsense, Miss Ashton. There is little about us that resembles these days." As if bolstering his strength, Basingstoke turned to his brother at last, stood stiffly before the Duke of Salterdon, his hands curled into fists at his sides. His voice was noticeably tighter when he spoke again. "Tell me, Miss Ashton, is there any improvement?"

"None, my lord. However, I've only been here a week—"

"God created the world in six days, Miss Ashton."

"I'm not God, my lord."

"No, I suppose not."

Lord Basingstoke slowly lowered to one knee before his brother. "Where the devil are you, Trey?" he demanded in a rough voice.

Maria hurried to her charge, fell to both knees beside Basingstoke. "Kindness, my lord, I beseech you."

"Kindness? My dear Miss Ashton, Trey Hawthorne, the Duke of Salterdon, never knew a moment's kindness his entire life. No doubt even this is a goddamn ploy to manipulate us somehow. Kindness? He doesn't know the meaning of the word."

Basingstoke lowered his eyes. His face—with its deep-set, smoldering gray eyes, high cheekbones, and strong jaw—drained of color. He curled his fingers around his brother's free hand. "I want him back, Miss Ashton. Bastard that he is, I want him back. There is part of me inside that's empty—a black void—and it's incredibly cold. Sometimes I think that if he dies . . . he'll take me as well, dragging me down some black well straight to hell."

"Have faith, my lord."

"Faith?" Basingstoke raised his head, looked directly into her eyes, and for the first time she was struck by the realization of how incredibly magnificent Salterdon had once been—refined, dignified, aristocracy personified. The most beautiful man she had ever met, had ever imagined. She felt . . . dumbfounded, mesmerized beyond words.

"My grandmother's heart is breaking," he said. "For the last twenty-five years the duchess's every waking minute has been consumed in raising us to fill satisfactorily our father's prestigious place in society. To perpetuate the title, and name. But more than that, she loved us. Regardless of the fools we made of ourselves, and of her, she continued to grasp the hope and dream that we would succeed at life's battles. She watched her husband die, and her son. I think it grossly unfair to watch her grandson die as well. Please, Miss Ashton. You're his—our—last hope. Help us if you can."

Help us if you can.

The words plagued her, as did Basingstoke's face— those searching, desperate gray eyes, not unlike his brother's—the troubled countenance as, having spent several hours at his brother's side, Basingstoke had yet to reach him. What bothered her most, however, was the intense fascination she found in Lord Basingstoke . . . handsome, attractive, imposing. All that aristocracy should be . . . everything his brother wasn't.

She learned from Basingstoke that His Grace's favorite respite at Thorn Rose was the extravagant hunting room, a massive chamber of eighteenth-century paneling, royal furniture, bear rugs and stuffed tigers with fierce snarling teeth and glass eyes brought to life by the fire in the pale gray-green Cippolino marble hearth. As Maria took her place in the rear of the room (offering the brothers their privacy, yet close enough in case Basingstoke needed her), surrounded by potted ferns and fringed and tasseled curtains, she fiddled with needlework and glanced time and again at the brothers, unable to fathom that once they had been identical.

How could Salterdon, so raw in appearance, have once reflected the sophisticated bearing of his distinguished brother? There was a certain feminine beauty to Basingstoke, finely sculpted marble polished by some past master's artistic hand, a visage which beckoned the eye, encouraged the flutter of a woman's appreciation, while Salterdon . . .

Frowning, she focused again on her knitting and purling, biting her lip as she dropped a stitch. A moment passed before she allowed her gaze to lift again— directly into Basingstoke's eyes which regarded her intensely.

"Come join us," he directed and motioned toward a companion chair near the fire. "You look much too cold and lonely there."

Gathering her needles and yarn, she moved to the chair, pausing long enough to adjust the blanket over Salterdon's legs. Settling into the wing-back leather seat, she resisted the urge to raise her cold toes toward the fire.

Basingstoke watched a moment before turning back to his brother. He spoke softly, matter-of-factly, as if this were any normal conversation.

"My wife sends her love, as do your nephews. Peter turns five tomorrow. Keith began walking only last week. Grandmother, as always, prays for your complete recovery. I'm afraid she grows more feeble every day—her memory isn't what it once was. Her spirit is feisty as ever, of course."

Basingstoke leaned forward, his elbows on his knees. "Tell me, Miss Ashton, do you imagine that he can hear us?"

Maria put down her knitting, her gaze lifting slowly to Salterdon's face, then to Basingstoke's.

He turned his head. "Why do you stare at me so?" he asked gently.

" 'Tis difficult to imagine . . ."

"That we're identical? Yes, I suppose it is. Tell me, Miss Ashton, are you frightened of my brother?"

"Occasionally."

"No doubt the help has enriched your imagination with tales of mania, etcetera."

She clasped her hands in her lap; blue yarn spilled through her fingers and over her knees. Her cheeks grew warm, her throat tight. " 'Twasn't only the help, m'lord."

"Ah. I assume you mean our less-than diplomatic guests, the Ladies Draymond." His lips thinned. One heavy eyebrow drew up. "Should matrimony to my brother be wagged before their noses even now, I wager they would pounce on the opportunity with as much enthusiasm as a starving dog on a rat carcass. I might add that the viscountess herself would be happy to entertain the idea of . . . entertaining the Duke of Salterdon, if given the opportunity . . . I see you're not convinced."

Lord Basingstoke left his chair and offered her his hand. "Come along, Miss Ashton. Come, come. I appreciate your dogged responsibilities, however, I hardly imagine he's up to getting into too much mischief should we step down the hallway for a few minutes."

Reluctantly, she put aside her knitting and joined His Lordship.

As they wandered down the immense gallery, Basingstoke pointed to portraits on the walls: images of ancestors forever forged with oil on cracking canvases. There were three-hundred-year-old vases and centuries-old furnishings whose fine grains were buried beneath hundreds of layers of darkened beeswax. Still, Maria only vaguely listened. Her gaze continue to stray to her host; his tall stature, his impeccably tailored clothes, which, she thought, looked more like a finely dressed country gentleman than those belonging to one of the most distinguished men in English aristocracy. And beyond that . . .

Oh, but he was incredibly handsome!

They entered a room, lit only by the dimmest daylight spilling through the row of massive windows along the distant wall.

"My lord," she breathed quietly, her gaze sweeping the incredible chamber of soaring paneled walls and plush carpeted floors. In the center of it all was a pianoforte. Its ebony case glistened beneath the crystal-tiered chandelier overhead.

Basingstoke walked to the instrument, lightly ran his hand over the polished surface. For a moment, his expression took on a pained look. His hand curled into a fist. When he spoke again, his voice sounded tight and rough.

"Once upon a time, Miss Ashton, there was a very talented young man who was born with a very special gift—an ability to hear music in his mind—incredible music that would rival the masters. From a very young age he burned with the desire to bring that music to life . . . to exorcise it, so to speak. Late at night, he would leave his bed and come here—when everyone else was sleeping—and for hours he would sit at this instrument and allow each note to flow through his fingers onto the keys."

Basingstoke slid down onto the pianoforte bench, his long legs spread slightly, his fingers floating over the keys without really touching.

"Occasionally, I would sneak out onto the veranda, sit in the dark, close my eyes, and listen. I would jealously wonder why I had not been gifted with such a talent."

"Are you speaking of His Grace?" she asked.

"Difficult to believe, isn't it, Miss Ashton? Difficult to imagine that the man, or what is left of him, was, as a child, a prodigy of music."

Basingstoke plinked on a key and the sound resonated through the room. When he looked up at Maria again, his eyes looked fierce and as maddened as his brother's. "You must understand, my dear, that such a frivolous pastime simply wasn't acceptable for the future Duke of Salterdon. There were business matters to bone up on—God forbid that a nine-year-old future duke not fully comprehend the workings of an estate that had been in the family since God created England. Can you imagine that once, I was envious of him— galled by the fact that while I was allowed to roam at will with whomever I chose—allowing they were my peers—he was holed up with my father, becoming a man before he was ever allowed to be a child. The title of duke, and his representation of it, was all that mattered. I shudder to imagine what the burden of that responsibility would do to anyone."

He left the bench and moved across the room, to a

cluster of chairs near a window. Maria followed, tiptoeing so as not to disturb the weighty stillness and quiet pervading the austere chamber.

Basingstoke stopped at a shrouded object tucked back in a dim corner beyond the chairs. Carefully, he removed the linen drape, exposing the partially completed painting of a breathtakingly handsome Basingstoke poised by a chair occupied by the faceless portrayal of a feminine figure in a flowing red gown.

"My brother, Miss Ashton, or what once was the Duke of Salterdon."

She swallowed and shook her head in disbelief. "I don't believe it. 'Tis yourself there—"

He moved up beside the painting, posed as the man was on the canvas, one hand resting on the back of the chair, the other leisurely tucked into a pocket on his breeches.

Her gaze locked on the realistic image on the canvas, Maria moved toward the painting, unable to look away from the eyes staring back at her—deep, intense, and as fiery cold as the blade of a saber.

Those were not the kind and gentle eyes belonging to Lord Basingstoke! Nor was the dangerous, stony virility of his sharply honed features. Yet . . . neither did these features belong to the man she had been employed to companion. Nay, the man depicted on the canvas was no savage, no beast at all, but a portrait of supreme sophistication.

"The woman," she said, forcing her attention on the unfinished figure in the chair. "Who is she?"

For an instant Basingstoke's eyes became hooded, his

jaw stony, his mouth curling in a sort of smile that likened him to his notorious brother. "My dear Miss Ashton, this is the next Duchess of Salterdon—Trey's beautiful, prehensile future wife . . . the Lady Laura Dunsworthy Ronsaville."

Chapter Six

Maria tried one last time to pen words on the ivory stationary emblazoned with the duke's family crest—another letter to John and her mother she knew she would never send. John, of course, would be thrilled to receive any word from her; he would be encouraged by her note—believing there was still some hope for him—for them. He might even come to Thorn Rose and convince her to leave with him, to marry him . . . to spend the remainder of her life becoming a reflection of her mother . . .

She wadded up the paper and flung it to the floor. Why could she concentrate on nothing but the images portrayed on that canvas? That man had been no beast. No monster. Only the epitome of power and sophistication—nay—outright arrogance. A man of extreme self-confidence. A man who exuded a certain virility that made her feel . . . how, exactly, did she feel?

Breathless hardly seemed sufficiently descriptive.

Yet . . . daft girl. Demented child. Obviously her father had been right about her all along.

From Salterdon's room came the sounds of Gertrude's hustle-bustle as she flitted from table to chair, dusting, rearranging pillows, collecting soiled laundry. By now, Thaddeus and his helper should have removed the duke from his bath and dressed him.

Maria joined the activity, pausing in the doorway, her eyes scanning the glowing room until locating His Grace, as usual, positioned at the window, his back to her as he stared off over the countryside. As usual, after Salterdon's bath, the scent of violets wafted in the air.

Gertrude looked up from her dusting and smiled. "Have ya done with yer letter, love?"

She nodded and moved into the room, hesitated at the dressing table long enough to rearrange the bouquet of yellow and purple flowers in a crystal vase, her gaze drifting reluctantly to her image in the mirror. The female peering back at her, with wide blue eyes, oval face framed by slender coils of silver-white hair, and pink slightly pouting mouth, was, indeed, little more than a child—no woman—no matter how adult-like she tried to behave.

"'Tis no wonder Lord Basingstoke was shocked upon meeting me," she mused aloud. "I *am* a child. What was Her Grace thinking when she employed me?"

Gertrude hurried to her, her dust cloth flapping like a flag from one hand. "Yer a kindhearted soul, love, and that's what His Grace needs most. Someone with compassion and understandin'."

Maria moved to the window, stood for a moment

with her gaze locked on the hills before facing her patient at last. The image in her mind was of chiseled, hard-as-granite features, of burning gray eyes. She knew fully now what His Grace had *once* been.

"Gerti, Basingstoke is a handsome man, wouldn't you agree?"

"No more handsome than Salterdon," the servant declared with appreciable pride and a flap of her dusting cloth.

"Basingstoke's features are so perfectly honed."

"As was . . . is . . . His Grace's."

"His lordship's smile is kindly and sincere."

Gertrude paused in her dusting, and looking somewhat bemused, replied, "I reckon kindly and sincere don't describe Salterdon's smile, exactly. Rakish and cheeky were more like it. A bit on the acerbic side, but then, while the two were as alike as two peas in a pod, their personalities were as different as night and day."

"So you've said," Maria replied absently and moved around the duke's chair, regarding his wild hair and face hidden beneath the unkempt beard. She brushed his shoulder lightly with her fingertips. "Judging by what I've been told, his present guise would suit him best, yet . . . can any man be so truly manipulative and cunningly hedonistic as those closest to His Grace have described him?"

She bent and searched his gray eyes, slightly mesmerized by the intensity with which they appeared to stare back at her. Unlike Basingstoke's, there was a madness there, a vacuity that would so easily impair his capacity to function normally in his society.

"Obviously you've lived too sheltered a life with yer saintly father if ya don't know the answer to that one," Gertrude replied. "Not meanin' to impugn the honor of His Grace's name, but hedonistic don't come close to describing Salterdon's lifestyle. If his position in society didn't reward him with what, or who he wanted, his good looks usually did."

"Understandable," she said thoughtfully, recalling the manner in which Basingstoke's good looks had held her (not to mention the irritating Ladies Draymond) fixated throughout the last days.

"Yet His Grace has come to this," she said softly to herself. Straightening, she turned to Gertrude. "Bring me hot water, shaving lather, and a razor."

"Beggin' yer pardon, lass?"

"I intend to shave him."

"But—"

"I've seen now what he's supposed to look like, and it isn't this. Now do as I say, quickly before reason takes hold and I change my mind."

Within ten minutes, Gertrude was back, required objects stacked on a tray and placed at Maria's side. The servant hovered like a bothered hen.

"That will be all," Maria told her.

"But, miss, when we've attempted to groom him before—"

"Please! I'm nervous enough as it is, dear Gertrude."

With a grunt of reluctance, Gertrude quit the room, muttering to herself and wringing her hands.

Her hands trembled as Maria dabbed the warm lather onto his bearded face, across his cheeks, beneath his

nose, over his jaw and chin. The first time she had
shaved Paul, she had nicked him—not much, but
enough to make him *ouch!* and stare at her with so
grieved a look she had almost cried.

Carefully, carefully. God, make her hand stop trembling. "There's nothing to be nervous about," she
whispered aloud. "'Tis only anxiousness making my
fingers quiver . . ." And the ridiculous desire to see
his face, the same face which had entranced her since
the moment she met his brother—since the instant
Salterdon's visage was revealed to her on that wedding
portrait.

One swipe.

Breathe deeply.

Not too fast.

Gently. Lightly.

Just skim, as Paul had instructed, and keep the razor
clean.

"A dull razor will tear the flesh as opposed to slice,"
Paul had proclaimed, just before she had nicked him a
second time.

Closing her eyes, Maria swallowed and tried to calm
herself.

The hand closed around her throat so suddenly and
fiercely her world went momentarily black. She tried to
scream. Impossible! She couldn't breathe. The world
was a red haze of pain and suffocation. Her arms flailed.
She kicked the washstand and sent the china basin of
steaming water to the floor with a crash.

"Lud! He's at it again! Help! Somebody help! He's
got Miss Ashton!" shrieked Gertrude from the doorway.

Maria clawed at the hand—the vise—cutting off her air, crushing her neck.

"Let 'er go! Stop it. Yer killin' 'er!"

"Bleedin', murderin' bastard!" Thaddeus yelled and attempted to wedge the fingers from her throat.

"Pl-please," Maria finally managed in a strained whisper, forcing her eyes to his—Salterdon's—which were no longer vacant and staring, but wild with fury and more horrible than anything she had ever witnessed. "Your . . . Grace . . . please . . ."

For an instant, the eyes widened, then narrowed. He hissed something through his teeth that sounded like *Ishellickufikenfler!* and his fingers clutched at her throat more tightly and shook her as she were a Christmas goose destined for the roaster.

"I . . . don't . . . understand . . ." she tried to cry before he shook her again—so hard this time her feet left the floor and her world became a fiery pinpoint of his eyes that were murderous.

"Bastard!" Thaddeus yelled again and dashed for the firepoker, causing Gertrude to shriek in alarm and fly at him with flailing arms, only to hit him with such impact both tumbled to the floor, smack amid the strewn soapy water and shattered china dish.

Her hands clutching Salterdon's, Maria, as calmly as possible, focused on his enraged face and tried to reason. *Impossible!* Dear God she was going to die; he was killing her, the very man whom she had tried so devotedly these last days to help and had actually harbored an amorous thought over (daft, moronic, imbecilic, and naive child!) had every intention of

murdering her, even as his lips clumsily formed words
that to her own ears sounded little more than the
incoherent ravings of a maniac.

"I . . . shel . . . licki . . . fickin . . . fler!" he
shouted again.

She did her best to focus on his mouth that was fast
becoming a blur.

Dragging her closer—so close she felt his breath on
the burning flesh of her face, he growled painfully
slowly:

"I . . . smell . . . like . . . a . . . fucking . . .
flower!" Then, with a roar, more animal than human,
Salterdon sent her flying, spilling over Gertrude, who
had managed to scramble to her hands and knees, and
sprawled onto the floor.

Maria gasped for air that, for a terrifying moment,
would not come, then it swept like a burning flood into
her deprived lungs, scraping the inside of her throat like
the razor she had flung to the far side of the room.

A melee of sound bombarded her, intensified by the
raging ringing in her head: Women shrieking, glass
breaking, Thaddeus cursing.

Someone called her name. "Miss Ashton? Miss
Ashton! Wot should we do with 'im now?"

Maria struggled to sit up, hand clamped to her mouth
because she feared she might scream—a delayed reaction, no doubt—or she might cry—which she always
did when she was frightened or angry. Blood buzzed
like bees behind her nose and in her ears.

"Wot would ya have us do with 'im now?" came the
voice again. This time she recognized it as Gertrude's,

but still she could not seem to focus her eyes. The room was a haze of blurry forms moving back and forth, and there was that other noise, that hideous growl, like a wounded wolf. "Miss Ashton?"

Shaking, she managed to climb as far as her hands and knees, swayed back and forth while the world careened into a solitary figure lying procumbent on the floor, arms and legs outstretched and pinned to the carpet by Thaddeus and several manservants.

"The chair," she managed before coughing furiously into her hand.

With a heave of strength, the duke was put back in the chair. His riot of hair falling over his as-yet unshaven face, his teeth showing in a feral sneer, her master centered her with his glowing eyes and growled, "Who . . . the *hell* . . . are . . . you?"

Thaddeus helped her to stand. Fortified by his arm around her waist, she continued to press one hand to her throat, to draw in deep, burning breaths until, little by little, her brain began to function and anger replaced her shock.

"Her Grace, the duchess, has employed me to—"

"Get . . . *out!*" he snarled and looked around for something, anything to break.

Flinging soapsuds and her shoes squeaking with water, Gertrude lumbered toward her. "Best to leave 'im, lass. He'll calm down eventually—"

"Nay, I shan't leave him!" she replied hotly, shoving Thaddeus away and advancing on her patient where he sat in his chair, hands like claws clasping the chair arms. "It seems His Grace has seen fit to break his basin of water, Gertrude. Will you be kind enough to fetch me another?"

The servant gasped. "Ya can't be thinkin' to try again."

Maria began collecting the shattered china scattered over the floor in puddles of soapy water. When reaching the razor, she rolled it in her fingers before turning back to Salterdon, who regarded her with narrowed, suspicious eyes.

"He didn't mean to hurt me, I think," she declared in as firm a voice as possible, considering. Neck throbbing and throat feeling as if she had swallowed a burning coal, she cautiously approached the duke.

"I think he awakened from his . . . nap . . . and became frightened."

Salterdon followed her with his wolf eyes, his upper lip slightly twitching.

"When fear clashes with our will to survive, I suspect our reactions, although human, can be, occasionally, beyond our abilities to control them. Take me, for instance. There were moments, when His Grace was attempting to murder me, when I would have done anything to stop him, even hurt him, if I must."

"Lud," Thaddeus groaned. "Yer daft as he is."

"Not totally, Thaddeus. Even an animal can be reasoned with, if shown sufficient patience and kindness. Of course, His Grace is *not* an animal, but a human. A man. A reasoning, intelligent person capable of acting with the dignity with which he was born."

Salterdon took a swipe at her with his fist.

She jumped away, slid on a ball of scap, before

sitting down so hard on her backside she felt momentarily stunned. "On the other hand, fetch me the ropes we tied him with before. Occasionally even animals must be taught to respect the hand that feeds them!"

The bruises were wickedly vivid against her pale skin. There were five of them shaped like little purple discs, four on one side of her neck, one on the other.

There had been not a solitary utterance from His Grace's room in the last quarter hour. Thank God. The show of strength she had managed to muster for Gertrude's and Thaddeus's benefit had left her depleted enough to excuse herself from the room on the pretense of changing her damp clothes.

For the last half hour, she had rocked back and forth in her little chair before the dressing table mirror and watched her neck swell. She had rehearsed a hundred excuses of why she must suddenly leave Thorn Rose and return to her father's home, but the mere thought of doing so had thrust a cold spear of dread through her heart.

No doubt she would spend the next year of her life on her knees pleading for God's absolution for dishonoring her father.

What, she wondered, would be the greater hell? Remaining at Thorn Rose . . . or returning to her father's house?

At last, she garnered her courage and returned to Salterdon's room.

He sat quietly in his chair before the fire, his wrists bound to the chair arms. Thaddeus hovered nearby, hands tucked into the waistband of his loose trousers, his red hair spilling over his forehead. Upon seeing her, he stopped and stared.

Only then did she notice Basingstoke, poised near the bedroom window, long arms crossed over his chest. At some point he had removed his jacket, exposing his well-made shirt. He regarded her with one raised eyebrow and his mouth in a grim line.

Maria self-consciously touched her neck, her gaze shifting from him to Salterdon, who continued to gaze into the flames. Had he reverted again, back into his own private hell?

God help her, but she hoped so.

"Miss Ashton," Basingstoke said softly, kindly, concernedly.

"Don't," she replied a bit hoarsely. "I fear I'll only get emotional again. I'm not at my best when I'm emotional."

Basingstoke joined her, lightly placed one finger beneath her chin and tipped her head slightly to one side. "Bastard," he murmured under his breath, then did his best to relieve his anger with a less than believable smile. "I'm certain it's little consolation, but I assure you, were His Grace in his rational mind he never would have treated you in such a manner. While he's always been somewhat cavalier about matters of the heart, I've never known him to physically harm a woman. You may cry, of course. I won't think any less of you if you do."

She shook her head in refusal even as her eyes filled up with tears. She did not dare blink or they would surely spill. Still, few people had ever treated her so kindly and with such genuine concern. That alone threatened to make her crumble.

Basingstoke moved away, circled his brother—the duke—who continued to glare into the fire, his bound hands in fists. His Grace looked, Maria thought, like one on the verge of shattering.

Placing one brotherly hand on Salterdon's shoulder, Basingstoke rewarded his brother with an emotionless smile. "During your absence, Miss Ashton, I spoke with Trey at length. I assume he listened. I can only assume he comprehended. I reminded him that you, like the others before you, were employed by the duchess to help him. However, the duchess has grown overly weary of the reports of verbal and physical abuse, which have found their way back to her over the last year." His tone becoming gruffer, he added, "If His Grace doesn't wish to find himself interned to an asylum for the remainder of his life, he might do well to curtail his bouts of temper and intimidation. He might also consider rousing himself out of this *pity me* attitude. Personally, I find it repugnantly tiresome."

The duke shifted, unclenched and clenched his hands.

Lowering his mouth to his brother's ear, Basingstoke whispered, "Then again, Trey and I have always disagreed on what is an acceptable manner with which to deal with the world in general. Haven't we, dear brother? And haven't I often mentioned that were the duchess's vast holdings passed along to me I would see that they would be invested cautiously, if not prudently?

By cautiously, I mean meagerly—such as allowances to recalcitrant prodigy, etcetera. Miss Ashton?"

"Y-yes, your lordship?"

"I believe you desire to clean him up?"

She nodded.

"Bring the razor and lather."

She joined Basingstoke as he rolled up his shirt sleeves, exposing very brown wrists and forearms. His hands, she thought with some surprise, looked hard and rough as a farmer's.

When she offered Basingstoke the razor and cup of lather, he shook his head. "I'm only here for support, Miss Ashton. I'll remind him, however, that should he behave unnaturally, as he did earlier, I'll take charge of the cutter myself." He winked at his brother, who continued to ignore him.

Only then did Maria allow herself to look at Salterdon, at those eyes that had glittered with such anger and hatred moments before. Slowly, slowly, they turned up to hers. No fury now. No desperation. Those gray orbs reflected a sort of confusion and fear that left her suddenly as shaken as his previous bout of bad temper.

"We don't intend to hurt you," she assured him in as steady a voice as she could manage. In truth, the very effort of speaking made her throat throb; each purple bruise felt like sharp stones pressed into her flesh.

As she cautiously touched the lathered brush to the side of Salterdon's face, Maria felt the penetration of those eyes into hers, watched the fine sheen of sweat materialize across his brow and bead at his temples.

"He's frightened," she said softly to Basingstoke.

"Because he knows I'll cut his throat if he thinks to harm you again," he replied with a taunting smile. "Or better yet, I'll invite the Ladies Draymond up to have a peek at what's become of His Grace. I've discovered them snooping about Thorn Rose's corridors half a dozen times the last few days, hoping for some glimpse of the *howling monster*. No doubt London will be abuzz with the graphic descriptions of our belligerent duke before the week's end."

Had the occasion been less serious, Maria might have laughed, for no doubt his lordship's threat had touched a sore nerve. Salterdon's wolfish eyes narrowed. He made a sound, so guttural in his throat as to be menacing, had the circumstances been more in his favor.

Her heart beat furiously in her chest and throat and ears. Again, the lather, across his jaw, beneath his nose, over his chin. The air became charged.

"In case you don't recall, Your Grace, my name is Maria Ashton," she told him in a dry voice, focusing on his cheek and not on his eyes that continued to rivet her. Oh, if her hand would only stop shaking. There was nothing to be frightened over, his wrists were bound, and Thaddeus hovered somewhere in the background. Basingstoke stood at her side, solid as a sentinel, his very demeanor a blatant threat to his brother should he try anything terrible. "Her Grace has employed me to companion you. I suspect you become quite lonely here, alone as you are."

With a sudden angry grunt, he turned his head away sharply.

The razor nicked his cheek.

Maria gasped, her frustration mounting as blood seeped from the cut and pinkened the surrounding white lather. "Now see what you've done," she cried, then bit her lip, closed her eyes and prayed for patience and calm. "I beseech you, Your Grace, to remain still unless you wish to be restrained."

A moment passed. When he made no further move or sound of rebellion, she continued the task, carefully, so carefully, anticipating another bout of temper, for surely he looked ready to shatter with the slightest provocation.

Yet, he made no further protest, just fixed his stare on some distant object in the room, and gritting his teeth and clutching his fists allowed her to finish the terrifying chore of peeling away the thick thatch of beard, until it lay on the floor and in the washbasin, clotted by blood-tinged lather.

At last, Maria stepped back, took an unsteady breath of relief, and with razor still in hand, regarded her handiwork.

"Oh," she whispered, with a lightening of her spirit—for those mesmerizing features that had fascinated her since Basingstoke's arrival were revealed to her eyes, which searched each detail and found them as utterly marvelous—if not a great deal sharper and harsher than his brother's, or even those portrayed on Salterdon's wedding portrait.

Forgetting Thaddeus, who had stopped his pacing near the door, forgetting even Lord Basingstoke, who stood near her shoulder, with his hands in his pockets, she swept up a mirror and held it before Salterdon.

"Look and see," she implored him. "Is it not an improvement, Your Grace? Is this not the image of a most dignified aristocrat worthy of his title?"

Cautiously, reluctantly, Salterdon's eyes moved to the mirror.

Her smile growing, her eyes becoming misty with pleasure, she went to her knees beside Salterdon's chair and peered with him into the looking glass at his— their—images. Pleasure kissed bright color on her cheeks. Excitement torched her eyes. "Is he not a handsome duke after all?" she said softly. "No beast, sir. No dragon. No wolf. A man blessed with extraordinary beauty."

He regarded his image without blinking, as if studying a stranger distrustfully. A myriad of emotions came and went over his features: confusion, frustration, despair.

Closing his eyes, he turned his head away. The anger returned, flooding his features, turning his jaw to granite, furrowing his brow. Cords stood out on his neck as he strained to escape both the mirror and the bonds anchoring him to the wheeled chair.

Dropping the mirror to the floor, jumping to her feet, Maria hesitated, uncertain for an instant, then took his face in her hands, even as he rolled it from side to side in denial.

"Stop!" she pleaded. "I beg you, Your Grace. 'Tis nothing frightening there, I swear it. 'Tis not the face of a stranger, but your own. Why would you deny it? Why would you run from it?"

He made a sound, more pain than anger, and twisted

from her again, forcing her to grip his hair with her fingers so that she might look him squarely in the face. His features appeared ravaged by emotion.

"Want me to get more rope?" Thaddeus shouted.

"Nay, no rope," she snapped. "He wants compassion not cruelty."

"He wants to snap yer bleedin' neck," Thaddeus argued and shuffled nervously, ready to spring at the first hint of trouble but obviously kept at bay by Lord Basingstoke's presence.

"Please," she implored softly. "I only meant to help, Your Grace. There's nothing to fear. Nothing to shame. You are most . . . remarkably handsome."

Her words seemed to soothe him. Or, perhaps, he simply wearied of his internal battle. Little by little, his body relaxed, and though he continued to hold his face away from her, his expression of pain and anger became, once again, a mask of blankness.

※ *Chapter Seven*

It was a soft February morning, with a warm mist going up from the brown grass, and breaking at last into sunshine so bright that the air felt just like summer. It seemed that spring had come remarkably early, and though the second calendar month was yet within a day or two of its closing, the birds and the budding leaves seemed bent on putting all almanacs to shame, and making those residing at Thorn Rose believe that winter was surely behind them.

Often, a blithe bright morning—a mere gleam of sunshine—will make one feel, if not happy, at least eager to receive happiness. Although Maria had spent a long night of tossing and turning, and had risen from her tangled bedclothes to discover the image in the mirror belonging to that of a haggard and sleepless waif, she had revived at the first instant she had thrown wide her window and allowed the influence of the spring-like day to surround her with soft fresh air.

It was obvious that she had overslept, and she made

haste to finish her toilette, first her hair, which she brushed until it shone then fixed into a bun on the back of her head—very proper, surely. Her master was aware now. Her hours and days of daydreaming girlish fantasies were behind her. No more musings of frolicking across the moor with butterflies, or playing games of tag with chattering squirrels.

Besides, Basingstoke had announced at dinner the previous evening that he would take his leave of Thorn Rose this morning and had warmly insisted to the Ladies Draymond that they accompany him back to London; he would make certain their driver, Clyde, found his way home as soon as he was capable, though Maria suspected he would be hard pressed to bid adieu to Gertrude anytime soon.

Maria fixed her lace cap to her head and tied it under her chin. Swiftly, she donned one of her two black dresses and kid slippers, hopping on one foot toward the door of Salterdon's bedroom, pausing at the threshold while her mind ascertained the mood of the room, which was bustling with late-morning activity. Molly bent over Salterdon's bed, stripping away sheets, the backs of her ankles and calves peeking from beneath her starched skirt. Gertrude was busily slapping away a cobweb from a lamp shade, and yet another servant was on her knees plucking lint from the carpet.

"Where is he?" Maria asked, bringing the servants' heads around in surprise. "His Grace, where is he?" she said.

"Lord Basingstoke thought His Grace could do with a bit of fresh air," Gertrude replied. "I believe he's wheeled him to the stable house. Enjoys that, His Grace does, watchin' from the veranda as his horses are worked."

"Then he's . . . aware?"

"Aye." Gertrude nodded. "Unsociable as always but at least he ain't hurlin' and hellin' us. Run along, love. Ya might enjoy the beasts yerself."

"Aye, that I will," she replied with an excited giggle.

Upon leaving the manse, Maria found her way down one meandering paved-stone walkway after another. Here and there were natural and man-made pools and ponds, both dotted with arc-necked swans that glided effortlessly over the glassy water. There were ivy-grown stone walls and occasional strands of bramble that crowded the footpaths. Here and there steep small slopes crowned with brown grass rose up to block her view, then dissipated into flower beds of pale crocuses' shoots that were bending toward shafts of intruding sunlight.

The entire area felt mystical, making her feel like a giddy child. If Paul were here, he might even tease her about fairies hiding beneath eyebrights and anemones. Oh, but he did love to tease her!

At last, she discovered her charge sitting where his brother had deposited him—on a tiny veranda that, at first, appeared to be little more than a green plateau surrounded by fans of brown-tipped ferns. The plateau, however, upon closer inspection, became a lichen-covered stone floor attached to a charming little cottage near a cluster of vastly sprawling stone stables.

For a moment, the image gave her pause. Her heart fluttered in her chest.

Where was the normal severity of his features? How smooth was his brow! How soft were his lips, which appeared to be almost smiling.

Nay. Impossible. 'Twas only the dance of sunlight around his head and shoulders that made him appear to look so at ease and almost . . . happy. 'Twas only the chill of the wind that made him flush, and look like a man on the verge of laughing aloud in pleasure.

Yet, there she stood, unable to move, irrevocably mesmerized by the play of light and shadow on his features. How beautiful and almost childishly innocent he looked in the sun, the wind caressing his chilled face and flirting with his flowing hair. His lap blanket lay in a heap by his feet. The muffler Gertrude had wrapped around his neck and shoulders dangled off the back of his chair and fluttered in the occasional brisk wind.

"Miss Ashton."

She jumped and turned. Basingstoke poised in the shady tunnel of elm limbs, his coat collar turned up around his nape.

"Good morning." He smiled. "I had gone looking for you. I thought you might enjoy a tour of the stables with my brother and me."

Before she could respond, he caught her arm and urged her along. "I assume you've been thoroughly educated about my brother's passion for Arabian horses."

"Somewhat, sir."

"Exotic creatures, Miss Ashton, as you'll soon discover. My own father held a fascination for them.

Traveled all the way to Arabia to attempt to purchase several. It was on our voyage home that our ship . . ." He took a long breath and slowly released it. "Watch your step. Careful. Seems the path has fallen to disrepair since my brother's become housebound. Never mind about the ship. That doesn't matter any longer. Best not to dwell on it. We were talking about horses. Arabians, Miss Ashton. My wife, Miracle, owned a dozen or more when I met her—"

"Miracle?" She stepped through a frail veil of down hanging strands of brown ivy, paused only long enough to turn her face toward the sunlight, then continued on at Basingstoke's side.

"Yes, Miracle," he said.

"How delightfully unusual, my lord."

"*She* is delightfully unusual, Miss Ashton. As were her cache of horses. Soon after our marriage, she gifted my brother with several: a stallion called Noblesse; a mare named NapPerl, and a colt by her stallion Napitov that my brother has since named NapPoleone. I vowed these horses have—or had—changed my brother's life. He spent far less time at the gaming tables than he did aback Noblesse."

"I have often said, my lord, that a man who is kind to horses is a good man, not only of heart, but of soul. 'Tis said, sir, that gypsy gold does not chink and glitter. It gleams in the sun and neighs in the dark."

"Saying of the Claddagh Gypsies of Galway, I believe," he said with a flash of a smile.

She laughed gaily and skipped ahead, uplifted by the clean rinsed morning and brisk air that made her flush with energy and vibrate with renewed enthusiasm over her task ahead. Dear lord, how long since she had felt so light and carefree?

Reaching the veranda, she declared in a bright, clear voice that might have roused the heaviest daydreamer, "Good morning, Your Grace," yet he made no noticeable start.

She moved up beside him, keeping a good distance between them, and regarded his sun- and wind-kissed profile as he stared out over the oblong arena where a groom exercised a high-prancing mahogany-bay horse. How lean was His Grace's clean-shaven face, and stoic. Mayhap she had earlier imagined the pleasure on his features. Certainly, there was little about him now that hinted of serenity.

"Good morning," she repeated more firmly. "Isn't it a grand morning, Your Grace?"

No response.

She gathered his lap blanket, wadded it in her hands, and rolled it over and over before cautiously bending to replace it over his legs. "Don't you look handsome and distinguished this morning, Your Grace. What fine leather breeches and—"

He snatched the blanket from her hand and flung it to the stone floor. All without looking at her, without uttering a sound.

Heart quickening, breath momentarily catching in her throat, which was yet throbbing from the previous fiasco, Maria tottered uncertainly on her tiptoes, glancing with caution and fear, first at Basingstoke, who regarded his brother with mild irritation, then at those hands, hard as anvils, that had almost murdered her last evening.

Again, she retrieved the blanket. "The air is chilly, Your Grace. If you could but see your cheeks, how the cold has given them bright color, and your lips are slightly blue—I would not have you falling ill with pneumonia, sir." She spread the woolen blanket over his legs again, tucked the ends beneath his thighs, then cautiously reached for the muffler.

He grabbed her wrist. Only then did he look up at her with his hard gray eyes, his clean-shaven jaw working with anger and belligerence. Only then did she realize how near his face was to her own, indecently so, it seemed. His warm breath brushed her cheek and mouth. Those ashen-colored eyes were tinged with flakes of gold that she might never have noticed before.

"Sir," she declared in a dry voice. "You're hurting my arm."

Still, his fingers bit into her tender wrist another eternal moment, and she wondered if she would be forced to plead help from his brother.

At last, little by little, his grip eased, until she withdrew her hand and held it to her breast, rubbing away the fierce ache in it with her other. She would not cry, would not acknowledge her own sense of anger and frustration over his continued outrageous behavior. She noticed, then, the discarded cart of food dishes placed to one side.

In an attempt to alleviate the tense moment, she declared in a light tone, "I see you refused your breakfast. But surely Your Grace is hungry. Let me see, what has Cook brought you?"

She whisked aside the silver plate domes to reveal cooling kidney pie and mushrooms, partridge legs, sausages, eggs à la George, grilled tomatoes and fresh fruit. "A veritable feast, sir. Certainly there's something here to your liking. I'll prepare you a plate with a bit of everything—there's nothing like a beautiful chill morning to rouse the appetite."

Managing a smile, she put the tray over his lap and stepped back, anxiously waiting.

He glared at her.

"Eat," she told him, her smile thinning as he neither moved nor spoke. "Mayhap you need help," she offered more softly, and with a deep breath, glanced around for a chair, which she pulled before him and sat down. With fork and knife, she cut his sausage and eggs and sliced the sugared berries into bite-size pieces. Upon heaping the fork with food, she poised it at his mouth.

Nothing.

"Just a small bit, sir. I'm certain you'll find it delicious—"

He turned his face away.

Determinedly, she followed his mouth with the fork. "You must eat. A man of your stature cannot survive on air—"

He turned the other way.

"If not for yourself, then think of your grandmother and your brother and—"

Again, he snatched her arm, causing egg and sausage to scatter over her lap and feet. His grip anchored her while his free hand extracted the fork from hers in a jerky fashion that seemed more mechanical than human. Then he released her.

Fiercely, his countenance creased with concentration and intense emotion, he struggled to manipulate the utensil over the food. Again and again he attempted it, to no avail. In a fit of exasperation and anger, he shoved the tray of food from his lap. It crashed at Maria's feet.

Basingstoke made a move toward her. She threw up her hand to stop him.

She didn't move at first, then she left her chair, shook off the egg that clung determinedly to her ankle and stepped over the shattered pottery, retrieved another plate from the serving cart and piled it high with food again.

" 'Tis obvious, Your Grace, that you wish to eat, and you wish to feed yourself. 'Tis understandable, considering you're obviously a man of considerable pride, that you would become frustrated at your current inability to manage on your own. However, there is such a thing as cutting one's nose off to spite one's face. I beseech you . . . allow me to help you."

He stared at her.

She stared at him.

Finally, he opened his mouth, and she promptly fed him his breakfast.

In the distance, encouraged by the proficient groom, the stallion Noblesse trotted above level, hooves flashing, haunches and shoulders rippling, each breath the stud blew from its extended nostrils forming a vaporous stream in the cold morning air. Salterdon watched the magnificent Arabian through narrowed eyes, recalling those brisk mornings when he, himself, had mounted Noblesse, and the two of them had ridden down Thorn Rose's wooded bridle paths. More often than not, he had been companioned by a beautiful woman, resplendent in trailing habits and hats with veils and feathers. At some point, he would seduce her from her pony and make love to her under the skies and trees.

God, he wanted to sleep. Wanted to drift away. Wanted to forget that he could no longer manage the spirited horse, or the spirited woman. He was a goddamn invalid. A goddamn eunuch. He couldn't string two words together, much less make a woman scream with desire and passion.

But she—this new stranger, invader, troublesome little gnat of a girl, simply would not leave him alone. She was there when he tried so fiercely to wrap himself up again in the solitude of his mind—that fairy's voice would come to him, drifting through his foggy thoughts, and like some pied piper lure him out of the comforting quicksand darkness.

Where was she now?

Planning his midday meal, no doubt, with the intention of spoon-feeding him again. Next time he would choke her with *both* hands. Perhaps that would get rid of her—send her flying out the door like the others, never to return.

Good riddance.

If that were not enough, he now had his goody-goody brother to contend with. His grandmother's favorite.

The one Hawthorne who could repeatedly fall into a cesspit and come out smelling like a rose. Let Clayton Hawthorne, Lord Basingstoke, walk into a drawing room and all of bloody England would fall to its knees.

So where the blazes *was* the girl?

No doubt she would turn out to be like his third companion—what was his name?—Dirk or Dick—a sniveling little upstart with one goal in mind, and that was to pocket the duchess's wages with the least amount of expended effort possible. He'd eaten. He'd napped. He'd pilfered the silver. He'd crawled into the duke's bed one night and proceeded to nuzzle. Trey had broken five of his fingers and three ribs before the pervert had managed to fling himself out of the window and flee the house in his nightclothes.

Oh, yes. He could so easily send—what was her name? God, why could he never remember? Miss . . . Aynesworth? Afsley? . . . Ashton!—the way of all the others.

A bustle beside him—she was back (at last); he refused to look at her, but continued to watch his stallion while she made a grand show of dragging chairs and setting tables with a straw bowl of yarn balls and pegs and cups and saucers.

Her face flush with energy and exercise, appearing as she always did when she at last managed to worm her way into his reluctant consciousness—butterfly-like, flitting hither and thither, looking as if she would soon fold her gossamer wings and transform into a new existence, she finally sat herself down in a chair beside him so her small shoulder was barely touching his.

My, but wasn't she becoming quite courageous?

"The idea has occurred to me, Your Grace, that much of your dispiritedness may stem from exasperation and frustration. You desire to accomplish certain tasks, but are unable to do so, due to, and I beg Your Grace's pardon for seeming indelicate and no doubt bruising to your manly pride, but *your lack of coordination brought about by your injury*," she finished in a tone so hushed he could scarcely hear her, then she plucked a blue ball out of the bowl and sat it down on the table. "If it pleases Your Grace, pick it up."

He slowly turned his head and stared at her eyes, which were wide and more brilliantly blue than the vast cerulean sky behind her.

She beamed him a smile; her teeth looked white as pearls, her cheeks like peaches. "The ball, sir. Pick it up, if you please."

What the blazes was she up to? And where in God's name did she find that medieval-looking cap that had slid somewhat lopsidedly to one side of her brow?

Patiently, she picked up the ball herself, lifted it up into the air in a great show, then put it down again. "Now you," she declared and smiled again.

He narrowed his eyes. She treated him like a goddamn idiot—just like all the others.

"Mayhap you need a bit of help. Very well." Again, she removed the ball from the table, and balancing it on her small white hand, presented it to him like a treasure.

"Take . . . the . . . ball . . . Your . . . Grace," she enunciated as if she were speaking to the deaf.

He glared at her, then at the ball. He smacked it from

her hand so suddenly she jumped in her chair and cried, "Oh!" as it sailed off the veranda and plopped into a clump of marjoram.

Hot color suffused her face. Her blue eyes became dark as midnight, her breathing ragged. She looked like a bird on the verge of flight—an *agitated* bird on the verge of flight.

He made no further move, and, gradually, she relaxed, collected herself, and took a deep breath. "Allow me to explain," she said patiently. "Concentration is the key to success in any of life's endeavors. Focusing upon one's goals, no matter how tedious and tiresome, will, ultimately, accomplish the most grueling feat. Shall we try again? Mayhap you like the red ball better?"

Up came the red ball from the bowl, and balanced on her fingertips. "Your Grace may take the ball . . . please."

His Grace knocked it the way of the first, then he slammed his fist on the table, sending pegs scattering and china bouncing.

As the fairy girl leapt from her chair, he snatched her skirt; its crude stitches popped from the fitted bodice and sprang open exposing a flash of ivory skin and undergarment beneath her arm, and the swell of her breast.

Stumbling away, she cried, "Oh! Were I not a Christian woman, sir, I . . . I . . . no, I shan't even contemplate such an act or thought. Understanding and forgiveness will right the occasion. Patience is the ultimate virtue, and . . ." She gulped for air, blinked away her shock long enough to collect her nerves, then, with as much *virtuous patience* as she could muster, excused herself and exited the balcony with the gracefulness of a ballet dancer. No doubt she would stalk toward his brother, who stood just outside one of the stables, running his hand down NapPoleone's arched neck. Clay would return and mutter some threat in his ear—vow to tell their grandmother what an ass he had become—all that muddlycock that he had long since grown deaf to. What difference did it make? She wasn't going to leave her inheritance to an imbecile anyway.

Salterdon sank back in his chair, white-knuckled fists clenched atop the chair arms. Pegs and yarn and china lay scattered over the table beside him. Again and again, his gaze drifted there, and each time he experienced the rise of anger, the moistening of his brow with sweat that even the bracing morning breeze could not extinguish.

Again and again, he saw the flash of white skin beneath the Ashton girl's arm, the flush of anger and frustration over her face—a flush as deep and hot as passion itself.

Teeth clenched, he tried to open his hand—ah, God! The effort! Didn't she understand it was so much easier to strike? Fury was without restraint, without control. He raised his arm, which felt heavy as an anvil, which wavered uncontrollably; he reached toward the china cup laying on its side. *Concentrate you bloody idiot; an imbecile can pick up a goddamn cup; you don't need her to teach you how to drink a bloody cup of tea—you were sipping tea at George's court when she was nothing but some commoner's daughter scrubbing floors on her hands and knees.*

He closed his fingers around the cup—or tried to. They wavered over the delicate white and gold china, knocking the cup to one side, then the other, never quite managing to grasp the gilded scrolled handle that sparkled in the sunlight as if taunting him.

Again, and yet again! Until his brow grew damp with sweat that ran into his eyes and made his vision blurry, until his body felt like a tightly wound coil that would unravel at any moment.

With a roar of frustration, he slammed his flattened hand upon the cup, shattered it, sending jagged pieces flying off the table, and burying into his palm.

Clay cupped his hand above his eyes and looked his way.

Miss Ashton appeared from nowhere—had she been watching his pitiful attempt to prove her and all the others wrong? *Damn her, damn her to hell.* Grabbing up his hand, which was severely cut and bleeding, she wrapped it with a lacy kerchief, never uttering a word or looking at him with those childish heavenly eyes, but going about her task with the efficiency of a nurse, her cheeks pale as milkwash, her lips tight with emotion.

When she had finished, she stepped back. Still clutching her bodice closed, she regarded him fixedly a long silent moment before slowly reaching for the last ball of yarn on the table. Her voice became a monotone, and with the tenderness of a tolerant and loving parent, she put the ball into his unharmed hand and closed his fingers around it.

"In my exuberance, I fear I've expected too much too soon. Of course the logical first step will be to bring coordination and dexterity to the hands and fingers. Squeeze and release the ball, Your Grace. Nothing more. Squeeze and release. Can you manage?"

He stared down at the yellow ball, at her fingers wrapped around his, gently inducing him to squeeze.

He squeezed.

"Very good." Her breath smelled sweet and fresh, and felt warm on the side of his chilled face. When she backed away, he felt, suddenly, very odd—cold and desperately vulnerable—more vulnerable than he had allowed himself to feel in a very long time.

Squeeze, release. Squeeze, release. Yes, he could do that. *Squeeze, release.* A little harder, a bit more gently—not so rough—softly, softly, as if it were a woman's breast. Yes, yes. He could close his eyes and imagine . . . and remember—remember the way her breast swelled heavily beneath the worn simple lace of her chemise.

Raising his head, he looked around for his companion; she was gone.

Chapter Eight

The smell of sweet hay and grain swirled in the air around Maria as she, having dashed back to the house to change her dress and inform Gertrude that Basingstoke (and the Ladies Draymond) would be leaving for London within the hour, entered the stable at Basingstoke's side. His lordship carefully maneuvered his brother's wheeled chair along the bricked aisleway between the rows of clean stalls while Salterdon looked neither right nor left, refusing to speak.

The stable boys solemnly stopped their mucking and grooming and removed their caps as Salterdon approached.

"It's a right pleasure to have ya back," a lad with yellow hair offered meekly.

"Aye," another joined in. "The place ain't been the same without ya."

In that moment the far double doors were flung open. The rider and horse Maria had earlier watched trot so impressively in the arena filled the entry. Steam from the stallion's body made a vaporous cloud in the chill air. The bay's glossy hide shimmered with froth. Its massive neck arched and its polished hooves struck the bricks with a flash of sparks as it trotted, barely restrained by the rider, toward Salterdon and his brother.

Maria forgot to breathe, while around her horses stirred in their stalls, threw up their heads, and trumpeted a greeting to the advancing stallion. *Aye,* she thought, *they are exotic, heavenly creatures, with dished faces and liquid brown eyes that reflect an intelligence that seems almost human.*

The rider astride Noblesse stopped the stallion mere feet before Salterdon, and he flashed the duke a smile that seemed far too cheeky for a mere groom. Sweeping the hat from his head, giving his shaggy sun-streaked blond hair a shake, he said:

"You've damn well taken your sweet time about joining us, Your Grace. I was beginning to wonder if you had lost all interest in your horses. Ol' Noble here asks about you every day. Don't you big guy," he added fondly and scratched the stallion's sweaty neck. With a lithe leap, he jumped to the ground and offered his hand to Salterdon.

Salterdon stared straight ahead, refusing to acknowledge the friendly, and quite handsome, young man.

"Ignore him," said Basingstoke. "He's being an ass."

"I'm glad to see some things don't change," the man replied, and winked in a most shocking manner at Maria.

Her cheeks flushed; she almost giggled.

"Who's the lovely lass?" the man asked with a lopsided grin that made Maria flush even more.

"My brother's companion. Miss Ashton, you have the extreme honor of meeting Lord Lansdowne, my brother's best friend—cohort in deviltry, equestrian extraordinaire. There isn't another rider in all of England who can sit a mount as exceptionally as he. He drops by occasionally to make certain Trey's horses are moving properly. Between you and I," Basingstoke added behind his hand, "it's just his way of enjoying the bounce without buying the flesh."

A grin inching up one side of his face, Lansdowne took Maria's hand and slightly bent over it. Flashing a look at Salterdon, he said, "Your grandmother's taste in companions is improving, which, perhaps, explains what the duke is doing here at the stables. His Grace's moods were always roused by a pretty face." He winked at Maria again.

Withdrawing her hand, intent on stifling the humor bubbling like spring water in her throat, she retorted, "You, m'lord, are too fresh to be healthy."

"Only *fresh?* Good gosh, I must be slipping. The pretty ladies once called me wicked."

"I don't know you well enough to call you wicked."

"No?" He wiggled his eyebrows at her. "Would you care to?"

Slapping a hand on Lansdowne's shoulder, Basingstoke shook his head. "She's far too innocent for the likes of you. Besides, I had heard that you'd turned over a new leaf; something about vowing off cheap gin and becoming celibate . . . ?"

He coughed and clutched his chest in an exaggerated manner, staggered slightly backward, causing Maria to laugh into her hanky.

"Swear off cheap gin?" He coughed. "Never!"

The watchful stable hands chuckled among themselves and returned to their chores; some hefted buckets of warm mash that steamed in the chill air of the stable. Others meandered from stall to stall, shoving dung-crusted wheelbarrows and carrying pitchforks.

Finally, a solemnity replaced the men's lighthearted banter. Lord Lansdowne went to one knee beside Salterdon, who continued to stare straight ahead, refusing to acknowledge his friend, as well as the horse who continued to stand patiently, his muzzle lowered practically into the duke's lap.

"Your Grace," said Lansdowne in a soft, fond voice. "You see Noble still remembers you. He was wondering only this morning, before I rode, just when you intended to mount him again. Seems I don't have near the touch that you do. The ol' boy won't give me half the trot." He withdrew a small apple from his pocket and placed it carefully, gently, into Salterdon's hand, then he looked up at Maria. "You see, Miss Ashton, my devotion toward His Grace runs deeper than mere friendship. I owe Trey my life. It should have been me in this chair . . . or, more likely, in a grave. I was one of the four bucks with the duke that fateful night. We'd spent the day at the races, and when returning home we were jumped by thieves. I was a bit of a wiseacre then, too cocky for my own good. When I thought to confront one of the robbers the lot of bastards jumped me and proceeded to thrash me with the butts of their guns. Salterdon, my friend . . . threw himself among them . . . they turned their energies on him instead."

With color creeping into his face, his voice becoming tight, Lord Lansdowne covered Salterdon's free hand with his own, and squeezed. "You'll hear a great many tales about Salterdon, Miss Ashton. Some, perhaps most, are true. He is—was—cavalier, and a bit too fond of the highborn ladies and their potential dowries. Alas, it was his burden in life to fulfill certain ancestral obligations—that included marrying comfortably. But I've never known him to let down a friend if the need arose. I'm alive today because of him. My only goal in life is to somehow repay him."

Focusing again on Salterdon, he said softly, "Trey, if you can understand me, please know that all the fellows send their best. Their thoughts and prayers are with you. My God, Trey, you aren't alone no matter what you think or feel. If you'll only allow us to help you . . ."

Lansdowne looked back at Maria in dismay, like one about to be swallowed by an emotional landslide that he was helpless to stop. Swiftly, he leapt to his feet and strode from the barn, paused momentarily in the bright sunlight, then continued on his way.

Basingstoke muttered something under his breath, then followed. Both men disappeared beyond a hawthorn hedge in the distance.

Maria tugged at her cap string that felt, suddenly, much too tight against her throat. With a sigh of exasperation, she untied the thin cord and slid the frilly object from her head. It dangled lifelessly from her fingers while she studied the back of her master's head.

"Occasionally," she said softly, "I think you use this unnatural silence as a sort of punishment. 'Tis no one's fault that this has happened other than the culprits who beat you."

Going to her knees beside him, she regarded the apple in his hand, which lay in his lap. The stallion's reins made a leathery coil on one of his knees. The horse pricked his ears forward and offered his black muzzle to Maria to stroke. Guardedly, she raised her hand, felt the animal's hot breath upon her flesh, and experienced a tingle of thrill rush over her.

From the corner of her eye, she saw Salterdon move—just barely; his head turned slightly toward her. His fingers closed more firmly around the apple. Should she acknowledge him, would he, like some creature who had, little by little, come to trust her, flee back into the dark forest of his mind?

Without speaking, she took the hand gripping the apple and gently lifted it toward the stallion. Noblesse nickered and, in a most gentlemanly fashion, sank his teeth into the fruit.

Clear, sweet juice flowed in a stream over their entwined hands.

Maria laughed, and laughed again as the hungry horse took the remaining apple and tossed his head in appreciation. Her chest tightened as, glancing at His Grace, she acknowledged the easing of his jaw, the flickering light of pleasure in his gray eyes.

Standing, she took charge of the chair and rolled it down the swept brick aisle. "Gertrude and Lord Basingstoke were right, Your Grace. These are the most incredible animals I've ever seen. 'Tis understandable that you should feel such pride; I've never known such an intelligent eye in a horse, nor have I ever seen such loyalty and devotion from a horse for his master."

A lanky lad stepped from a stall, whistling to himself. Upon looking up, he stopped, grinned, and swung the stall door open further, revealing the heartstopping image of a heavenly white mare, a gangly newborn chestnut filly at her side. Only it wasn't the heartstopping picture the mare and filly made that caused her eyes to fill with tears, but the expression of pure pleasure on Salterdon's features. The hardness melted from his brow. His shoulders relaxed. It seemed in that instant that his entire body became fluid as air.

He leaned forward, outstretched his hand. He whispered, "Nap . . . Perl," and the mare nickered, and nudged the clumsy little filly as if saying, *Look what I have given you, my friend.*

"Aye," the stable boy said quietly. "'Tis yer own NapPerl, Yer Grace. She's given ya a lovely filly, as precious as all the sands of Arabia. Ye'll be the one who names 'er, o'course."

On delicate spindly legs, the foal, only days old, wobbled toward the door, regarding the intruding humans with huge brown doe eyes. Like her dam's, the filly's head was dished, tapering to a muzzle tiny enough to fit in a tea cup. A bold white blaze streaked down her forehead between her eyes. Her front left foot boasted a white sock.

"Oh," Maria breathed. "Your Grace, is she not beautiful?" She cautiously stepped into the stall, her hand extended. As the foal raised its whiskered muzzle to her, Maria eased down into the thick straw, her skirt forming a soft black pool around her legs.

Propped up on his pitchfork, the stable boy grinned and informed her with some authority, "She'll be gray, ya know. Aye, His Grace taught me that a gray is born either black or chestnut."

As the filly nuzzled her chin, Maria laughed and looked at her charge. Salterdon regarded her with one eyebrow lifted. "She deserves a name as beautiful as she is, Your Grace. I trust you'll give some thought to it."

Salterdon shifted in his chair, his only response.

Strange that he should find himself so mesmerized by such an image that in a few hurdling moments felt as if it were branding itself into his mind's eye: the lass upon her knees amid the clean, fragrant straw, the little filly nestling her muzzle into the cup of the woman-child's hand . . . ah, God—those wide blue eyes as innocent and vulnerable as the precious filly's—those gently curving lips the color of ripe plums. Hers was not the sort of smile a man, even a man as jaded and furious as he, could stiffen or disapprove of; her sort of gaiety could only be responded to with a smile. A younger, more naive knave might foolishly respond with a passionate reciprocity of emotion, perhaps fling himself into the straw beside her and whisper sweet, nonsensical murmurings into the ivory shell of her ear—but he, the Duke of Salterdon, had never been nonsensical . . . or naive.

Still, he found himself smiling—not with his mouth but with his eyes . . . smiling, nevertheless.

She pondered dreamily, mistily, with the warming sun on her face and the buds of the trees rattling overhead. With her back against the elm trunk, Maria sleepily searched for the proper encouraging phraseology with which to inform Her Grace, the Dowager Duchess of Salterdon that her beloved grandson had roused from his ennui at last. But how did one pen such soul-shaking news? How could one put into proper words the expounding sense of accomplishment and encouragement she, alone, had experienced the last hours as she had managed, finally, to form a sort of tenuous bond with her master?

Had she imagined it?

"Ah, me." She sighed, and allowed her lids to grow drowsy as she gazed out on the gentle slope of garden, the tender blades of grass appearing upon their gray shoulders like some glaucous mantle. Had she and Salterdon finally managed to form some fragile truce? Would he, at last, cease this penchant to wreak havoc over the entire household? Could the Duke of Salterdon go from being the most crude, cruel, and terrifying human being she had ever had the misfortune of encountering to one so docile and gentle that he had come very close to weeping at the very sight of a new-born filly? How very ironic that just hours ago she had determined that she would rather spend the rest of her life under her father's thumb and wicked lash than to walk back into Salterdon's presence again with no

means to protect herself against further physical outbursts.

"I wouldn't be so quick to write that," came the
intruding voice behind her, and she sat up straight so
suddenly the quill pen and paper tumbled from her lap.

Thaddeus leaned against the twisted old elm and
hooked his thumbs over the waistband of his breeches.
"He might seem better now but 'e could go back to the
way 'e was just like that." He snapped his fingers. " 'E's
done it before, ya know. Wouldn't take much to send
'im back in 'ere." He tapped his forehead. " 'Er Grace is
too bloody old for many more disappointments."

Maria frowned. "I'll simply convince him that I only
want to help."

Thaddeus dropped onto the blanket beside her and
proceeded to chew on a blade of grass. " 'E ain't ever
had much respect for kith or kin. Not as long as I've
worked for 'im, at least, which is goin' on five or six
years. Thought the world owed 'im cause 'e was first
born to a duke, then became duke himself when 'e was
only ten. 'Is folk drowned, ya know, off the coast of
Africa. Sharks ate their bodies whilst their sons watched."
Silent for a while, he stared out over the moor with its
sprawling patches of sienna heather. "I reckon that could
do somethin' to a man's mind and heart. And speakin' of
heart. You left any broken hearts back in Huddersfield?"

"Broken hearts?"

"Heartsick beaus. Men friends. I bet you 'ad a dozen
of 'em, pretty as you are."

She shook her head and watched a yellow-crested
finch hop along a bough overhead. Thaddeus was

flirting with her again, and not so subtly this time. He had bathed and donned clean breeches; his boots shone. Even with her limited experienced, Maria recognized that there were certain changes that came over a man when he became interested in a woman—something about the eyes: they became . . . searching and eager, almost . . . hungry. She had seen it in John's eyes a time or two, before he had reminded himself that all passion was to be directed heavenward. She had also witnessed it in Paul's, when he had fancied the wife of the blacksmith who had ultimately broken his back.

She had no desire whatsoever to see it reflected in Thaddeus's pale eyes. The very idea of it made her shiver, as did the sudden, unwelcome image of his squirming atop Molly . . . and that there was little of her own anatomy that he had not had visual privy to.

"His Grace should be rousing from his nap at any time," she announced, and reached for the quill and paper.

Thaddeus caught her chin between his fingers. His eyes searched her face intensely. "Don't ya ever get tired of talkin' 'bout nothin' but 'im?"

"'Tis my lot, Thaddeus. 'Twas what I was employed to do, to see to his needs. There is something to be said for loyalty, you know."

"Aye, but ya can carry loyalty to extremes. Now take yerself, for instance. A lovely lass such as you should be daydreamin' 'bout beaus and such. 'Bout findin' yer ownself a lifemate and settlin' down to birth a dozen babes or so."

"I suppose I shall," she replied with a lift of her chin

and a rise of one eyebrow. Pointedly, she added, "When I find a man who suits me."

He leaned toward her, a crooked smile on his face. "And wot kinda man would that be?"

"I . . . don't know."

"I reckon he would be young, and tall, and strong. Someone like—"

"I fear you're becoming outrageously bold," she declared.

"Wot if I am?"

"I should remind you of Molly, I think."

"Molly!" His eyes widened briefly, then narrowed. His ruddy cheeks turned even redder. "Ya can't blame a lad for takin' wot's freely given. We've got needs, ya know. Same as women." Leaning closer, he said silkily, "Take you, for example. Lass as lovely as you, with a body that would make any man ache with wantin' ya. It's enough to make me heart stop. I ain't thought about anything or anyone else since you come to Thorn Rose. Molly's just some dollymop with an itch I scratch every now and again."

She caught her breath as he pressed closer, brushed his lips across her cheek, and flicked her earlobe with his tongue. As she shied away, he grabbed her wrist and squeezed it fiercely. "Need I remind you, Thaddeus, that *I* am *not* a dollymop," she cried with conviction.

"O' course yer not," he declared with a look that made her eyes widen. "Ya can't help that yer shapely enough to make a man crazy with wantin' ya. That ye've got a way of lookin' at a man that makes 'im 'ard with desire. It's them damn eyes, lass . . . yer tits don't help a mite either."

With a sudden move he shoved her back on the ground, pinned her shoulders with his arms and smugly grinned down at her as she continued to struggle. "I figured you for one of them hard-to-get lasses. Guess I was right, but I don't mind. Makes things int'restin', I wager."

She narrowed her eyes. It seemed her entire body turned hot.

"I bet you ain't ever even been kissed before, huh?" Thaddeus's reddish eyebrows shot up and he laughed. "Damn me but I'm right. Imagine that. A lass of your age, 'avin' never been kissed."

"I hardly think there's anything wrong with that—"

"Course there is. It ain't natural," he declared in a raspy voice, then he planted his wet, open mouth on hers with a forcefulness that stunned her.

She didn't move, or breathe. Just stared at his closed lids that were as freckled as his face and recalled Molly's face ravished with ecstasy and her body writhing with apparent pleasure. On and on, the kiss continued until Thaddeus's breathing became ragged, his body tense and squirming, his long skinny leg dragging over hers and bunching her skirt up to her knee.

He grabbed her breast. She gasped and shoved his hand away, struggled to turn her face from his. The taste of his mouth made her feel ill suddenly, and angry.

"Enough," she said through her teeth, and at last extracted herself from him long enough to scramble to her knees. Her hair had fallen from its chignon and tumbled across one shoulder, and down one side of her face. Her mouth felt swollen and her cheek abraded.

Thaddeus grinned back at her, his face flushed with the same emotions as Molly had those nights before. "Liked it, didn't ya?" he asked hoarsely.

"Nay," she replied flatly, then wiped her mouth with the back of one hand.

"Sure ya did. A man can tell these things. A woman has a certain smell about her when she's horny—"

A bell rang in the distance. Briefly closing her eyes in relief, Maria jumped to her feet. He made a grab for her ankle, and she danced aside. "You grow far too familiar—"

"And whose fault is that?" he retorted, then grinned so lasciviously Maria blanched.

Maria fled for the house. Gertrude stood at the threshold, her hands on her hips and her lips pursed in apparent displeasure. She tapped her foot.

"He's awake, lass, and as grouchy as a bear. Ye'll do well to put on yer best face for him this evenin'. And while yer at it ya might do somethin' 'bout yer hair; it's a bloody mess. And get rid of the grass on yer skirt tail—"

"Is there aught else wrong with me?" she demanded as she hurried down one corridor after another, Gertrude hot on her heels.

"Aye, there is: You can stay away from that ne'er-do-well of a stable boy. A lass like you can't afford to 'ave 'er reputation spoiled over the likes of 'im."

"I doubt that the daughter of a meager vicar would warrant anyone better," she snapped so irritably Gertrude momentarily slowed her step, then hurried to catch up.

The servant followed Maria to her room, and while Maria made haste to brush out her hair and twist it back into its usual braided chignon, Gertrude flung open the wardrobe door and snatched the dress she had mended earlier in the day. "I'll be washin' the grass stains out of the one yer wearin'," the woman said with a huff of displeasure.

"For heaven's sake, you make it sound as if we were tumbling in the heather. 'Twas only a kiss. I didn't care much for it at that." Maria stared disconcertedly at her reflection in the mirror, her abraded lips.

Gertrude moved up behind her. Though her countenance was yet one of concern, her mien was agitated. "Heed me well, love. Twice we've lost good help 'cause o' 'im: decent girls afore 'e got 'is roving hands on 'em. Shamed they were, with a bastard brat in their bellies and 'im unwillin' to marry 'em."

"You needn't worry about that," Maria declared firmly, and thinking of his hands on her again, she shivered.

"Famous final words from the mouths of innocents. Will ya deny that ya find yerself attracted to him?"

"Aye!" she snapped. "I deny it."

"Then yer lyin' to yerself. Ever'time 'e comes in the room ya go all flushed and bothered."

She opened her mouth to argue that the only reason she grew flushed and bothered was because she had seen the man butt naked and fornicating with Molly on the kitchen table, and he, in turn, had chanced a glimpse of her own self naked . . . thanks for her penchant for reverie. Instead, she kicked aside her dirtied dress and snatched the mended one from Gertrude's hand.

Gertrude shook her head and clucked her tongue. "I'll tell ya wot yer dear mother told ya since ya were old enough to sprout tits: The goods God planted between a woman's legs was meant to give to one man and one man only—the one true love of yer life. There ain't no greater gift, or sacrifice, ya can make in the name of love than yer maidenhood."

"My mother told me no such thing," she declared with a huff and made for Salterdon's door.

"Well if she didn't she should have," Gertrude called behind her.

With a groan of exasperation, Maria fumbled with the ribbons at her throat, grabbed up her straw basket of yarn balls, and ran to the duke's room, leaving Gertrude mumbling to herself.

As usual, Salterdon refused to acknowledge her when she joined him, but sat stonily, as always, before his window, the breeze kissing bright color on his cheeks.

"Sorry I'm late," she said. "I was . . ." Chewing her lip, she considered a hundred excuses for her tardiness, all of which were lies. "I was . . . writing to your grandmother," she hurriedly confessed, which wasn't a lie . . . nor was it the entire truth, she acknowledged with her habitual twinge of guilt.

He made a harsh sound—a laugh, deep in his throat, that made her start. The grunt was as offensive as it was surprising, and was as infuriating as any cryptic words he could have uttered. Then he turned his gray eyes up to hers, and his lips curved in so cynical a manner she took a step backward and glanced away, her gaze falling on the distant scene below his window of the patchwork quilt spread out beneath the leafless elm tree . . . where she and Thaddeus had visited only minutes before.

She briefly closed her eyes; her face flushed with heat. "Am I to be deprived completely of privacy?" she demanded hotly. "Am I to have no personal time for myself?" She flung the basket into his lap. "What I do with my off time is no one's business but my own."

He laughed again and continued to smirk. Eyes narrowed, he looked her up and down as if she were some tavern wench, causing her to set her chin and clench her teeth.

"You mucky minded, ill-humored sod," she blurted, and turned to leave.

He caught her wrist, and with a yank, toppled her across his lap, facedown, her head near the floor and her derriere in the air. "Oh!" she cried, then he grabbed and squeezed her buttock through her dress, and she screamed, squirmed, then screamed again as he slid one hand beneath her and planted his fingers around one breast.

Flailing and kicking, she spilled to the floor. Salterdon laughed.

Throwing back her head, scrambling to her hands and knees, she glared at him through her tumbling hair, her eyes filled with hot tears. "You crude, despicable beast of a man!" Her voice cracked and trembled. The tears spilled down her cheeks in torrents. "And to think I had almost come to like you; to believe you were simply misunderstood and a rather likable fellow."

Little by little, the smirk on Salterdon's face faded.

"They all warned me you were an animal," she said through her teeth. "But I didn't believe them, not totally. I didn't believe any one man could be so completely decadent and lacking in moral fiber." She choked, covered her mouth with one hand, and did her best to swallow back her rising outrage. Body shaking, she tried vainly to climb gracefully to her feet, keeping a good distance from Salterdon, whose features had become as expressionless as a statue's as he continued to stare at her eyes.

At last standing, leaning momentarily against the windowsill until she was certain her legs were sound enough to hold her, she did her best to breathe evenly, to count away her anger, to recite a proverb under her breath: "Your own soul is nourished when you are kind; it is destroyed when you are cruel," which did not seem to fortify her much, if any, when she thought again of his hand squeezing her breast.

Grabbing the basket, which had spilled to the floor, and clutching it in her arms, she ran from the room, collapsed against the corridor wall and closed her eyes.

Dear God, how much more of this could she tolerate?

As a child, such an angry outburst would have brought a thorough washing out of her mouth with soap. The consequences of this, no doubt, would result in her termination—as if she cared. If she never set eyes on the malfeasant again it would be too soon. How dare he toss her about like some gunnysack. And how dare he

fondle her so brazenly? The very idea of it made
her . . . tremble and shake. Even now the imprint of
his fingers on her breast felt like tiny hot brands searing
her flesh . . . making her think of Molly and Thaddeus again . . . Molly's features contorted in some
blissful but mysterious agony . . .

Closing her eyes, she swallowed and clutched the
yarn basket to her bosom. Her knees suddenly felt
liquid. Her breast began to throb.

She moved again to the door.

Salterdon continued to gaze out the window, his back
to her, the cooling breeze riffling his long dark hair
occasionally. He looked in the evening light like a boy,
and suddenly she was chilled by the awful words she
had flung at him, the hateful acerbities that no decent
woman or man in their right mind would or should cast
at another human being.

With an inward cry of self-disgust, she returned to
her room, flung the basket of balls to the floor and
grabbed an ewer of water, splashed a goodly amount
into the washbasin and took a handful of soap.

She proceeded to wash her tongue with it: her teeth,
her lips, scrubbing them wickedly (as her father had so
often done) until her self-contempt drained from her,
leaving her to lean upon the bedpost limply, to feel
abashed, both at her behavior toward her master and
toward herself.

"What have I done?" she said aloud, and, as if in
response to her question, a considerable wind roused
and billowed the curtains over her open window,
causing pale daylight to tiptoe over the ferocious image

of St. Peter on the ceiling. He appeared to shake his finger at her, and she thought, *Aye, I'll apologize.*

She eased to his doorway. Still, he sat, brooding and remote. Drawing back her shoulders she moved to his side and gazed out on the dimming garden. Her master neither moved nor spoke, and occasionally she glanced at him askance, hoping he would, eventually, offer her some avenue of approach. His brow looked stern, his mouth set grimly. Obviously, he had no intentions of making this easy for her.

Then, suddenly, the idea came to her . . .

Grabbing the back of his chair with no warning, she spun Salterdon around and pushed him toward the door, out of the room, down the corridor, first one way, then another, eyes searching frantically for familiar objects, until . . .

At last, they came to the music room.

In the daylight the music room gave her pause. Skylights and sprawling windows spilled failing sunlight over the portraits and still lifes hung from gilded mountings between burgundy damask wall coverings. Settees and benches, as well as gilded chairs placed comfortably apart to accommodate the ladies' billowing gowns, were clustered near the center of the room, so that those in attendance could not only enjoy the music of the pianoforte, but also have unhampered viewing of the breathtaking masterpieces.

Looking down at Salterdon, she noted his shoulders had become very rigid. His hands gripped the chair arms in a stranglehold.

"Occasionally, Your Grace, a change of scenery will

accommodate a mood, as will a change of routine. Mayhap exercising with yarn balls has grown too tedious for a man of your temperament and intellect."

He made a move—an attempt to turn the chair away—to escape the room . . . and her.

"I think not," she said. "Lord Basingstoke told me this was once one of your favorite rooms. He said that as a lad he would hide here and listen to you play."

His head turned, albeit slightly.

"Didn't you know, Your Grace? It seems that Lord Basingstoke greatly envied you and your talent. He said that you might well have been one of the finest virtuosos of your time."

He made an angry sound in his throat and tried again to wrench control of the chair from her.

"He also mentioned that your father considered music was for women and parlors. Said no son of his would spend time partaking in such feminine frivolities. That it wasn't manly and becoming of the future Duke of Salterdon. Men were supposed to be financiers, rascals, hunters. I'm told that after your parents died, you would spend hour after hour playing the pianoforte, sometimes with tears running down your young face.

"How very sad," Maria mused softly, her gaze still locked on the back of Salterdon's head, "that one with your incredible talent should bury it. There is too little music in the world, I think. Such a gift could only bring joy to those in need of comforting—"

"No . . . more!" he suddenly exploded, and crashed his fists down on the chair arms.

She jumped, then forcing her suddenly trembling

hands around the push bars of the chair, she wheeled him toward the pianoforte.

"No." He growled it.

"There really isn't any need to deprive yourself—"

"Get . . . me . . . out!"

She positioned him at the instrument and backed away.

Salterdon stared down at the keyboard, his fingers gripping the chair arms fiercely, his jaw working, then he raised one fist, and brought it down with a crash.

The discordant clash reverberated through the room. Again and again, he pounded, until, unable to stand the tremendous noise any longer, Maria captured his fists with her hands and gripped them to her breasts, feeling them shake almost uncontrollably.

"Stop it," she implored him. "You'll hurt yourself again. Nay, I will not release you until you promise to calm down."

"No!" he shouted with a fury that terrified her, then with a shove he sent her backward, crashing into the piano with an unharmonious *twang* of notes. "Let . . . me . . . the hell . . . alone," he hissed through his teeth.

"I'd like nothing better, Your Grace. However—" She made another grab for his hands. "I would be remiss in my duties if I allowed you to continue this abhorrent, self-destructive behavior—quit fighting me; I'll tie you again with ropes if I must—"

"Bitch!"

"The duchess is depending on me—"

"Slut!"

He shoved again, flinging her backward and sending the chair rolling from beneath him, and him flying forward, toppling onto Maria, as she sprawled with a squeal over the pianoforte.

Keys digging into her buttocks, the fallboard gouging into her spine . . . His Grace's weight crushing the breath from her, she glared up into his face, only inches from hers, and tried to swallow. Her heart beat erratically. Her breathing quickened. She thought of his hand on her breast moments before, and the image of two bodies entwined before the kitchen fire roused before her mind's eye—a woman's breasts exposed and a man's lips and tongue gently, hungrily, caressing them. Only, it wasn't Molly and Thaddeus, but Salterdon and—

She gasped and cried, "I am *not* a slut!"

The terrible anger that had burned in Salterdon's eyes only seconds before, gradually extinguished, becoming something smoky and smoldering. He stared at her mouth with a heavy liddedness that seemed almost drowsy, that made her feel odd, as if her nerve endings were exposed.

"You're the most infuriating man I've ever known," she said against his mouth, then added as his weight began to slide, "I should let you fall, right here. I should leave you lying right here—'twould serve you right."

He flashed her a smile that was as disarming and staggering as his invidious behavior, then he grabbed the piano with both hands to better leverage himself. The muscles of his shoulders and arms became rock solid; the cords on his neck momentarily stood out.

With as much effort as she could muster, Maria wrapped her arms around his waist, stretched for the floor with her feet, and pushed herself and Salterdon off the piano.

For a moment, they tottered, his arms clutching her small shoulders, hers wrapped securely around his waist. Balance shifted, from her, to him, to her again— back to him. She swung him around and allowed him to drop into the chair.

"Perhaps after this—" She struggled for a breath. "Your Grace will reconsider before allowing your temper to get the better of you."

Drenched with perspiration, he wiped his forehead with his shirt sleeve and blotted his cheeks.

"Mayhap I'll try harder to control my temper as well," she added more softly, and managed a smile. "I understand Your Grace enjoys playing the pianoforte. Would you care to try?"

He shook his head and his countenance became belligerent again.

Maria dragged the piano bench from beneath the ebony instrument and positioned it by his chair before the keys. She sat, then reached for his hands, which were fisted in his lap. Opening his fingers, she placed them on the keys.

A strained moment passed.

He shook his head angrily and jerked back his hands. "Have you forgotten how to play?" she asked nonchalantly, and replaced his hands on the keys. "Or are you simply denying yourself because of your father?"

He grabbed her forearms before she could move away and squeezed so fiercely she thought her bones might shatter. Pain shot up her arms and robbed her of breath.

Fingers digging into her flesh, he said through his teeth, "N-no. N-none of your business—what I do just shut up and go away."

He released her, and she thought she might faint with relief. Arms throbbing, Maria swallowed back the lump of emotion at the base of her throat and watched as he turned his chair away from the pianoforte and wheeled it toward the door.

"I was thinking," she said in a strained, almost desperate voice, "that we might utilize the piano for therapy."

He stopped, hands still resting on the spoked wheels of his chair.

Moving up behind him, she took the chair and turned it back to the instrument. "Concentrate on gently stroking the keys one at a time, Your Grace. Mayhap it will help your dexterity and ability to focus. I'm certain your father wouldn't disapprove, considering the circumstances. 'Tis only for exercise, after all, and not for enjoyment. I'll leave you alone, if you like . . . while you refamiliarize yourself with the instrument."

Maria backed toward the door, noting that he had not moved, but continued to sit with his hands buried in his lap and stare down at the keys. At last exiting the chamber, she walked steadily until reaching her room. Closing the door, she sank back against it, slid to the floor, and buried her face against her knees.

The shadows lengthened, and little by little, the room became quite dark.

He was a boy again, shivering in anticipation, counting the long minutes until he was certain his parents had settled in for the night—God forbid that his father find him here again; there was French to study, after all, and a dozen tomes of facts and figures that made his head hurt when he attempted to comprehend them all.

Oh, but it was there, swelling up inside him, the need, the music; he could hear it as distinctly as church bells. His palms grew wet; his fingers ached. He flexed them open and closed, held them poised over the keys that shimmered dimly in the failing light.

Why would they not move—his hands, why would they not move? And the music . . . why, suddenly, did it warp into this nonsensical buzzing, cymbals crashing, violins screaming, and screaming discordant melees.

Oh God! He covered his ears with his hands and curled over, face driving sharply into the keys as his body shook. The abyss was opening again; he could see it, yawning there, black and inviting, luring him in to that place where reality could not intrude on his memories, on the music that spiraled sweet as birdsong round and round inside his head. That place was safe—so safe. No anger. No frustration. No regrets. No goddamn regrets.

So why was he so desperately fighting it?

Why, when he closed his eyes, did the image of blue eyes and moonlight hair fill up the blackness? How dare she unsettle him, haunt him, call out to some hidden self that he, until now, refused to acknowledge.

Damn her for forcing him to care . . . to hope . . . to

*dream. Damn her for slamming the door to his mental
lethargy . . . that woman-child with her peculiar face
alight with both seductiveness and innocence. If he retreated into that abyss again, she would leave.*

*Then where would he be? What would he have?
Who would believe in him at long last?*

Chapter Nine

Through the predawn haze, Salterdon could see the wheelchair next to his bed. His clothes for the day were hanging on the door of his wardrobe, had been for the last week, and he had refused to use them, just as he had refused to allow the lot of sniveling domestics near him with their bloodthirsty-looking razors; they would like nothing more than to cut his throat. Soon they would come stringing through the door like a lot of army ants to attempt once again to dress him, feed him—then *she* would come—Miss Ashton—with her pugnacious chin that raised with the slightest provocation, and she would prod at his conscience, his will-power, his temper and dignity, and she would make him want to murder her.

Infuriating little chit, with the looks of a seductive madonna. Once he might have found her . . . stimulating—despite her penchant for obstinacy. Not that he had ever fancied the common wenches—he had made certain all his affairs had been with women of equal class, with an occasional fling with the lesser wife or daughter of a mere lord or baron or some such . . . although there had been one girl—oh, yes, he had almost forgotten—a lass he had happened across in a tavern in Sussex, with raven hair and lips full and red as cherries. He had felt . . . fascinated by her . . . slightly enraptured . . . and he had not even slept with her; he had liked her too damn much . . .

Lips pressed, Salterdon flung aside the sheets and counterpane and stared down at his legs wearing the same rumpled breeches he had worn the last five days. He had taken to sleeping in his clothes just to agitate his *companion*, receiving a perverse sense of pleasure in watching her mouth pucker like a keyhole each morning that he greeted her wearing the same clothes, not to mention the dark growth of stubble that had begun to shadow his lower face.

Dammit, but the Ashton girl scraped at his nerves, always flitting about, talking to him as if he were a damned idiot mute . . . except she had not done much talking the last few days. She had kept to her room, taken her meals alone, intruded on his privacy only when she made some pitiful attempt to deal with his stubborn and infuriating antagonism.

Goddammit, where was everyone? Since when did the staff sleep away half the day?

He glanced at the chair, just making out its bulky form in the half-light. He could easily touch it, and did so, tentatively, before gritting his teeth and, with his shoulders and arms quivering from the strain, dragging himself onto the wheeled contraption with a grunt and groan and a muttered curse as it began to creep away from him, inch by inch, his body beginning to sag between the chair seat and the bed. Heart pounding in his ears, skin becoming damp with sweat, despite the coldness of the air, Salterdon clutched at the chair like a man scrambling for a fingerhold on the edge of an abyss.

His bedroom door opened.

Shit, he thought.

Thaddeus moved on tiptoes to the hearth, his arms full of firewood and peat. Seeing Salterdon stretched between chair and bed, body shaking with the effort not to fall, he stopped and stared through the dawn shadows, his countenance obliterated by darkness.

"Well, well," Thaddeus said softly. "Wot 'ave we got here? 'Is Grace is becomin' quite venturous, by the looks of it. Quite venturous indeed."

Shoulder pressing into the chair seat, head resting on the chair arm, Salterdon swore under his breath again.

Thaddeus dropped the wood into the hearth, swept dust and bark from his arms and hands, then he moved toward the chair, freckled hands clenched at his sides. He smelled a bit like horse dung and sour sweat.

Dropping to one knee beside the chair, Thaddeus said, "Looks like Yer Grace could use a bit of 'elp. Eh?"

"D-do it myself."

"I don't think so . . . sir. I think yer just about to fall, and once ya do, yer gonna lie there like some beetle on its back." Thaddeus chuckled, then stood and slid his hands under Salterdon's arms and, with a grunt and a huff, dragged him from the bed and dropped him into the chair.

Thaddeus bent near his ear. "Once I would've given anything to be in yer shoes. Not anymore, no sir. I can't imagine wot it would be like to be forced to sit back and watch the world spin round ya, to be forced to watch other folk go about their lives normally. So tell me, Yer Grace, did ya enjoy watchin' me make love to Miss Ashton last week?"

"Lovely," he grunted and elbowed Thaddeus's hand away from his arm.

Thaddeus pushed the chair to the window. "I knew you was there, o'course. It's a bit ironic, in't it, that once upon a time it was me who stood back watchin' you make love to the beautiful ladies. Aye, there were some lovely wenches wot strolled through Thorn Rose and Park House and Wyndthorst. If ya don't mind me confessin', sir, I offtime imagined meself makin' love to 'em. But then, they wouldn't have aught to do with me . . . only bein' a stable hand and all. Yer shakin', sir. Let me fetch yer lap blanket. Couldn't do with ya gettin' a chill or aught."

He flung the blanket across Salterdon's legs, tucked it around his knees and thighs, then he grinned again and squeezed Salterdon's shoulder. "Just between you and me, Yer Grace, I quite fancy Miss Ashton. I could see me settlin' down with the likes of 'er. Lud, but 'er mouth is sweet—like ripe cherries, it is. And 'er tits . . . 'ere now, yer feelin' all tense, sir. 'Ow about a shoulder rub? Aye, she's got lovely tits, full enough to fill me hand and then some. The trouble is, Yer Grace . . . Gertrude tells me that she's leavin'. Aye. Seems after the tiff you two 'ad she wrote to the duchess and declared that she would rather swim in a cesspit with Satan 'imself than to continue takin' yer abuse. She's vowed to stay only until the duchess finds a replacement . . . preferably a male."

Thaddeus turned away, made busy with stacking wood in the grate while Salterdon focused on his own reflection in the windowpanes, wild hair spraying across his shoulders, his eyes looking somewhat mad.

So, the angel with moonlight hair and coral lips was leaving. She had had enough of him, just like all the others. Only . . .

Maria Ashton was not like all the others. Was she?

At last, he turned back to find Thaddeus gazing down into the fire, face painted by yellow flames.

"Yer wonderin' if I've had 'er," Thaddeus said, his mouth drawing to one side in a smile. "Admit it. Yer wonderin' wot it would be like to bury yer body into 'ers . . . not that ya can anymore. Just imagine my peelin' 'er dress off, little by little, exposin' 'er white shoulders, then 'er tits with their erect little nubs of nipples that taste as sweet as honey on the tip of me tongue. Imagine 'er dress slidin' over 'er hips and tanglin' 'round 'er ankles. The 'air between 'er legs is no doubt pale and curly, the skin beneath pink as blood. I reckon she's deep enough to take all of me; she'd be tight, and 'ot, and liquid as quicksilver. Now, 'cause of you, I might not ever get to know."

His eyes glazed somewhat, he grinned at Salterdon and swallowed. "I'm truly sorry for wot 'appened to you," he said in a monotone. "But life goes on, don't it? We make do with wot we're given. Make the best of it. Ya should've given the scurrilous lot yer money and horse then they wouldn't have been forced to whack ya upside the head. It were a damn fool thing to do, sir."

With that, Thaddeus quit the room, leaving Salterdon to stare into the flickering flames, the memory of that night hammering inside his head like the blow that had left him senseless . . . and the image of Maria Ashton spread out beneath Thaddeus Edwards making him inexplicably ill.

"Bastard," he said to himself. "Perverted bastard."

With the help of numerous servants, Salterdon was moved to the library. His grandfather, the former Duke of Salterdon, had taken great pride in Thorn Rose's library. The towering walls were lined with leather-bound books pertaining to philosophy, medicine, poetry, plays, with an occasional fictional novel wedged in between works of the eighth century poets Notker, Balbulus, and Mutanabi. By the time Trey turned fifteen, he had read most of them.

Half an hour later, Miss Ashton arrived looking somewhat pale (as she had the last days), her big eyes ringed by dark shadows.

"Good morning, Your Grace," she greeted as she moved graceful as a butterfly to the desk, righting the lacy cap, which continued to slide askew over her forehead. As always, she wore her typical black dress (neatly starched and pressed, thanks to Gertrude) and a pair of kid slippers that were wearing through at the toe.

A rather tattered looking petticoat flashed briefly beneath the hem of her skirt.

"I trust you rested well last evening? I understand from Thaddeus that you were up particularly early this morning, and that he found you in a rather perilous position." She looked at him directly at last and regarded his appearance with her typical disapproval and disappointment. He wondered what bothered her most: his crumpled clothes or unshaven face. He wondered if the circles around her blue eyes were caused by anything other than her unhappiness over being cloistered at Thorn Rose with a lunatic.

"Do you think it wise, sir, to try something so foolish as attempting to leave your bed yourself? You might have found yourself on the floor, or worse, you might have been injured."

He said nothing, only thinking that black did not suit her at all, any more than the tacky, ill-dated swatch of lace hiding her hair—any more than Thaddeus Edwards suited her, with his mucky boots and barbarian manners.

Red was her color. Scarlet would blaze against her pale skin, exaggerate the fiery blue of her wide eyes. Only . . . those eyes were not so fiery now. They continually looked on the verge of tears.

Her mouth smiled; her eyes did not. "Did you rest comfortably last evening? Yes? No? Will you please make an attempt to answer me, Your Grace? A simple nod or shake of your head will suffice."

He narrowed his eyes, noting how the cinched bodice of her dress made her waist seem all the smaller. She had the kind of body that would suit a corset, her breasts flowing over the ruched décolletage like white pillows.

She swallowed. Her shoulders stiffened and the recognizable frustration returned to her face. Standing behind the desk as she was, with her hand resting on a stack of books, she looked like some prim, spinsterish nanny and tutor. Then again, maybe not. More like a child playing at the part.

"I spent the better part of the evening considering your inability to communicate. Then the idea came to me—books." Pasting on a smile, she declared, "You shall read aloud!"

The proclamation jarred him from the ridiculous trance. *The hell you say,* he thought, then swung his chair toward the door and proceeded to push.

In a flash, she was there before him, barricading his way. "Why must you fight me constantly?" she demanded in a voice quivering in agitation.

"Out!" he snapped and attempted to go around her, plowing into her shin in the process.

"Damnation!" she cried, and hopped up and down before grabbing the arms of the chair and planting her feet solidly in an attempt to hold him. Her face level with his, her eyes and cheeks flaming, she declared through her teeth, "I realize you don't want me here, Your Grace, any more than I want to be here. However, I promised your grandmother that I would do what I could to help you until she locates an adequate replacement. While I . . . may not care for you particularly, I *do* feel a certain attachment to the duchess. She loves you very much, and I fear this terrible thing that has happened to you is breaking her fragile heart."

An emotion crossed her face, anger and pain together. Still, it was not the intensity of the feelings that held him rapt, but the sudden flood of sorrow in her weary eyes.

"'Tis nothing more horrible than the helplessness one feels when one is forced to watch a loved one disintegrate little by little before one's eyes, to watch someone who was once so vital with life become a shell of himself, to wither and die." Her voice dropped an octave, became soft and dreamy and husky. Her lids grew heavy, and that recognizable pout returned to her lips—that child's pout that seemed to grab his vision in so fierce a hold that like one rapt he couldn't look away.

"One moment you pray to God to end their suffering, Your Grace—to end their misery and your own. The next you pray for mercy, that if He will only spare their pitiful life you will happily spend the entirety of your own life seeing to their every need."

Several seconds of intense repressed emotion passed; silence crackled the air as flagrantly as the jumping flames in the hearth. She looked for an instant as if she might crumble, yet, he could not look away. It seemed to him in that moment that her eyes, those wide, drowning pools of blue were the most captivating, ravishingly beautiful eyes he had ever encountered.

"Then you realize," she finally whispered and drew away, "that you cannot help someone who will not help themselves."

With effort, she turned the chair back to the room and

pushed it toward the fire. For an instant he wondered if
she intended to thrust him into the flames—have done
with him at last. Instead, she moved to the desk and
grabbed a book, returned to him, and plunked it
unceremoniously into his lap.

"For the next hour you will read aloud from the book.
Not only will the exercise stimulate the mind's ability to
think, it will also help the tongue to communicate more
easily, just as playing the pianoforte will limber the
fingers of your hands. The work belongs to Oliver
Goldsmith. It's entitled, *The Vicar of Wakefield*. Begin
with page one, please."

Dropping into a companion chair, she stared down
into the flames, her silence filling the room as she
waited. After several minutes, she lifted her head, a
sullen movement, and without looking at him, said,
"There is no disgrace in trying and failing. The disgrace
is in the failing to try."

He glared at her profile a few hurdling moments,
infuriated by her ennui. So that was that. She had given
up; decided her life as a vicar's daughter was far more
agreeable than her independent existence seeing after a
mental and physical moron. He considered flinging *The
Vicar of Wakefield* into the flames. Then he considered
flinging it at her.

Instead, he flipped open the book, fumbled with the
pages, then stared down at the printed page while the
tiny words appeared to swim and smudge, forcing him
to concentrate, which made his head ache. The realization occurred to him that he had not so much as looked
at a book since the goddamn highwaymen had left him

lying in the middle of a road with his brains leaking out into the mud.

Squeezing closed his eyes, he muttered, "Can't."

"Yes you can. Concentrate. One word at a time."

Teeth clenched, he focused again. The word, as a whole, looked as foreign as hieroglyphics. "Can't," he blurted again, slammed closed the book, and flung it into the fire.

Maria leapt from the chair, snatched the poker, and fished out the smoldering book. Her hands slapped at the sparks; her lips blew away the ashes. Without so much as a muttered recrimination, she then dropped the book back into his lap, reseated herself, and said, "Begin."

"What are you *Dumb!* as well as *Deaf?*" he barked, the only words to explode through his lips being "dumb" and "deaf." He flung the book again, just missing her head by inches. I *don't remember* how!

Again, she retrieved the book, turned it over and over in her hands before, more cautiously, returning it to his lap. Bending to her knees beside his chair, she opened the cover and lay her fingertip beneath the first word. "When you were very young," she said, "your tutors taught you how to read by sounding out the letters. Do you recall the alphabet, Your Grace?"

Her silvery hair reflected the firelight like a mirror. Her smell washed over him. He felt suddenly, inexplicably, riveted by her nearness.

"Your Grace?" she repeated, and turned her big eyes up to his.

He shook his head.

"Nay, from now on you'll speak," she told him, but when he stubbornly refused to respond, she sat back on her heels, and with her fingers laced together in a show of patience, released a weary sigh. "You could rile a bloody saint, I wager. I'm not certain I've ever dealt with someone so unreasonably determined not to yield, whose disposition is to resist constantly, whose unwillingness to brook opposition is tantamount to the Rock of Gibraltar. I'm beginning to understand now why the others left. It is beyond our capabilities to work miracles. What must I do to get through to you, sir?"

A sad smile crossed her face, then she stood, put the book on the desk, and moved to the distant window where dreary light turned her form into a silhouette.

He glanced at the desk, at the book, then back at her.

" 'Tis a dismal day," came her sad voice. "Yet, there was a time when I was stimulated by the wind and rain. My being was uplifted by the sharp cold. There is something about the iciness of winter that hones the senses to every nuance of the human anatomy, makes one aware of their fingers and toes and nose, clears the vagueness from the sluggish mind so all perceived is vibrant, as it was when we were children. Do you recall, Your Grace, how, when we were children, each new season was the prelude to new experiences? Spring brought birds and flowers, summer the long warm days of sunshine and fragrant heather. Autumn was a time for harvest and colors, of gold and red falling leaves in which we frolicked and daydreamed of winter snow. Winter was roaring fires and snuggling deeply beneath goose-down comforters and listening to the howl of wind and sleet scratching at our windowpanes. It was a time to share secrets with our best friend, and to dream of the coming spring. I wonder, Your Grace, when exactly did the seasons become so monotonous and something to be dreaded? When did the summers become too intolerably hot and long, and the winters too cold? Why did the autumn leaves become a drudgery to be raked and burned? Why did the springs become far too dismally wet and chilly? I wonder," she whispered. "I wonder when exactly did our every aspiration, dream, and hope become simply another anticipated disappointment."

At last, she turned, the pale light streaming through the window at her back silvering one side of her face. Had she been crying? He could not tell, could not see her eyes clearly, shadowed as they were. Then she sniffed and swept the back of one hand across her nose. Her voice sounded tight and husky when she spoke again.

"You're the most exasperating person I've ever known."

"Sorry," he replied after a time, realizing he had been staring at her and suddenly feeling self-conscious about it. He was not sorry at all, of course—not in *that* way.

"Distinctly spoken, if lacking in genuineness." Moving again to the desk, she picked up the book, thumbed the charred pages, and said, "Shall we try again, Your Grace?"

Maria could not sleep this night any more than she could sleep the last fortnight, since the incident in the library—more to the point, since she had sent her written letter of resignation to the duchess. Any day now, her replacement would arrive. She would return to Huddersfield and continue her life as the vicar's daughter and all her aspirations of saving herself and her mother would be nothing more substantial than those ridiculous notions she had spun in her romantic mind of saving the Duke of Salterdon from an asylum. Salterdon lived to spite her—to spite the world, not to mention himself.

Certainly, the mood he had reflected the last two weeks had not ingratiated him to anyone at Thorn Rose. His personality had gone from bad to horrible. His belligerence had become insurmountable. Everyone tiptoed about as if on eggshells. They plotted to burn the house down . . . with him in it.

It seemed that Salterdon had every intention of sliding back into his mental inertia; repeatedly she was forced to coerce him from sleep, only to be confronted by a temper that was reminiscent of Beelzebub himself. She had liked him better when he was unconscious, and there had been times the last weeks when she would have gladly encouraged his mental hibernation, had the memory of the duchess's suffering not spurred her to rally, to face the dragon again, sword of contumacy raised in challenge.

To say that he disliked her as much was an understatement. To say that he would like nothing better than to murder her with his bare hands was too.

That thought alone continued to plague her.

Why should she care what he felt?

Why was she continually nagged by some odd spark of emotion she had experienced for him that brisk morning in the barn when she had seen something in his eyes and face that, suddenly, made him appear all too human and vulnerable . . . and likable.

Oh, yes, that emotion had nagged her. It bothered her sleep. She could not eat. It made her heart break all the more now when he reacted toward her so furiously.

Dear merciful Father, please help the duchess to understand why I can not remain here.

She sat up in bed. The air felt frigid and cut uncomfortably through her thin nightdress. The idea of leaving the cozy warmth of the bed did not appeal to her, but tonight the feeling of disquietude would not leave her alone. The air felt charged and disturbed . . . as if someone had been there, in the dark, watching her as she slept. The fact that rumors had reached Thorn Rose of recent robberies had not helped. Only last week Melcombe Manor, just a stone's throw across the downs, had been seized by the awful thieves and ransacked; Lord Melcombe's daughter had been dragged to the wine cellar by a pair of hooded giants and . . .

She didn't want to think about it. Obviously, she was becoming as jelly-spined as Molly, who ran about the halls always in a twitter and vowing that Thorn Rose, vulnerable as a motherless lamb, would be next.

As always, the door to Salterdon's room was ajar. With candle in hand, she tiptoed to the foot of his bed, peered into the sheers like Beowulf gazing into Grendel's dark lair.

Empty!

Raising the candle higher, she focused harder on the tossed back counterpane and flannel sheets, the pillow with the indentation of his head—she spun around, causing the tiny candle flame to flicker threateningly— her eyes searched the room and discovered his chair was gone.

Maria ran to the bellpull to summon Gertrude, then reason took over and she froze, shaking, fingers gripping the tasseled pull as if it were a lifeline while her heart ran wild, as did her imagination.

"Think rationally," she said aloud. "No need yet to rouse the help. Panic won't help the situation."

Where the blazes was he?

She, of course, would be held responsible if something happened.

But what could have happened?

He could have fallen down the stairs, of course. *Oh God.* She had not meant it when she imagined him buried in a worm-eaten coffin!

He might even have thrown himself out a window: funereal personalities were known to take their own lives on occasion—Paul, in his lowest moments, had even spoken of it—*Oh God.*

Running into the corridor, she plowed straight into Thaddeus and screamed, dropped the candle on her foot, causing her to dance backward and step on her gown hem that trailed the floor by two inches.

"Blimy," he muttered, and scooped up the candle before it burned out, held it between them and looked her over with raised eyebrows. "I reckon it's too much to hope you were lookin' for me."

"His Grace," she said, still shaking. "He's gone."

Thaddeus moved around her, into Salterdon's room while Maria hugged herself and curled her toes from the cold. The halo of light from the sputtering candle gilded one side of Thaddeus's face as he turned to look at her again. "So 'e is. I reckon it's too much to hope that the demons from 'ell come to collect 'is miserable soul. Shall we break open a bottle of 'Er Grace's best champagne to celebrate?"

"Don't be daft," she replied, and took the candle from him.

Thaddeus moved after her down the corridor. "The duchess could do us all a favor and commit him to Royal Oaks."

Coming to the staircase, she paused, searched the lower darkness that looked as deep and black as hell's pit. "He's not insane."

"The crazies . . . they all line up at the barred windows and spit on folk as they walk by. Some howl like dogs."

She looked back at Thaddeus, the disturbing image his words painted making her shiver. "He's *not* insane," she repeated.

A sound came to her then, so indistinct she might have imagined it. Again! By-stepping Thaddeus, she moved back down the corridor, past Salterdon's room, her senses honing on the *plink plink plink* that little by little became musical.

"The music room!" she cried aloud, and ran with her

gown hem flapping around her ankles down one corridor after another, until reaching the music room, where she paused on the threshold, breathing hard, the candle dripping hot wax on her fingers.

In the pale orange glow of a solitary lamp, Salterdon slumped over the keys of the pianoforte, long fingers of one hand stroking a solitary ivory note.

Plink. Plink. Plink.

His hair, a riot of tumbling waves and unruly ends, curtained one side of his unshaven face and spilled over his shoulders.

Plink. Plink. Plink.

With the lamplight flickering across his intense features, he looked a little like the devil in contemplation. He looked like the little boy he once had been, sneaking into the music room against his father's wishes, practicing by the light of a candle, countenance a mixture of ecstasy and pain.

Thaddeus moved up behind her. She pushed him away. "I'll speak to him alone, Thaddeus."

"Think that's wise, considerin' how yer dressed?"

He flashed her his typical cheeky smile, and Maria frowned. "That will be all," she reiterated, and stared at him more sternly, until he put up his hands and backed away, dissolving into the darkness.

With a fortifying breath, she turned back to the door, hesitated only briefly at the threshold, then moved stoically toward her charge, who, upon seeing her from the corner of his eye, sat up abruptly and looked around. His eyes, normally so resolute in their obstinacy, were

startled and desperate, making her pause, and shiver—
as much from trepidation as from the cold.

Her throat and lips suddenly dry, she said, "Your
Grace . . . you frightened me out of my wits. When I
discovered you gone I couldn't imagine where you were
this hour of the morning, or how you came to be here."
With a sigh of exasperation, she added, "I thought
perhaps we had been set upon by those dreadful thieves,
and that . . . Well," she sniffed. "Never mind."

He slowly sat back in the chair, yet one hand lingered
along the keys, fingertip lightly stroking up and down
the length of it.

"I suppose I reacted rashly, but I *am* responsible for
your well being, whether either of us like it or not."

As usual, he did nothing but regard her with those
infuriating, enigmatic eyes while his long finger continued to slide up and down the piano key. Surprisingly,
he had changed clothes and had done a fairly respectable job of it, except for his slightly wrinkled shirt,
which was buttoned crookedly at his throat . . . and
his bare feet.

"I suppose this is as good a time as any to tell you
that I've decided to leave Thorn Rose," she announced,
and the words seemed to reverberate the very air around
them. "I realize your grandmother will be disappointed;
I fear I was her last hope; she did so hold the faith that
I could help you. At some point these last few days I
realized that no one, least of all myself, can help you
unless you desire to be helped." She attempted to smile.
"Shall I see you back to your room, sir? Or, if you
prefer, I could summon Gertrude."

No response, not even a flinch of surprise.

Her shoulders sinking a little, she turned away. Foolish girl. What had she expected? That he would plead with her to stay? No doubt he would be more than happy to see the back of her.

Plink. Plink. Plink.

She stopped.

Little by little, the simple *twang* of the singular note became two, then three, forming a rudimentary tune. Maria turned, her gaze locking on his fingers that moved a bit stiffly, slowly, but without the recognizable awkwardness, across the piano keys.

"Oh!" she cried, then covered her mouth with her fingertips, dropping the candle from the other, but hardly noticing. By now, his hands had found their comfortable rhythm, and the music lifted from the instrument like beautiful birdsong.

Swiftly, she moved to the instrument, danced around it on her tiptoes, hands fluttering over the highly polished instrument but not touching, like a butterfly hovering above a petal before dropping softly, lightly onto it.

At last, she landed, leaned upon the massive fixture, feeling the slight tremors of the music pass through her body while her gaze followed every movement his hands made upon the ivory and ebony keys. Dare she breathe? Mayhap she was only dreaming again. Mayhap she would awaken any moment to discover she had been caught up in another one of her silly fantasies— but, no, not even in her dreams could she have imagined such a moving, lyrical poetry of sound.

At last, she forced her eyes back to his, which were

deep gray and gold with lamplight and watching her
every reaction, even while his fingers continued to
move, to fill the room with heartrending music.

He smiled.

Oh, God, *he smiled!*

Nay, not the droll and sarcastic twist of his lips
denoting hate and anger.

It was a smile that touched his eyes, that lifted the
grim and harsh lines from his face. He became human,
suddenly, and breathtakingly beautiful.

Tears filled her eyes and beaded on her lashes. For an
instant, the music faltered. "Don't stop!" she pleaded.
"Nay, don't stop, Your Grace. 'Tis the most beautiful
music I've ever heard. Nay, don't stop. I would stand
here forever and listen."

His smile grew. His hands moved, fingers growing
more supple, stretching, stroking while his body moved
and swayed, feeling every nuance of every note; experiencing it as if it were a living, breathing being inside
him.

Closing her eyes, Maria allowed the music to absorb
her. Then it fell silent, and she forced open her burning
eyes to discover Salterdon regarding her with a shadow
of his old mood. Only then did she realize that she had
allowed the tears to stream down her face, and her
throat to tighten with emotion.

" 'Tis the most beautiful music I've ever heard, Your
Grace."

"Bach," he said, the word rattling slightly in his
throat.

"Bach," she repeated simply, and he smiled again,

and touched his fingertips lightly—so lightly—to the base of her neck.

"From . . . here, Miss . . . Ashton."

His fingertips touched like warm coals on the flesh of her throat, brushing as lightly as they had his worshiped piano keys. Dear God, he had actually spoken a complete sentence and all she could do was focus on the discomforting sensation the touch of his fingers caused in her. No fear now, but something else.

"You spoke," she murmured breathlessly, noticing in that very instant the book wedged between his hip and the chair arm. *The Vicar of Wakefield.*

"You've been reading as well. Your Grace, is that why you've been so closeted the last days? So moody and tired? Have you been coming here at night to study?"

He opened his mouth to speak.

She did not give him the chance.

Grabbing the chair, she spun it toward her, fell to her knees before her master, and melting against his legs, grabbed his hands. "You *can* communicate, sir. I know you can. Speak to me. Anything. Tell me I'm the most infuriating 'chit' you've ever had the misfortune of knowing. Tell me I'm a nag. That I'm disrespectful. I'm a termagant and a witch. One sentence is all I ask and I swear I'll never demand anything of you again."

"My head . . . hurts to read," he said with hardly a bobble, closing his fingers around her hands that lay in his lap. "But . . . it's getting better."

"Indeed. 'Tis certain to grow stronger with exercise, don't you think?"

"Yes," he said, and smiled, and squeezed her hands,

not roughly, but gently, controlled, almost . . . fondly. *No, not fondly, surely not fondly!*

With a laugh, Maria jumped to her feet and flung her arms around his shoulders, hugged him fiercely, her face pressed into his soft, flowing, fragrant hair that felt like silk against her cheek.

Eyes closed tight (God forbid that she cry any harder—he would certainly think her an emotional ninny) she smiled and clutched him more tightly, her lips brushing his ear as she spoke. "I prayed every night and morning for you, Your Grace. Your family will be so very pleased, as will everyone at Thorn Rose. I cannot wait to see the looks on their faces when we tell them."

They remained that way for several minutes, silent, with her arms wrapped around him, his face pressed into her shoulder, her breath falling softly, warmly against the back of his ear. Then his hands slowly, tentatively lifted, and he placed them along the small of her spine, palms flat, fingers spread.

She felt, suddenly, very small. Her skin grew warm beneath his hands, even through her nightdress.

The nightdress.

What a frail barrier! It seemed to float away from her body; its folds pooled over Salterdon's legs; her unbound breasts, oddly heavy and sensitive, felt flagrantly conspicuous. For a hurtling moment she imagined him touching her breast again, and imagined her allowing it.

She pulled away, intending to flee, refusing to look at his face that, once terrifying, now was stealing the strength from her legs, causing her heart to thrum like thunder, her ability to breathe vaporizing like the smoke rising from the oil lamp hissing on the piano. A vision of his reaching out and cupping her breasts in both of his hands distracted her momentarily from her own acute discomfiture, and she could do little but stand rooted before him, watching those strangely burning eyes moving over her, and knowing she should be doing something to cover herself, but shamelessly doing nothing.

Suddenly she felt herself blushing, hideously embarrassed.

Turning away, she ran toward the door, her foot knocking aside the forgotten candle that had long since sputtered out and lay in a pool of its own warm wax.

"Wait," he called behind her, and the tenor of his deep voice resonated like the stroke of the felted hammer upon the piano wire. Clutching the closure of her nightdress, she looked back swiftly, long enough to acknowledge him sitting in the pool of gold lamplight, no longer the beast, nor the tyrant, nor the invalid. Simply . . . the man.

She fled to her room.

Chapter Ten

She awakened the next morning with the sweet melody of piano music still floating through her mind, with the image of Salterdon's unfathomable gray eyes smiling at her, with the warm feeling of his hands pressing into her back. For an hour, she lay in her bed, suspended in an odd sort of pleasure, as if the soft mattress beneath her were little more than clouds and the mural of St. Peter above her was, literally, heaven on earth.

He—the Duke of Salterdon—had actually smiled, and, oh, what a fascinating and awe-inspiring transformation it had been! The choir of thrill that had surged up inside her at that very instant had resonated like a thousand harmonious tones sounding together.

At breakfast, she perched on the edge of her chair and watched her master manage his breakfast with little problem. He poured his own tea and cut his own meat. They even staggered through a brief conversation, with her trilling like a bird and him rumbling like imminent thunder:

"Good morning, Your Grace!"

"Morning, Miss Ashton."

"Isn't it a wonderful morning, Your Grace?"

"If it pleases you to think so, Miss Ashton." (With a touch of his old sarcastic drawl.)

Obviously his disposition was still sadly lacking. She had not managed to coerce a solitary smile, or even a smirk from his handsome?—oh, my, now she was considering his lips attractive!—the entirety of breakfast but she was certain that even his good humor would rally in time. No doubt the gloriously positive turn of events had left him feeling somewhat overwhelmed.

In truth, the entire exhilarating experience the evening before had left her . . . dizzy. There simply was no other way to describe the incredible sense of lightness that seemed to lift her.

When learning of the sudden turn of events, Gertrude wept with pleasure, danced up and down with Maria until the two of them collapsed in a fit of laughter.

" 'Twas the most incredible moment of my life!" Maria confessed as, spinning on her toes, she hugged herself. "He smiled at me, Gerti, he actually smiled. And held my hand!" Holding her hand up before her, she gazed at it as if it had suddenly turned into gold.

Gertrude watched, eyes round and little teeth biting her lower lip.

"His music—oh, his music—I have heard a thousand choirs sing and not one of them could compare to the heavenly sounds roused by his magnificent hands.

Oh, but his hands *are* incredible. Wouldn't you agree, Gerti? Has he not beautiful hands?"

Gertrude nodded, and her eyes grew rounder.

"And when he smiled." She spun again and laughed, grabbed the bedpost for support and sank against it. "'Twas radiant. Transforming. I was . . . mesmerized." She sighed and her eyes grew drowsy. "When he spoke to me my very being trembled as if with thunder. My every nerve seemed to vibrate. I couldn't breathe. I felt as if . . . I would faint. Yes, as if I would faint."

"Oh my." Gertrude pursed her lips. Her brows drew together.

"His voice," Maria mused, "is dark blue velvet. Rich and deep and soft. Deeper, I think, than his brother's. I felt . . . impassionedly jarred to the very marrow of my being."

"Oh lud," Gertrude muttered and clasped her hands together.

"Forgive me if I act the ninny. No doubt these emotions are not unlike that which a mother feels upon seeing her infant manage his first step at last. Months of training, of waiting in anticipation and then . . .

"In truth, Gerti"—she laughed lightly, if not tightly, and hooked her arm around the bedpost "I often suspected that such a triumph would spring from here." She pressed her fist to her heart. "And it did. It does, only, from here as well." Her stomach. "And here." Her throat. "My entire body feels as if it wants to fragment and scatter like sparks in a whirlwind!"

With one raised eyebrow, Gertrude moved toward

Salterdon's door and asked, "And how do ya imagine *he* feels 'bout all this, lass?" She pushed the door ajar and peered in.

Maria danced up behind her; they gazed secretly into the room, finding Salterdon dressed and sitting in a winged-back chair before the crackling fire, an open book in his lap. He, however, stared into the flames, his features far less hostile, but remote.

"Isn't he remarkable?" Maria whispered. "Is he not grand? Handsome? Distinguished? Oh, Gerti, is he not the most incredible man you've ever seen?"

"We *are* talkin' 'bout the Duke of Salterdon, right? The same man ya was callin' a beast, incorrigible, and detestable just yesterday evenin'?"

"I was blind then. Now I'm . . . I'm . . ."

"I got a disturbin' idea wot ya are," the servant muttered under her breath, and shook her head. "God help ya, love, if I'm right."

The cold, fresh air of the overcast day appeared to revive her duke of his morning doldrums, as did their time spent in the company of NapPerl and her frolicking filly. In yet another paddock paced a sleek, silvery stallion that snorted to his mare occasionally, then pranced, knees breaking level and neck arched, from one end of the paddock to the other. Now and again, the horse tossed its head in a circular motion, then turned its muzzle into the breeze and nickered.

"Drinkers of the wind," Salterdon explained. "The Arabs are known for their ability to withstand extraordinary challenges. They drink in the hot desert winds then blow them out. Their nostrils are like fire. Their stamina and endurance is unsurpassed."

"What do you call him?" she asked, awed by the brilliance of the gray stallion.

"NapPoleone."

"He seems, Your Grace, to challenge. Is he dangerous?"

"If I could leave this chair I would show you how dangerous he is. Dangerous? A child could climb on his back, Miss Ashton. A girl as fragile and delicate as . . . you."

A blush touched her cheeks. She looked away, into the trees, then toward the sky whose horizon had grown dull throughout the day and dark with impending weather.

"Tell me, Miss Ashton, if that filly were yours, what would you name her?"

A moment passed before she could find her voice. "NapPerl's filly, Your Grace?"

He nodded, causing his woolen scarf to fall askew.

Busily, she adjusted the scarf more closely around his shoulders and neck, allowing her fingers to brush lightly against his hair—to linger, to toy, unbeknownst to him, with a singular curl that lay coiled upon the back of his chair. Odd that that which she had once found so repugnant now drew her hand to it like a magnet. "I would call her NapTeesta Rose, your grace."

"Why?"

"I . . . don't know. Because it sounds so feminine, and she is feminine. Rose, of course, to honor your home."

Silently, he watched the filly run across the brown grass, then he said, "Then NapTeesta Rose it shall be."

For the next hour they sat beneath a tree, and she listened as he read aloud from *The Vicar of Wakefield.* Like the music he had spun the night before, his words seemed lyrical. Had it only been days ago when he had managed an occasional slur or groan? When his very presence had appalled and frightened her? Now she could only lean upon the strong and knotty trunk of the old oak and, with eyes closed and her shawl drawn more tightly about her, for the weather was changing rapidly, and not for the better, listen to the tenor words and feel as if she were floating on the swirling, chilling breeze. The idea occurred to her suddenly that she could remain here—at Thorn Rose—forever—see to Salterdon's every need and wish—forever. Spend every waking minute of every day in his company, float on his music at night, and pray that once more in her lifetime he might reward her with an embrace.

Only when the sudden silence struck her did she look up to discover Salterdon staring at her, a shadow of his old anger in his dark eyes, the book tossed on the ground at his feet.

"Your Grace?"

"Tell me what good that will do me," he demanded and made a dismissive motion toward the book, "without my goddamn legs."

Like the sudden, unexpected slash of freezing rain and the pitiless east wind that swept over the moor, driving both human beings and beasts inside, the

Duchess of Salterdon arrived at just after noon . . . with no warning.

Maria was perusing the library shelves for some tome that might stimulate the duke out of his apparent dismal mood, when Gertrude burst into the chamber, arms flapping in agitation while behind her servants were scattering like frightened hens. "It's the duchess," she cried simply, then dashed from the room again with a flounce of skirts and petticoats.

Her gaze fixed on the empty threshold, Maria swallowed and said, "Oh God. The letter. I forgot about the letter." Her spirits plummeted even further when she learned that the duchess was not alone . . . obviously Her Grace had wasted little time in locating another companion for her grandson.

Maria was immediately summoned by the duchess.

For two hours Maria sat outside one of the half dozen salons, waiting to be received by Her Grace and watching the staff, most of which had traveled from Wyndthorst with the duchess, hustle up and down the corridors, arms full of bed linens, silver chocolate services, and vases of fresh flowers brought up from the conservatory. One would have thought King George had arrived instead of an eighty-odd-year-old duchess.

There were a minimum of four chamber and parlor maids, a laundress to wash only the duchess's garments and a linen woman to iron them, a maid whose entire job consisted of packing and unpacking the duchess's trunks, a butler who snapped orders constantly at the four footmen whose job was to jump at his every command. There was also a French chef (with two assistants in tow), who sent Thorn Rose's cook scrambling from the kitchen in a huff, not to mention a pâtissier to cook the duchess's daily bread, tea cakes, and confections. By the time the duchess had been in attendance an hour, the entire west wing of the stately mansion had been dusted, swept, furniture rearranged, and windows washed. Smells of cinnamon tea cakes wafted from the kitchen.

Maria paced up and down the gallery, then to the staircase where she stood with one foot on a step and one hand gripping the banister. Silly ill-tempered child to have written that detestable letter of resignation. How could she have allowed her temper to so overwhelm her?

Would the duchess allow her to see him—the duke— one last time before she was sent packing back to Huddersfield? Even now Gertrude was with him, bathing, shaving, dressing him in his finest when it should have been herself brushing his hair, preparing him for this most auspicious moment.

The door of the salon opened. Sydney, the duchess's butler, a tall gaunt man with a hooked nose and lips like a cod's, looked down his nose at her and sniffed. "Her Grace, the Duchess of Salterdon, will see you now."

Sydney led her into the salon where the immense Italian marble hearth roared with fire, even as a cold breeze tumbled into the room through the open windows.

The duchess, wearing a loose-fitting vibrantly red silk kimono, waited until Maria had curtsied before pointing to one of two chairs—one empty, the other occupied by a roundly built fellow with a scattering of hairs brushed over a wide bald spot atop his head . . . Edgcumbe, the duchess's physician.

The portly gentleman immediately leapt to his feet and rewarded her with a nod of his head and a smile, peering at Maria through a monocle that made one of his protuberant brown eyes look bigger than the other.

"How do you do, Miss Ashton. I'm—"

"I know who you are," she declared with a sudden burst of emotion that made the rotund little man rock back on his heels, and the duchess to raise both eyebrows. "You, sir, have come here to take His Grace away."

"Indeed," he said.

"It must be stated," she said, drawing back her shoulders and lifting her chin, "that upon commencement of that dismal missive I was not of a rational mood. I . . . am not certain, exactly, what sort of fit had overcome me; I fear occasional failure, no matter how brief, can make even the most stoutminded and -hearted falter in their endeavors."

The man exchanged looks with the duchess, then Maria said, "Not that His Grace's temper can't yet be decidedly reprehensible—yes, I believe that's how I described him in the letter," she stressed to the duchess, who regarded her with bemused brow and slightly pursed lips. "I feel, nay, I'm certain you'll find him much improved."

"You don't say," said Edgcumbe.

"Oh, yes. I do. Much improved." She smiled and nodded.

At last, the duchess relaxed in her chair. "Sit down, Miss Ashton."

Maria sat stiffly on the lip of the chair; a servant appeared from nowhere to present her with chocolate in a gold-rimmed black china cup.

The duchess waited until her own cup was refilled before speaking. "I haven't the foggiest idea what you're talking about, my dear. I've received no letter. My purpose in coming here was to have Edgcumbe visit with my grandson one last time before I make my decision."

"Decision?" She peered at the duchess through a ribbon of rising steam, the words "I've received no letter," rolling over and over in her mind.

The duchess had not received the letter of resignation—the hysterical plea to employ a replacement as soon as feasibly possible because she could not survive another fortnight in the company of her reprehensible grandson.

It was not too late after all.

She would simply explain that she had reconsidered—

"Disturbing rumors have reached me of Trey's recent behavior."

Boiling chocolate caught in her throat, Maria briefly closed her eyes. The Ladies Draymond.

"Of course I summoned Edgcumbe immediately," said the duchess in a tight voice, casting the physician a despairing look.

"Oh, but—" Maria began.

Edgcumbe leaned forward. "I'm certain you're

aware, conditions such as Salterdon's show a distinct tendency toward intense melancholy with sporadic displays of extreme aggression—not uncommon with the sort of injury he sustained, being the blow to his head, of course. I fear our hospitals are overflowing with such dementia and will continue to be so until we have a greater understanding of the workings of the mind."

"Yes, but—"

"Therefore," the duchess interrupted, "we have come to the regrettable conclusion that, in the best interest of my beloved grandson, he be taken to an environment that more suits his situation and needs."

"Someplace where he'll be attended by individuals more . . . shall I say, possessed of a level of efficiency and ability to better govern his behavior and well being," Edgcumbe intruded.

"Royal Oaks," Maria gasped aloud, her cup clattering on the saucer and sloshing chocolate across her knee.

"Certainly not." The duchess raised one eyebrow.

"But a hospital, nevertheless. To be housed with lunatics who howl like dogs!"

"Good God," said the duchess under her breath. "A very melodramatic portrait I'm sure, but unlikely. We're speaking of the Duke of Salterdon, my dear, not Tinker Tom or Billingsgate Moll."

"But—"

"Did he not vilify you?" asked Edgcumbe.

"Yes he did, however—"

"Did he not choke you?" asked the duchess.

"He did, but—"

"And practically wrenched your arms from your body?" asked Edgcumbe.

"He—"

"And did I not impress upon you that you, Miss Ashton, were my last hope of somehow saving my grandson from this last drastic but necessary decision?"

Her head swimming, Maria sank back in the chair. "Yes, Your Grace, you did. However . . ." She closed her eyes briefly, took a fortifying breath, waited for yet another interruption, then said so softly the duchess was forced to lean toward her to catch the words, "I'm happy to report, Your Grace, that his ability to verbally communicate has vastly improved. He feeds himself, and dresses himself, and reads to me aloud. I'm most happy to add, that he has again taken up the pianoforte!"

"You don't say!" expelled Edgcumbe.

"And his . . . disposition?" prodded the duchess.

"I can only relate that our meeting last evening and this morning was without its normal discord. He seemed, Your Grace, most agreeable."

"Which is not to say that his mood will not relapse if provoked," Edgcumbe pointed out. Brow creasing in concern, he left his chair and took the duchess's hand. "My dear Isabella, you mustn't take such a turn too much to heart. He's rallied before only to suddenly, without warning, plummet to the depths of dementia again."

Her eyes bright and her chin quivering, the duchess said in a tremulous voice to Maria. "I must see him for myself immediately, of course."

"Gertrude is preparing him even now," Maria replied, and set her chocolate aside. "If it pleases Your Grace, I'll go up before you to make certain he's ready."

"Of course."

As Maria left her chair, the duchess caught her arm with fingers that were frail yet surprisingly strong. They gripped her with a fierceness that touched her gray eyes with a glint of hope and desperation.

With a confident smile, Maria pulled away and hurried from the room, pausing long enough to stare blankly, like one in shock, down the sprawling gallery.

Dear God in heaven, they had come to take His Grace away, to put him in a horrible place to be treated little better than some dangerous, mindless animal.

"But he's better now," she reminded herself aloud. "Much better." Glancing toward the ceiling, where gilded cherubs frolicked among the scrolled vines of olive branches carved into the plasterwork, she whispered to God, " 'Tis nothing less than a miracle that His Grace should improve so dramatically now, the very eve before they would take him away. Mayhap You haven't given up on me after all."

With that, she bounded up the stairs two at a time, coming to an abrupt stop as she came face to face with a white of cheek, round-eyed Gertrude whose uniform was torn and drenched with water and soap.

"It's His Grace," the housekeeper finally managed to mutter. "I fear, lass, that he's taken a sudden turn for the worse."

Maria moved around her. "That's not possible—"

"The instant I told him that Her Grace had arrived—"

"He was fine two hours ago, Gertrude. He was feeding himself and chatting—"

"It were like hell opened up and Old Scratch himself appeared. He would not have aught to do with me or anyone else or anything we tried to do with him. I fear Molly will be sportin' a black eye come tomorrow, and as far as my own bum is concerned—"

There came a sudden crash and scream from down the corridor. A maid fled Salterdon's room, ducking as an object flew over her head and smashed against a wall.

Maria entered the room just as a china vase streaked by her head and exploded against the doorframe. Broken glassware lay strewn over the floor. Tables and chairs had been upturned. But it was the vision of her charge that made her heart and soul go numb.

Cautiously, she approached him where he sat in his chair, staring out at her from behind his disheveled hair, broad shoulders heaving from anger and exertion. The wolf was back . . . the dragon. His eyes were like fire. His teeth were showing. She thought she might faint.

"No." She shook her head. "Not now. You won't do this now. I won't let you. You've come too far. I've seen what you can do. What you can be again."

"Get—out," he growled.

"Nay, I won't. I won't let you do this to yourself, or me, or your grandmother." She approached him guardedly, disregarding her fear of him and allowing her anger to rouse her. "Remember who you are, sir. What you are—"

"I know what I am," he sneered. "I needn't have

someone like you to remind me. I'm the fucking Duke of Salterdon, my dear, and you are . . . a drudge employed by my grandmother to conform me into reasonable likeness of what I once was. Well, in case you haven't noticed"—spreading his arms, he finished with a mocking curl of his lips—"I am not the man I once was."

"So that's it." She dropped to her knees beside him and gripped his chair, searched his emotion-ravaged face, uncaring in that instant if he chose to strike out again in anger. "You're afraid."

He grabbed her head between his hands; his fingers twisted cruelly in her hair, forcing back her head as if he intended to snap her neck. Tears of pain sprang to her eyes and flowed down her temples, but she repeated through her teeth, "You're frightened of your own vulnerability, Your Grace. Frightened because you suspect the world will perceive you as less than a man because you're in this chair."

He dragged her closer, gripping her so fiercely she felt paralyzed with splintering pain. Still, she managed, "Takes more than legs to make a man, Your Grace."

"Agreed," he snarled, then released one hand from her hair and grabbed her wrist, thrust her palm up against the warm bulge of his crotch, held it there as she gasped and tried futilely to pull away. "It takes this to be a man, sweetheart, and I haven't got the use of that either. So tell me, Miss Ashton, m'lady companion who pleasures herself with virile young stable boys, what's left for a man who has neither the use of his legs or his cock? Hm?"

"He has his dignity," she whispered, her cheeks burning, her eyes continuing to overflow. "He has his spirit and soul; the immaterial essence which makes him worthy of heaven or hell."

"Is that so?" His face now only inches from hers, he wrapped his hand around her throat and slightly squeezed. "But what of us who have no souls, Miss Ashton?"

"There's goodness in you, sir. 'Tis there if you will only acknowledge it. I saw it in your eyes last night, shining brighter than any star in the universe."

"My, my. Don't we wax poetic for a whore?"

"I am not a whore, sir."

His mouth curved cynically; his nostrils flared. He stroked the soft pulse in her neck with his thumb while he bored her with his slate eyes and wolf's regard.

At last, he released her. She slid away, relief draining the strength from her legs, forcing her to rest on her knees while her scalp throbbed and the imprint of his fingers on her neck felt like hot little punctures. Only then did anger rise up in her throat. Her sudden disappointment (had she really floated through the previous night contemplating that she had felt a spark of something other than obligation toward the ill-tempered aristocrat?) made her shake. Finally, she managed to climb to her feet and move toward the door without looking back.

"Miss Ashton," he said behind her, and when she still did not stop he called more harshly, "Maria!"

She whirled, hands fisted at her sides, her hair at last spilling from its loose chignon and across one shoulder. "I have not given you permission to call me that, Your

Grace. Nor do I intend to. I don't think I like you much, no, I'm certain of it. I've tried to keep an open mind these last weeks, to disregard the rumors and innuendos I've heard regarding your character, but, I'm sorry to say, I fear they are all true. No doubt you deserve the cruel fate that awaits you next.

"Oh yes," she added in higher voice that verged on cracking, "I forgot to inform you: The duchess has brought along a companion, a physician named Edgcumbe who firmly believes the only remedy for your situation is a home for howling maniacs and lost souls. I, of course, have attempted to convince them otherwise. However, I'm certain that after they see you, and the evidence of your foul temper, they'll make haste to carry out their plans and with any luck you shall be spirited away from all of us by nightfall, and I hope you *rot like a sewer rat in that despicable place because it's what you deserve!*"

She ran from the room, straight into a half dozen servants who crowded together, necks craning, eyes wide as saucers as they apparently eavesdropped on her inexcusable tirade. They all gaped at her as if she were the grim reaper himself.

Gertrude wedged herself between two slack-jawed servants and stared, round-eyed, at Maria a full half minute before speaking. "What would ya have us do with him now, love?"

"I . . . don't care what you do with him."

A gasp and mutter went through the crowd.

"Lud," said Gertrude, wringing her hands. "I reckon that means His Grace will be leavin' us soon."

"Undoubtedly."

"Wot a shame. And him havin' come so far since ya came. Why, he were only sayin' this morning afore breakfast that 'e 'as you to thank for it."

Maria frowned. "Gertrude, 'tis a sin to lie—"

"Oh, I wouldn't lie 'bout somethin' like that, lass. He said, 'Miss Ashton whorled through my mental blackness like spring air and sunshine.'"

She frowned again. Her shoulders sagged.

"And he smiled when he said it," Gertrude added with a sniff.

A servant rounded a distant corner. Skirt hiked to her shins, she ran down the corridor with a flash of petticoats and a bounce of her big bosom. "Her Grace is on her way up!" she announced in an exaggerated whisper.

They all stared at Maria.

Gertrude moved closer. "If he's to be took off to the home I reckon it don't matter wot he or his chambers look like."

"Have we time—"

"Ye'll just have to stall her, lass."

"How does one stall the Duchess of Salterdon?"

"I reckon you could do it if anyone could."

"He may resist again."

"Somehow I don't think so, not after catchin' the look on his face when you tol' him that his grandmother was about to put him away. Went white as chalk, he did."

She tried to think, realizing she had been too carried away with anger to acknowledge anything but her own wounded feelings and disappointment. Yes, perhaps she *had* noticed, just that flicker of fear that had flashed from those normally lifeless gray eyes. The memory of it made her queasy.

"Yes," Maria said softly. "I'll try and stall her."

With a smile, Gertrude clapped her hands. "To it, ladies, and be quick about it."

Molly stepped forward and pointed to one eye that was fast becoming black and blue. "You expect me to go back in there after this?"

"It ain't no more'n ye've come draggin' in with after a night spent down at Bill and Beaver's Tavern on a Saturday evenin'. Now get to it afore I blacken the other eye."

With that, the group marched into the dragon's lair, clutching their brooms and dust pails as if they were weapons and shields. Maria closed her eyes and waited for the explosion, the shrieks, the servants to come flooding back into the corridor with fear in their eyes—the same fear that had riveted her motionless a few short minutes before.

They did not.

Still she waited, unable to move, to breathe, the memory of those last few minutes bringing a hot flush to her cheeks. Silly, naive, ignorant ninny. After administering her brother Paul for two years, listening to his confidence about unfulfilled dreams and fantasies, she should have realized Salterdon's anger and lack of confidence stemmed from more than his inability to walk.

But why, she wondered, would that rouse now to so trouble him?

"Miss Ashton."

Blinking, she looked around at the duchess.

"I will see my grandson now."

"No."

"I beg your pardon?"

"He's . . . not ready."

"But you said—"

"There were a few last-minute preparations to make— Gertrude is overly thorough, I think . . ."

The duchess stepped closer, so close Maria could clearly see the gold flakes sprinkled through the dowager's eyes—just like her grandson's. It was *his* eyes staring back at her, their humanness masked by the steel curtain of aristocracy.

The door opened in that moment and Gertrude stepped out. She looked at Maria, then at the duchess. "His Grace is ready to see ya now."

"Is he?" the duchess replied with a lift of one eyebrow, a sideways glance at Maria, then a curl of her lip. She waited until Gertrude stepped aside, then moved into her grandson's chamber.

Maria followed at a respectable distance, afraid to look, to breathe, finding the strength to remain standing only as Gertrude moved up beside her. Only then did she focus on Salterdon.

"Cleans up right nice, don't he?" Gertrude whispered. "Thought he was gonna use that damned razor on me own bloody throat afore I was finished shavin' him. Alls we got to do now is to convince him to let us cut his hair."

"I've grown quite fond of his hair," she heard herself murmur in reply, her gaze still locked on her charge where he reposed in a high-backed chair before the fire, his face as fine-honed and strong as chiseled marble in the dancing light. He had never looked so . . . handsome. So distinguished. So . . . arrogantly self-confident—hardly the same man who, moments before, had purposefully planted her hand between his legs and called her a whore.

She was not a whore, *damn him*. She was not . . . but for that instant, that very moment his body heat and the reaction from the contact of her hand on his crotch had sluiced up her arm to her brain . . . she had felt like one . . . she still did—God help her.

"I dressed him in his finest, o'course. Always liked the threads, he did. Spent a fortune on London tailors, havin' his clothes brought all the way from China. Looks right commandin' in 'em, don't he?"

The Duchess of Salterdon stopped before her grandson's chair. They regarded one another silently before he said dryly, "Forgive me for not standing, Your Grace. You do understand . . ."

"Of course. What I don't understand is your anger toward me."

He took a moment to reply. To someone else, he might have appeared simply aloof, mildly bored by the conversation he would rather not be having. He was not, of course.

He was concentrating, mentally rehearsing, repeating the words over and over in his mind until he was certain he could say them coherently and distinctly. As Maria watched him, forgetting to breathe, her body turning rigid as granite, she recalled again last evening—those final hours after he had played Bach's *Mass in B Minor* and before the first streaks of pale sun had broken through the horizon's foggy barrier—when he had read to her from *The Vicar of Wakefield,* stumbling over words, cursing his ineptitude, trying again and again until his body became wet with sweat, until the words flowed freely as water from his tongue. She had buried her face in her hands and wept, and laughed, and wept again.

Watching him now, recognizing the tension in his shoulders, the working of his jaw, the manner in which he gripped the chair arms with his hands, she thought to herself, *Slowly. Carefully, Your Grace. You needn't rush it. It will all come back if you simply relax and allow it . . . and I didn't mean the terrible things I said earlier. Forgive me, forgive me, forgive me.*

Gertrude took her arm and nudged her into the hallway, shutting the door and closing off the image of Salterdon being offered a drink by the duchess's attendant. Her heart skipped a beat, but as she opened her mouth to protest, Gertrude shook her head and clucked.

"He'll do just fine, love. Leave it alone."

"He has trouble yet holding a glass, Gertrude. What if he drops it? He would be horribly humiliated, and—"

Gertrude forced her down into a chair and proceeded to rectify the damage caused to her hair by her earlier tussle with Salterdon. "Why should you care?" the servant asked nonchalantly. "Ye've made it more'n clear wot ya think about him. Called him a sewer rat—"

"I didn't!" she cried, and twisted around to face her

friend. "I said I wished he would *rot* like a sewer rat."

"Right. So ya did. But ya can't hardly deny that ya did say that ya didn't care for him much, and that he deserved to be sent off to a place where folk howl like maniacs."

"Oh God." She sank back in the chair. No wonder her father had prayed for her soul every waking minute of every day. "Occasionally, I think he needs someone emotionally stronger. He frightens me sometimes and infuriates me more than anyone I've ever known. Still, at other times, despite the frustration and fear and anger, I feel this warm place in my heart and stomach . . ." Her voice trailed off and she bit her lower lip.

"That's to be expected—these motherly feelin's. It's the nurturin' part of a woman, I suppose."

"Is that what it is?" she asked with feigned brightness. "Motherly nurturing?"

"Wot else *could* it be?"

"I . . . don't know. It doesn't matter, I suppose, because in light of the hateful things I just said to His Grace I'm certain to be leaving now whether I want to or not . . . just as soon as he informs Her Grace what a despicably ill-tempered companion she's employed him."

Chapter Eleven

Salterdon remained silent as his grandmother paced the room, her brandy in one hand, the diamonds on the other casting flashes of brilliant light across the richly paneled walls. Only when she paused by the fire, one knotted and pale hand bracing herself against the mantle, did he meet her stern eyes and say what was on his mind, but not before taking one last look at the door through which Maria had vanished.

"I must be more weak-minded than I thought, Your Grace. I actually imagined that you would weep with delight and relief when you witnessed my vast improvement."

"Is that why you continue to glare at me and brood?" she asked. "Need I remind you that I'm not, nor have I ever been, witlessly sentimental."

"No." He looked away. "You needn't remind me."

"You must know how pleased I am, if not surprised. It seems that Miss Ashton has managed to accomplish miracles since her arrival to Thorn Rose."

"She's . . ." He searched for the word, the phrase to describe the woman who, just minutes before, had verbally clawed his eyes out . . . the same woman who, the night before, had danced in joy, barefoot and in her nightgown, around the music room floor as he clumsily plunked out a tune on the tuneless pianoforte. ". . . a dichotomy of emotion," he finally said.

"An understatement." She looked at the glass of port he held in one hand and waited for him to drink. Carefully, he lifted it to his mouth, drank, felt the liquor slide like fire down the back of his throat. He squeezed his eyes closed until the inferno eased to that oozing, ember-like heat in the pit of his stomach. He wanted to cough, but would not. That, of course, would be a sign of weakness, and if the duchess looked down on anything, it was weakness.

"You look well enough, considering," she said. "A bit thin, perhaps, and ruffianly. Why you've chosen to grow your hair in such a manner is a mystery; you look more like your brother now than you ever did. No doubt you'll be digging furrows with your bare hands and sowing cabbages for your tenants."

"That hasn't lowered Clayton in your esteem, as I recall."

"While that may be acceptable for Clayton, my second-born grandson, it is not acceptable for you. Dukes do not toil with tenants."

"Nor do they play the pianoforte," he said to himself, and took another drink.

Finally, the duchess sat down, back straight, chin set. His gaze locked on his diminishing port, Trey asked,

"Why have you come here? And why did you bring Edgcumbe?"

"Why do you think?"

Again, he glanced toward the door, watched it hard, as if he could will it open. Was she there still—Miss Ashton—waiting for some sign from him before she came charging in, casting orders like a soldier. Of course not; he had sent her away, had he not? Virtually ordered her to get the devil out of his life, and for what?

Simply because, in her innocence and enthusiasm, she had believed that she had saved him from an existence worse than death.

He almost laughed. Instead, he drank again.

Where was she?

Not that he needed her . . . he could hold his own against his grandmother, always had, only now . . .

Jesus, he felt tired suddenly. His head was beginning to ache, his mind to blur. He was having trouble thinking coherently—could not seem to come up with just the right words that would appease the duchess.

The port went down more smoothly this time. He barely noticed it burning his throat, was only vaguely aware that a servant appeared from nowhere to replenish his glass.

"Why do you think?" he repeated his grandmother's words aloud. "Why do you think? Let me think . . . because . . . you had every intention of putting me away. Of burying me in some chamber as if I were little more than some distasteful secret best hidden."

"Yes."

"Ah." Port sloshed on his knee. He watched the

splotch creep like a shadow over his fawn-colored breeches. "Well, this may come as a surprise to you, Grandmother, but the secret has long since been out. In case you were unaware, my peers ceased dropping in long ago. Couldn't seem to understand my inability to cope with my new role in life. Not that I believed for a moment their interest in my welfare had anything at all to do with concern. Fallen aristocrats, especially dukes, make for incredible conversation at dinners and soirees."

Turning the glass round and round in his hand, he said through his teeth, "Shocking what you hear when people think you're an imbecile. As for you, Your Grace, you were always shockingly honest, but never mind. I forgive you . . . as always. I really haven't any other choice, have I?"

"Not as long as you wish to inherit my fortune."

"Ah," he repeated, and flashed her a smile.

"I'm not getting any younger, Trey. For the last fifteen years I've waited patiently for you to settle down, grow up, marry, and produce me some heirs. Now this. I can hardly bequeath my assets to a vegetable."

"And with me tucked away nicely in a hospital you can get down to the business of passing on your assets to my more deserving brother Clayton."

"Who doesn't want it or need it," she supplied somewhat wearily. "But all that is beside the point now. You're better, thank God—"

"Thank Miss Ashton," he intruded, and raised his glass a bit shakily toward the door.

The duchess raised one eyebrow and sank back in her chair.

Over the past weeks, Maria had not given much thought to the opulence of her surroundings, particularly her bedchamber, mostly because nearly every waking minute of the day had been spent with Salterdon . . . as had been her evenings. By the time she had fallen into bed, she had been too exhausted to appreciate the extreme beauty of the white paneling, rosy pink curtains, and pale Aubusson carpets—all reflections of the Louis XV period—all, certainly, fit to accommodate a princess.

Now, as she folded her last mended stocking and tucked it, along with a patched petticoat into her little valise, she regarded the cheery interior with a sense of disconsolateness.

She was leaving. Obviously the duchess would not have a companion for her grandson who maligned him to his face. He was the Duke of Salterdon, for heaven's sake, and she had likened him to a sewer rat. There was no one but herself to blame, of course. It was because of her rebelliousness that she had applied for this position in the first place. It was due to her frustration that she had resigned, and, last but not least, thanks to her burst of temper she had spoiled any chance of changing her mind about leaving.

She sat in a little straight-back chair with bowed arms before the fire, held her hands up to the heat, and waited.

The door opened. Gertrude filled the threshold. "Her Grace will be seein' ya now."

"Very well," she said stalwartly. With a lift of her chin, she swept up her threadbare cloak and declared, "I'm ready."

She walked down the long galleries, glancing right and left, mentally saying good-bye to the paintings on the walls and the statuaries cluttering the tabletops while she hurried to keep up with Gertrude, who walked ahead. However, instead of Gertrude escorting her to a salon, or even to the duchess's own private wing of the rambling house, she was led straight out the front door, onto the vast marble steps that declined to the sweep of curving drive. An open carriage was parked there, its two occupants swaddled in mufflers and fur-collared cloaks, their hats pulled low and tight over their brows as a soft, fresh snowfall danced silently around them. A moment passed before Maria realized they were the duchess and her grandson.

"Come along," called Her Grace. "Quickly! While I can tolerate the cold while moving, sitting dead as an iceberg tends to make my joints throb."

Good Lord. They were so eager to be rid of her they were whisking her away from Thorn Rose without so much as a meeting to dismiss her formally! But that was not what concerned her in that moment.

Swiftly as possible, considering the increasingly icy condition of the steps, she slid her way to the conveyance, her gaze locked on Salterdon, who sat in the plush leather seat opposite his grandmother, eyes downcast, his cheeks gray from cold, his lips tinged with blue.

Without boarding or taking her gaze from His Grace,

she said, "Do you think it wise to bring him out on such a day, Your Grace? The cold is bitter, and—"

"Edgcumbe suggested it," the duchess snapped. "Felt the fresh air and briskness of temperature would help rouse the mind and fortify his resistance to illness. Now get in before we all freeze to death."

Maria scrambled aboard, sank into the seat beside Salterdon and dropped her valise to the floor. She reached for the duke's lap blanket and tucked it more securely under his knees. "You're trembling," she said to him softly, and wrapped her chilling fingers around his kid-gloved hands.

The carriage, pulled by four high-prancing white Arabian geldings, lurched under way, the driver whistling and popping a whip in the air.

"You shouldn't coddle him so," said the duchess. "He's not a child, Miss Ashton."

"Neither is he well enough to withstand this cold, Your Grace. He needs time to build his strength."

Nestled in layers of mink and fox fur, regarding Maria with eyes as gray as the countryside, the duchess sniffed and raised one eyebrow. "He's the Duke of Salterdon, young lady. He comes from hardy, irascible stock. For over eighty years I have not gone one day without a ride in the countryside, come rain or snow, nor did his grandfather, my husband, when he was alive."

"He died of pneumonia," Salterdon murmured without so much as a flick of an eyelash, catching Maria and the duchess by surprise. "And I would appreciate it if the two of you would stop talking about me as if I weren't here. I may be a trifle . . . slow in getting the words out, but I'm perfectly capable of speaking for myself, thank you."

Flashing a glance at Maria, he lifted one heavy dark brow as if in challenge, or humor, she could not tell. She really could not think of anything at that moment but the stab of disquietude she experienced hearing the soft rumble of his voice and suddenly realizing that for the last long weeks she had prayed every night and morning to hear him utter a distinguishable sound and now that she had she was about to leave and never hear him again.

She sank back into the seat and pulled her cloak snugly around her. Her ears burned from the cold, as did her fingers. Her nose began to run and her eyes to blur. The toes on her right foot, thanks to the worn thin tip of her shoe, were swiftly going numb. That all seemed secondary to the sense of maudlin emotionalism that suddenly overwhelmed her, made her shiver and squeeze close her eyes.

Salterdon tugged loose one edge of his lap blanket and flung it over her knees, then he caught hold of her arm and tugged it. "Closer," he told her. "Before you freeze to death."

"No." She shook her head and refused to budge. "I'm fine."

"You're also stubborn, a fault which, in retrospect, is good for me but not so good for you. Very well, I'll go at this another way: I'm freezing, Miss Ashton. Won't you share my blanket with me . . . because *your* body heat will help keep *me* warm and therefore *I* won't die of pneumonia."

"Well," she said, and chewed her lower lip. "If you put it that way . . ." Reluctantly, Maria slid herself closer to Salterdon, sat stiff as a poker as he tucked the blanket around her legs, hips, and waist, making certain her hands were buried beneath it.

"Better?" he asked with a thin smile.

She nodded.

The snow fell faster, thicker, danced in swirls and eddies along the meandering roadway.

He glanced askance at Maria. Her nose, chin, and cheeks were bright red, her eyes vibrantly blue and watering slightly. And her mouth . . .

He looked away and frowned.

"So tell me, Miss Ashton," said the duchess. "What have you there in your bag?"

"My belongings, of course."

Salterdon exchanged glances with his grandmother.

They rode in silence for a while, watching the snow cover the undulating downs in a blanket of white. When they came to the crossroads, one leading to Haworth, the other deeper into the downs where a scattering of tenant houses cast yellow light through tiny square windows, the driver directed the horses down the winding lane away from Haworth.

Maria sat forward, gazed hard down the road to Haworth, then looked at Salterdon. Her long dark lashes were glistening with snowflakes. The icy crystals glinted like jewels upon her silver hair. Trey said nothing, just winked and closed one hand over hers beneath the blanket and gave it a squeeze of reassurance. Her eyes widened; lips parted. Her small hand opened and clasped his, clung, trembled as her smile turned the cold air warm and the overcast sky blindingly bright.

The realization occurred to him in that instant that he had never squeezed a woman's hand in reassurance before. It also occurred to him, as the driver whistled and drove their carriage down into a tiny village where the staring white houses lining the banks of a freezing lake looked like rows of teeth in the gloomy daylight, that he continued to hold her hand . . . and she continued to hold his.

"Hopefully, my examination will further enlighten us as to his ongoing condition," Edgcumbe said as he moved down the corridor slightly ahead of Maria. She hurried to keep up while doing her best to balance phials and medical instruments she carried on a tray. "You say, my dear, that he's shown no improvement whatsoever in his ability to move the lower portion of his body?"

"None," she replied.

He shook his head and frowned. "I simply cannot understand why. While the blow to his head was sufficient enough to cause trauma to the memory coherency, I've found no reason why his mobility should be so permanently impaired. In short, there is no physical reason that I can find that he should not get up from his chair and waltz right out through the door."

"He withdrew mentally and emotionally," Maria said. "Might he not have done the same physically?"

Edgcumbe looked thoughtful before shaking his head. "Perhaps. But the man is the Duke of Salterdon, my dear, in line to inherit one of the greatest fortunes in England. He has everything: youth, wealth, good looks. He has an obligation, doesn't he?"

Edgcumbe continued down the corridor until disappearing into Salterdon's room. Maria trailed behind, her mind on that afternoon when she had walked from the house to discover him shivering in the cold, eyes down, his breath smelling heavily of liquor. That far too familiar and discomfiting emotion had roused inside her, had leapt up like a startled hare the moment he had wrapped his hand around hers. It had sung as vibrantly as a bird the instant she realized that she would not be leaving Thorn Rose after all. For an instant, as their carriage had made its way down the meandering slippery road and he had continued to hold her hand, she had been silly enough to actually fantasize that they were lovers, out for a brisk romantic ride in the snow.

Daft girl.

And she had relived that moment in the music room when he had held her—gently, so gently, and the warmth of his body and hands had made her feel liquid and on fire.

Obviously the strain of the last weeks had wrecked havoc on her sensibilities.

And the memory of her hand on his private body— the heat of his body—the fullness of it . . .

"Coming, Miss Ashton?" came the physician's voice from Salterdon's room.

She took a breath . . . and wondered if she were coming down with something; her entire being felt uncomfortably feverish all of a sudden.

The pungent smell of medicinals greeted her as she hurried into the room that was thick with a foul-scented vapor that made her nose burn and her eyes water. Along with a roaring fire in the hearth, tins of red hot coals had been placed around Salterdon's bed. Molly hovered in the background prepared to pour the rank smelling liquid on the embers, which hissed and spewed steam into the air.

"Come along, Miss Ashton, quickly," called Edgcumbe.

Carefully, she made her way through the cloistering fog, sliding the tray onto a table where Edgcumbe pointed. Only then did she turn for the bed and froze.

"The duchess mentioned you had nursed an invalid brother," Edgcumbe said as he poured a thick oily fluid into his hand. "And that you are perfectly capable of assisting me without embarrassment."

She swallowed and faintly nodded.

"Good." Edgcumbe caught the white sheet covering Salterdon from the waist down, and flung it aside.

He lay on his stomach, totally nude. His broad back was slick with sweat and narrowed sharply to a thin waist and slender hips. His buttocks were round and firm, his legs incredible. From mid-thigh down, they were sprinkled with coarse black hair.

"Miss Ashton?"

She blinked and forced her gaze to Edgcumbe, and the flask of oil he extended to her. "Concentrate on the waist down, rubbing briskly. The steam will open the pores and allow the elixir to absorb. 'Tis said the heat increases the circulation, encouraging blood to the muscle and bone, as well as limbers the muscles so they become more pliant."

Maria moved around the bed, just as Molly tossed a cup full of water on the coals. Already her clothes felt damp and clung to her skin. The collar of her dress felt like a noose. Maria glanced around at the maid, saw her eyes narrow and her mouth part in something less than a smile, as if she recognized Maria's embarrassment and relished in it.

Taking a deep breath, she allowed the warm oil to spill from her hand onto his back where it pooled and glistened in the lamplight and slid along the ridge of muscle running along the length of his spine. Hesitantly, she reached out, caught the stream with one finger that touched his skin so lightly she hardly noticed, until he stiffened, caught his breath, and twisted his fingers into the bedding.

She closed her eyes, drew her oily hands down his waist, over his firm buttocks, and down the backs of his hard thighs, rubbing, massaging, learning the feel of him, the smoothness, roughness, softness, only vaguely aware of those around her who spoke occasionally, of Molly splashing the coals with the pungent liquid that formed a heavy cloud around Maria's shoulders.

This was not a boy's body—not like Paul's, whose early manhood had been obliterated by a blacksmith's hands—whose body had not matured to such extremes. Paul's had been pale and soft.

This was not even Thaddeus's body—or what she had seen of it as he was making love to Molly.

She shivered. Her breath seemed to catch somewhere deep in the pit of her stomach and the sudden over- whelming need to flee shook her. Yet . . . she did not, but allowed her hands to move over him gently, firmly, experiencing the feel of her skin sliding against his, skimming on a frail barrier of slick warm oil, luxuriating in the feel of his flesh. Learning him as few women ever had, from the tiny scar along his left hip (a burn?) to the unusual scattering of brown beauty marks on his right buttock.

"Miss Ashton?"

She blinked and slowly looked up at Edgcumbe.

"I said we should turn him over now."

"Turn him over?"

Edgcumbe nodded.

Molly made a faint noise of amusement and tossed medicine on the coals. A geyser-like spray of steam and water spewed into the air, coating Maria's face in moist, cloying heat that made breathing impossible.

Leaning near her ear, Molly said, "No doubt yer thinkin' 'bout Thad. Well I'm here to tell ya that it'll be a cold day in hell afore you ever set hands on him like this. Aye, he likes oil poured in a slow warm stream over his body, but I'll be the one pourin' it. And furthermore—

"You," Edgcumbe said to Molly, cutting her off

midsentence. "Give me a hand, please. Miss Ashton seems to be preoccupied."

"Right," Molly said, and pushed her way by Maria, shoving her hard enough to unbalance her slightly.

For heaven's sake, what had come over her suddenly? It was not as if she had never witnessed Salterdon in partial undress; obviously the last weeks she had touched him hundreds of times in hundreds of ways. She had seen to his every need: fed him, shaved him, brushed his mane of hair, helped him clean his teeth, and manicured his nails. Now she stood at his bedside unable to move or breathe, oddly agitated and nervous at the prospect of seeing this man undressed, and of touching his flesh.

Setting her chin, she grabbed Molly's arm and shoved her away. "I'm perfectly capable of handling the situation, thank you."

They rolled him.

Maria turned away, bumping the hod of coals and upsetting the pitcher of water. Catching it before it toppled from the table, she clutched it to her stomach and shut her eyes.

"The oil, Miss Ashton," Edgcumbe called.

Slowly, she set aside the ewer and turned again to the bed, relief flooding her at the sight of the fleecy towel draped over Salterdon's loins. Her gaze drifted to his face to discover that he regarded her—*only* her—his gray eyes the color of smoke, dark hair clinging to his damp brow, his skin flushed by heat and steam. And his mouth . . . tipped up at one end, flat at the other—as conflicting in its message as his too-often erratic behavior.

Stiffly—dear merciful God in heaven, her arm felt as if it weighed ten stone—she reached for the oil and poured it from the bottle into her hand, allowing it to spill through her fingers in a thin amber thread and pool on his lower belly, just beneath his navel.

His skin quivered in response; the muscles in his stomach grew tight.

She nudged the toweling aside just slightly, swept the oil over his pelvis, then his hard thigh, rubbing gently at first, then briskly until her own fingers began to ache. All the while, Edgcumbe chatted amiably, muttering comments about how well His Grace's body had held up to its year of incapacitation.

Maria touched the scar on his hip. It was as big as her hand and slightly pink. "A burn?" she asked, more to herself than to Salterdon.

"Yes," he replied. "A burn."

"How?"

"When I was ten, my brother and I traveled to the Far East with my parents. On the return journey, our ship caught fire during a storm. I fell beneath a burning mast. My father saved me."

"Your parents were killed."

"My mother first. She drowned."

"And yet you survived."

His brow knitted. His eyes became distant and hard. For a moment, it was as if the past opened up and swallowed him. In his eyes, she saw terror. His body became tense with fear.

"Sharks," he finally whispered, his voice dry. "They took most of the crew and passengers who hadn't already burned to death or drowned. We drifted for days clinging to a bit of wood that was only large enough to hold three of us. We all took turns in the water. I had begun to run fever because of my injuries and when it came time for me to go in the water, my father wouldn't allow it. He went in for me . . . The sharks came during the night . . ."

His voice trailed off. It seemed that the silence magnified with every beat of her heart, deepened as heavily as the shadows in the darkening room. The image of turbid seas, of terror and blood rose up before her, made all the more riveting by the sense of fathomless pain and self-blame reverberating in the steamy air around her master. She was beginning to understand, oh yes—the reasons for his lifelong anger and belligerence—

He blamed himself for his father's death.

"There were screams all around us," said he in a soft, guttural voice. His face had become a caricature of itself, eyes wide, nostrils flared, lips pressed against his white teeth, his body rigid as stone. "The water was still as glass, the night incredibly clear and bright with a full moon suspended just above the black, undulate horizon. All around us there were men, women, and children crying, 'My god, my god help us, save us.' The screams of terror and pain were bloodcurdling."

Salterdon swallowed. His eyes never leaving hers, he said emotionlessly, "With no warning the monster came up from the depths and cut my father in two. I was looking into his eyes the very instant it happened, Miss Ashton. He didn't scream. He was too damn dignified, you see."

He closed his tormented eyes briefly. His breathing became labored.

"It should have been me, Miss Ashton. Had he not taken my place that night he would be alive now, relishing his role as duke, living up to his ancestors' reputations and expectations. He was so damn good at it, too. Always reasonable. Always rational. The most intelligent man I've ever known. In the blink of an eye, barely ten years old, I became the Duke of Salterdon. How the hell was I to live up to my father's reputation as a gentleman, as head of this family, as a hero who would sacrifice his life for his family . . . when all I wanted—all I had ever wanted—was the freedom to enjoy my childhood."

Silence ensued again. Only then did they realize they were alone. When had Edgcumbe departed, and Molly? While the coals continued to radiate heat and blink hot red eyes in the dwindling light of the room, the steamy vapor dispersed little by little, leaving in its wake a brittle coldness that settled into every fold of her clothes, to permeate her skin and grip her bones.

When had she last managed to breathe?

When had she sat on the edge of the bed, her body pressing almost indecently against his?

When had she reached for his hand, closing her own around it, offering the same comfort he had offered her that afternoon?

When had she become lost in those dark eyes, sucked

like a vacuum into his tortured memories so her own heart pounded and her breath seemed to catch in her throat so long her lungs burned?

When had he ceased being simply her patient?

When had he become a flesh and blood man— overwhelming her judgment, vibrating her senses so acutely she could feel the heat of his naked flesh through her dress. It burned like a brand into her hip. His body was youthful yet, despite his thirty-five years, and she imagined that even in his youthful prime—a male at his peak of manhood—he would have looked no differently. The difference was in his eyes, lurking there, barely concealing a weariness and pain and anger that stabbed her fiercely in her heart—as did the sudden realization that the emotions she was experiencing at the moment had little to do with pity, or even the simple fondness and responsibility a companion might feel for her master.

Discomfiture assailed her. She tried to release his hand; he wouldn't allow it. His hot moist fingers, slick upon her flesh, held her in place though she tried with as much dignity as possible to escape.

"Let me go." She struggled again. *Let me go,* she pleaded in her mind, though her body—her traitorous body—seemed, on its own to draw to him, a weakened supplicant for his nearness.

He slid her hand over his belly, her palm skimming the last of the oil that made a tiny pool in his navel and glistened on the sprinkling of dark hair disappearing beneath the towel.

"Perhaps I should call Gertrude," she said faintly, her

eyes following their locked hands over his well-defined chest, slowly circling his nipples that looked hard and the color of copper coins, then down again, over his ribs, to his belly, round and round, then lower, until the tips of her fingers brushed the towel, and slightly beneath.

"I don't want Gertrude," he replied.

"She's just as capable—"

"But not nearly so pretty."

Her body flushed as she glanced at his face—his eyes—his mouth that had mocked her, taunted her, cursed her. He looked on the point of saying something else that would further unnerve her. The air between them crackled almost tangibly, and she knew in that moment that she could not remain another second—not feeling as she did, swirling with all those confusing emotions: fear, nervousness, sympathy . . . and unaccustomed desire. Then—

His free hand came up and curled around the back of her head, twisted fiercely in her hair and dragged her down so the tips of her breasts grazed his chest; her face just above his, his lips near hers; her mind cried to her to struggle, but she did not. She should have reminded him that even though he was a duke and she was nothing more than a hired domestic he had no right to treat her as if she were some dollymop like Molly. Neither was she one of those females who were flattered by his indiscriminate attentions. But she didn't.

She tried to wet her lips, but her tongue, like the inside of her mouth, was dry as dust.

What is he doing?

Why?

Didn't he realize what she had come to feel for him?
Of course not. How could he? She had only realized
it herself that very moment—

He dragged her face to his, and kissed her. Roughly.
Urgently. Thrusting his tongue inside her mouth and
swirling it round and round her own, robbing her of
breath, of strength, while his other hand slid hers deep
beneath the towel to that foreign and forbidden part of
him—just a brush, a touch—

Gasping, tearing herself away, she stumbled back,
away from the bed, and fled toward the door.

"Am I that monstrous, Miss Ashton?" he called in a
loud angry and bitter voice that stopped her in her
tracks. He laughed harshly. "You needn't worry, you
know. I'm incapable of forcing my attentions on you.
The bastard who bashed in my skull left me a eunuch,
Miss Ashton. The rakehell of London society, seducer
of virgins, and consummate wrecker of marriages has
finally got his comeuppance."

She ran for her bedroom and slammed the door
behind her.

Chapter Twelve

Nights such as this, cold, blustery, black as pitch and achingly damp, he might have spent in the company of his cohorts: gentlemen such as he, with more money and idle time on their hands than intelligence. Slouched before a fire in some club or tavern back room, they would gamble away the monies in their purses; they would embalm themselves with ale or inferiorly distilled beverages; they would coerce bawdy serving wenches to a cot up the stairs where they would spend the next few hours pretending they actually meant something to one another.

Instead, here he lay, exactly where Miss Maria Ashton had left him hours before, naked but for the sheet wrapped around his hips, inebriated (thanks to his grandmother), shivering with cold.

Where the hell was she?

Just who the devil did she think she was, fleeing his company as she had those hours ago? Miss Maria Ashton. No more than a grossly overpaid domestic who owned two plain and threadbare garments to her name . . . who did not even have the grace to be embarrassed about it.

Why the blazes should he care what she thought of him? Furthermore, what the blazes had come over him that he would have remotely entertained the thought of seducing her?

As if he could have done anything about it.

He drank again.

No doubt about it, his grandmother had incredibly good taste when it came to choosing liquor. Like her clothes, her homes, her jewelry, and her friends, it was the best her money could buy.

Turning the crystal glass in his hand, he stared into the amber liquid, watched how the light from the distant fire played amid the exquisite cut prisms of glass, then he quaffed the port and flung the glass to the floor.

He reached for the tester drape, twisted his fingers into it, and with teeth clenched, pulled himself upright. In the dim light his legs, motionless, as always, were wrapped like a mummy in the binding sheets.

He ripped the bedcovers away and flung them aside.

His body burned both hot and cold. It sweat and shivered. The room whirled around him, and he wondered if the cause was due to his grandmother's outrageously expensive port or this unaccustomed exertion. When had he last attempted to walk? Not since the night of the attack, when robbers had swooped down on him and the half-dozen young swains who had accompanied him to Epson Races, all as pompous and full of themselves as he, their purses bulging with their day's good fortune, their bodies glutted by spirits, their minds on the shapely slatterns who awaited them in London's notorious East End. For an hour he had lain in the mud, facedown, watching the steam rise from the seeping blood that formed a warm black puddle beneath his cheek. He had almost died, had experienced an odd moment when it seemed that he had actually left his body, hovered over the scattering of groaning young men and saw himself, the Duke of Salterdon, white-faced and covered in blood. It seemed a millennium had flashed before him in sequences of blinding light: his past, his present, his future: a child with his nose pressed against the windowpane, watching his brother play in the sunshine while he, himself, vaguely listened to the dronings of a stiff-lipped tutor who waxed on and on about the immense responsibilities of filling his father's shoes.

"Bastards," he said aloud, and as if in response, some minute crackling sound came from the dying fire, a shard of kindling collapsing, perhaps, or sap hissing amid the glowing embers.

His bedroom door opened. Light from the hallway spilled over his floor briefly, then a feminine figure moved into it, nothing more than a black silhouette as it paused, obviously taken aback to find him perched on the edge of his bed, naked but for the sheet twisted around his hip, sweating from exertion, breathing heavily.

"Maria?" he called out, his hands clenching as he acknowledged the escalation of his heartbeat, the relief that she had not, after all, packed up her pitiful

belongings and hightailed it away from Thorn Rose—
away from him and his idiotic and fruitless tauntings.

"Well now," came Molly's unexpected, curiously
seductive greeting. "Wot have we here? I reckon ol'
Edgcumbe was right, eh? Give a man a bit of tender
loving care and he suddenly find himself amazin'ly
recovered." With a swing of her hip, Molly closed the
door behind her then moved toward him, balancing a
tray of pastries in her hands. Slipping into the light
beside the bed, she smiled down at him and winked. "I
was thinkin' you might be feeling a mite lonely, trapped
up here all by yerself. Thought you might enjoy a tart or
two . . . or three." She giggled and put the tray down
on the bedside table.

"Where is Miss Ashton?" he demanded.

"Miss Ashton, is it? 'At's right formal when just a
minute ago you was callin' 'er Maria."

"Where is she?" he repeated.

"Does it matter? There ain't aught she can do for ya
that I can't."

He looked at her breasts, which, for a change,
appeared extraordinarily full. She wore no chemise. Her
nipples were hazy dark coins behind the translucent
material of her blouse. What the blazes was she doing?

She broke off a piece of tart, slid her fingers into the
warm cherry filling and scooped out a portion of fruit
that was plump and as richly colored as a full-bodied
wine. Syrup dripped down one side of her finger.

"What the devil are you doing?" he finally asked,
his gaze locked on her fingers. "That was a perfectly
good tart."

She offered the cherry up to his lips, allowing the sticky juice to dribble in a stream onto his naked thighs. Her lips parted in a half smile. Her eyelids grew heavy.

Slowly, he lowered his gaze to her offering.

Good God. She was seducing him . . . or attempting to. The flush of embarrassment rushed to his face, his neck, his shoulders, even as he opened his mouth and allowed her to slide the cherry and the tips of her fingers between his lips. The syrup was warm and slick and sweet, the fruit plump and firm. He sank his teeth into it, gently. His eyes drifted closed, even as his mind tumbled backward, to other women—lovers—whom he had caressed with his lips and tongue, savoring the rich taste and smell of them, cupping his tongue inside them and allowing the nectar of their desire to drive him mad with the need to bury his body into theirs with an urgency that made them scream with pleasure and gratitude.

Beautiful women. The most desirable women in England and the Continent. Women who wore nothing to bed but their jewels—long strands of pearls and diamonds and sapphires which looped around their exquisite breasts and sparkled with candlelight when they slid over their ivory flesh.

Oh, that ivory flesh—soft, smooth, fragrant like flowers—like violets . . . like Maria.

Yet, he had come to this, a doxy housemaid with dry yellow hair, whose rotten and missing teeth were made more desirable by dim light and shadows, whose overly thin body and sagging breasts smelled of sour sweat.

Molly slid her blouse off over her head, tossed it to

the floor. Grinning, she smeared one nipple with cherry syrup, cupped the pendulous breast in one hand and lifted it toward his mouth.

"Give it a try," she crooned and parted her legs so she could press the sensitive mound between her thighs upon his knee and rub. "Just a lick, Yer Grace. Might do worlds for ya. Ya never know unless ya try, right?" She slid the sticky bud of her nipple across his lower lip.

He turned his head.

She twisted her fingers into his hair and forced his face back around. "You forget yourself," he snapped, and grabbed her wrists, causing her to clench her teeth and hiss.

"Wot's wrong, Yer Grace? 'Fraid ya can't rise to the occasion? Well that's wot I'm here for, sir. To see if we can't help things along a bit."

"And what, may I ask, makes you think I would even consider your advances?"

"Beggars can't be choosers, now can they?"

He flung her backward. She tripped on a rug and spilled heavily onto her butt, her skirt hiked to her knees exposing her sprawled thighs. "Bloody lunatic," she declared. "Don't know what I was thinkin' to agree to such a scheme. I've a good mind to tell 'Er Grace to—"

"To tell Her Grace what?"

Molly's mouth twisted. Her eyes narrowed and her voice became surly. "Ya don't think I come 'ere for me bleedin' 'ealth, do ya?"

His body turned rigid.

"That's right," she said. "To make a man out of ya again."

He stared at her fiercely—so fiercely she scrambled away, snatching her blouse before stumbling toward the door, flinging it open, and disappearing into the dark.

Teeth clenched, brow sweating, he slid his body off the bed, clung to the bedpost with one shaking hand as he allowed his weight to sway from side to side, forward and backward as he struggled to find his balance, anticipating his legs to give out at any moment—

"Your Grace?" came the soft, distressed cry from the threshold of Maria's bedroom, and suddenly she was there, her simple nightgown a shimmery white in the gauzy light of the room. Flinging her arms around his waist, her light body atremble with exertion, she cried, "What can you be thinking, sir? Quickly, allow me to ease you back onto the bed—no, don't struggle—stop fighting or we'll both surely fall."

"Leave me the hell alone," he growled and tried to shove her away.

She clung all the harder, her small face pressed into the hard, sweating musculature of his chest, her hair cascading like moonbeams over her shoulders.

Burying his hand in her hair, he dragged back her head so fiercely she cried out. Her eyes looked hollow, her face gaunt and full of despair. "Odd that you would come flying in here like some angel of mercy when only hours ago you thought me despicable," he sneered through his teeth. "Has she gotten to you as well, Miss Ashton? Just what is your loyalty worth?"

She shook her head frantically. Her features twisted in pain and confusion.

He shoved her away. She spilled to the floor with a stunned and angry cry.

Even as the great house became quiet she paced about her chamber with the smell of burning oil and peat in the hearth giving the air a pungent scent of staleness. Her mouth felt raw, swollen, and bruised.

How could she have done something so daft as to allow him such liberties? To have kissed her so brazenly? To have turned her, with one touch of his mouth, into a mindless, compunctionless hussy like Molly who wanted with every fiber of her being to stretch her body out against his, to give him the freedom to do what he wanted with her mouth, her body, her hand—oh God, her hand. Beneath the towel. Fingertips brushing against his flesh and wiry hair . . .

She saw the bed from the corner of her eye, its immense down mattress piled high with silk and tapestry pillows. A small lamp cast enough light to paint only a very small part of the room in a red-orange glow; it splashed gyrating patterns on the floor, the bed, the pile of multicolored cushions.

How could she face him again?

Mayhap she had misread his intentions, just as he had misread hers. She had not fled the room because she found him monstrous—how could he imagine such a thing?—but because the sudden flood of feelings in which she had found herself drowning were too much to bear. Too much to control. In a heartbeat she had wanted nothing more than to be as flagrantly willing as Molly—as free to enjoy the same wild pleasure that would drive a woman to copulate with a man on a kitchen table—so wrapped up in the gratifying act she did not give a flying leap if anyone discovered them.

Even now, hours later, her disquieted state of mind and body kept her pacing—a stranger to herself—that ember of sexual appetency becoming more discomforting by the moment. It gripped her—her chest, her stomach, and low, deep between her legs—a pressure that roused any time she thought of him, which was constantly.

She felt insane.

Dear God, would she never again experience a moment's peace? Would she never again manage to put this apparent obsession from her mind—this mindless devotion for a man who despised her literally?

When, exactly, had the fear she had first experienced over his appearance and savagery turned into willful duty; when had duty become comradeship; when had comradeship become fondness, and fondness into . . . what?

"No," she said aloud. "Daft girl, don't admit it even to yourself. You've not fallen in love with Salterdon. You wouldn't dare! To even falsely acknowledge such a ridiculous thought would force you to pack your pitiful bag and flee Thorn Rose this very minute. Imagine his reaction if he got wind of such an asinine thing. Imagine his grandmother's reaction!"

Imagine her *body's* reaction if he touched her again.

*   *   *

The morning dawned dreary and cold. Upon rising Maria wearily sponged herself the best she could with water from the ewer. She splashed her face, allowed the water to trickle down her neck while flashes of the day before paraded, one after another, across her mind's eye.

She thought, *I must be truly insane for remaining here. I should have insisted that Her Grace see me to Haworth. From there I could have gone anywhere—to London or Liverpool—far away from this awful lunacy. How can I face him again? How do I occupy the same room, the same house, the same damned country without being reminded of what I had nearly allowed to happen? Had he sat out to intentionally crush me he couldn't have succeeded more thoroughly.*

She walked to her window and nudged aside the heavy damask drape. The panes were coated with frosty ice; she rubbed a circle in it and peered out onto the bleak countryside. The house was silent yet. As silent as the gray hills.

A distant lantern from some tenant's house winked faintly in the mist and she recalled a time when she and Paul would sneak out of their bedroom window and run, with vapor pouring through their lips, to the cemetery at the top of the hill. From there, they would play a game of guessing which neighbor's window would flicker with light first, then second, then third . . . she always won, though she suspected Paul had allowed it. After all, she had never known anyone as clever as her brother. He had a solution for every problem.

If he were only here now, perhaps he could explain what was happening to her. Why she would continue to sacrifice her own sense of dignity in an attempt to help and encourage a man who wanted neither. Why she continued to tolerate his sarcasm, his taunts, his belligerence, his degrading insinuations. Why had her philanthropic objectives (not to mention her duties as companion) suddenly become confused with this all-consuming ache to be physically near him every waking minute—despite his extreme arrogance, and bitterness—despite his behavior last evening . . . *because* of his behavior last evening.

Heaven help her.

Sighing, she turned away from the window and froze. Molly stood just inside the room, hip cocked to one side and her arms crossed over her chest. As usual, her cap looked crumpled and her hair streamed in strands from beneath it.

"Well now," Molly declared. "Seems yer just full of surprises, Miss Ashton."

"What are you talking about? And who gave you permission to come into my room without knocking?"

"I'm takin' 'bout 'im, o'course. Yer vis'tor."

"Visitor?"

"Ya mean ya ain't heard?" Molly chuckled. "I reckon not. 'E arrived fairly late last evenin'. You was a'ready abed, I suppose."

"Not my father," she said aloud, the panic in her voice causing Molly's eyebrows to lift.

"I reckon ye'll find out soon enough. 'E's takin' coffee in the blue salon with the duchess."

With that, Molly turned on her heels, and with a last taunting laugh, left the room.

Dear God, not her father. Surely not her father. He would not dare antagonize the duchess by coming here unannounced.

She dressed quickly, then brushed out her hair, braiding it so tightly her head began to ache, making certain every hair was in place before scrubbing her face once, then twice, until she reminded herself that she was not a child any longer and would not be forced to stand still for his inspections, terrified that he would discover a solitary smudge of dirt—cleanliness was next to godliness, of course.

Should she check on Salterdon?

No. Not yet. She would need all of her strength for the confrontation ahead.

She fled the room, running almost blindly down the dimly lit corridor. Why had he come? To force her to return home? Perhaps her mother was ill—oh, please, not her mother . . .

The door of the blue salon was closed. Her heart pounding, her body shaking, Maria paused at the threshold, briefly closed her eyes, then pushed open the door.

At the distant end of the salon a man sat with his back to her, conversing softly with the duchess, who looked up from her regal chair and acknowledged Maria with a lift of one eyebrow.

"She's here now," came the duchess's muted voice.

The visitor stood and turned.

"John!" she cried, relief causing her knees to slightly

buckle; then she ran down the long room, forgetting all propriety, and, as she had since she was a child, flung herself into his outstretched arms.

He laughed and held her tightly, but briefly, before taking hold of her arms in a firm fashion and pushing her away. "Maria." He laughed again. "I see you've not changed a whit. Look at you, lass; just as full of verve and impishness as you were the day you left Huddersfield."

"It hasn't been so long ago," she bantered.

The duchess put her cup and saucer aside. "Mr. Rees arrived late last evening. We thought it best not to wake you, my dear."

"But why have you come?" she asked, searching John's familiar features, which had so enthralled her the last years—*before* coming to Thorn Rose. "Is Mother well?"

"Your mother is fine. And so is your father," he added more sternly. "Since I was in the area I promised your mother I'd drop by and say hello, and to check on you, of course, to make certain you're well and happy." Catching her chin with one finger, he frowned and asked softly, "Are you happy, Maria?"

"It seems," said the duchess, "that word of the county's trouble with highwaymen has reached Huddersfield."

"We're quite safe here," Maria assured him, backing away and averting her face. Few people knew her as well as John. She could detect from the concerned and suspicious look in his eyes that he did not for a moment believe her.

Glancing about the palatial room, John said, "Apparently so."

The duchess left her chair. "I'm certain the two of you should like a few moments of privacy. Breakfast will be served in an hour. I hope you'll join us, Mr. Rees."

He bowed slightly. "Thank you, Your Grace."

The duchess left the room; only then did John turn back to face Maria, where she sat on a bench before the brightly dancing flames in the hearth. She regarded him pensively. "You don't approve of Thorn Rose, I take it."

"Can I be faulted for believing that the monies spent decorating this room alone would feed and house the hungry and homeless of three counties?"

"Dear John, you'll never change." She smiled brightly, or tried to, and patted the bench seat beside her. "Come here where it's warm."

There came a moment's hesitation, then he moved almost woodenly to the bench and slowly lowered himself onto it. He held his hands, palms up, toward the fire. He said, "I must admit I don't altogether approve of your companioning such a man as Salterdon. We were all under the impression you were to nursemaid a child."

"So was I."

"Yet you've remained."

"As the Bible says, 'We are our brother's keeper.' Besides . . . he's harmless." She blushed at the lie. The memory of Salterdon's behavior the previous night pressed like a hot poker at her temples.

"I would have little qualms about your remaining

here if the duke wasn't known for his enormously and flagrantly shocking reputation with . . . women."

Tipping her head, lightly touching his arm, she smiled. "Were you any other man, John, I would take this concern for jealousy."

He stared at her for a long, intense moment before suddenly leaving his place beside her. Pacing, he asked, "Have you given any serious thought to coming home?"

"Oh, yes." She nodded, laughing a little to herself. "All the time."

Spinning around, his long black clergy's coat swirling around his legs, he opened his arms enthusiastically and cried, "Praise the Lord! My journey here will not have been for nothing. I'll speak to the duchess immediately, of course. We'll explain that after much consideration—"

"No."

"I beg your pardon?"

"I'm not leaving."

"But you just said—"

"That I've thought of it frequently." She shook her head. "There's nothing for me there, John."

"And what have you here? Never mind. That's most obvious, I suppose. I could hardly supply you with these decadently lavish accoutrements, even if I chose to."

"My reasons for not marrying you had nothing to do with what you were willing or unwilling to give me monetarily."

Standing, Maria moved to him. Tall and slender, he watched her fiercely, his dark eyes turbulent, his face flushed with emotion. As always, the battle raged inside him; it was there in each tiny pearl of sweat forming on his brow, in the tremble of his body, the almost agonized twist of his mouth. Only this time, she was struck with the realization that like a desperate man balanced upon a lip of an abyss, the smallest encouragement would cause him to plummet over the edge. He would succumb to his desire for her. Would give up everything to have her. That was really why he had come, whether he realized it or not.

As she stood there, staring up into his despondent face, her hand frozen on the verge of caressing his cheek, the many times she had wept into her pillow for want of his undivided attention flooded her memory— how she would have done anything to win him away from his obsessive devotion to God—and now she could. He had come here to be seduced from that obsession. At long last, he had made his choice, and the unnerving truth occurred to her that her former reasons for wanting this man had had nothing to do with love, or even desire—God help her, she now knew true desire . . . and love. Her father's handsome young curate had offered her a means of escaping her father . . .

Now that she had escaped her father, did she care enough for John to spend the rest of her life with him?

A noise sounded behind her. She looked around, her heart seeming to skip in her breast, and her breath to catch.

"Salterdon," she said aloud. "Your Grace."

Salterdon moved his chair out of the shadows and into the room, and the air became electric. His hair was tousled, as if he had just climbed out of bed—just as he had looked last evening, when he had kissed her and demanded more of her than she had been willing to surrender at the time. His face looked red from exertion, and unshaved. His white shirt looked damp with perspiration.

"I wasn't aware we had visitors," he said. "Normally, the head of the house is informed when guests arrive. Then again it's normal for a domestic to seek permission from their employer before entertaining her or his guests."

John stepped forward. "Your Grace, I'm—"

"I know who you are are. A . . . friend?"

"I've known Maria for years, since she was no bigger than this." He held one hand waist high and flashed her an embarrassed smile. "I lived with her family during my tenure as curate to her father."

His lips curling, Salterdon said in a low smooth voice, "She's hardly a child now. Wouldn't you agree?" He wheeled his chair toward them, stopping short of the lamplight, yet his eyes reflected the firelight like icy glass. "Please, don't let me interrupt your conversation. I believe you were about to convince the young woman to return to Huddersfield with you."

Maria stepped toward him. "You've been eavesdropping. How long were you there?"

"Long enough."

"Have I no right to privacy?"

"You have no rights at all as far as I'm concerned. So tell me, Mr. Rees, have you come here to steal Maria away from me?"

John lowered his eyes.

"I should consider my vows before answering, if I were you. The church doesn't take kindly to lying."

"Yes . . ." He smiled at Maria. "I came with news that I hoped would change her mind about returning to Huddersfield. I came to tell her that I've been offered the position of vicar in Bristol."

"John," she cried happily. "That's wonderful!"

"Yes." He nodded. "I'll be supplied a comfortable house, and the tithes, I understand, are more than adequate to keep our larders full."

"Our?"

"I've come to ask you for your hand in marriage, Maria."

"Isn't that sweet," Salterdon murmured in a deceptively pleased tone, his eyes narrowing, his lips becoming firmly pressed together. "But you seem to forget that she's made a commitment to me."

"None that cannot be broken . . . Your Grace. Above all else I would have Maria happy."

"Is Maria *un*happy?"

By an act of will, Maria kept her face composed as she responded, "Yes, Your Grace. Maria is very unhappy to be talked about as if she were little more than a bloody mote of dust in the air."

"Maria," John scolded. "Remember yourself."

Salterdon threw back his head in laughter. "Obviously you don't know Miss Ashton as well as you think, Mr. Rees."

"Maria has always been . . . spirited."

"Is that what belligerence and rebelliousness is known as these days?"

"If you're so disenchanted with her," John stated calmly, and with a patient smile, "then you should have no qualms over allowing her to leave."

There came a rap at the door. Thaddeus entered the room, dragging his cap from his head. "The duchess says for me to inform His Grace and Miss Ashton that she'll be takin' her ride in an hour. She respectfully requests that they join her."

"I've seen the house," said John. "It's very pretty. There are three rooms: a mid-size parlor/kitchen arrangement, and two loft bedrooms . . . one for us, as well as for our children . . . certainly should we need more room we can always build on." He cleared his throat as color crept into his fair cheeks. The coffee in his cup had long since grown cold, yet he continued to stare into it as if it offered some sense of strength, and the courage he was so apparently lacking.

"The cottage is set among a copse of gigantic elm trees, and there are well-tended garden areas, which receive a great deal of sun. The soil is rich and black, which accounts for the locals' great success with their crops. I assure you, Maria, you would not want for comfort."

"Tell me about the church."

"'Tis small yet, but growing. I've met with several members of the congregation and found them warm and friendly."

"Have you spoken to my father on the matter?"

"I have."

"And what did he say?"

At last, John set aside his cup and saucer. "I was reminded that you are no longer his daughter, and that should I decide to sacrifice my life to wed one so morally corrupt then he would pray for my soul every day for the remainder of his life."

John looked at her at last. "I thought you would be pleased over my proposal."

"I'm only taken off guard."

"It's not as if we haven't spoken of this before. I recall a time when you twittered for hours about spending our lives together. You vowed to love me more than anyone else in the world."

"Aye, but as I recall you were most adamant about not returning the compliment. Your one great love is God, John. Or has that changed?"

"You're well aware of my devotion—"

"To God. Only to God."

"And to you."

The day was overcast and bitter. As Maria stepped from the house, she paused, catching her breath and blinking her eyes, focusing on the coach at the bottom of the stairs, and its only occupant.

John regarded her closely. "Are you afraid of him?" he asked.

"Do I appear to fear His Grace?"

"You appeared disturbed by him. A moment in his company and you became . . ."

"What?" She looked up at him.

"Tense."

"He hasn't the best of temperaments."

" 'Twasn't that sort of tenseness, I'm afraid."

She looked around as Thaddeus joined them, a full-length sable cape tossed over his arm. He carried a sable muffler and a hat whose wide brim was sable as well. "Yer to wear these," he announced, and thrust them toward her, his gaze, sharp as a lance, flashing toward John.

Even in the dullness of the day the thick, rich fur shone like black fire. "I couldn't," she said. "Tell Her Grace—"

"Don't belong to Her Grace. They belong to him." Thaddeus nodded toward the carriage, his lips curling in something less than a smile. "Or rather one of his last paramours. His Grace felt these would keep you warmer than *that lot of rags,* as he called yer own."

"Did he?" she said, feeling her cheeks grow warm. "Well, you may tell His Grace . . . never mind, Thaddeus, I'll tell him myself." Snatching the heavy cloak, slipping on a thin coat of ice covering the steps, she marched the best she could to the coach and flung open the door. Sunk in his seat, the fur collar of his own coat pulled up around his ears and his hat brim shielding his dark eyes, Salterdon slowly turned his head and regarded her.

"I don't want your mistresses' furs, Your Grace. I would rather freeze—"

She let go a cry as he closed his gloved hand around her arm and dragged her into the coach, slamming the door as she dropped into the plush seat with a gasp of indignation; then he called out the window to John, who had started down the steps the instant Salterdon forced her into the conveyance, "I believe the duchess has taken ill, Mr. Rees. I'm certain your company and a prayer would benefit her more than your attempts of heroism toward Miss Ashton ever will."

Stopping at the top of the steps, his face bright red in the gloomy day and the wind whipping his cloak furiously around his legs, John said nothing as Thaddeus hurried to the coach and handed the hat and muffler through the window, then scrambled up to the driver's seat. With a last malicious smile, Salterdon snatched closed the shade and sank back in his seat, his gaze now locked on Maria where she shook irately across from him.

"You have no right, or reason, to treat me so despicably in front of my guest, Your Grace."

"I have the right to do anything I goddamn want, Miss Ashton. I could pitch your beloved vicar out on his ear, should I decide to do so." A smile curling one corner of his lips, he added, "One word from me and he could be excommunicated from the entire church."

"Why would you want to? He's done nothing to you—"

"Hasn't he?"

"Tell me what he's done."

"Trespassed."

"By coming to Thorn Rose?"

He sank in the seat. His features became closed. Spine conforming to the cushion, long legs slightly splayed and swaying with each motion of the coach, he continued to regard her with such intensity her entire body turned as rigid and cold as the icicles forming on the distant tree limbs.

Finally, he said, "Do you intend to leave with him?"

"I've hardly had time to consider it."

"Do you love him?"

"That is none of your business."

"If it affects my future it is my business."

"Yes!" she cried furiously. "I did . . . I do . . . he's . . . he's been a loyal and trustworthy friend since I was a child. As I was growing up my greatest dream was to marry him."

"He would never make you happy."

"You don't know him."

"I know he loves God more than he loves you. If that weren't true, you wouldn't be at Thorn Rose now."

Huddled deep into the corner of the plush seats, she stared out the window, tried to focus on the scattering of crystallized trees and the drifts of ever-deepening snow.

"I don't for a minute think he could make you happy," Salterdon said. "You're the type of woman who'll expect one hundred percent of her husband's attention. You'll demand it, of course, and if you don't get it you'll cheat."

She slapped his face.

He only laughed. "You'll destroy him, little by little. You'll shred his loyalties. He'll preach about adultery and sins of flagrant copulation to his mesmerized masses, then he'll return home to a wife who wraps her beautiful white thighs around him and demands more of his body and soul than he's capable of giving, because every time he buries his body in you, God is going to be there tapping him on the shoulder, reminding him of his priorities."

"You'll despise any man who can . . ." She bit her lip.

"Can what, Miss Ashton? Make love to a woman?" He laughed softly. "There can be a vast difference between fucking and making love. Take us, for instance . . . Were I capable, I could toss up your skirts, glide my body into yours and take my pleasure as quickly or slowly as I so desire. On the other hand, I could forget about my own enjoyment and focus totally on yours— never finding the need to bury myself between your beautiful legs at all."

"Stop it," she cried, and covered her ears with her hands. "I want to go back to Thorn Rose now. I demand it!"

He leaned forward, caught the hem of her skirt with one finger, and eased it up.

His eyes seemed almost catlike in the cold gloaming— they held her transfixed and incapable of responding. Oh God, why could she not move? Why could she not claw his arrogant face? Why could she not cry out for Thaddeus to save her?

His fingertips brushed her calf, and she gasped. They slid up, and up, to the bend of her knee, then to her thigh, and when she attempted to draw her legs together, he nudged them apart with a flick of his fingers.

"Come here, Miss Ashton," he said, and reached for her with his other hand, curling his arm around her shoulders as she leaned toward him like some helpless puppet. She might have whispered "No" "Don't" "Can't." But the words buzzed incoherently in her brain and defied what her body craved—had craved since the night before.

She slumped into the seat beside him, head fallen back, offering her throat to his open mouth that breathed wet, warm vapor on her flesh before he gently sank his teeth into her skin, touching her skin with his hot tongue and lips while his hand cupped the throbbing mound between her legs and stroked the aroused cleft as gently as he had his beloved piano keys.

It was not a conscious decision; her mind did not voluntarily capitulate; but her body had become an entity of its own. For hours—days—it had sought a kind of release, foreign as it was, that only he could give her—he—the duke—her master—with his burning, taunting eyes and surly lips and wolfish disposition. She had become like Molly, a prisoner of her own desires.

His mouth found hers and ravaged—teeth, lips, tongue—making low guttural sounds in his throat while he sank his fingers deep inside her, causing her arms and legs to thrash, her mouth to open further, her breasts to press against his hard body, her hips to writhe, her legs to quiver, to spread, to curl around his own while she ground her body against his hand and whimpered and strained, finally tearing her mouth from his and throwing back her head, losing herself completely to the magic his hands conjured inside her, around her, turning the frigid air into cauldron heat.

And then he stopped.

"Please, please," she heard herself plead, though she did not know exactly what she was pleading for, only an end to her misery, that glorious surcease she had seen on Molly's face—that heavenly ecstasy Paul had whispered about that came from joining with someone you—

"Hush," he said and slapped his hand across her mouth. His body rigid, he flung back the window drapery, allowing a rush of cold air to hit their faces.

The countryside flashed by as the conveyance swayed with each bounce of its wheels. Then the sound: a gunshot, voices shouting.

"Bastards," he said through his teeth, then, hefting himself partially out the window, shouted to Thaddeus, "Can we make it back to Thorn Rose? Damn you, man, answer me!"

"We're no match for their horses!" Thaddeus shouted back.

"Do your best, goddammit!"

"Aye, Yer Grace."

Salterdon fell back into his seat, and when he turned to Maria again his face looked damp and frigid. Grabbing her skirt, he yanked it down over her knees. She could not move, could not think. Her entire body felt wound like a clock spring that would shatter at any moment.

With a growl of exasperation, Salterdon curled his fingers into her forearms and shook her. "Snap out of it, Maria. Dammit, listen to me." He shook her again, just as a cacophony of gunshots rang out. The coach shook, careened to one side, then the other, forcing Salterdon to grab hold of the squabs to steady himself.

Then the world appeared to blur, to turn topsy-turvy. Salterdon threw himself against her, wrapped his hard arms around her, and dragged her up against him as the conveyance seemed to float momentarily in the air, its windows and seats shifting in an odd arc around them before falling, slamming into the ground and rolling end over end, until reality became black as midnight.

Chapter Thirteen

Salterdon awoke slowly, shaking with cold.

"Simpleminded bastard, wot the blazes were ya about? Ye've gone and killed 'em, no doubt. Imagine the sort of trouble we'll be in for murderin' a bloody duke."

"We were only 'avin' a bit o' sport. Wot's it to ya? Ya gone and sprung scruples on us or wot?"

The voices faded.

He drifted.

When he opened his eyes again it seemed the chill had bored into his bones. Raising his head, he took in the scene: the scarred and razed snow, the scattering of lines and harnesses (fast becoming covered by falling snow), the almost indecipherable form of a dead horse. And beyond that, at the bottom of the craggy hill, crushed and crumpled into a mess of splintered black wood and what was left of velvet casings, ripped and strewn over the white snow like streaks of crimson blood, was the coach.

"Maria," he said aloud in the still air, then shouted it, "Maria!" while doing his best to pull himself up on a boulder, out of the snow. His head throbbed. His fingers burned. The image in his mind of her frail body crushed within the tangle of debris made him groan. He drove his fist into the rock until the pain overwhelmed him, and he collapsed, rolling onto his back in the snow. He closed his eyes.

A sound.

A sigh.

A murmur.

Rousing, he looked around.

The cleft of rock whereon he lay curved to the right and was crowned by a beard of brushwood and thistle. Near the crest, rimmed by shear black rock, lay a form. Salterdon pulled himself up onto the boulder again, blinked the frozen water from his eyes, and focused.

Maria!

He clawed his way to her, found her lying on her back in the snow, her hair a silver web around her head. She was shoeless. Her small pink toes peeked through holes in her stockings. Her chin was scuffed. A large purple knot had begun to rise just above her left eye.

Upon dragging his body up against hers, he slid his arms around her and pulled her close. She moaned, moved, rolled her head toward his as her eyelashes fluttered open.

"Your Grace?"

"Don't move. Don't talk. Jesus." He laughed in relief. "I thought you were dead."

"Do I look dead, sir?"

"Dreadfully dead, my love. Like an angel. A snow angel, with ice-crystal lips."

"I'm cold, sir."

"Come here. Careful. Can you move?" He managed to open his coat, and collecting her pliant body against his, closed the cloak around her. She nestled against him, her form molding to his, the top of her head barely reaching his chin. Her slender arms wrapped around him; one leg drew over his hip and thigh as if she were some sated lover ready to nap.

He kissed the top of her head, which smelled like snow-drenched violets. She snuggled again and murmured, "Not to worry, Your Grace. I'm here if you should need me."

If you should need me.

Christ, how deliciously innocent.

Occasionally, he ran his hands up and down her arms; he kneaded her back, massaged her neck—anything to kindle her body warmth as the minutes crawled into hours and the daylight dwindled.

Where the blazes was Thaddeus? Had he gone over the precipice with the coach and horses?

Certainly someone would come looking for them soon. The storm was escalating, the winds groaning and sending sprays of snow driving like sharp little needles through the air. He did not dare close his eyes; he would die. *She* would die.

He held her tighter, shook her, roused her from her dreamy state, forced her to look at him squarely. Her wide blue eyes rimmed in ice reflected a dullness that speared him with panic.

"Talk to me," he demanded.

Her eyes drifted closed.

He covered her mouth with a hard kiss, holding her chin while his fingers bracketed her jaw. He kissed her harder, forcing open her lips, sliding his tongue inside her—she moved and groaned—"Kiss me," he said through his teeth, and felt her body flutter. Her breathing escalated. Her cold skin turned warm and supple, and she moaned deep in her throat.

His hand moved down her chest, found her breast, closed on it gently at first, then harder, rougher, until he felt her small hands twist into the shirt on his back. Her leg drew him closer, so close he could feel the heat between her thighs. She turned her soft open mouth against his shoulder and sighed deeply.

His blood warmed.

His brow began to sweat.

Heart pounding, he dragged his hands out of her clothes, folded his arms around her and crushed her to his chest . . . until her breathing became even again, until she lay quietly in his arms. Turning his face into the falling snow, he began to laugh. He laughed so hard tears leaked from the corners of his eyes and grew thick as treacle on his freezing cheeks.

At last, Maria raised her head and blinked at him. Her blue lips whispered, "I fail to see what's so funny about freezing to death."

Grabbing her face between his hands, he said, "Maria . . . my toes are cold."

She frowned.

"Maria . . . my legs hurt."

"Your legs?"

He nodded and kissed her fully on the mouth before laughing again.

Woozily, Maria struggle to her knees. Conscious at last to the import of his discovery, she fumbled with her hands down his body, to his legs, and squeezed.

"Yes!" he cried out, and beat the snow with his fists. "I can feel that, Maria."

"And there?"

"Yes!"

"Here? Can you move them?"

Gritting his teeth, he tried—nothing—then tried again. Exhausted, he fell back in the snow, took a long deep breath then . . .

"Your Grace!" she cried. "Your foot. Did you move it?"

He nodded and forced himself up on his elbows. Perched on her knees, her flimsy cape a pitiful barrier from the cruel elements, she appeared little more than a spectre in the failing light and driving snow. Hands clasped at her chin, her face turned up toward the heavens, she wept so softly he barely heard her.

"Come here before you freeze," he said.

"Nay, not until I've thanked God for His favor," she replied.

"If you don't come here and keep me warm, Miss Ashton, I fear both of us will be speaking to God face to face before long."

"But—"

"God is patient, lass. I'm not." Grabbing her arm, he pulled her down, wrapped his wool and fur coat around her shivering frame and concentrated on the tingling sensation working up his leg, from his toes to his calves to his knees. Damn if he could not wiggle his toes. If he tried hard enough, he might manage his ankle—

"Think how thrilled and relieved your family will be," Maria said against his chest.

His smile faded.

"You can go on with your life now, just as you had planned. You'll be as good as new. Imagine the duchess's pleasure—"

"Hush, Maria."

"She'll—"

"Be quiet!" he shouted, then digging his fingers into her upper arms, lifted her up to face level and shook her fiercely. "You're not to breathe a word of this to anyone. Not to Edgcumbe. Not to my grandmother. Do you understand me, Maria?"

"Nay, I don't understand."

"Promise me. Swear it. Not a solitary word until I'm ready."

At last, she nodded. Again, he wrapped his arms around her and stared unseeing through the flying snow.

For two days Maria lay in her bed shivering first with cold, then with fever. Gertrude slipped in and out of the room, mopping her brow, stoking the fire. Now and again snippets of conversation came to her, but the words made no sense. Faces came and went: Gertrude's, whose brow was constantly creased in concern; Edgcumbe's, which regarded her as if she were some specimen to be poked and prodded.

Once, she roused enough to recognize John's face smiling down at her. His hands were cool when he touched her brow, and soft. Other times . . . his hands felt warm and strong. They cupped her face in so caressing a manner she wanted to weep. Those times always came late at night, when the fire had dwindled to glowing embers; when only a solitary lamp near her bed filled the immense quiet with soft hissing.

She dreamt they were her master's hands. That the litany of *"Maria, Maria, don't die"* whispered near her ear were spoken by Salterdon's lips.

Had she imagined it all in her feverish mind? Had he held her? Touched her? Kissed her?

And had she realized, at long last, that she had fallen hopelessly in love with the Duke of Salterdon?

On the fourth day she awoke with a clear head and sat straight up in bed. John sat in a chair near the fire, his head bent over the open Bible in his lap. He looked up, surprised.

"His Grace," she cried. "Where is he?"

Putting aside the Book, John left the chair.

Maria scrambled from the bed, swayed back and forth, clutched the bedpost for support, then stumbled toward Salterdon's bedroom door.

"Wait!" John called, and ran after her.

Flinging open the door, she fled into the chamber, paused only long enough to note that his bed was empty—she scanned the room—her sight locking at once on his form in the wheeled chair by the window. With a cry of relief, she dashed over the carpeted floor, and throwing her arms around his shoulders, pressing his shaggy head against her bosom, she wept, "You're alive! Thank God. Precious master—" She covered the top of his head with kisses. "You saved my life. How can I repay you?"

John looped his arm around her waist and tugged her away. She fought him, arms and legs flailing.

"Stop this," John demanded.

"Nay, I won't! Can't you see that he needs me?" At last, she managed to shove John away. Turning to Salterdon again, she dropped to the floor and flung herself upon Salterdon's knees. She grabbed his hand and clutched it to her breast.

His features appeared haggard, his face unshaven. Staring out over the frozen countryside, his eyes looked glazed and vacant as glass.

"No. Not again," she told him frantically. "You won't hide from me—from us again. I would rather die than lose you again to that dreadful madness!"

Briefly, he closed his eyes; his shoulders drooped.

Wearily, Maria lay her head on his lap and entwined her fingers through his. "I didn't imagine it," she whispered. "You're not insane. You're not ill. And your legs—"

He touched one fingertip to her lips. Lifting her head, she regarded his countenance and his eyes that were far from remote now, and regarding her so fixedly she could scarcely swallow.

"You promised," he breathed. "You promised."

"You can't imagine how frightened we were when Thaddeus returned to Thorn Rose looking as if he had been beaten with a cudgel. He babbled frantically about thieves and a mishap—of the coach careening from the road and plummeting down the hillside. I thought I had lost you . . . again."

John reached across the lap tray and took the cup and saucer from her. "My relief upon finding you alive was too great to fathom. Since you left Huddersfield I continued to tell myself that you would come back— that once experiencing the ofttimes harsh and cruel realities of the world you would come flying back to the security of your own home. As days turned into weeks I realized that I had been too complacent in my expectations. I should never have allowed you to leave in the first place. I want you to come back to Huddersfield with me. We'll be married. We'll go immediately to Bristol—"

"No," she said softly.

Without looking at her, John left his chair. He proceeded to pace back and forth before the fire. "You need never have to see your father again, Maria. We'll make arrangements for your mother—"

"No."

He paused his step, held his hand over his eyes for a few moments, then turned his grave, quiet, affectionate smile on her again. His voice, at first tremulous, and always low, was touched with a solemnity that reflected how intensely moved he felt. "I shouldn't ask it, but I must. God forgive me, but I must. Is there something between the two of you? Between you and that . . . the duke."

"What do you mean?" she averted her face.

"I was there when you were found together at the base of that chasm. It was I who pulled you from his arms. No, I see that you don't remember. You wouldn't. You were sleeping as soundly as a baby with your head on his shoulder."

Color drained from his face. "Are you in love with him, Maria? No. Don't answer me. The scene I witnessed earlier convinced me. Maria. Maria. 'Tis a tired cliche; a domestic falling in love with her employer and he taking advantage—"

"He hasn't," she cried hotly. "He wouldn't."

"Does he love you? Has he proclaimed himself thus?"

"Nay!"

"But you believe it here." He thumped his chest. "You want it . . . here. Maria, don't you see; his kind gobble up children like you then toss them aside. You want to believe in fairy tales, Maria. You always have. But reality isn't like that. Reality is stability. Strength. The ability to make intelligent choices and to reach intelligent conclusions rationally with the mind—not the heart.

"You were always mindlessly devoted to the helpless. To the broken. To the dispirited. You hoped your devotion would endear you to them. You wanted them to love you . . . . didn't you realize, sweet Maria, that they would have loved you regardless?"

He picked up his Bible and turned it over and over in his hands, then he muttered, "The devil with it," and strode angrily toward Salterdon's door.

"What are you doing?" she demanded, and flung the

counterpane aside. "Where are you going? Leave him alone, John. John!"

Reaching the threshold, she sank against it as John's voice reverberated through the quiet.

"Were I not a man of God I would see you at dawn. I would demand satisfaction. Tell me, sir, have you spoiled her?"

Salterdon gazed into the fire, his countenance fixed. At last, he said in a monotone, "Do I look like a man who could *spoil* a woman, Mr. Rees?"

"Are you aware that she's in love with you? Do you even care? Of course not. Your kind never do. You collect women's hearts and souls as if they were mere butterflies to assemble under glass. Were you any kind of gentleman at all you would direct her immediately to gather her things and leave with me for Huddersfield."

"But I'm not a gentleman, Mr. Rees . . . as you have so adeptly reminded me."

John looked up then and saw her, clinging to the doorframe, her gown forming a pale pool around her little feet, her sleep-tousled hair a halo around her head. He swallowed convulsively and moved toward the distant exit—obviously too shaken to go near her.

"John," she called. "Friend!"

Swinging around, he shouted, "Friend? I would rather rot in hell than be considered your friend—*only* your friend."

He trembled and for a brief moment looked as if he yearned to escape the torture of seeing her there and knowing then that he would be forced to leave her to another. That this perhaps would be the last hour—the last moment—that he would stand in her presence, hearing her voice, receiving the tokens of her unconscious affection. He gazed with mad, dumb passion on her stricken features before saying, "God help you when you finally realize what he is. God help you when you're forced to experience this terrible stab of rejection. *God help me* . . . but I'll be waiting . . ."

With that, he quit the room.

A stillness ensued, shaken only by the rattle of wind against the windows. The room felt frightfully cold.

At last, Salterdon looked up. "Come here," he ordered her.

She obeyed. Dropping to the floor at his booted feet, her shoulder toward the fire, she rested her head upon his knee and pulled her gown down over her toes. At last, he caught her chin with his fingers and forced her to look at him squarely. There was something dark and bothered about his face. His cheeks looked flushed, and there were strong workings in his features. An odd light lit his eyes.

"You should have gone with him," he said.

Chapter Fourteen

There come at times in life deep, still pauses; when the spirit rests upon its full content, as a child lies down on the grass of a meadow, fearing nothing, desiring nothing, ceasing almost to think, and satisfied only to feel. The days following John's leave from Thorn Rose Maria existed in a sort of rapture. What else could she call it? For the first time she exhilarated in her own frailty, looking forward to those moments when her master would join her. For hours he would read to her; he fed her soup; he sat near the fire—not so far away—and scribbled musical notes on paper when he thought she was sleeping.

He seemed, in those moments, like a soul adrift, hearing music where none existed except in his mind.

Where now was the beast? The dragon? The wolf?

Lost in a sonata.

She gave herself to a dreamy kind of delight—there seemed over her a sort of golden haze through which all her life's realities, bitter and sweet, were seen from afar like shadows. The world beyond her chamber ceased to exist.

Occasionally, she dreamt that she awoke from a deep sleep to discover Salterdon's chair empty before the fire; he stood at the end of her bed, his arms crossed over his chest, his face a mixture of pain and promise.

Those were the times she fought her awakening. Oh, but she was beginning to understand why Salterdon found more solace lost deep in the oblivion of his mind. The illusions were so much kinder there . . .

Alas, duty forced her from her bed as, after a week's recuperation the duchess requested her appearance in the blue room. As Gertrude brushed and plaited Maria's hair, preparing her for the meeting with the duchess, the housekeeper regarded Maria's reflection in the mirror.

"Yer right radiant," Gertrude told her.

"I've never been happier, I think," Maria replied with a smile.

Her eyebrows raised and her little red mouth pursed in concentrated effort, Gertrude ventured, "I reckon I ain't never seen 'Is Grace in quite so congenial a mood . . . that is, after 'e got over 'is concern for ya."

"Was he concerned, Gerti?"

"Hardly left yer bedside, 'cept to wheel down to the music room. Thrice I found him deep in the night makin' music on that pianoforte." Bending toward Maria's ear, she said softly, "I think 'e's become quite enchanted with ya, lass. And if I'm any judge, I'd say the feelin's are mutual."

Gertrude then presented Maria with a freshly laundered and mended gown and, upon wrapping a shawl securely about her shoulders, ushered her to the blue room, just as Molly was exiting, her normal smirk a bit more self-righteous than usual.

"I ain't right sure I like the looks o' her," Gertrude muttered, and continued to eye Molly as the girl sauntered down the corridor, glancing back over her shoulder occasionally, and still smirking.

Maria found the duchess poised by the hearth. Edgcumbe hovered nearby.

"Your Grace." Maria curtsied.

"I trust you're better?" the duchess offered with an odd sort of aloofness in her tone.

"Much, thank you."

As the duchess nodded at Gertrude, the housekeeper hurried to collect the scattering of cups and saucers around the room.

The duchess gazed up at a portrait of her husband. Young, handsome, imposing, he was the epitome of aristocracy—as was the portrait of his son—the former Duke of Salterdon—which hung next to his father's.

"I look at these images," she said, "and I am filled with despair. For generations this family has prided itself on its distinguished heritage. Scandal was virtually nonexistent. Failure was not a word in our vocabulary. Now . . ." She sighed and lowered her head. "I am constantly bombarded by controversy. Is it any wonder why I am forced to continually seclude myself in shame?"

"There, there, Isabella." Edgcumbe took the duchess's hand and stroked it fondly. "It will all work out."

A soft smile turned up her mouth as she gently pulled

away from the adoring physician. She then turned her attentions to Maria.

"I'm relieved, my dear, that you're better. You might have been grievously injured, if not killed. Were it not for my grandson's rather . . . heroic measures, you might have frozen to death."

She added in a low, contemplative tone, "Imagine my surprise when I was informed that the coach departed without me. I was even further stunned to learn that I was supposedly ill and could not join you . . . Trey has a most vivid imagination when it suits him. Still, I suppose it's rather fortuitous that I didn't accompany you as I had intended as I rather doubt I would have survived such a tumble. Still in all, I'm not accustomed to being undermined, especially by my eldest grandson. Trey has always had a proclivity for bending over backwards to please—or appease me, should the need arise . . . which it did on more occasions than I choose to remember . . . unlike his brother who has invited me to hell as many times as he has affectionately kissed my cheek.

"Early on I learned what sort of shenanigans to expect from Clayton. Roughhousing with a lot of plowman's boys wasn't unusual. I wasn't at all surprised to find him sitting at my dinner table sporting a black eye or skinned knees or knuckles as he grew older. As a young man he didn't have much time for nonsense; he was too busy making his own fortune so he wasn't dependent on mine.

"Trey, on the other hand, was busy depleting mine. Gambling. Womanizing. Occasionally I wondered if his actions stemmed from some buried animosity he might have harbored for me and my attempts to control his behavior . . ." Pausing, the duchess took a breath and appeared to collect her thoughts just long enough for Maria to offer softly:

"'Tis against human nature to be controlled, Your Grace."

Her eyebrows lifted. "Is it? Then why, I wonder, did he so ingratiate himself on me throughout the last years? I'll tell you why, my dear. Because there is nothing more important to Trey Hawthorne, the Duke of Salterdon, in this entire world than the power and position left to him by my husband and his father. The wealth he will inherit upon my demise is beyond your meager comprehension. He couldn't gamble away my fortune in a hundred lifetimes. Imagine the opportunity: the duration of his existence spent in unadulterated dissoluteness. Even now . . . regardless of his apparent condition . . . I suspect there is nothing he wouldn't do, or sacrifice, to guarantee my continued financial support.

"Against nature to be controlled, Miss Ashton? I think not. At least, not when a five-hundred-year-old ancestry depends on it. Aside from the monarchy itself, there is not another branch of the aristocracy that is more dependent upon its reputation, and the passing on of its heritage.

"But all of this rambling is neither here nor there. I didn't bring you here this morning to prattle on about our personal affairs. After much consideration, Miss Ashton, I feel it necessary to relieve you of your duties.

I'll make arrangements immediately to return you to Huddersfield."

Gripping the bedpost with one hand, Salterdon shifted his weight from one leg to the other, gritting his teeth against the discomfort that sliced like knives up the backs of his thighs. His body broke out in a sweat. His breathing caught as knots formed in the muscles just below his buttocks and burned like hot pokers all the way up his spine. He had managed so far to walk around the bed, holding fast to the posts and mattress. The temptation to fling himself onto the bed, to stop the excruciating pain, made him curse aloud. Instead, with his body sweating, he managed to turn, to focus on the distant, despicable and loathed chair in which he had spent the last grueling year of his life, and start back the way he had come.

The door flung open behind him.

He looked around, anticipating Maria—she would scold him, of course, for clambering out of that deviled steel contraption without her, then she would flit around like a fairy in enthusiasm over his accomplishment.

"Yer Grace!" cried Gertrude, and suddenly the rotund little housekeeper was beside him, her face flushed, her eyes wide as two farthings. "I know it ain't none of me own business, Yer Grace. I'm just a servant 'ere and wot goes on 'round me I'm to see and hear blind and deaf as a bleedin' poker, but I just come from the blue room, yer grace, where the duchess had called a meetin' with our Maria . . ."

The servant paused to take a much needed breath,

and as she continued to stare at Salterdon, the look of
angst on her features dissolved into stunned amaze-
ment.

"Bloody hell," she muttered. "Yer walkin'."

"Never mind that," he snapped, biting back the
discomfort gnawing at his lower body. "What the devil
is my grandmother up to?"

"She's gone and dismissed our Maria," Gertrude
replied, still in shock over finding Salterdon afoot.

"The hell you say. Get me that goddamn chair,
woman, and be quick about it."

The duchess waxed on about appreciation, about
continuing all financial support until Maria had located
another position. She would, of course, supply Maria
with a letter of recommendation, assuring Maria that
there would not be a door in England that would not be
open to her now that she had succeeded so smashingly
at Thorn Rose.

She would send a note immediately to Maria's
parents, informing them that she would be returning to
their home within the week. She would also send a short
message to John Rees . . . as she was certain Maria
would now reconsider the young man's offer of marriage.

"He'll make you a most appropriate companion, my
dear, being that he's of the same class. God should look
favorably on such a match of . . . equals.

"You must understand, my dear, that my reasons for
employing you were to bring about some form of
reformation to my grandson. Now that you have more

than adequately achieved that, Edgcumbe and I believe
the need for a companion is unnecessary and would
prove to be a waste of your valuable time."

A door opened.

The duchess looked around. Her features became
masked.

The sound of Salterdon's voice made Maria's knees
slightly buckle. She grabbed the back of a chair for
support but she refused to turn her face toward his. Her
disconsolateness was too raw. She would reveal her
emotions for what they were.

"Obviously someone forgot to inform me a meeting
had been arranged," came his deep, deceptively calm
voice as he moved his chair into the room.

"I thought it best not to disturb you," Edgcumbe
supplied with a slight bow and a smile that quickly
faded as Salterdon pinned him with a look.

"I wasn't aware that my actions were being dictated
by a mere physician . . . or have I already been exiled
to Royal Oaks?"

"Hardly," snapped the duchess.

He looked toward Maria. Still she refused to acknowledge him, but stared straight ahead, willing a
strength to her legs that was fast diminishing the longer
he regarded her.

At last, he spoke. "Rumor is you've decided that
Miss Ashton's services are no longer needed. I should
think I would be included in such a decision."

"I simply felt that due to your vast mental and
emotional improvement you're perfectly capable of
residing on your own. Besides, you've never been one

to care a great deal to participate actively in business resolutions, choosing instead to allow me to make whatever decision I thought best for your welfare and the future of our family. I think it best if Miss Ashton leave Thorn Rose."

With that, the duchess turned stiffly toward Maria and with a dismissive nod, said, "That will be all, my dear. I'll have my secretary draw up the necessary papers this afternoon."

How long she stood there, staring into the duchess's gray eyes, she could not fathom. What was she waiting for? Some miracle change of heart on the dowager's behalf? Perhaps to be informed that this sudden befuddling "business decision" was nothing more than a jest?

Or, God forbid, that she fling herself on her knees before the duchess and plead for her to reconsider—to explain what had brought on this sudden turn of events—beg the duchess not to send her away because the idea of never seeing her grandson again would prove to be more than she could bear.

Why did he not speak up? Say something? Do something?

Had she been so horribly naive that she had misread his feelings toward her? Mayhap the fondness in his eyes and smile had been some ruse to simply seduce her.

Somehow, Maria forced herself to curtsy, to woodenly turn toward the door, refusing to allow herself to look down at Salterdon.

He grabbed her arm.

She closed her eyes.

"No," he said.

"I beg your pardon?" replied the duchess.

"Miss Ashton will remain at Thorn Rose . . . until I see fit to dismiss her . . . As head of this family, I make the decisions on who we will employ, and when."

"As head of this family—?" Her tone mocked him.

"My birthright, grandmother . . . as you've reminded me for the last twenty-five years of my life." To Maria, he said, "Sit down, be quiet, and wait. There." He motioned toward a chair on the far side of the room.

"Your Grace," she whispered urgently. "I would not be the cause of a breach between you."

"Sit down," he stated more firmly, never taking his gaze from the duchess.

Maria crossed to the chair and sat, her fists buried within the worn folds of her skirt. She wondered if it were her past illness that made her feel as if she might faint.

Having taken her chair, the duchess regarded Salterdon with a fixed intensity, a flush of emotion on her normally pale cheeks, her frail, bejeweled fingers gripping the chair arms fiercely. It occurred to Maria in that instant that while the duchess, until her death, controlled the majority of the family wealth, Salterdon was in the position of authority. The sudden clash of wills resounded in the air between them.

Voice tight, lips thinned, the duchess finally said, "While I'm accustomed to butting heads with Clayton, I'm not inured to confrontations with Your Grace. Forgive me if I seem . . . taken aback. Obviously, I underestimated your dependency on Miss Ashton."

"Obviously."

Another silence ensued, making the stillness in the room almost palpable.

At last, the duchess took a deep breath, drummed her fingers on the chair arms and set her chin. "In light of this determination on your part, I will ask Your Grace if we might have privacy to discuss a rather important family matter."

"As Miss Ashton has accompanied me during some of my most private moments, I can't imagine what you could say that she won't, eventually, be subject to."

"Perhaps you're right." Raising one eyebrow, a smile drawing up one side of her mouth, her expression one of sudden excessive satisfaction, she said, "Of course you're right. As long as Miss Ashton remains at Thorn Rose, we might as well make the most of her abilities.

"The realization occurred to me last evening that because of your emotional and mental improvement and as portrayed by your behavior today, that you, as head of this family, will desire to give some thought to your responsibility to Lady Dunsworthy."

Lady Dunsworthy.

Maria fixed her gaze on a portrait of a boy and hound on the distant wall. Her body turned unbearably warm.

How had she forgotten Lady Dunsworthy?

The duchess said, "In case you were unaware, Miss Ashton, at the time of my grandson's mishap he was just one week from marrying Lady Laura Dunsworthy, a young woman of his peerage of whom I much approved. At the time of their joining I had intended to reward him with half of his inheritance—enough to see him fixed for the remainder of his life. Another quarter would be awarded him upon the birth of his first son.

"Certainly, after the tragic occurrence, all plans were put on hold. For the last year the young lady has patiently and devotedly waited for his improvement, at which time she fully intends to honor the vow she took to marry His Grace. She's quite beautiful. And bright. She'll eventually mature into a more than satisfactory duchess. As I recall . . . His Grace was most fond of her."

Focusing on her grandson again, she added, "I'm certain that His Grace will approve of my writing to Lord Dunsworthy informing him of Salterdon's vast improvement." Reaching for an envelope on a side table, she turned it over in her hand and said, "They'll be arriving day after tomorrow."

Maria locked her doors. She took to her bed. Throughout the remaining hours of the day, she stared up at St. Peter's image and considered this black turn of events was God's retribution for so vainly believing that she somehow fit into the duke's life as something other than a mere domestic.

Occasionally, someone came to her door and lightly knocked.

Long after dark, she quit the room, slipped through the deep shadows of the corridor and left the house.

The night was starless and cold. A wet drizzle crept into the folds of her thin cloak and clothes, making her flesh shiver and her bones ache. She fled to the stables. The horses were bedded down for the night. The grooms had long since turned in to their cots. For a long while Maria sat on the edge of an overturned crate, hugging herself, feeling her toes go numb with cold while around her the horses shuffled in their straw and occasionally let out a long, contented sigh.

She would leave Thorn Rose, of course. Life with her father would be preferable than spending these next weeks helping Salterdon prepare for his wedding to Lady Dunsworthy. The duchess's directives had been explicit:

"You'll work with His Grace until his speech is impeccable. Until he can eat and drink as effortlessly as he did before his injuries. You'll continually remind him of his obligations to this family, and to the future Duchess of Salterdon. If you care for Trey as much as I suspect you do, you'll concern yourself with his happiness and well-being. You'll not wish for him to be publicly humiliated or maligned in any way. Above all else, you'll consider his future, and the future of this family above your own happiness.

"Of course, I wouldn't demand such an undertaking with no promise of reward on your behalf. Once my grandson is married, I'll see that you're allocated a goodly sum of money—enough to purchase a cottage of your own . . . and enough allowance each month for the next ten years that you may comfortably care for yourself . . . and your mother which, as I recall, was your objective upon accepting this position in the first place."

What have I done—what sin have I committed other

than loving your grandson to bring this bleak burden upon me? she had yearned to scream at the duchess.

But that question in itself had brought a reply from her conscience:

The mistake, the sin, has been falling in love with a man who is, and will be, forever forbidden to you.

Terrible moment! To leave now would mean the end of her dream of helping her mother. To stay would mean she would be forced to see her beloved every day, to touch him . . . to make him ready to marry another woman.

Angrily, she drew her cloak about her and left the stable. She wandered the grounds, looking neither left nor right, barely noticing when a steady chill rain began to fall.

At last, she came upon a row of cottages far removed from the house and barns. Meager light emanated though the solitary window of each abode. Moving closer, shielding her eyes with one hand, she gazed through a window and noted a number of lads clustered about a table talking among themselves. At their hands were a scattering of objects she could not make out because of the rain.

Then Thaddeus moved to the window and appeared to search the dark outside the cottage.

Maria stepped behind a tree, wearily lay her head against it until she finally managed to rally her strength. With rain running down her cheeks, she returned to the manse.

Chapter Fifteen

Once, during a foray of good health and passably good spirit, her mother had taken Maria for a walk in the countryside. Just budding into womanhood and feeling not unlike an ugly duckling, Maria had spent the last days in a sort of mope: she had fallen hopelessly in love with a local landowner's son; he, of course, was infatuated with a young beauty of his peer who, as rumor had it, had spent a great deal of time on the Continent—who was proficient in foreign languages, played the harp, and sang like an angel.

With her mother holding Maria's hand, they paused in a field of wheat. For a brief moment, with the sun kissing her face and the breeze teasing her wisps of pale hair, Mary Ashton, the vicar's wife, had looked young and beautiful again. She had taken Maria's face between her hands and smiled.

"Daughter, it is a lesson worth learning by those young creatures who seek to lure by their accomplishments or dazzle by their genius, that though the man of

301

their devotion may admire them, no true gentleman ever loves a woman for these things. He loves her for her woman's nature and her woman's heart."

The memory of her mother on that summer day stayed with Maria that night after the duchess's announcement. It was the first thought in her mind when she roused the next morning and prepared herself to see Salterdon. It bolstered her courage as she paused outside his room, her hand on the door, her heart beating in her throat.

He would marry another woman.

Because of her, he would marry another woman.

She would nurse him, teach him, encourage him so he could marry another woman.

At last, she entered.

He sat at a desk, his back to her, his head and shoulders bent over a farrago of papers. Around him on the floor were papers: crumpled, torn, shredded. For an eternal minute Maria regarded the back of his head, his long waving hair that spilled softly over the collar of his dark blue suit coat. How many times had she touched that hair? Stroked it? Learned the heavy silken feel of it? Allowed those luxurious curls to twist around her fingers, to lay like shadows upon her pale skin?

He had no idea, of course.

"Your Grace," she finally called.

His head came up sharply, but he did not turn.

Maria moved across the room, noting the wheeled chair remained in its place beside the bed. Upon retrieving a book from a table, she turned it over and over in her hands before crossing to Salterdon, who had gone back to his scribbling on paper. Again and again he thrust the quill tip into an ink bottle then proceeded to draft bold, black musical notes onto a scale.

Finally, he looked up. The light from the window showed every fine line in his weary face, every minute gray thread sprinkling his dark hair. It seemed he had aged overnight. The wildness that had once reflected upon his demeanor showed now in a sullen despondency.

Yet, his eyes looked mad.

A fine film of moisture beaded his brow, and his mouth was savage. He glared, first at the book in her hand, then at her eyes.

"What the devil do you think you're doing?" he demanded in a rough voice.

" 'Tis time for your lesson, Your Grace."

"Go to hell."

He jabbed at the inkwell, splashing ink onto the tips of his fingers. Turning on her again, he declared, "You needn't remind me of what my responsibilities are, Miss Ashton. I'm well aware of my responsibilities. My grandmother slyly and adeptly reminded me of them yesterday. God forbid that I attain the upper hand with the dowager duchess."

"Why are you angry?" she asked. "If it's true that you were fond—"

"Fond?" He laughed sharply. "Yes, I was fond of Laura. Who wouldn't be? She's exquisite. And wealthy. And so fragile I could crush her in my fist."

He made fists of his stained hands; his knuckles shone white.

"The one and only time she came to Thorn Rose after I was hurt, she looked at me and sank to her knees in a puddle of French satin and velvet. She wept on her father's knee to spare her from marriage to *a monster*." He removed the book from Maria's hand and flung it against the wall. "For better or worse. In sickness and in health, Miss Ashton. Common vows for common people. *Not* the aristocracy."

Slumping back against the chair, he fell silent while Maria went to collect the book. She felt his gaze follow her; it burned like embers into her back.

Finally, he said, "Tell me why you didn't return to Huddersfield with John Rees."

She brushed away nonexistent dust from the book before responding. "I don't love him."

"You care for him. Isn't that enough?"

"No."

He laughed. His words were keen, even fierce in sarcasm. They revealed the grinding sense of his anger and frustration that gave a sudden wild look to his countenance. "Ah, the plebeian ideals of happily ever after. Tell me, Miss Ashton—Maria—what is your idea of love?"

"Sacrifice. Compassion. Understanding. Devotion, uncompromised. Wealth is what you build together. Fortune is amassed by participated dreams. It is a spark . . . here." She lightly touched her breast. "It is the yearning you feel to see him, or her, succeed at their life's aspirations. The spark never flickers, but burns hotter through the years."

For an instant, he lowered his eyes. His brow

softened. His lips parted. Slowly, his hand came up and closed gently around her arm. "Naive child," he said tenderly. "You believe in fairy tales."

She pulled away. Emotion flushed her cheeks. "Don't touch me. Please. Don't ever touch me again. I should never have allowed you to touch me before. I don't know what I was thinking. My only excuse is that in my enthusiasm over your vast recovery I allowed myself to become overly infatuated. 'Twas not my intention. 'Twas not my reasons for coming to Thorn Rose."

"No? What were your reasons for coming here, Miss Ashton?"

"Employment, sir. A way to earn money so that I might save enough to purchase a cottage for myself and my mother. I would save her from spending the remainder of her life shackled to a man she no longer loves . . . perhaps never loved. You needn't look so smug, Your Grace. Mistakes of the heart are made even in our class. 'Tis easy for any innocent young girl to be seduced by good looks and power."

"And now that you've had sufficient time to dwell on your parents' mistakes you've decided not to make the same error in judgment. Look at me, dammit."

"I would remember my reasons for coming here, Your Grace. I would remember that you're betrothed to another, that you have an obligation to your family and to your heritage. I would remember that there is nothing so important to you than rising to your father's expectations. A multitude of generations have come down to you, after all. A relationship between us would hardly signify . . . or benefit."

With a sudden, terrifying roar of rage, he jumped from the chair, sending it crashing against the little desk, scattering loose papers over the carpet. Maria stumbled backward, crying out as he made a desperate grab for her, only to be brought up by a sudden spasm of such intense pain he threw back his head and clutched at his legs. His visage went white.

With a gasp of despair, she flung herself onto him. They staggered. He tilted and turned and fell against the wall, dragging her with him. The impact shook the furnishings. Glass rattled in the window. But he did not fall. And while his lower body quivered in pain and weakness, he gripped her arms fiercely and lowered his head over hers.

"You needn't remind me of my obligations. They have been driven into my brain like nails since I was born. Right now I don't give a damn about my obligations. Only one thing has driven me out of mind these last hours and that's been you. You and your goddamn blue eyes and sultry mouth. I lay in bed at night and I try to imagine myself seducing you. Of robbing you of your innocence, of stealing your virginity. I was once very good at that—of driving women out of their minds with desire. I knew exactly what to do with their bodies to make them beg me to take them. Now . . ."

He covered her mouth in a hard kiss. She struggled briefly, until he succeeded in sliding his tongue into her mouth. She twisted her hands into his coat lapels, intending to push him away, but all she could do was sway against him, curl her fingers inward, allow a low groan to escape her and dissolve against his lips.

Oh, that she had come to this: a slave of longing for her master; a wanton who would gladly disregard the feelings of a young woman who waited patiently to become his wife.

Suddenly, he pushed her back. His breathing came heavily; his face was agonized.

He shoved her away, pivoted awkwardly before stumbling against the desk. With one swipe of his arm, he sent papers, quill, and ink onto the floor and shouted, "Get out! Just get the hell out!"

Her jewel-headed cane making a determined thump on the floor, the duchess, with Edgcumbe at her side, moved down the corridor, chin thrust, her eyes locked on Maria who, along with Gertrude and a number of other servants, had gathered outside Salterdon's door.

"What is the meaning of this?" the dowager demanded. "Answer me, for Godsake. What is this poppycock that Trey has locked himself in his room and refuses to respond?"

Visibly trembling, Gertrude stepped forward, extending her ring of keys. "The key to His Grace's room has gone missin', Yer Grace. I've sent Lilly to fetch the spare."

The duchess turned toward the door, glared at it a long minute, then declared, "Trey, you will open this door this minute."

"Go to hell," came the reply.

"You're acting like a spoiled, ill-tempered brat."

He laughed, a maniacal sound.

"You will open this door this moment or I shall have someone break it down."

"I'll shoot the first person who tries."

"Oh, you will, will you?" she muttered under her breath, then turned her attention to a gawking servant who had just retrieved the supper tray from Maria's room.

"You," the duchess barked. "Here."

The girl elbowed her way through the cluster of fascinated domestics. The duchess grabbed a knife from the tray, thrust it at Edgcumbe, and declared, "Do what you must, my good man."

Gertrude leaned toward Maria and whispered, "I reckon he's wishin' he could use that on his own throat 'bout now . . . or on hers. I s'pose the outcome of this little foray ain't exactly goin' to put Edgcumbe and his healin' medicinals in a right pretty light."

Countenance drained of color, Edgcumbe gaped at the knife in his hand, then at the door. Fingers trembling, he slid the blade into the crack between the door and its frame by the keyhole as far as it would go and gave it a jiggle. Then another, harder, causing the door handle to gyrate up and down.

An explosion erupted.

Servants scattered.

The teacup balanced on a saucer on the tray the servant was carrying shattered and sent slivers of china flying.

They all stared at the thumb-sized hole in the wall.

"Gorm," the servant squeaked. "It's a bleedin' bullet hole. The loony devil be shootin' at us now."

With that, the servants took off running.

Edgcumbe studied the hole through his monocle before turning slowly back to the duchess. "By gosh," he said, "I do believe she's right."

With that the duchess sank to the floor in a swoon.

Gertrude shrieked.

Edgcumbe gasped. Dropping to the floor on his knees, he slid his arm beneath her neck and grabbing a kerchief proceeded to fan her ashen face with it. "There, there, Isabella. Breathe deeply, my dear. It will all work out. We'll send for Physician Sivenwright at Royal Oaks immediately."

"Royal Oaks?" Maria said in a sudden panic. "A hospital?"

"We have no other choice, my dear. The man is beyond our help. He has resorted to murder!"

"He's murdered no one!"

"The gun," cried the duchess coming out of her faint. Grabbing hold of Edgcumbe's coat, she dragged herself into a partially upright position. "He has a gun. Dear God. He is liable to do himself harm."

Maria stood, that realization as splintering as that dreadful, deadly bullet through the wall. She moved toward the door, pressed her ear against it and listened. Finally, she called softly, "Your Grace. I beg you to open the door. I won't allow them to take you to Royal Oaks."

"Won't allow—" Edgcumbe began furiously.

"Hush!" Gertrude snapped, causing Edgcumbe's eyebrows to shoot up and his face to go red.

"Your Grace?" Maria forced herself to breathe evenly. "Think about what you're doing. There comes a time when we must all accept our lot in life. While I can dream of fairy-tale lives, I realize that being born the daughter of a meager vicar I must content myself with such a destiny. You were born into greatness, into wealth and power. It was your destiny, sir."

She listened hard, feeling her heart pound at the base of her throat. Her eyes closed, she imagined his image, slumped in his chair surrounded by discarded remnants of his passion—his music—his dark, chiseled face framed by glorious wild hair. A gun lay in his lap, his long fingers lightly cradling it.

"Think of the beautiful children you shall have, Your Grace. Think of the values you might instill in them. Think of their own hopes and dreams and aspirations, and how your power and wealth will enable your sons and daughters to achieve them. You needn't make the same mistakes your parents made with you. You'll revere your children for who they are, not what they are."

A servant scurried up, wagging a key. "I found the spare," she whispered and slapped it into Maria's hand.

Her fingers closed around it. She slid it into the lock and slowly twisted it.

"Gorm, lass, be careful," Gertrude said. " 'E's liable to plug ya the minute ya walk in."

"He won't hurt me," she declared, and eased open the door.

Just as she had pictured him, he sat at his desk, legs slightly sprawled, the gun in his lap.

"Did I kill anyone?" he asked with a slight smirk on his handsome lips.

"Nay, Your Grace, although you didn't do a particular teacup and saucer any favors . . . or the poor maid who was holding it at the time."

"A shame," he replied simply.

"Your grandmother, however, is recovering from a swoon."

He smiled.

"Will you give me the gun?"

"Say please."

"Please," she replied softly.

He tossed it onto the bed and relaxed again into his chair. "Who's to say that I'll be capable of having children?" he said in a weary voice.

Reclining on a chaise, with Edgcumbe hovering and fanning her face, the duchess glared at the lineup of servants and Maria.

"I demand to know how my grandson came to have that gun. Obviously one of you got it for him. Well? Speak up. Confess. Do you expect me to believe he sashayed down two flights of stairs, sauntered to the hunt room and retrieved the weapon himself? Need I remind you that he's incapable of walking?"

Maria looked away.

Had he managed it somehow?

Impossible. A mere movement of his legs sent his muscles into spasms.

The duchess lifted one hand. A maid hustled to hand her a cup of chocolate.

"I don't understand," said the duchess. "He seemed so much improved. What's brought on this sudden spate of dementia? Everything he's ever wanted is right at his fingertips. All he need do is to marry the Lady Laura, something he was more than happy to do before he was injured. Not only would he be entitled to half of my money upon marrying the girl, the dowry that comes with Laura is exceptional. Considering that Laura is Lord Dunsworthy's only beneficiary, the estates which will pass to Laura upon her father's demise will make my grandson one of the wealthiest men in the entire country. It's what he wanted," the duchess declared in exasperation, then realizing she was rambling to the mesmerized servants as if they were cherished confidants, she frowned and thrust her empty cup at Edgcumbe. "For the love of St. Peter you'll be interning me to Royal Oaks soon . . . and I'm not so certain it would be such a displeasing opportunity."

Chapter Sixteen

"It is a strange truth that although the human heart may know peace, contentment, serenity, even thankfulness, it never does and never can know happiness—the sense of complete full-rounded bliss except in the joy of happy love . . ." So Maria's mother had often said when reminded by family or friend that she should be thankful for the comfort and respect her husband's position offered her. Of course, such a confession had not been made to anyone except Maria and Paul.

Maria pondered this late into the night.

Obviously, her time at Thorn Rose was drawing to a close. As soon as Salterdon married Lady Dunsworthy Maria would return to Huddersfield, where John Rees waited. He would offer her marriage, a home, a future . . . something she had always wanted—to spend the rest of her life in the company of a good, kind man who was her friend.

Once, she had desired him . . . or thought she had. Then desire had been the titillation over a forbidden kiss, a mysterious yearning. He had been a prize to win, an objective to lure away from God—to no avail.

Desire now was something uncontrollable. It obsessed her every waking minute.

Her better judgment warned her to leave this minute. Why put herself in the position of watching the man she loved marry another woman?

But he needed her.

Her heart simply would not allow her to say goodbye just yet.

Having paced her room for hours, having walked a hundred times to his door, refusing to allow herself to enter, she quit her room and wandered down the corridors. Perhaps Gertrude would be up. Or Cook. It suddenly occurred to her that she had not eaten the entirety of the day. She felt weak and light-headed.

As she passed a salon, she paused and peered into the room where a solitary candle burned on a table. Obviously, some servant had forgotten to blow it out. She hurried to the candle, and as she bent over to blow it out, raised her eyes to the chair on the far side of the room, and the figure of a man sitting there in the dark recess.

The candle sputtered out.

"Your Grace." She bumped the table with her leg. "I hadn't realized you had left your room. You should have called me."

Nothing.

"I'm sorry you were forced to have your dinner alone. I . . . beg your forgiveness for my recent susceptibility to glumness. I fear I've become too conscious of myself—a grievous sin, according to my father. For the last hours I've given a great deal of thought to my motivations, and I suppose it all comes down my wanting your happiness above all else. What happened between us . . . 'twas wonderful, Your Grace. I admit I've allowed myself to become . . . overly fond. But is that not the nature of a woman, sir? Alas, I fear we're ruled by heart."

Drawing back her shoulders, she raised her chin. "Regardless, I shall endeavor to stand by you until you've taken your wife. I am committed to you entirely . . . for as long as you want me. There. I've confessed. Now you know that my affections for Your Grace are not strictly motivated by my desire to help my mother, as I earlier declared. I trust you won't make light of me. Then again, I'm well aware of the scores of women who have loved, Your Grace, so I'm certain you're accustomed to such silliness from naive young women."

At last, he spoke softly. "Are you saying that you're in love with His Grace, Miss Ashton?"

"Aye, I am, sir."

The shadowed figure left his chair and came toward her. No stiffness. No limping. No groan of pain. Then he moved into the pale light emanating from the corridor. Maria stared up into his face a long, silent moment before the realization set in.

"Basingstoke," she breathed.

She turned to flee.

He grabbed her arm.

She struggled, briefly, before he managed to usher her to a chair and push her determinedly into it. She covered her face with her hands and wished in that instant to die.

"Your pardon, m'lord. I thought you were Salterdon."

"Obviously."

"I suppose it would do little good to plead with your lordship to disregard all that I've confessed these last few minutes."

"No good at all."

He dragged over another chair and sat down before her, gently took hold of her hands and eased them away from her face. Catching her chin with one finger, he tipped back her head.

"You're not the first young lady to spill out her feelings over my brother to me, so that is neither here nor there. I would know, however . . . if he's done anything to compromise you."

"Compromise, m'lord?"

"Has he bedded you, Miss Ashton?"

"No, m'lord."

He took a relieved breath and sank back in the chair in a weary manner. "Then that little problem is obviously not what brought me here."

"Sir?"

"I've ridden two days to get here because I couldn't shake the notion that something was wrong. The curse of being a twin, Miss Ashton. When some problem plagues my brother, it plagues me as well. Trey is troubled, Miss Ashton. Tell me why."

"I'm not certain I know. He had rallied, then, when the duchess announced that she had continued with plans for his marriage to Lady Laura, and that she and her father would be arriving immediately, he regressed. He locked himself in his room and threatened to shoot us if we entered. He went so far as to shoot through the wall, causing your grandmother to faint."

"The duchess fainting? Good God, I would have liked to have seen that. So would half of England for that matter. Imagine the old iron mare succumbing to a fit of vapors."

"Fortunately, Edgcumbe was at hand."

"Edgcumbe? Christ." Basingstoke stood and proceeded to pace through the shadows. "What the blazes is Edgcumbe doing here?"

"He's trying to convince the duchess to have your brother committed to Royal Oaks in Menston."

"Committed! The devil you say. Edgcumbe cannot commit a man of my brother's peerage with no less than twenty witnesses to attest to the fact that without a shadow of doubt he is mentally incapacitated and no longer able to function in a normal or rational manner."

"There are as many witnesses living in this house," she said.

"Are you telling me, Miss Ashton, that my brother is insane?"

"Your brother is the most brilliant man I have ever known, m'lord."

"But is he insane, Miss Ashton . . . or simply desperate?"

"Desperate, sir?"

"You tell me my grandmother is going through with plans for his marriage. You tell me that Lady Laura and her father are due to arrive here . . . ?"

"Tomorrow. Sir, why would His Grace become so desperate as to undermine his own future? Marriage to Lady Laura will secure his financial well-being—which is always what he's wanted, according to the duchess. And it's not as if he's committing to a woman he cares little for. He's very fond of her, m'lord."

"Yes," he replied thoughtfully. "He was."

"My greatest fear, m'lord, is that because of this rebellion of sorts, your grandmother will finally send him away."

"We can't allow that to happen, Miss Ashton."

"What do you propose we do, sir?"

Silence. He paced again through the dark, moving into and out of the light through the doorway, giving Maria an occasional glimpse of his profile. He wore a simple white shirt with blousy sleeves, tight riding breeches, and knee boots. Her heart constricted because he was the image of his brother.

"I wonder . . ." he said, "what's caused my grand-mother to instigate this marriage so precipitously? That she would toss caution to the wayside—so totally disregard Trey's health and state of mind in order to make certain he marries Laura."

He walked to the doorway, leaned his shoulder against the doorframe and slid his hands into his pockets. When he faced her at last, his countenance was obliterated by the light at his back. He appeared to regard her for a long time before speaking again. "Christ," he said softly, drawing one hand through his hair. "I fear I'm beginning to understand."

* * *

Lord Dunsworthy and his daughter arrived at ten the next morning, preceded by an hour by an entourage of outriders, servants, butlers, ladies maids, and grooms.

"What shall I do?" fretted the duchess. "I can hardly deny the extent of my son's condition if I'm forced to send Dunsworthy and his daughter packing the moment they arrive."

"You're the Duchess of Salterdon, my dear Isabella," Edgcumbe declared with a pompous air. "You may tell them to take a leap off the Buttertubs if you so desire."

"You forget that I sent them a letter just days ago professing my grandson's much improved health. You forget that I've contacted numerous associates so they might proceed with all necessary arrangements for the wedding—"

"Isabella, you're becoming flushed. I must insist that you take a deep breath and—"

"For Godsake, cease mollycoddling me." She shooed him away as if he were some incessant insect, then she turned on Maria again. "Miss Ashton, you seem to be the only person residing in this house who can communicate with Trey. What have you to say over this behavior?"

"Your Grace, I'm as baffled by it as you. My only thought is that he's yet uncomfortable about facing his bride-to-be in his current condition."

"Poppycock. Edgcumbe feels confident that it's only a matter of time before he regains the use of his legs."

"Perhaps, although however confident Edgcumbe

feels is irrelevant. 'Tis how His Grace feels which matters."

The duchess's eyes narrowed. "Obviously you're totally ignorant of the ways of the aristocracy, Miss Ashton. Emotionalism has nothing to do with our lives. We're born for a purpose. We live for a purpose. We refuse to die unless that purpose is passed on to the next generation. I'm eighty-five years old, young lady. I haven't a great deal of time left to waste on recalcitrant children. If my grandson proceeds to thwart me, I'll have no other choice but to allow Edgcumbe to begin proceedings to commit him to Royal Oaks."

"That won't be necessary, Grandmother."

They turned.

The Duke of Salterdon, dressed impeccably, sat in his chair just inside the doorway.

Only it wasn't the duke, Maria realized after an initial rush of shock.

Basingstoke.

The duchess sat upright. Edgcumbe grabbed his monocle, fumbled with it twice before managing to situate it properly in his eye. "Incredible," he muttered.

As Basingstoke rolled the chair into the room the duchess stood, tottered, shoved Edgcumbe's hand away when he attempted to steady her, then moved toward her grandson. Stopping before him, she said, "I should have known immediately, of course. But then, the two of you were always very good at dupery. This, however, I find in bad taste, Clayton."

"Agreed," Edgcumbe barked. "My good man, your grandmother is delicate—"

"My grandmother hasn't been *delicate* a day in her life. Sit down and shut up." He smiled at the duchess. "You have to admit you were fooled for a moment, Your Grace."

"Cruel boy. What have I done to deserve this deplorable behavior?"

"Quite a bit, as I recall."

"Why are you here? When did you arrive?"

"Last evening. As for why . . . ? We both know the answer to that. What affects Trey affects me. Have you ever known me to disregard that pull between us? I sensed he was in trouble—"

"He's resorted to murder."

Clayton glanced at Edgcumbe. "Seems his aim could be better."

"I resent that," Edgcumbe blustered.

"I resent your attempting to manipulate my grandmother. In fact, I resent your entire existence. I resent your association with the duchess, and—"

"Enough! Now get out of that chair and tell me what the blazes you think you're doing."

"About to save my brother from being humiliated."

"Meaning?"

"In your haste to get Trey married at last I fear you've forgotten a small detail . . . his dignity, which has already suffered much over the last year."

"Dignity," she huffed. "What about *my* dignity?"

"I don't give a damn about your dignity any longer, Grandmother."

Stiffly, she turned her back on him. Finally, she asked, "What will this guise accomplish?"

"Perhaps it'll buy us some time. Miss Ashton can continue in her attempts to draw him out again. In the meanwhile, Dunsworthy will be presented a future son-in-law who, if still unable to walk, is at least capable of coherent conversation, and who is not howling at the moon . . . as rumor in London has it."

Lord Dunsworthy was a statuesque man, a handsome man, some years younger than Maria's father—the typical Norman ruggedness of the ancient gentry of England stamped upon his fair complexion. His daughter, Lady Laura, was a tall, slender creature with skin the color of rich cream and eyes the color of emeralds. She floated into Thorn Rose on her father's arm, gaze downcast, kerchief gripped in her hand, or possibly it was a vinaigrette. From his place atop the stairs, situated behind a fall of velvet casings, Salterdon couldn't tell—but he suspected it was a vinaigrette. The girl chewed her lower lip and tried desperately not to noticeably sob.

"She's very beautiful, Your Grace," Maria said. "But then I suspected she would be. A man of your extreme good looks would hardly settle for less than perfection. I can see why you became so fond of her."

"I became fond of her money," he replied. "There are a great many beautiful women, Maria . . . but few with her father's fortune. Besides . . . the duchess approved. What the duchess wants . . . the duchess gets."

Maria continued watching the goings-on below, her small white hands resting lightly on the balustrade. He could read nothing on her face; her brow was smooth, her eyes clear of emotion. Her pink lips, as always, were turned up slightly in an unconscious smile.

"What are they doing now?" he asked.

"They are lost within an ocean of servants." She laughed lightly. "There is Gertrude, of course, directing them hither and yon, dashing about like a plump little bumblebee from flower to flower. There! She's speaking to Dunsworthy—"

"Doing her best to explain why the duchess won't be greeting them immediately. 'Er Grace is taken a bit peaked. She's 'avin' a lie down and will see yer lordship and 'er ladyship at tea. 'Is Grace will be joinin' ya then as well."

"Will you?" she asked without looking at him. "Be joining them?"

"His Grace will see them when he's good and damn ready. I'm not ready."

"You're being stubborn."

"Perhaps."

"You're simply delaying the inevitable, Your Grace."

"Good God, you're beginning to sound like her. Whose side are you on, Miss Ashton?"

Her eyes suddenly widened. "They're coming," she whispered.

Gritting his teeth, Trey turned on his heels, took a fortifying breath and moved stiffly down the corridor. Maria took hold of one arm and supported him with her slight weight.

"Quickly," she urged him, causing him to stumble

slightly. "I should never have allowed you to come this distance without your chair."

They hurried on, the sounds of chattering servants and conversing guests urging him to move faster. By the time they reached his room, his body was sweating; his legs were racked by pain. Still, he fell back against the wall as Maria slammed his door, and he began to laugh.

"I don't see what's so funny," she decided, breathing hard. "You profess to want nothing to do with this arrangement until you're ready, yet you would run the risk of being found out by your grandmother. You're fully aware that should she discover your ability to walk you have no further excuse to delay your marriage to Lady Laura."

"Certainly I do. I'll just tell her that I've fallen in love with you and have every intention of running away and living the life of a farmer."

She turned on him, her blue eyes ablaze—a certain alteration of her previous unusual state of malaise. "Despicable oaf. How dare you tease about such a thing."

"I didn't realize marriage to me was so offensive."

"And I didn't realize how truly cruel you could be."

She grabbed the door handle, attempting to flee.

He took hold of her arm, fiercely at first, then more gently. She would not look at him. Instead, she stood away, her hand frozen on the brass knob; she looked as if she might shatter, as if any word from him would bring tears to her eyes. Or perhaps they were already there, shimmering and swimming, threatening to spill like crystal beads down her cheek.

"Look at me," he said softly.

"Nay, I won't."

"You're upset. Tell me why."

Maria shook her head, pulled away and slowly, as if she were trying futilely to collect her pride, opened the door. Halfway out, she paused. Looking toward the hall, one hand resting on the doorframe, the other on the door's edge, she squared her shoulders and said matter of factly, "You never struck me as a stupid man, Your Grace."

Then she left the room, softly closing the door behind her.

Laura Dunsworthy lay like some fallen swan upon her bed, her silk gown spilling over the mattress like silver water. A pale mouse of a woman hovered nearby, occasionally dipping a fine lace linen into a bowl of cool water and, after wringing it out, folded it neatly and placed it lightly upon Laura's forehead.

Maria waited patiently in a chair across the room, dreading the moment the young lady, barely older than herself, would rouse from her nap to acknowledge her . . . yet wishing to get her mission over with as soon as possible. She wasn't accustomed to subterfuge—that alone was bad enough. Sitting in the presence of Salterdon's future wife was agony. She would certainly find her deplorable. Vain. Selfish.

Maria wished desperately that she had some finer dress to wear—that she owned combs for her hair, and pearl earrings for her ears—that she were as beautiful as Laura. Maybe then she might win Salterdon's admiration and affection. But no . . . she had neither Laura's birthright nor her fortune.

At last, Laura stirred. Her companion hurried to her side, spoke to her softly, then gently, as if Laura were made of the most fragile china, helped her to sit up. She plumped the pillows at Laura's back, spread her skirts like a magnificent fan over the bed, then turned and nodded at Maria.

"M'lady will see you now."

Her knees shaking, Maria stood, self-consciously smoothed a loose tendril of hair back from her temple, ran her hand over the mended bodice of her dress—the memory of Salterdon's ripping it flashing before her mind's eye like a bolt of lightning—the memory of his kissing her and touching her burned like a brand on her cheeks. She moved across the room, her gaze riveted on Laura's face—her eyes were wide, green, and watchful. Maria wasn't certain she had ever seen skin so pale.

"My lady—" she began.

"Your hair is beautiful," Laura said, and smiled.

For a moment, Maria was taken aback.

"And so are your eyes."

"You're very kind, m'lady."

"Not at all. Please, sit down, Maria. You look dreadfully nervous." She patted the bed beside her, then dismissed her companion with a nod. When the woman had left the room, Laura sighed. "It's nice to talk with a woman my own age. I've lived such a secluded life, you understand, since my mother died. What have you there?"

Maria looked at the note in her hand. "From His Grace," she said.

"Oh." A look of trepidation crossed Lady Laura's face. She shrank into her pillows. "He's capable of writing, then? My father mentioned he was much improved, however, I had hoped . . ." Laura bit her lip and averted her eyes. "He speaks now as well? And knows his family?"

"He reads frequently, to himself and aloud."

"You've accomplished miracles, Maria."

"He's worked very hard, m'lady."

"And how does he look?"

Maria smiled, more to herself than to Laura. "Distinguished and handsome."

Frowning, lowering her voice, Laura said, "And his behavior?"

She had marched into this room prepared to dislike the young woman, through no fault of Laura's, equally ready to go to any lengths to live up to her commitment to the duchess—but all the lies were there, burning in the back of her throat as bitter as bile. The truth could and would end any hopes of a marriage between Salterdon and Laura for now . . . it would also end any hope of bettering her mother's plight. And what of her master? With the duchess's last hope of a marriage between her grandson and a young woman of noble birth, would she not bend to Edgcumbe's notion to inter him at Royal Oaks?

Maria looked away, focused on a bust of Eros, and replied, "You can be certain that His Grace would never intentionally hurt you."

"Oh. I see." Laura sighed and laid one hand, palm up, upon her forehead. "Very well, Maria. You may read me the note now."

With a deep breath, Maria opened the missive. "Lady Dunsworthy. I would request the honor of your company in the Gold Room at half past eight. Salterdon."

Closing her eyes, Laura sighed again and replied weakly, "Of course."

Maria sat with an open book on her lap, her gaze fixed on the flames dancing in the hearth. The meeting between Laura and Basingstoke had gone off without a hitch. While the duchess had sat in her regal chair, looking as if she might shatter with nerves at any moment, Laura, with her father hovering around her like a watchdog, sat across from the man whom she believed to be her fiancé, her eyes downcast, her fingers twisted together, looking for all the world like a young woman just sentenced to hang.

Like she had during Maria's visit to her room earlier, Laura had shown little joy over the fact that her betrothed had apparently made such a miraculous recovery, nor did she show the slightest inclination of excitement over the prospect of finally marrying the Duke of Salterdon.

What woman would not have been enchanted by Basingstoke's banter? His charisma? His seductiveness?

Yet, an hour into their meeting, Laura had whispered to her companion that the last two day's journey to Thorn Rose had obviously taken its toll, and had begged

His Grace's pardon and returned to her room, looking pale as milkwash. Just before Maria had returned to her own room for the evening, she had passed by the girl's chamber, and was certain she had heard Laura softly crying.

Maria closed the book and wearily left the chair. She would try one last time to coerce Salterdon to unlock the door. She would try her best to convince him that this act of rebelliousness would accomplish nothing; there was his grandmother's health to think about; there was Laura's happiness. This was his destiny, after all.

She was surprised to find the door unlocked. The room was empty. Maria glanced at the tall case clock; the hour was nearly midnight. She hurried to the music room only to discover that the room was totally dark.

Where could he be?

She rushed to the library, the hunting room, the kitchen, passing several sleepy-eyed servants. Certainly she didn't dare ask if they had seen His Grace wandering the corridors. No one but herself and Gertrude were aware that he had regained the use of his legs.

After a half hour search she returned to her room and collected her cloak, made her way out of the house and into the misty night, pausing momentarily as the cold bit into her cheeks, then continued down the meandering path toward the stables.

The sound of angry voices brought her up short. Carefully, she descended a set of lichen-covered stone steps, stepped over a fallen curtain of ivy, stopping again at the sight of several shadowed figures standing together on the path.

She recognized Thaddeus's lanky form immediately. It took a moment to realize that the smaller figure, shuffling its feet from cold, was Molly. No matter how she tried, she couldn't make out the third person, as they stood partially concealed behind a spray of bushes.

A gust of wind whipped up, causing the trees to tremble and dead leaves to rattle. Maria backed away and continued toward the stables, occasionally glancing back over her shoulder, only briefly wondering why anyone would choose to visit amid the bone-chilling wind and drizzle, at midnight no less. Her mind was on Salterdon.

The stables were dark and quiet and warm. The horses shuffled in their stalls while she moved as silently as possible down the long, bricked aisle checking each cubicle until coming to one whose door was thrown open, revealing an empty stall.

Noblesse.

Throwing open the doors, she ran from the barn shielding her eyes from the drizzle.

A form came at her from the dark with an explosion of clattering hooves and streams of steam flowing from distended nostrils. Its hot body brushed hers, causing her to stumble back with a cry, to nearly topple before a hand wrapped around her arm and swung her up from the ground. For an instant she floated on air while the stallion pivoted on its powerful back legs and spun around, then she was easily dropped onto the animal's withers and situated by a pair of strong arms.

Left shoulder buried against Salterdon's chest, Maria blinked the rain from her eyes and managed to catch her breath. "Your Grace—"

"Nice of you to join me," he declared in her ear. "I never cared for riding alone."

With that he gave a shrill whistle and heeled the stallion in the flanks. The animal reared slightly, arched his dark neck and let loose a snort that seemed to echo in the night. Then Noblesse leapt into a canter, his long, powerful stride carrying the riders out of the stable yard and down the sodden riding path beneath an arc of rain-soaked trees.

Breathless, Maria grabbed hold of Salterdon and clung fiercely to him as the animal's forearms rose like springs ungathered and flew into the wind, scattering the clouds of mist and fog. Their speed was made all the more frightening by the pumping of the horse's shoulders and his mane whipping like trees in a tempest.

Maria dug her nails into Salterdon's cloak, allowed her body to sink deeply into his and turned her face into the sharp cold wind, gasping for an occasional breath, blinking the mist from her eyes even as an odd sense of security overtook her. For once her master would comfort her; he would protect her; he would coerce her from her earthly bonds and take her flying beyond all human cares.

They had ridden an hour it seemed when Salterdon finally crooned softly to the stallion and the beast's powerful stride began to diminish until they stopped beneath a canopy of trees. His arms around her yet, his warm breath falling softly against the side of her face, Salterdon said nothing for a long moment, then he cupped one large hand along her jaw and tilted her face toward his.

"I once thought I would die without the prestige and fortune due me because of my birthright; I would cease to exist. But this last year . . . I was already dead and no one gave a damn except you. Maria . . . how can I let you go?" He brushed her ear with a kiss; his breath was hot and made her shiver. "You are my sanity, Maria. My strength. My . . . desire." His voice died away into a low growl, the purr of a lion, his lips grazing the soft skin behind her ear. "Oh yes," he breathed. "I desire you."

Helpless, oh God, she felt helpless. Weak and timid. She ached to turn her face up to his, to open her mouth beneath his, to experience his tongue once again—and his hands on her body. But he belonged to another—a frail, dewy-eyed young woman who waited, had waited the last year to become his wife. A girl of his peer, chosen by his family, and hers, to become the next Duchess of Salterdon—to give him children—a son so that he might continue their dynamic heritage.

Yet, as he slid from the horse's back, sweeping her with him, cradling her effortlessly in his arms, she felt powerless, helpless, conscious only of the tumult in her heart, and loins, knowing if he kissed her and touched her again she would not, could not deny him any more than she had been able to deny him that fateful afternoon in the coach.

He crushed her to him, arms gripping her fiercely, one hand buried in her silvery hair.

"Do you understand what I'm telling you?" he demanded in a rough, almost desperate voice. "I want you, Maria. I want you so goddamn badly I could explode." Catching her hand, he slid it down his body, to the swelling at the apex of his legs. Her fingers touched him through the straining cloth of his breeches, molded upon the shocking length and shape of him even as the startling realization of what he was telling her set in—even as that foreign and frightening part of him moved against her fingers like a being unto itself.

She could say nothing, do nothing, as rigid with anticipation as she was with indecision. He smelled of mist and wind, of leather and horse, of sweet brandy and sweat.

Don't touch me! she longed to beg. She would surely shatter—her resolve would crumble—her pride would dissolve like the misty vapor swirling around them.

"I want you," he murmured. "Maria, Maria," he whispered as his hands ran over her, dragging away her thin cloak—her mantle of poverty—no fox or mink cape for her, there never would be.

Why could she not fight him, turn him away? Why had her body become this trembling, weak stranger, pliant beneath his hard, warm hands that were gently lowering her to the ground amidst a wet cushion of musty fallen leaves? His hands then ran over her damp body, tugging at her clothes gently, then almost angrily, ripping the seams and buttons until the frail dress her vicar father had forced her to wear lay in tatters beneath her.

Exposed, shivering, Maria lay naked before him, watching desire carve creases in his incredibly handsome face, feeling her own body respond with a sort of power and need that obliterated her control.

She opened her arms to him, and her legs.

With a groan, he threw aside his woolen, rain-heavy cloak and impatiently dragged his shirt over his head. He tore at the hooks on his breeches, peeled the cloth down over his hips—she looked away briefly, then back again, losing her breath at the sight of his arousal. For an instant she wanted desperately to run, to deny her own cravings. But then he touched her—there— where he had touched her before, sliding his gentle fingers into the warm, silken folds of her intimate body, cupping her mound in his palm and squeezing and releasing in a rhythm that made her arch and quiver.

For a moment, he left her, removed his boots and discarded his pants. His body looked pale and powerful in the rainy night as he came to her again, easing down over her, bending his head to her breasts and taking one sensitive, erect nipple into his mouth, teasing it with his tongue, causing her to gasp, to whimper. The sudden bolt of pleasure was so fierce and enjoyable she clutched at his shoulders, feeling them shift, bunch, ripple beneath her hands.

"Easy, easy," he murmured before kissing her, before stroking her lips with his tongue, then plunging it inside her mouth to do a passionate battle with her own.

The sudden burning pressure between her legs made her gasp, arch, flail wildly for an instant with her legs—then he was inside her, stretching, filling her up, his body melding into hers, flooding the burning spear with an odd delicious pain that made her grind her hips against his and groan deep in her throat.

He continued to kiss her, his mouth harsher and more

demanding as he slid a hand beneath her buttocks and lifted her off the spongy ground, driving his body further into hers, moving into her and almost withdrawing with a careless speed that was driven by necessity.

The spasms overcame her suddenly, like heat flashing from a stormy heaven, rendering her completely without will, driving her to cry aloud and writhe beneath him, even as he continued to pump his body in and out of hers, faster and harder, almost desperately. As her own body trembled with its final release, he threw back his dark head, and with a soundless cry, spilled himself inside her, until the strength left him and he allowed his body to collapse on hers, his mouth near her ear, his soft voice whispering so she barely heard:

"Maria. Sweet Maria. Dare I love you?"

Chapter Seventeen

Maria sat before the diminishing flames in the hearth, Salterdon's cloak wrapped around her. It was wet and smelled like him. The lining was red silk and felt smooth and cool against her naked flesh, which even now tingled with the memory of his kissing her. Her body ached. That place between her legs burned like an ember. Her feet were dirty. Her legs and thighs were spotted with leaves and grass. Her hair, falling limply over her shoulders, was matted with mud and flecks of brown velvety moss.

Upon returning to the house she had fled to her room and locked the door. Several times her master had tried the door only to find it locked against him.

"Open the door, Maria. Dammit, open the door."

She hadn't, of course. How could she face him again?

How could she look into those gray eyes that had once so frightened her and know that she had given herself to him so wantonly, so unabashedly, all in the name of love?

How did she admit that she had come to love him so devotedly? Yet, what other excuse for her irrational behavior could she offer him—and herself? That she had only wanted to prove to him that he was yet a virile and desirable man? That there was no cause to fear marriage to Laura—no reason to believe he could not live up to the requirements of a husband? One could carry duty and obligation only so far. Besides, that was one lie she was certain she would never be able to pull off believably.

Wearily, she walked to the door, listened hard for any sound.

Wretched fool! Already she ached to see him again, to hold him, to make abandoned love to him before she was forced to face his fiancée and pretend to be nothing more than some devoted, compliant servant.

With a will of its own, her hand went to the key, turned it, waited for the subtle shift of the lock, then, with her heart pounding in her throat, she pushed open the door and stepped into the hallway.

His hands moved up and down the keys, stroking lightly, filling the predawn hour with a crescendo of harmonic sounds that reverberated from the walls and caused the crystal prisms of the chandeliers to shimmer like raindrops. His upper body bent slightly over the keys, his jaw clamped and his dark hair spilling wildly over his brow and eyes, Salterdon manipulated the instrument as he had Maria's body hours before. He breathed raggedly. The magic of the sound was as seductive as her breath had been in his ear.

Christ, he hurt: his legs, his back. Yet the pain ran deeper, the frustration burned. Did she realize what she had done? *Maria.* That alluring voice had seduced him from his safe, comfortable sleep. *Maria.* Those eyes had taunted his resistance. *Maria.* Her naivete and innocence had roused the passion he had thought gone from him forever.

A movement. He looked around.

She stood in the doorway wrapped in his cloak, her hair a pale spray around her dirt-smudged face. His hands fell still, and the room echoed with silence.

On bare feet, Maria crossed the floor, her steps slow, hesitant, her blue eyes huge and her moist red lips slightly parted. The cloak fell open, slid from her white shoulders and pooled around her ankles.

As her lithe, warm body swayed slightly toward him, he reached for her, took her fiercely into his arms, crushed her against his straining body. He could feel her trembling. Her naked back and buttocks were still sprinkled with bits of brown grass and leaves from the glade in which he had made love to her earlier.

In one swift, smooth effort, he swept her up and around, sliding her onto the piano with a discordant clash of sounds. He took her breasts in his hands and lifted them, kneading them almost roughly, then gently, before suckling each one as though sipping little drinks from them. Maria gave a desperate whimper; her body quivered. She arched her back, struggling momentarily as her nipples grew hard between his lips and teeth. Then he touched her *there*, within the soft pelt between her legs. Her hips writhed, lifted; she made a soft guttural sound in her throat that was as helpless as it was desirous.

"My breeches," he told her softly. "Open them."

She complied—eagerly, releasing each hook until his sex was free: a hard, throbbing arc that was almost too painful to endure, made all the more aching by the memory of his taking her before; the feel of his body between her white legs, filling her, stretching her virginal opening and awakening that pleasure which had caused her to claw his back and scream aloud in the rain-drenched night.

Eagerly, he drove his body into hers. She cried out, then wrapped her legs around his hips. With arms thrown wide, she fell back on the piano like some sacrifice on an altar, scattering papers of music onto the floor, her hair a glistening silver web strewn over the ebony wood.

"My God, my God," he moaned, his voice a ragged tear of sound. "For weeks I made love to you through this instrument. I've wooed you, seduced you, kissed you, raped you, thinking I would never know you like this—believing I couldn't. Then, the music was enough—not now. The music in my head that's driven me mad has been replaced by you. You and your angel hair and succubus eyes. Damn you, damn you—forcing me out, thrusting me back into this abhorrent responsibility I never wanted. I could have hidden there forever, denying my identity, my worth, even my manhood. Thanks to you, I'm healed. Thanks to you, I'm doomed. Thanks to you, I now know how deeply I can feel for a woman—and I cannot have you."

He drove into her again and again. When he came at last, he did so with a curse, a shiver, a collapsing of his body against hers as they sank onto the piano, sweating, struggling for a breath.

At last, he took his body out of hers, kissed her mouth and hooked his breeches. Retrieving his cloak from the floor, he wrapped it around her, drew her close, held her tight, feeling her heart race against his chest as her small hands twisted in his shirt and gripped him fiercely. Finally, she whispered: "I love you."

He closed his eyes and held her tighter.

"Well, well," came a sudden voice from the door. Trey looked around, directly at his brother. "My sense of intuition must be slipping, Your Grace. I had no idea you were capable of walking . . . or seducing innocent young women on pianos. Really, Trey . . . you never had a great deal of self-control, but this is beyond even your low moral standards."

"That coming from a man who intentionally seduced the woman I was to marry."

"Jackass. We both know you had no intention of marrying Miracle. You have every intention of marrying Laura Dunsworthy, however, so tell me what the hell you're doing taking advantage of Miss Ashton while your affianced is residing down this very corridor. Quickly, Trey, and while you're at it explain to me why I've been forced to play out this pitiful scam these last days, believing your resistance to meet with Laura was strictly because of your inability to . . . walk."

"I don't love her."

Basingstoke laughed dryly. "What's that got to do

with anything? You've never loved a solitary soul your entire life, Trey. You've loved the power and prestige your position in life afforded you. You found a means to an end in Laura Dunsworthy and suddenly you talk about not loving her?"

"Yes," he replied softly, almost wearily. "I don't love her, Clay."

Basingstoke said nothing for a long moment, his gaze shifting from Trey to Maria, who huddled behind Trey, her face averted, her cheeks white with discomfiture. Salterdon did his best to protectively block his brother's view of her; she trembled against his back.

Briefly, Basingstoke closed his eyes, ran one hand through his dark hair. "Christ," he muttered. "What a bloody mess."

Laura Dunsworthy looked particularly frail, her cheeks washed of color, her thin fingers repeatedly twisting her hankie and occasionally dabbing it to her tiny, slightly upturned nose as if she were sniffing vinaigrette to rouse her energy and courage. Every few minutes she flashed a look toward the man she thought to be her fiancé—Basingstoke stared right through her, his jaw set, his smoldering eyes reminiscent of his brother's. He didn't want to be there any more than Maria did. But she had a responsibility to fulfill. She had been employed to nurse and companion the Duke of Salterdon, and for all intents and purposes, the man brooding in his brother's wheeled chair *was* the Duke of Salterdon . . . for now. Maria wondered just how long he would tolerate this apparent fraudulent and deceptive act of chicanery before blowing up in anger.

She wondered how long she could tolerate it before she screamed in frustration.

Maria watched the meeting between Lord Dunsworthy, his daughter, and the duchess all from a distance, her chair situated well away from the goings-on. She felt numb—a witness to a despicable crime. She wanted to leap from her chair and announce to Lady Laura and her father that the Duchess of Salterdon was a liar. That she was only buying time. That she was controlling and manipulating everyone's lives in a manner that could, would, destroy them all—all for the sake of securing her own damnable blue-blooded heritage.

"Certainly we desire the union between our children to take place as soon as possible," Lord Dunsworthy said to the duchess. "I trust Your Grace won't mind that I drop an invitation or two to a few of our mutual acquaintances—invite them to Thorn Rose just so they can assure themselves and others that all is . . . shall I say, right—and well—with His Grace."

One eyebrow lifting, Dunsworthy studied the man he believed to be his daughter's future husband, an appearance of worry and frustration working across his features. "You must understand . . . considering His Grace's history . . . and the, ah, disappointment and, er, discomfiture my darling Laura experienced due to His Grace's unstable state of mind, I would not wish for her to endure any further humiliation brought on by the outrageous conjecture concerning His Grace's stability and his relationship with Laura which flies about so rampantly among our peers."

His Grace allowed His Lordship a thin smile, and said in so caustic a voice that the duchess sank a little in her chair, "No one is exactly holding a gun to your daughter's head and forcing her to marry the duke, are they, Dunsworthy?"

"Indeed," Dunsworthy replied smoothly, his own smile just as acerbic. "But considering His Grace's circumstances—" His gaze swept Basingstoke's legs, and the chair in which he sat. "I would think that he would consider himself fortunate that a woman of my daughter's breeding and beauty would care to go through with the marriage at all."

"The fact that the alliance will eventually make her one of the wealthiest and influential women in England hasn't a thing to do with it either, I'm sure."

"Any more than your marrying my daughter will assure you of inheriting your grandmother's influence and assets . . . Your Grace. Besides . . . as you can readily see, my daughter is desperately in love with His Grace. Her greatest wish is to spend the remainder of her life complying to His Grace's every wish . . . as any devoted wife should."

For a moment, all eyes turned on Laura—her wan cheeks, her slightly trembling lower lip. She returned their study from behind her hankie and did her best to hide her immense discomfort by righting her shoulders and lifting her chin. Then her wide green eyes shifted, not to her own companion, but toward Maria, as if looking for some emotional rope on which to grasp.

To her own surprise, Maria smiled.

The air around her seemed to buzz. Her body became warm; her heart squeezed. The breath caught in her chest and a lump formed in her throat that she couldn't swallow. She was giving encouragement to the woman who would marry the man Maria so desperately loved. She had spent the previous night wrapped up in Salterdon's embrace . . . and she was giving encouragement to the woman with whom he would spend the remainder of his life.

Hypocrite.

Dunsworthy continued. "By the time we've prepared for the wedding there won't be a family of our peers who won't be sniping to attend the ceremony. By gosh, but it will be a wedding England shan't forget for centuries!"

The duchess raised her head a bit stiffly and regarded Dunsworthy. Her lips were pressed, her brow furrowed. For an instant she looked on the verge of blurting out the truth—that the man sitting across from Dunsworthy's daughter was not the Duke of Salterdon. The Duke of Salterdon was holed up in his room like some hermetic lunatic—or so she thought. In truth, known only to Maria and Basingstoke, Trey Hawthorne, the Duke of Salterdon, was astride his high-prancing Arabian stud, riding hell-bound for leather over the downs, drinking in the wind. Living wildly. Freely. Thumbing his nose at everything his grandmother represented.

Finally, the duchess said, "And how many guests did you have in mind, Lord Dunsworthy, to attend this . . . gathering here at Thorn Rose?"

"A hundred. Perhaps two hundred."

Basingstoke coughed into his hand, flashed the duchess a speaking glance, and shifted in his chair. His face grew darker, if that were possible.

"The invitations are being written even as we speak, Your Grace. I feel a week from today should give us sufficient time to make arrangements for their arrival. I'll handle everything, of course. Your Grace need only worry about your health and doing your best to grow stronger the next days."

The duchess sighed. "Were that all I had to worry about, my dear Dunsworthy, I would be a most incredibly healthy woman."

Dusk had come late due to the clearing of the clouds and the casting of sunlight across the rain-kissed downs. Having searched for her master the better part of an hour, both at the house then at the stables (she had promised Basingstoke that she would speak to him once more and try to convince him of the folly of his continued rebelliousness), Maria made her way back up the path, her walk made shorter as she cut through an ash tree covert. The little light that intruded there seemed to spring up from the ground, strewn with an occasional blanket of last year's foliage and the lichened claws of chalky twigs.

"Maria," called a voice softly from behind a fall of brown ivy.

Stopping short, Maria peered through the shadows, her mind still occupied by thoughts of Salterdon and when she would see him again—and hold him, and pretend no one else in the world existed. "Lady Dun-sworthy?" she replied, surprised to find her master's fiancée hidden behind a tangle of vegetation.

Laura stepped onto the path. Her pale hair was partially fallen and her frock was touched with wet where she had brushed against the damp leaves. The dress was bright, rich and sumptuous. Her eyes were dark as the forest and troubled. "I had hoped to see you," the girl said.

Maria looked around for Laura's companion.

"She's not here," Laura informed her. "I plead guilty of subterfuge, I fear. I told her I intended to nap. Occasionally I find the company of a companion dreadfully tedious—oh, I'm sorry. I tend to forget you companion His Grace. You don't seem like a nurse."

"No? What do I seem like, m'lady?"

"A . . . friend."

Maria looked away, her face suddenly burning.

"I don't often get the opportunity to visit with girls my age," said Laura. "Will you come sit with me for a while?"

A thousand excuses flashed through her mind, all enabling her to escape quickly, to avoid facing the woman Salterdon would eventually marry—with whom he would share his life, and children. Dear Lord, it was enough that she had made love with him the night before; how could she possibly hold a conversation with the girl? She felt as if the same harlot's brand with which her father had burned Paul's lover was radiating off her cheek.

With reluctance, Maria nodded and followed Laura to a pair of matching marble benches nestled within a grouping of rose bushes. They sat, facing one another, their hands clasped in their laps, both nervous, both no doubt thinking of the same man.

Salterdon. Her mind's utterance of the name made her quiver.

At last, Laura sighed. "For a moment, Maria, might we forget our vast differences in situations and speak to one another like friends?"

"If you so desire, m'lady."

"First of all, you may stop addressing me as 'm'lady.' My name is Laura."

Soon to be Salterdon's wife, Maria thought with a growing sense of despair. Dear Lord, what was happening to her that she could sit here before this charming child when the night before she had been wrapped up in the girl's soon-to-be-husband's arms.

"Tell me truthfully, Maria. I simply must know. His Grace . . . is he really healthy? Is he prepared to marry me?"

"Do you doubt it, Laura?"

Laura chewed her lower lip, and once again her eyes became troubled. "I only wonder if there is any hope— or possibility—that he would decide otherwise."

Stunned, Maria stared at the suddenly flushed young woman. It seemed in that instant that Laura's being began to frazzle. She shook; tears filled up her eyes and spilled down her cheeks.

Covering her face with her hands, Laura began sobbing. "Oh, I am a dreadful child! Irresponsibly selfish and self-centered. I should be grateful that a man

of Salterdon's esteem should choose me to marry, but
I'm not. I'm not, I tell you."

Maria took the bench beside Laura and, after a
moment's hesitation, put her arm comfortingly around
the weeping girl's shoulder. "There, there," she con-
soled. "I assure you His Grace is neither monster
nor—"

"He's a stranger to me, Maria. Simply a man my
father deems as acceptable for me to marry."

Shrugging, gazing off into the bramble of twisted
rose bushes, Maria mused softly, "I admit, at first he
seems intimidating. But he's no different than any other
man, and much more human than some. He loves
pudding, m'lady. And bread with treacle. He enjoys
reading late at night beneath the flame of a goodly
beeswax candle—he says the light is clearer than with
tallow . . . and besides, dukes don't stoop to using
sheep fat unless they're sinking in a mire of debt—says
they smell like a rutting ram when they smolder.

"He loves horses—oh, not just any horses, but
Arabian horses. Drinkers of the wind. Beasts beautiful
enough to inspire royalty. Animals full of fire and spirit,
whose every stride is like the movement of a celestial
ballet.

"He . . . plays the pianoforte, deep, deep into the
night. He hears music when others perceive noise. His
genius is surpassed only by his immense desire to fill
the air with heavenly sonatas.

"His only fault is in refusing to recognize and
acknowledge his own identity—that aside from what

he is, the duke, he is a man worthy of respect and admiration, even without his grandiose title."

"But I don't love him, Maria! Oh, I respect him fiercely. I think him incredibly handsome. A girl would have to be insane not to find the prospect of becoming the next duchess the realization of a dream. He is—or was—after all, the most sought-after bachelor in all of England."

Laura left the bench and paced, wringing her hands, doing nothing to stem the flow of emotion pouring down her cheeks. "You see . . ." Her voice grew tighter, almost painful as she appeared to struggle with her next confession. "I—I'm in love with another!"

With a stomp of her little foot, she turned on Maria with a swirl of her velvet skirt. Her countenance became tormented and angry—hardly the demure, shy, doe-like creature she had portrayed the last days. "You cannot know how dreadful it is to love a man forbidden to you, Maria. To crave him with every fiber of your being. To close your eyes and see nothing but his face, to recall the desirous ecstasy of his touch and know he is only, can only be, an impossible fantasy."

Eyes brimming and burning, Laura said, "Please don't tell me I shall learn to love Salterdon. I have heard it a hundred times, Maria. I would rather die than be forced to marry a man who would care for me only because I suit his purpose, knowing there's one who would cherish and adore me if only . . ."

"If only what?"

"If only he were born of the same class."

"So that's the way of it," Maria said gently, almost to

herself. What dreadful irony. What a wretched twist of fate!

"Oh, Maria." Laura dropped onto the bench beside Maria, took one of her hands and gripped it fiercely. "If only I could be as unencumbered as you. To be free to marry the man you love, never having to worry over this despicable responsibility expected of us by our fathers. Oh, if I could only change places with you, Maria, I would be the happiest woman alive."

Briefly closing her eyes, Maria replied softly, "And I as well, dear Laura. And I as well."

The moon was lifting well above the shoulder of the surrounding hills when Salterdon swept into the room with a rush of cold wind, the smell of leather and horses clinging to him. Sitting at her dresser, brushing out her hair, Maria barely had time to turn from the mirror before Salterdon swept her up from the cushioned stool and spun her around the floor. She laughed despite herself and the sudden onslaught of upheaval that overwhelmed her each time he stood near her. He kissed her throat, her shoulder, the soft skin beneath her ear.

"Your Grace, I've searched hours for you. You're making it extremely difficult to continue to hide your improvement from your grandmother—"

"I don't care to talk about my grandmother," he said in her ear, and twirled her again. "I want to tell you about where I've been and what I've seen."

Maria pulled away, backed against the dresser while watching his face and his eyes which were no longer wolfish, or hard, or angry. In truth, he looked like a boy full of mischief. "Obviously Your Grace is growing stronger by the day—"

"By the hour, sweetheart." With his fists, he pounded his long legs, which were encased in tight leather breeches, then he reached for her again, forcing her to dance aside, to put distance between them or she would surely succumb to her desire to fling herself against him and invite his body into hers.

"Your guests will begin arriving tomorrow. Do you expect Basingstoke to continue this dupery forever?"

"I'm surprised that he would play into Grandmother's hands as easily as he has."

"Edgcumbe continues to press Her Grace into sending you to Royal Oaks. He believes any man who would continue to close himself up in his room, refusing to see or speak to anyone as you have supposedly done, has lost all fiber of sanity."

"Edgcumbe is an ass. He and Thackley have leeched off my grandmother since the day my father died. With me buried away in Royal Oaks they can continue to control her estates and finances after she dies. Thackley realizes that the moment I inherit my grandmother's estate I'll let him go. It's called self-preservation, my beautiful Maria. More than one family has been ruined by unscrupulous administrators."

"If you think them unscrupulous, then why have you not insisted to your grandmother—"

"To get shut of them?" He shrugged. "I have. So has my brother. In her own perverse way, she's fond of them. Hell, the old lady's mind is sharp as a blade; she's aware of their occasional pilfering. Thinks it's harmless. Besides, who the devil else would put up with her? Who would coddle her? Fawn over her? Make her feel more important than she really is?" He laughed to himself and added, "I used to be very good at that as well, not so long ago."

He slid one hand into his breeches pocket and pulled out a folded paper, turned it over and over in his hand before offering it to Maria.

She opened it, revealing a splash of musical notes. Scrawled across the top was: *Maria's Song*.

"My masterpiece," he said and began a slow waltzing move around her. "Every morning before dawn I've ridden out to a lea beyond the hills. I sat with my face in the wind, watching the sun inch up over the horizon splashing velvety streaks of light across the downs. I saw your face in the crimson and silver bursts. I smelled your body in the wafting of sweet crocus. I imagined making love to you amid the pale green and brown grass. And the music came as if on angels' wings."

"Your Grace—I beseech you—"

"To what? Make love to you? Here? Now? Come to the music room and I'll give you *Maria's Song*, then I'll lay you on the piano and make you scream."

She turned to leave. He moved, blocked her escape with his body which had become as familiar to her as the air she breathed.

"I can't . . . not any longer. I loathe the lies. I despise myself when I sit at Lady Laura's side and pretend to be someone I'm not. I'm weary of the foolish fantasies that occupy my every waking and sleeping minute. But most of all, I abhor myself for this wretched helplessness I feel when you're near." She backed away. "I detest what you are and represent. The absurdity of your way of life appalls me. This preoccupation of marriage without love and only for the sake of materialism is repugnant. I am infuriated by your cowardice."

His eyes narrowed; his jaw tightened. The wolf was back, there in the burning light of his steely eyes.

"Aye," she nodded. "You're a coward, Your Grace. Running from the inevitable. You profess to want nothing to do with this marriage, yet you hide away, too frightened of your grandmother's threats to disinherit you to defy her."

The crème de la crème of aristocracy converged like some hungry army on Thorn Rose in their shiny black coaches pulled by high-prancing horses. The sprawling house teemed with laughter and chatter—and conjecture.

Was His Grace truly cured?

Was Dunsworthy daft enough to sacrifice his daughter to a lunatic?

And what about the rumor that the duchess's health was declining rapidly?

Salterdon stood in the shadows, watching the throng of men and women below. Once, they had been his friends. He had danced with them. Seduced them. Drank with them. Gambled with them. They, in turn, had turned their backs on him and called him a lunatic. A beast. A monster.

His nostrils still full of Maria, her taste still lingering

on his lips, he focused on Laura Dunsworthy, who stood at her father's side, congenially greeting the curious guests and no doubt making excuses for his absence.

Once, he had thought her incredibly attractive—for a child. She still was, but there was no spirit there, no fire, no rebelliousness. She was like a conservatory flower, beautiful to look at, but easily snapped with the gentlest wind of controversy.

She was certainly intelligent. She could recite a plethora of facts and figures from highly respected books, enough to occupy an evening with idle chit-chat . . . but what about her ability to make intelligent choices on her own, to reach intelligent conclusions or decisions about her own future—without relying on his directives? After all, she would undoubtedly outlive him by a number of years . . . how would she hold up under the responsibilities of a duchess?

Once, he had felt a sort of desire for her—the same sort of desire any man would experience over a woman's beautiful body in bed. But that desire suddenly seemed so inadequate; like a solitary ember amidst the forest fire he felt for Maria.

Maria: The antithesis of everything he had ever considered necessary in a woman he would care to . . . marry.

Yet, he did consider it. Lately, the thought had replaced the music in his head. The ache to own her had obliterated the nagging hurt in his body.

A door opened down the corridor. He stepped behind a drape and watched Molly exit a room—Edgcumbe's room—a pair of muddy boots tucked under her arm.

About that time, Thaddeus rounded the corner. He spoke briefly to Molly, then tapped on Edgcumbe's door before entering.

Salterdon moved down the hall.

As always, he experienced a twinge of nervousness before stepping into the duchess's room. As grand as the salons in the palace, the ostentatiously magnificent chamber glittered with gilt and crystal. Rich tapestries splashed brightly colored images of warriors riding blowing steeds on the paneled walls. There were portraits of his grandfathers, and his father. Several of himself and his brother were scattered among them—likenesses of their youth, before they had become such sardonic and cynical bastards.

At the far end of the apartment, was the duchess's bed. She lay on it like a corpse.

Quietly, he moved to the bed, his gaze never leaving his grandmother's body. The silence in the room reverberated like drums in his ears. His body began to sweat—as it always did when in her presence.

A movement caught his eyes. Startled, he looked up.

Having left her chair, Gertrude hurried to his side, her eyes wide with concern.

"Lud, sir, wot are ya doin' up and about? The place is crawling with people, ya know. If someone saw ya now—"

"Is she dead?" he demanded in a hoarse voice.

"O' course not," Gertrude whispered. "She's only sleepin'."

"Jesus. When did she become so old?"

"She's eighty-five, Yer Grace. She's been right old for a long time."

He shook his head. "Not like this. Is this what I've done to her, Gerti?"

Gertrude chewed her lip. "She's been right worried, sir."

Running one hand through his mussed hair, Salterdon shook his head. "I came here to tell her I have no intention of going through with this marriage. I came here to tell her that I'm in love with Maria, and if she cannot accept that then she can go to hell. I fully intend to stand up to her for the first time in my life . . . but how can I when she looks like this?"

The duchess moved.

Gertrude grabbed his arm. "She's wakin', Yer Grace. If she finds ya here the jig is up fer sure. If she discovers yer up and walkin' there'll be no turnin' back. Remember, she thinks ye've hold up in yer room, legless and threatenin' to shoot yerself and ever'body else if they disturb ya."

"Not an altogether intolerable idea."

"But I ain't right sure she could stand the shock of seein' ya like this, and besides . . ." Gertrude lowered her voice even further. "Think about the sort of humiliation she'd experience if ya marched down them stairs right now, lookin' as ya do, and announce to them hundred or so folk that ya have no intention of marryin' the Lady Laura."

The duchess stirred again. Her eyelids fluttered. Her hands weakly clasped, causing the diamonds on her fingers to sparkle.

Salterdon backed away, the old frustration and anger centering in his belly like a gnawing dog. With a muttered curse, he spun on his boot heels and quit the room, stalked back to his own chamber and slammed the door so hard the windows shook.

Chapter Eighteen

With her bare feet tucked beneath her skirt, Maria laid her head against the back of the chair and listened to the last strands of *Maria's Song* float through the midnight air. Each note resounded in a series of heartrending echoes. They vibrated the stillness. They made her cry.

Thank God for the inadequate illumination from the solitary candle on the pianoforte. Thank God that the curious guests had long since found their way to their rooms and beds. If she could only hold back her emotions until she had kissed Salterdon good night one last time, but that was impossible. As she watched her master wring each melodious tone from the piano, watched the tumult of feelings wash like pure light over his features, she knew to the core of her being that he had made his decision.

He would marry Laura Dunsworthy.

He would do so out of duty. Out of respect for his heritage. Out of love and concern for his grandmother.

Oh, God.

Leaving the chair, she moved to the open French doors, catching her breath as the cold wind tumbled in. The room fell silent. Turning, she watched Salterdon continue to stare down at his hands that yet lay spread and in position on the white and black keys. Slowly, he raised his head, and his eyes met hers.

Then Basingstoke appeared at the door, his form a black silhouette with broad shoulders and an angry stance. "There you are," he declared to his brother; then, noticing Maria, he stayed his step briefly, hesitantly, until she allowed him a smile.

"You're just in time, m'lord. His Grace was just about to inform me of his decision regarding Lady Dunsworthy."

"You don't say," he replied sharply, his attention again focused on Salterdon. "Wonderful. I would say it's about time, wouldn't you, Trey? Especially in light of the fact that I've just spent the last hours coaxing Grandmother back from death's door, and do you know why, Your Grace? Because she vows she awoke from a nap to find you standing at her bedside. Standing is the key phrase here. Moving at will around her room. I managed at last to pacify her by convincing her it was only a dream."

"Why did you bother?" Salterdon said, and gently closed the cover over the keys.

"I've asked myself that repeatedly the last hours. I cannot guess why I continue to protect you. My only excuse is I care more for her state of mind and health than I do for your own twisted reputation. The humiliation she would experience over being found out passing off one grandson for the other—to her peers, I might stress—would prove to be a wee bit more than she can endure right now. Not to mention the wallop she would get upon discovering you're not an invalid after all—much less a lunatic . . . or perhaps I'm wrong on that count."

Turning away, Maria stepped from the room, out on the balcony where the wind howled over the cement balustrade and cut like little knives into her exposed flesh. Occasionally, she heard their angry voices—spurts of heated accusations and confessions.

Tomorrow she would leave, pack her paltry little valise with her two dresses and tattered shoes, and return to Huddersfield. She simply couldn't stay here any longer. Even an existence of living under her father's vindictive brutality would be better than facing one more day of loving the Duke of Salterdon.

A sudden sharp and angry exclamation made her turn and rush to the door. Her heart stopped.

Lord Dunsworthy and his daughter stood just inside the room. Laura, her aghast gaze fixed on Salterdon, appeared on the verge of fainting. Her small hands gripped desperately at her father's arm.

"By God, what is the meaning of this?" Dunsworthy demanded with a ferociousness that seemed to shake the walls. "Imposters! Did you think to dupe my daughter into marrying some—some—good God, look at you, man!" he raged at Salterdon.

"I told you, Father," Laura wept on his coat. "He's a beast, a monster—"

"Nay, Laura!" Maria ran into the room. "No beast!

No monster! Simply a man who has long since grown weary of his responsibilities to everyone but himself. Believe me when I say that His Grace is good and kind and finds himself in this awful turmoil only because he doesn't wish to hurt either you or his grandmother. I should count myself lucky if I could trade places with you."

For a moment, Laura stared at her blankly, her eyes swimming with tears. Then her lips fell slightly open with realization.

More softly, Maria said, "I'm certain you understand, m'lady."

"I demand to see the duchess immediately," blustered Dunsworthy.

"The hell you say," Basingstoke replied.

"The hell *I* say," came the duchess's voice behind them, and they all turned.

Leaning her weight heavily upon her cane, she moved into the room, directing her words to Clay, but her gaze fixed on Trey. "I knew you were spitting out a lot of poppycock and balderdash. Dreaming my backside. You're old enough to realize that I've known every move either of you have made since the instant you took your first breaths. While you might have fooled the rest of the world occasionally, you never once fooled me. This time, however . . . I don't rightly know where my mind was. I suppose I was too bloody wrapped up in my own misery and grief to realize just how far His Grace would go to defy me without completely obliterating his chance to inherit my money. What a damnable choice he's been forced to make."

"Choice?" Dunsworthy barked. "What the blazes are you talking about?"

Stopping at the piano, she laid one hand upon it almost caressingly before focusing on Salterdon again. "The choice between devotion and obligation, Dunsworthy. Between freedom and that damnable albatross of responsibility we are born with around our aristocratic throats."

"Choices, you say?" Clenching his fists, his jaw working, Dunsworthy declared, "The only choice to be made here, my good woman, is his cutting that deplorable hair, dressing like the distinguished man he is supposed to be, and carrying out his commitment to my daughter."

The duchess raised one eyebrow. "And if he doesn't?"

"Then I will make certain that every guest residing in this house knows what a hoax you attempted to perpetrate on myself and my daughter. That you would have had this imposter (he shoved his finger at Basingstoke's face) trick my daughter into marrying a man obviously of irrational behavior and inferior intelligence."

"If he is so irrational and inferior," said the duchess, "then why would you care for her to marry him at all?"

"He is the Duke of Salterdon, madam. I would have my only daughter duchess someday. She *will* be duchess . . . whether the lot of you like it or not."

With that, he grabbed his daughter by her arm and dragged her from the room as she wept, "But, Papa, I don't want to marry—"

"Quiet!"

"But—"

"Quiet!"

The music from the orchestra below resonated through the house. The guests had gathered in the ballroom for the last hours, imbibing the duchess's best champagne, sparkling in their Parisian creations, supposing on the reasons why His Grace had not yet joined his obviously discomposed fiancée or her heavily perspiring father.

In truth, he hadn't shown himself at all—to anyone. Except Maria.

Her hands resting lightly on his shoulders, she gazed over his head at their reflection in the mirror. She tried to smile. Impossible. She attempted to speak. Not yet. Not until the act was done.

Taking a handful of his hair, she slid the keen edge of a razor through the thick, silken strands, watching as they drifted like feathers through her fingers and over his shoulder. Again, and the dark hair melted to the floor to lie like a coil of shadow over her toe. When the last long strands fell into her hand, she closed her fingers around them fiercely and clutched them to her breast.

"Delilah," he whispered. "You would rob me of my manhood and deliver me to the enemy."

"For your own good, Your Grace."

He turned in his chair and gently took her hand. His eyes were dark as slate. "You'll come with me downstairs."

"No." She backed away and reached for the fine black tailcoat with the rolled velvet collar he had tossed so carelessly onto the bed. "Besides, I've simply

nothing to wear for such a grand occasion. A black
nurse's dress would hardly suffice." She self-consciously
ran her hands over her skirt. "I'm certain you'll manage
well enough without me."

With only a momentary unsteadiness, Salterdon left
his chair. He adjusted the double-breasted waistcoat and
tugged at the linen stock round his throat. "Odd that I
never realized just how bloody suffocating these damn
things could be. No wonder my brother curses every
time he's forced to wrap himself up in one."

Maria held up his coat and averted her eyes.

He slid his arms gracefully into it. Slowly, he turned
to face her. "So tell me, Miss Ashton. Do I look
properly duked?"

"Aye," she replied without looking. "You're
quite . . . smashing, Your Grace. But then . . . you
always were."

"Pretty liar. I appalled you not so long ago."

" 'Twas your temperament that appalled me, sir. Not
the man. Never the man."

He reached for her again. She slipped away, toward
the door to her room. Though she tried—oh, how she
tried—not to look back, she did anyway, just long
enough to see him standing there, poised in his arrogant
glory—a man personifying aristocracy and aloofness.
Only it wasn't remoteness in his eyes which reflected
the splash of bright light from the chandelier overhead.

From her hiding spot behind the drapes, Maria
watched the Duke of Salterdon, with his grandmother
on one side, his brother on the other, slowly, cautiously,

descend the curve of stairs. Below them, the din of conversation had ceased the moment the guests looked up to discover that, at long last, their host had decided to join them. He would saunter back into their lifestyle with the ease and grace of an accomplished dancer. Tomorrow, he would be a different man. He would belong to them—and to her—the Lady Laura Dunsworthy, who did not love him—who loved another.

The crowd of his peers washed over him like a tide, swept him beyond her vision into the adjoining salon.

The music began again and Maria returned to her room, took up a book and opened it, knowing, even as she did her best to focus on the blurry words, to comprehend them would be impossible. Again and again she was forced to endure the sounds of frivolity from below: laughing, the strains of violin music that made her want to weep.

But she would not weep! She would not feel sorry for herself. She had known love for the first, mayhap the only time in her life, and that was enough.

Then she saw the dress.

It hung from a hook on the wardrobe: a flowing scarlet creation reminiscent of ancient Greece. A note was pinned to the bodice.

"I'll dance with you in the moonlight."

She couldn't! Dare she? Imagine her, who had never worn aught but gray and black. What could he be thinking, to tease her in such a way?

What harm could come of it?

Her hands trembling, she pulled off her clothes, allowing them to fall where they may, kicking them aside as she reached for the sumptuous gown that was finer than anything she might have dreamt up in her own vivid imagination.

In a breath, she slid it on, felt it fall soft and light around her body, flowing like crimson water down her legs to the floor. Then she spun toward the mirror.

Fitting beneath her breasts, accentuating her bosom, the gauze dress exposed her shoulders and much of her breasts. The back plunged low, to the small of her spine, and from there spilled in tiny gathered folds to an abundant train. All was edged in the most delicate lace dyed the same color as the dress. The train sparkled with some iridescence that looked like stars flung upon a sunset heaven.

With a quiver of thrill, Maria spun around, closed her eyes and allowed the distant music to uplift her. For hours, it seemed, until the candle burned low, she glided in and out of the shadows, little noticing when the fire grew dim and the room cold. Round and round she twirled, dipping and swaying to the sounds of the crooning violins, then . . .

She stopped.

The music. *His* music. Vague, at first. Soft. A piano litany that drew her to the door and out into the corridor, her feet hesitant, then swift as she flew down the sprawling corridor to the music room.

Maria's Song.

Alone in the vast, shadowed room, moonlight spilling through the open French doors, Salterdon looked up from the pianoforte, and his hands became still. His eyes narrowed. His face became impassioned.

"Don't stop," she pled. "I would hear it all to the end once more."

"I would end it with you in my arms," he replied, and stood, extended one hand, and smiled.

Too eagerly perhaps, she moved to him, touched one fingertip to his before melting against him, sighing as his strong arm closed around her waist and swept her up, crushing her momentarily as he kissed her mouth.

Effortlessly, they glided into the rhythm—one, two— one, two—one, two, three, four—spinning, dipping, the music coming low and from deep in his chest, purring through his lips against her ear, turning her knees to water and her heart into fire.

"Maria." He opened his mouth and breathed upon her shoulder. "I—"

A sudden shattering of sound erupted from below—a sharp explosion. In an instant, Salterdon twisted, his face contorted; he clawed at his back and gasped for breath.

"Sir!" she cried, grabbing him as he bent double.

"Not . . . me," he groaned, then pushed her away, stumbled toward the door. "Clay. Something's happened to my brother."

Maria ran after him, into the corridor where the sounds of screaming and shouting from below made her heart climb her throat. "Salterdon," she cried as he ran stiffly toward his room.

He emerged with the gun he had threatened the help with. "Get the devil to your room and lock the door."

"I won't."

"Dammit, Maria, now is not the time to turn stubborn

on me again." Pushing by her, he moved down the corridor that seemed eerily quiet all of a sudden. Maria ran after him, tripping on the hem of the scarlet gown.

Salterdon stopped at the head of the stairs and backed up slightly, raising his hand sharply to stay Maria.

Just below him on the steps stood a figure hidden within layers of clothes, a cloth hood pulled down over its head, a gun in its hand. Obviously, he was not yet aware of Salterdon's presence behind him.

In the foyer, guests stood frozen, all eyes fixed on the body sprawled facedown on the floor, a growing pool of blood oozing from beneath it.

Basingstoke!

Maria felt her knees go liquid. She clutched the balustrade with both hands and willed away the sudden faintness swirling like some bottomless black eddy in her head.

Suddenly the duchess shoved her way through the crowd. Draped in her finest Chinese silk, her silver hair spilling from its anchor of diamond-studded hairpins, she tottered momentarily, then fell upon the man's procumbent form with a mournful wail.

"Ya daft buggers," the figure on the stairs cried in an eerily familiar feminine voice. "Ye've gone and killed the wrong bloody man! Ye've shot Basin'stoke. Criminy, can't ya ever do anything bloody right?"

A second hooded man shoved his way through the terrified spectators, waving a pistol in their faces so they screamed and stumbled over themselves in an effort to give him room.

Slowly, Salterdon eased down the stairs, clenching his

teeth against the controlled exertion of moving his legs. The wolf was back—the dragon, his mien an unearthly mask of explosive outrage. His face looked bloodless.

The hooded figure below stooped over Basingstoke and the duchess, who sobbed at her grandson's body. Then he looked up, directly at Salterdon, and his eyes widened.

Salterdon grabbed the gun-bearing perpetrator from behind and slammed the barrel of his gun against his temple. "I would advise you to drop your gun now, you son of a bitch, before I blow his head off."

The robber dropped his bag of booty, then flung the gun to the floor. In a panicked voice muffled by his hood, he shouted, "This were all his doin'. Blackmailed me, he did. Said if I didn't do the duke in he'd see us rot in prison."

Maria sensed the movement behind her a second too late. An arm clamped around her waist. A knife pressed to her throat.

Salterdon turned, the gun still shoved into his captive's temple. His face, having already drained of color, became as smooth and still as stone. "Edgcumbe. You bastard."

Edgcumbe breathed rapidly in Maria's ear. "Too bad you couldn't have expired with dignity, Your Grace. It would have been much less messy for us all. Do you know what it's been like these last many years? Watching a worthless, self-indulgent wastrel dissipate money so foolishly while I—a gentleman of some esteem—am forced to pander continually to old women and disease-infested ingrates in order to make ends meet."

"Let her go," Salterdon said.

Maria winced as Edgcumbe squeezed her more tightly.

"I think not. At least . . . not yet." He nudged Maria toward the stairs. "Perhaps in a day or two when I've contrived a way to satisfactorily settle this distasteful circumstance. We should see then just what sort of sacrifice you're willing to make for a common little strumpet. How much will you be willing to pay for her life, Your Grace?"

Clutching the stair rail with one hand, Maria eased her way down the curving staircase, her breath burning in her constricted throat.

Reaching the foyer, looking neither left nor right, Maria allowed the pressure of Edgcumbe's body to direct her toward the door. Suddenly, the hooded thief who had earlier bent over Basingstoke stepped before them, blocking their exit.

Maria knew his identity the moment she saw his angry eyes through the menacing slits in the hood.

Thaddeus!

"Bleedin' bastard," he hissed to Edgcumbe. "Ya didn't say aught about nothin' like this. Ya said it would go off like clockwork, that we would go about our business of liftin' their damn purses, managin' to slip Salterdon a bullet—"

"You killed the wrong man, you idiot."

Edgcumbe attempted to shove Maria by him. Thaddeus grabbed her arm. "I ain't lettin' ya have 'er."

"No?"

Thaddeus slowly dragged the hood from his head. "Naw, guv. Ye'll 'ave her over me own dead body."

"Ah. Well. Suit yourself, sir." Edgcumbe raised the pistol to Thaddeus's forehead and pulled the trigger.

Maria screamed. For an eternity, it seemed, Thaddeus continued to stand there, his eyes wide and panicked, his forehead open and blood where his flesh used to be. Then, like a collapsing house of cards, he dropped to the floor.

A welter of cries erupted. Finally jarred from their earlier stupification, men and women, all in their finest Parisian attire, fell over one another as they attempted to stumble through the nearest doorway, leaving the pitiful image of the Duchess of Salterdon crumpled over Basingstoke's body. "Help him," she wept aloud. "Someone help him. He's bleeding to death."

But it was the shrill screams of the thief on the landing, still gripped by Salterdon, that reverberated the charged air.

"Lud, lud, 'e's gone and killed 'im! Bastard! I'll see ya hang along with me, I will, if it's the last thing I bloody well do!" With that, the figure lurched from Salterdon's grip and stumbled down the stairs, ripping away the hood, aiming the gun in a wild, wavering fashion toward Edgcumbe and Maria.

Edgcumbe shot her. The bullet drove Molly back and she hit the floor with a sickening thud, her blonde hair spilling like yellow and crimson sunbursts around her head.

"Perhaps you'll take me seriously now," Edgcumbe announced to the terror-struck onlookers. "Would anyone else care to die? I'll be more than happy to—"

A thump—an obscene noise that sounded nauseatingly like a melon cracking.

The arm gripping Maria tightened violently; she

thought her ribs would shatter, then she was falling, being dragged down from behind, hitting the floor so jarringly the world spun around her.

Laura Dunsworthy, a fireplace poker gripped in her hands, stared down at the carnage she had delivered to Edgcumbe's head. Turning her wide green eyes up to the shocked spectators, she declared, "Oh my. I fear I've killed him."

"Who would've thought it," Gertrude said. "Our own Thaddeus, ringleader of highwaymen. And Molly . . . daft girl. I always told her she'd find herself in more trouble than she'd know what to do with." Gertrude beamed Basingstoke a smile. "Ye'll rest now, m'lord. Ye'll be sore in that shoulder for a while, I vow. Just between you and me, sir, I hope yer a sight better patient than yer brother. Gorm, but he tried a person's patience, not to mention our sanity."

Basingstoke winced and looked at Salterdon. "I always said you would get me killed eventually."

Salterdon paced the room, his hands in his pockets. Then the duchess entered, a touch of her old fire and determination painting color on her cheeks. She looked from one grandson to the other before saying, "It seems my ability to judge character has become a trifle lacking in my advancing years. Edgcumbe has just confessed to the constable that Thackley was involved in this little scheme as well. I should have seen it coming, of course. Occasionally, however, we choose for whatever reason to deny what is most apparent before our eyes."

The duchess took a chair next to Basingstoke's bed.

She wrapped her hand around his and squeezed, still not taking her gaze from Salterdon. "I've spoken with Dunsworthy. He demands that we continue with this soiree once the guests have had time to calm down and collect themselves."

"Does he?" Salterdon sneered. "God forbid that a little human brains splattered over the foyer would get in the way of him roping his daughter a duke for a husband. I suppose we must get our priorities straight." Where the blazes was Maria? It had been hours since he'd last seen her. He walked to the door.

"She's gone," the duchess said.

He turned, stiffly. Knife-like pain sluiced through him as he focused on his grandmother's face. The realization occurred to him in that instant that never in his thirty five years had she refused to meet his gaze directly, but she did so now.

"I beg your pardon," he said dryly.

"Gone. I paid her her wages and sent her on her way. Now that you've obviously recovered so thoroughly I hardly thought it necessary to keep her on."

For a long moment, he said nothing, just absently rubbed his aching shoulder, realizing that it wasn't his shoulder at all that hurt so damn deep inside he couldn't breathe.

Again, he turned for the door.

"If you go after her," the duchess declared in a slightly panicked voice, "I'll disinherit you completely. You'll never see a farthing of my money or a stone from any of my estates. You'll be a pariah to your peers. You'll spend the remainder of your life in abject poverty. So tell me, Your Grace, is she so important to you that you would risk all of that?"

Salterdon said nothing, just left the room, closing the door behind him and briefly leaning back against it.

Maria was gone. Not so much as a word of goodbye. She was gone and he would go on with his life as it was intended to be . . . as his forefathers had intended it to be.

"Your Grace?" came the feminine voice.

His heart jumped. He swiftly turned, Maria's name on the tip of his tongue.

" 'Tis only I," Laura said, and smiled timidly. "By the look on Your Grace's features, you hoped I was Maria. I'm sorry to disappoint you."

Salterdon straightened. He adjusted the sleeves on his black coat and recalled how Maria had helped him into it earlier that day, before the madness and mayhem.

Laura moved to him. He noted there was something different about her. She appeared stronger. Her eyes were vibrant with determination.

"Lady Dunsworthy," he said, and offered her a slight bow. "I owe you an immense debt of gratitude for your act of courage this evening. Had Edgcumbe managed to get Maria away from the estate—"

"You would have done something very noble I'm sure to get her back. Maria has a way of doing that to people, I think. Bolstering their strength and courage. Perhaps because she's so brimming with both herself."

He swallowed.

"It took a great deal of courage for her to leave you, I'm sure. It took a great deal of courage to remain here as well. Her devotion to you was powerful and moving. Her strength of conviction inspired me. She made me realize that to love is to sacrifice. She sacrificed her heart and soul by remaining with you, knowing you were to marry me. What more can anyone sacrifice, Your Grace, than the very core of their being?"

"What are you trying to tell me, Laura?"

"What is all of this without love, Your Grace?" She looked around her, at the vast treasure-lined walls. "All the gold and silver cannot keep us warm when we're old or content when we're ill."

"You're in love with someone," he said softly and smiled at her gently.

"I would marry you, of course, as you would marry me. Because of obligation. I only know, that when Edgcumbe was killing those people, and the possibility crossed my mind that he might well kill me too, my thoughts were not of regret for never getting to experience being a duchess . . . but of never holding—"

"Mine and Maria's child in my arms," he said.

Laura smiled. "I knew Your Grace would understand." Laura turned and moved a short distance down the corridor before pausing and looking back. "She said you were special. I believe her."

He remained where he stood, his hands in his pockets while below him music began to filter up the stairs. Obviously, the help had managed to mop the blood off the floor and walls. God forbid that the deaths of two people (albeit servants) would stop the aristocracy from enjoying their own company.

Turning back for the door, he shoved it open and

walked inside. Basingstoke lifted his head from the pillow and raised one eyebrow.

The duchess looked up, her eyes briefly widening, her lips curling in smug satisfaction. "I knew you would be back."

Gracefully, Salterdon crossed the room, his gaze fixed on his grandmother's features.

He stopped before her and glanced at Basingstoke. His brother's eyes were twinkling. They said, *Go on, I dare you. Stand up to her. Make me proud for one time in your miserable life.*

Bastard.

The duchess lifted her hand to him. He bent over it, kissed it, and said, "My darling Grandmother . . . go to hell."

Noblesse shifted beneath him, pawed the ground and trotted in place, vitalized by the cold, midnight air and the anticipation of the ride ahead. Having reached the summit of the hill highest above Thorn Rose, Trey looked back on the manse. Sprawled across the lea, its every window ablaze with light, it glittered like crystal amid fire. He could hear music—only it wasn't the thin tones of the orchestrated violins, but the music in his head which kept singing. *Maria. Maria. Maria's Song* softly as angels' sighs.

Turning Noblesse into the dark, he rode the stallion down the road . . . toward Huddersfield.